FORGET
ME

Andrew Ewart was born in Chester in 1983. After teaching in Denmark he studied English at Cambridge, then spent ten years in London. He now lives in St Albans with his wife and daughter. He works as a production journalist and is overly fond of a pun headline.

Forget Me is his debut novel.

FORGET ME

ANDREW EWART

ORION

First published in Great Britain in 2020 by Orion Fiction,
an imprint of The Orion Publishing Group Ltd.,
Carmelite House, 50 Victoria Embankment
London EC4Y 0DZ

An Hachette UK Company

1 3 5 7 9 10 8 6 4 2

A CIP catalogue record for this book is
available from the British Library.

ISBN (Paperback) 9781409189695
ISBN (eBook) 9781409189701

Typeset at The Spartan Press Ltd,
Lymington, Hants

Printed and bound in Great Britain by Clays Ltd,
Elcograf S.p.A.

www.orionbooks.co.uk

For my parents, George and Marjorie

Prologue

The Crossing

The car rested on the tracks at the level crossing. She felt a kinetic thrum through her seat, filling her muscles with tension. He sat very still beside her, his forehead resting on the leather of the steering wheel. Horns blared around them with monotonous regularity; ineffectual, meaningless warnings.

'Reverse,' she said. 'Now.'

'Can't,' he replied tersely. 'Trapped.'

She shook her head in frustration. At this point there was only a tingle of fear.

How had they come to this in less than three minutes? The lights had flicked to red as they approached the level crossing. Three car-lengths away, perhaps less. She had told him to slow down, stop driving so fast, they had no chance of making the crossing in time. He had not replied. The day was hot, far too hot, and her husband's face was glowing florid, burning with that unhinged determination common to all men who feel their manliness challenged. Reclaiming that masculinity would require some great, pointless risk.

Muttering under his breath – the rhythmic chuntering, she realised now, so similar to the click-clacking of a train over tracks – he had increased the pressure of his foot on the accelerator and the small neon green vehicle burst forward. She had not been able to stop herself ducking as the first barrier swooped down, narrowly avoiding scraping their car. She could see her husband's lips drawing back from his teeth. He would make the crossing. He had to make the crossing.

The barrier on the other side of the tracks rapidly descended and a vision bloomed in her mind: the metal grille smashing through the windscreen like a diver's arrowed hands breaking the water, slicing her in two.

She had let out a small shriek which seemed to shock her husband back to his senses. .

He thrust his foot down on the brake pedal, his knuckles on the steering wheel turning red then white. The car jerked to a halt inches from the shining white teeth of the barrier.

They were stuck. Trapped in the centre of the rail tracks, a thick metal grille either side of them. That sight had brought him back to some sort of normality.

'Oh, Christ,' he had whispered.

'Jesus!' she shouted, scared and furious. It occurred to her, a little too late, that if she hadn't screamed then the car might have made it underneath the barrier. Maybe this whole mess was her fault. 'What stupid point are you trying to prove?'

He said nothing. She had snapped at him, in a shrill, hectoring tone that teetered on the brink of hysteria , to get them out of there, get them the hell out of there. He spun and twisted the wheel and the engine snarled with tinny desperation. Beads of sweat tracked down his jawbone, pooling on the collar of his shirt, and all the while there was no doubt that they were thoroughly wedged in their holding pen.

Eventually he had given up and placed his head on the steering wheel, letting out a long sigh. People had begun to congregate either side of the barrier, a sea of alarmed faces. Some motorists were beeping their car horns, warning them of the danger. *Thanks for that*, a petulant voice rose up in her mind. *Didn't know we were in trouble. Really helpful, there.*

Then the juddering of the tracks had begun, so lively and industrious.

The anger bled away. Calm determination overtook her. 'We have to get out,' she said, as softly as she could manage. 'A train is coming. We have to get out. Now.'

She slid the seatbelt from around her neck and laid a soft, cooling palm on his quivering shoulders.

'The car—'

'Forget the car, Euan. We have to get out. Now. Please.'

The blaring of car horns rose to a crescendo.

'Then what?' he asked. His voice was muffled. She realised he was crying.

'We find our way home. We sit down, pour a very stiff drink, and talk about … whatever. And I strongly suspect we'll need to buy a new car.'

'Then what?'

She breathed out heavily, fighting to maintain that air of control. 'Well, I suppose we pick up where we left off.'

He turned towards her, his eyes red-rimmed and pleading. 'Great. Wonderful. Such a tempting offer.'

Control, Hannah, she told herself again. Stay calm. There could be a simple solution to this problem; her husband was being completely irrational so she had to be entirely rational. But wasn't that the running theme of their relationship now? Euan was distraught and cold and distant and she was unable to console him. It had been an awful six months, so bleak and grey. Six months of her husband – once so brash, so confident – being morose and oh-so very cold. Six months since what happened with Jennifer. Six months that came down to this moment.

'What do you want?' she asked, caught between anger and pity. 'What's wrong, Euan? Tell me, please. What the hell's the matter with you?'

'I thought things would get better,' her husband said, blinking rapidly. 'I tried.'

His words made no sense. She shook her head. 'You're trying to make things better?' she asked incredulously. 'Making things better by endangering your life, both our lives? Real life's more complicated, I'm afraid.'

The second after the vinegar-tasting words were fully formed she clapped her hand over her mouth, trying to cram them back in.

He raised his head from the steering wheel and nodded slowly. 'You know, that's exactly what I've been thinking too, Hannah.' He let out a humourless bark of a laugh that chilled her despite the heat of the day. 'Real life is so very complicated.'

The thrumming of the tracks had magnified to the angry buzz of a wasps' nest. The car began to rock gently.

'Please, Euan,' she tried again, her voice wavering as panic began to compress her throat. 'You're really scaring me here. Just get out of the car. Come on now. Please.'

He let his head fall again onto the wheel. She reached for his hand and he tugged it away.

'Don't do this to me,' she begged. 'For God's sake, Euan, don't do this to us.'

'I think I've done enough,' he replied.

There were more words tumbling from her lips and later on she could not remember a single one. So perhaps none of those words had been quite right.

Eventually the words stopped. She pushed open the passenger door and stepped out of the car. The air felt hot enough to scorch her throat and the underarms of her blouse were soaked with sweat. She stared helplessly at the figures standing at the edges of the barricade, their faces pink blurred blotches. In the corner of her vision she noticed one person nimbly hop over the grille and hurry towards her.

She ran around to the driver's side of the bright green vehicle. Such a ridiculous colour, she thought. Far too garish. Yet it had tickled him; he had pointed out that they would never lose sight of it in car parks, where the vehicles blended into a sea of blues and greys. It shocked her that they had once talked about something so normal, so regular, so dull. Something that a married couple should talk about, rather than pain and loss and grief. It seemed like a half-forgotten memory of times long past.

Bending to the car, she rapped on his window. 'Please,' she said faintly, feeling as if the words were coming from very far away. She was floating some distance above the scene, watching a sweating woman with white-blonde hair tap on the window of a car resting in the centre of a railway level crossing. *This isn't happening*, that mind-voice whispered, and this time it was not whiny and petulant but insidious, coaxing her. *Don't worry, Hannah. This isn't really happening.*

But it was. As crazy as the situation might be, it was certainly no dream. She banged again on the glass, thumping it with her palm.

'Come on, please. Whatever … whatever it is that you've done, this isn't the answer. We can make it better.'

She felt a tug on her arm. She shrugged it away.

'Now!' her voice rose to a shriek. 'Get out, Euan, please!'

Then she sensed another presence approaching. A grey, hurtling bullet. There was a louder noise that rose above the merry blares of the car horns. She stared at her husband's face. That well-known, well-loved jawline with the aquiline nose and the curly dark hair thinning slightly at his temples.

'Please,' she repeated, softer now. 'Look at me. Please.'

His eyes squeezed slowly shut.

She felt hands grip her, nails sinking in above her biceps, and she was yanked backwards roughly. Then there was an enormous thump of displaced air that threw her to the ground and she collapsed on to a squashy human cushion who wheezed hot breath in her ear. The next day she would see the skin around the muscles had turned a vicious mauve shade, rimmed with yellow outrage.

Arms reached to wrap around her. She shrugged them away with a strength born of desperation. She scrabbled to her knees, lunging forward. Her fingertips came within three inches of brushing the train, then she stumbled and fell backwards once more.

Those words rose up again. *What stupid point are you trying to prove?*

Right up until the dull steel snub-nose of the train mashed into the passenger door of their car with a shriek of twisting metal and the reek of spent ozone, bunting the vehicle containing her husband down the tracks and out of her line of sight with such shocking velocity, she still believed he was only trying to prove a point.

I

Hannah and I: Our first meeting

Café Bellevue

The sun glints off the small circular patio tables, turning the metal into a chef's hotplate that sizzles to the touch. I sit with my back to the cave-like entrance of the bistro, my nostrils occasionally picking up the whiff of sharp continental hops from within. I listen to the background hubbub of cars, the shouts of traders from a nearby market, the whirring whoosh of trams.

This place is called Café Bellevue, the words scrawled in florid script on the napkins and menu. God knows how I ended up here. Maybe I was drunk, found my way into one of the wicker chairs and slept through my hangover. There are worse places to wake up than a café-bar in Paris. I think I may be in the 14th arrondissement, but again my memory's a blank.

So I sit at my table, a glass of beer in one hand and a demolished plate of steak-frites in front of me, idling away my afternoon. Café Bellevue belongs to me and an old gentleman with a neatly trimmed white beard who is reading a pink-shaded newspaper. The waiter – a skinny, moustachioed young man in a tuxedo – hurries around on unspecified errands, his expression one of perpetual harassment even though there are only two of us at his café. The fierce sun is inching its way through the gaps in the clouds.

Time passes.

Perhaps I nodded off again but when I turn my head, I see another person has joined us, three tables away to my left. A charge of adrenaline crackles through my body. The new arrival is a girl, sporting over-large sunglasses that bring to mind the blackly bulbous eyes of an insect. A bob of white-blonde hair – as bright as a flare of lit magnesium – falls over her forehead. Her complexion is as little suited to the sun as mine; her pale shoulders are already tinting pink. She is wearing a powder blue dress that floats away from her slender, milky-white thighs. I try not to leer too obviously.

Well now, Euan, where do we start? We're both tourists and somehow I even know we're both British. I've been in Paris for months now and I've come to accept I'll never look like I belong here. This girl doesn't belong here either. Surely this bonds us already, so surely I can think of a great line? Something witty, something wonderful. Something like … something like … isn't the weather nice? Isn't the food lovely? Have you been to the Louvre yet? Have you ever met a more boring person than me? I can't think of a single thing to say and she's going to get up and go, any second now. The moment, the chance, will be lost forever.

Instead someone saves me. The waiter glides to the girl's table – suddenly he is not harried, suddenly he has all the time in the world to attend to his customers – and places a large coffee cup in front of her with an unctuous smile and bow. She is staying. Yes, she is staying; long enough for a drink, long enough for me to think of something to say to her, long enough for me to regret that I'm still wearing this reeking, oil-smeared plaid shirt, last washed God knows how many days or weeks ago. I see she has ordered *café crème* in one of those massive cups which the Parisians unaccountably adore; the unwieldy soup bowls with handles too small to fit a finger through. The blonde girl's lips twitch. She is evidently at a loss as to how to tackle this gigantic beverage.

At last she takes hold of the drink, but for some inexplicable reason she lifts it by the saucer, not the tiny handles. Her hands are shaking and above the background hubbub – the trams, the workmen's drills, the market clatter – I can hear the crockery rattling. In fact, it seems her whole body is shaking.

Despite her eyes and most of her face being hidden behind those great blank bug-eyed lenses, I know that she is staring straight at me. That she has been staring at me for exactly as long as I have been staring at her.

Feeling my cheeks flush, alcoholic bubbles lightening my brain, I raise my hand in greeting. I mouth, *Hello, you.*

Gravity takes its toll and the vast cup tips forward, falling from its inadequate base. It tumbles for what seems like forever, as if it might be suspended for eternity in the midpoint between the girl's hands and the cobbled street. Then the porcelain connects with the rim of the table and shatters. White shards fly across the café. Brown liquid explodes in a rainbow-shaped spray. The girl lets out a gasp, rising to her feet, knocking the table to the ground with a musical clang, the front of her dress soaking and sopping and clinging yes-so-tight around those pale thighs, and I stand up, gracelessly bunting over my own table, sending my empty plate and cutlery and beer crashing to the ground.

We stand in front of each other. I am sure the shock on the girl's face is mirrored in my own. We have decimated Café Bellevue in a matter of moments.

Then there is an enormous blast like a bomb or an air horn and I feel a sickening rushing sensation and I whip my head around in anticipation of an earthquake or tsunami or explosion, then a great strike of empty white light blanks out all vision.

9

I gasp and cover my face with my hands and fall back in my seat, expecting oblivion.

When my eyesight returns to normal, nothing has changed in the scene. The old man is still engrossed in his newspaper. The waiter is polishing a glass. No one is concerned by seismic changes in the atmosphere or atomic explosions. I stare at the table where she sat. But the girl with the burning magnesium hair has gone.

The girl has gone, vanished. The table has been righted by an unseen hand, if it was ever tipped over in the first place. I scan the ground for shards of crockery or coffee rivulets winding their way towards me. Any sign of her presence. Any sign of her.

Nothing.

The girl has gone.

2

245 days since the accident

The photographs were spread out on the living-room table, their lives reduced to a series of snapshots. The man with the dark curly hair and the pink scar tracking from the left side of his temple to his jawbone stared intently at the images, occasionally taking one in his hands to trace his fingers over the surface. A young couple, barely out of their teens, embracing against the London skyline. Then the same couple – a few years older now – standing on top of Highland crags, clad in bulky raincoats, grinning defiantly against the elements. Then a man in a black morning suit and a woman in a flowing cream dress thrusting their left hands into the lens of the camera like children showing off new toys, twin silver bands gleaming on their fingers.

That familiar dull hopelessness throbbed through her body as she watched him squint at the photographs as if they were part of a jigsaw puzzle where the pieces didn't quite fit together. She would have preferred his anger. Instead it was her husband's confusion that tore at her heart.

The man in the pictures looked an awful lot like Euan and the woman in the pictures bore an uncanny resemblance to herself. But she knew that the happy couple beaming out from the photographs were strangers; unknown figures from the past, encased in acetate.

Her sister took her by the arm and wordlessly led her through to the kitchen.

'I knew it was shit,' Saskia said, reaching into the fridge for the near-empty bottle of Sauvignon Blanc and topping up her glass. Her hand trembled slightly as her sister poured the wine and the neck of the bottle juddered musically against the glass. 'But I didn't realise how cataclysmically shit it was.'

She shrugged, burying her face in her drink. 'This is how it is. This is life now. You learn to get used to it.'

'It's like he's revising for an exam,' Saskia said in a low voice, casting a concerned glance into the living room. Euan's shaggy head was still bowed over the photographs. Their mother was talking him through the pictures, her words riddled with false jollity. 'You can memorise every one of the facts but I'm not sure if it means anything.'

'He's trying. That's the best I can hope for.'

'I'm sorry I haven't been there for you, Han.'

She shrugged again. 'San Fran's hardly the next town over. I'm just pleased you're here now.'

Saskia pulled her into a crushing embrace. Her sister's solid form felt wonderfully comforting against her bony frame. Since the accident the weight had simply fallen off her. Food held no pleasure any longer – as if the time inside antiseptic hospital wards had cauterised her taste buds – and at the end of another long day of trying to tutor her husband back to his former self, she had to remind herself to eat.

'What do the doctors say?' her sister asked, leaning against the kitchen countertop.

Saskia was five years older, but with her West Coast tan and achingly fashionable razor-sheared haircut and gym-honed physique, a casual onlooker might have thought her the younger of the siblings. Certainly healthier, she thought, than the reflection that greeted her in the bathroom mirror each morning: a woman with lank, unwashed hair, dark grey circles cut underneath her eyes, her dowdy clothes hanging like the hide of a rhino. Increasingly it seemed that applying make-up was stretching gauze over an open wound. Two years ago, in a certain light, she could have passed for a girl in her late teens. That, however, was before her husband's accident.

'The doctors—' she started, then stopped. In the months since Euan had come out of his coma, the doctors' earnest and hopeful prognoses had slid into conjecture, then concern. After a while, she realised they were siphoning off her hopes, drop by drop.

She had spent countless hours talking Euan through his past life, as the people at the hospital had recommended. Dropping little reminders into their conversations. *Memory bombs*, the psychologist had called them. Depth charges designed to sink down into his subconscious and explode the past to the surface of his brain. Memory bombs, such a sick joke. The real memory bomb was that hurtling freight train which had crashed into their car on the level crossing, blowing his mind apart.

Her solace would come with the solution. The quest for a light flickering in the darkness, a light that now only burned in the most optimistic of her daydreams.

'The doctors have done everything they can,' she finished lamely, and she knew that wasn't true. It couldn't be true, because if it was true, it meant the end of hope, and it was hope alone that sustained her. The hope that one day she would open the front door to their home and Euan would be waiting for her in the hallway, his posture easy, a glass of brandy in one hand, his face cracking into that familiar crooked grin. His lips framing his old greeting, *Hello, you.* The first words he had mouthed to her in Paris. The greeting he had used a thousand, a million times over the course of their relationship, the sweet taste never diluted by repetition. *I remember you now, Hannah,* Euan would say, his voice trembling with emotion. *I remember you, I remember everything – absolutely everything.* Then she would throw herself into his arms, his lips pressing against hers with such hungry fervour, the world exploding into a kaleidoscope of wildly iridescent colours and . . .

She felt a hand squeeze her forearm. The beautiful mirage vanished. Shaking her head to clear her thoughts, she stared into her sister's eyes. Through the open doorway into the living room, she could make out the sound of her mother's voice as she explained the photographs to Euan.

'You drifted off for a few seconds there, Han,' Saskia said.

'Sorry,' she muttered.

Her sister sucked in air through her teeth, her lips pursing as if she had a foul taste in her mouth and needed to spit it out. 'Listen,' she said, 'there are some people I've heard about in Seattle. Neuropsychologists, memory specialists. Maybe . . . maybe they could help you. The Reel Memory Project. You heard of them?'

Apprehension wriggled in her gut. 'I've heard about them,' she said, trying to keep her tone emotionless. Of course she had heard of the Reel Memory Project. Ree-Mem had been the unspoken word on the lips of everyone at the hospital. Ree-Mem lurked between the lines of the sentences on each online support group. She tried to ignore the clamour but still those twinned sing-song syllables echoed in her mind like a child's nursery rhyme. But who were the people behind that simple, twee brand name? *Saviours,* said some. *Brain butchers,* said at least as many. Ree-Mem messed with your mind. Ree-Mem

14

played God with your psyche. Ree-Mem offered a miracle cure or mental obliteration. Ree-Mem could bring back the person you loved – or destroy them entirely.

'I saw a documentary last year,' she went on. 'There were lawsuits from former patients. They wiped a woman's mind in Oregon. She went into a trance and never came out. I want my husband back. Not a … not a vegetable.'

She tracked her sister's gaze over her shoulder into the living room. Their mother had given up on the photographs and cards and had turned her attention to the television. Euan sat beside her on the settee, his expression flat and unquestioning, seeing but not seeing.

'Surely anything's worth a try,' Saskia said. It was less a question than a statement. 'Why not arrange a meeting with those Ree-Mem guys? Talk to them. See what they have to say. See what they can offer you.'

There was a challenge in her sister's gaze, exasperation muddled with pity. The stare that asked her why she hadn't been brave enough to contact Ree-Mem before. She felt transported back to her childhood, when her elder sister had encouraged her along on another dangerous adventure, and little Hanny Allaker had been so fearful and cowardly and shook her head to send her blonde locks flying, and she said no-no-no, I won't, I won't.

'Hannah,' Saskia said. 'I'm sorry to have to say it like this, I'm sorry to be the bad person yet again, but please, answer me one question. What on earth do you have to lose?'

She stared first at her sister, then her husband. She wondered why she had spent almost half a year waiting for Euan to snap back to his former self.

'Dad always said you were the best at making the best of

things.' Saskia placed a hand on her arm. 'But … this isn't Euan. This isn't even you. You can't go on like this, Han.'

'Things are fine,' she replied, her voice barely a whisper. 'I can cope.'

'Talk to them,' Saskia went on implacably. 'You can't say you've exhausted every option until you speak to Ree-Mem. You owe Euan that much. Christ, Han, you owe yourself that much.'

She hung her head, defeated. She knew – she had known for a long time now – that there was only one path left to try. She imagined blank-faced men in white coats delving into her husband's mind, drilling through memories into the bedrock of his psyche. She was scared of what Ree-Mem might find. But, she had to admit, intrigued too. She felt a dark curiosity; a taste on her tongue like burnt sugar. There was a reason why the accident had happened. The desire to know the whole truth burned almost as fiercely as the need to have her husband back.

'They might even give you a few answers,' Saskia said, reading her mind in that casually spooky manner of siblings. 'A bit of closure at least? You never found out why he did it.'

She shook her head. It must have been a mistake, surely. Euan loved her and he would never want to hurt her. What had happened that summer's day was definitely an accident, a bad mistake. But it was possible that the Reel Memory Project could uncover the reasons behind her husband's mistake. Better still, she thought, a surge of adrenaline jouncing through her body, maybe Ree-Mem could fix that mistake and make everything better. She imagined how she would feel if she really did come home to find Euan with all his memories restored, as he had once been, as she had loved him – a reality this time, not a daydream – and allowed her lips to tilt into a half-smile.

'I'll call,' she said at last. 'I'm not going to promise anything else. But I'll call Ree-Mem.'

'Swear?' Saskia asked. It was as if she was nine-years-old again and her sister was making her promise – *swear, Hanny, swear it* – not to tell their mother about her first boyfriend. The word brought her back to their childhood; sisters' secrets, unbreakable bonds.

'Swear,' she replied.

3

251 days since the accident

From the first sip of wine she felt a glow settle inside her. Even if the kindling was only alcohol it was worth stoking that fire. The pub was carefully decorated to create the impression of a centuries-old coachman's inn. Yet the bridles mounted on the walls were plastic and she doubted the copper bedpans hanging from the ceilings would have been quite so clean.

Euan was staring down at the pint of ruby-shaded ale she had ordered, sniffing at the white suds. She knew one of his questions was coming. A question that showed he did not understand, would never understand, would never know and never remember.

Eventually the question came. 'Do I really like to drink this?' he asked, his nose crinkling at the almost untouched glass of beer.

She flinched. 'Euan, please—'

'Sorry. It's pretty disgusting. It's flat and gloopy. Too warm.'

'Well, have a nice cold lager then,' she said brightly. 'Or a brandy, you always liked brandy. Or do that thing with tequila where you sniff the salt and squeeze the lemon in your eyes. People liked to watch you do it at parties, especially when it seemed like you'd really blinded yourself. Your mate Barry always called it a Tequila Suicide.'

Inwardly she cursed herself for saying the word *suicide*. She had been warned by the counsellors not to use that word; what happened on the rail tracks had been an accident, they told her, and no one was to blame. She took a long swig of her drink and tried to smile, cheerful and supportive. But her weak grin crumbled before his puzzled expression. The white wine – lively tropical fruits and a perfumed bouquet, the bottle promised – turned to acid in her mouth.

'It's the sort of beer you used to drink anyway,' she went on. 'You loved those weird ales with silly names. Honeyed Strumpet. Or Badger Baiter. Or Old Bollockface. You'd spend ages at the bar quizzing the landlord about his beers. They were sick of the sight of you.'

Euan nudged the pint away with a forefinger. 'I'm sorry,' he repeated. 'I don't know, it's not to my taste.'

'Tastes do change, Euan,' she said with a frantic laugh. She was so determined for this evening to go well. It was her plan to make him feel comfortable, make him feel settled, then tell him about Ree-Mem. How could she tell him when he was staring at her in that way, so lost and confused? She thought for a moment and inspiration struck. 'Okay, okay. I've got a game for you.'

'A game?'

'Oh yes. Fabulous prizes to be won.'

He smiled a little and that was better, yes, that was better.

'Why do you always order a funny-sounding beer in a bar? A beer you might not even like?'

'I don't know.'

'Fine. Fine, no problem.' She drummed her fingertips on the table. 'Think of my dad. What was his name?'

He squeezed his eyes shut, concentrating hard. 'Mar … Martin. Martin Allaker.'

'Good. Very, very good. What were my dad's two great loves in his life?'

'Uh, I think … you. You and your mother?'

She was momentarily taken aback. For a short while she was lost for words. Her father had died of a brutally sudden heart attack seven months before their wedding, and her only regret of their marriage – her only regret before Euan's accident, at least – was that he had not been there to walk her down the aisle.

'Sorry,' she said with a slight choke, 'I wasn't being specific enough. Think more hobbies, not family values.'

He shook his head again. 'God, I don't know.'

'The answer's in front of you!'

He raised his eyebrows. 'Beer?'

'Yes!' she said, clapping her hands. 'One hundred per cent correct. My dad's two big loves were beer and cricket. And you, what do you think of cricket?'

'What do I think of cricket?'

'Yes.'

'I … I'm not sure, I …'

'You hate it.'

He nodded, perhaps in recognition. 'I hate cricket.'

'You hate cricket. Really hate it. Because it's … because it's … because it's what, Euan?'

'It's boring?'

She gave him a thumbs-up signal. 'And? And?'

He held up his hands. 'Sorry—'

'And Scotland are rubbish at cricket. But you were so desperate to get in my dad's good books that you told him you loved it. So every time we visited my parents' house—' she play-acted a bat hitting a ball '—what do you think you had to do?'

'I had to lie to him?'

'You did. You really did. You used to read up about batting averages and fielding positions so you had something to talk about. You sat together and watched the Ashes for hours drinking pints of his nasty homebrew. Why did you do that, Euan?'

His gaze was fixed on the shoddy reproductions of artworks on the pub wall. She allowed herself to hope, just a little. 'Because I loved you very much,' he said finally, 'and I knew how much you loved your dad.'

The hope bloomed into something wonderful. 'So you do remember?' she whispered.

For a second he held her gaze and she wondered if she could detect that familiar wry gleam in the depths of his eyes; the acknowledgement of the tiny complicities that all couples carry between them. Then he sighed, shaking his head, and the fragile illusion fractured. 'I know because you've told me this before. Not because I really remember. I can't lie to you, Hannah, can I? That's not what I'm supposed to do, the doctors said.'

Her smile fell apart like a shattered mask. He had defeated her. He had defeated her the same way as always: guilty yet blameless. He had defeated her without knowing because he did not know anything. His face had taken on that kicked-puppy look and she clenched her teeth together, feeling a steady pulsing of pressure behind her eyes.

'No,' she agreed, trying to keep her voice steady. 'No, Euan, you're quite right.'

He gulped at his drink. 'The beer's not that bad actually,' he said, his tone conciliatory.

'It is that bad, Euan,' she blurted out. She knew the words were wrong, the opposite of the *positive affirmation* urged by the doctors. She knew she was preparing a splendid banquet of guilt upon which she could feast during the night and the nights that followed. 'Everything really is that bad. It's completely fucked.'

He hung his head. 'I'm sorry. Should we go?'

She nodded. She could not trust herself to say any more.

Later that night, as she lay awake in the double bed that had once been theirs to share, she heard a tentative knock on the door. He stood at the doorway, wearing baggy grey boxer shorts and a worn-out T-shirt bearing the logo of an obscure punk band.

'Couldn't sleep,' he said timidly. 'Can I stay here tonight?'

He was embarrassed, she realised, his confidence blasted away. That spark of arrogance which simultaneously attracted and vexed her had been extinguished in the crash. She most certainly missed the good things about her husband – his love, his wit, his warmth – but she missed his flaws too. Euan's old personality was filled with valleys and crags, soft in places and rough in others. This new Euan seemed to be all malleable contours; there were no fault-lines for her to smooth over, no depths for her to trough. In his old life Euan George Stornoway had been many things, many brash, arrogant and infuriating things, but never timid. She missed his certainties. She missed his passion, his impulsiveness, his romantic recklessness.

Euan always had the ability to trick her. One year, in the back-before, she thought he had forgotten her birthday. *You can't expect me to remember*, he said in the face of her hurt glare. *What did you want, a party and jelly and custard?* Then, when she stomped out the door on her way to work, cursing him under her breath, she had seen his gift. The number 27, ten-feet high and six-feet wide, constructed out of thistles and white roses on the front lawn of their mansion block. *I called your work*, Euan murmured as he snuck up behind her, relishing her surprise and delight. *Poor Hannah has a terrible case of three-day flu. Doctors say the only cure is tapas and rioja in Barcelona.* He held up two flight tickets, offering her what he termed his Spy Hero Eyebrow. She hadn't suspected a thing.

Before, Euan had been a fine actor. A good liar. He kept an awful lot of thoughts to himself. Maybe if he had been more comfortable with the truth, if he hadn't locked so many of his emotions inside, he wouldn't have ... no, she couldn't allow her mind to travel down that path once again.

'You can stay if you like,' she told this new, guileless version of her husband, wondering why her voice sounded so indifferent.

Her husband slid into bed and pulled the duvet over them. He was a polite, chaste distance away from her and those few inches of empty space felt like a chasm.

He said, 'I hope it gets better.'

She rested a hand on the small of his back. She stared at the ceiling. She counted his long, shallow breaths until the first tendrils of dawn light flickered through the gaps in the curtains and it was time to face another day.

Her daily routine: she woke up, went into the spare bedroom where Euan usually slept now, she spoke to him. Not about anything much – but, as advised by the doctors, dropping in snippets of their past life in an attempt to provoke a reaction. Making contact, the doctors called it. He responded politely; he did not remember. They performed some domestic tasks, she spoke to him again. He responded politely; he did not remember. They ate lunch, she spoke to him. He responded politely; he did not remember. They sat in front of the vast television screen that dominated one wall of their living room. She would point out certain characters who reminded her of people they had once known. A truth or a lie, it barely mattered. He responded politely; he did not remember. They ate dinner, they watched more television, they drank a little wine in a parody of cosy co-habiting. She hated herself for the flush of relief, brief but strong, that she felt when he went upstairs to bed.

She reminded herself that long ago her greatest fear had been losing the intimacy she shared with Euan. The way he made her feel like the centre of the entire universe. Oh, they had lost that intimacy, in ways she could not possibly have imagined. She remembered the meeting with the clinical psychologist a month after Euan emerged from his coma. The questions, the answers. *Do you know who this woman is?* the man had asked, staring at them over the top of his half-moon spectacles. *Yes, she's my wife*, Euan replied. *Do you know her name?* the man asked. *Hannah Jane Stornoway, formerly Allaker*, Euan responded robotically, as if reciting from a crib sheet. *Do you love her?* the psychologist asked. She had held her breath. Then there was that stutter, complemented by a rapid camera-shutter blink. *Y… yes*, he said, not meeting her gaze, and that pause told her more about Euan's condition than she wanted to know.

It was only another little wound. One of a million paper cuts sliced into her skin every minute of every hour of every day.

She tried. She tried so hard. She tried to understand this version of Euan – outwardly identical but for the scar, yet emotionally so very different. She had tried to build a new life for them both. Her mother, her sister, the few friends who still came to visit – they all told her how hard she was trying, that she was doing everything she possibly could. She greeted her husband each day with a warm, patient, encouraging smile. No one had to know that this smile was painted on; that over the course of each endless day it threatened to crack and split, the colours running into a scream.

4

Hannah and I: Our first meeting

Café Bellevue

The girl takes hold of the saucer with both hands and lifts the cup to her lips. Her whole body is shaking; the crockery rattles on its base. She is staring at me, I'm sure. I raise my hand in greeting. My lips frame the words, *Hello, you.* The rattling of the cup increases to a crescendo.

The cup drops. The falling porcelain catches the edge of the metal table and shatters and a deluge of coffee sprays over the girl's dress and spatters on the cobbles.

She stands up, her dress sopping and clinging. I leap to my feet with no idea what I'm hoping to achieve and knock over my own table. My plate and beer crash to the ground and the glass self-destructs. Brilliant work, Stornoway, you complete numpty.

The girl and I stare at one another, our mouths perfect circles. We are bonded in our shared shock. Coffee and beer intermingle in rivulets between the cobbles. Shards of glass and porcelain wink in the sunlight. Café Bellevue, once a picture of tranquillity, now looks like the scene of a bar-room brawl.

'Oh fuck, sorry—'

'Jesus, I'm really sorry.'

Why are we apologising? To whom are we apologising? Having caused such devastation independently, we assume shared responsibility. The waiter, emerging from his lair, stops and silently assesses the carnage. The girl stands next to me, one bare leg hooked behind the other, her stance nervous. Her scent washes over me, light and delicate like apple blossom.

'What should we do?' she asks. Her voice is low, urgent. The complicity is thrilling. We are co-conspirators in the Great Ruined Café crime.

'I don't know,' I hiss back. 'Run away?'

'I think that's worse. We haven't paid.'

'Should we sit down then?'

I didn't mean this to sound like a line. The girl stares at me, her gaze evaluating. Suddenly I wish that I had shaved, that I had changed this shirt I've worn for days now. Despite her soaked dress she glows with strange inner grace; a coffee-stained goddess.

'Okay,' she says finally. 'What's the worst that could happen?'

The waiter reappears with a mop and broom. For an awful moment he seems to contemplate handing them to me. But instead he clears up the debris – our shared debris – with speed. Occasionally he glances upwards with a countenance so hangdog, so heartbreakingly put-upon, that I have to fight to avoid laughing. As she hides a smirk with her hand, I can see the girl has the same struggle.

'*Je voudrais une autre bière, s'il vous plaît,*' I tell the waiter.

With a deep sigh the waiter stumps away to replace my beer. The girl declines another cup of *café crème*. Instead she removes a packet of cigarettes from her handbag. Fumbling in my pocket, I bring out my lighter. Her hands are trembling and I have to follow the wavering line of the cigarette before it catches. The tip winks red. She breathes in and reclines. There is something unnatural about the way she smokes. Her attention is on the cigarette itself, how chic the slender white tube looks balanced between her index and middle finger. There is none of that inward-looking hunger of the nicotine slave. Then it hits me: she has seen this pose, this poise, in a movie. She is only smoking because Paris is the city of elegant smokers.

'So,' she starts.

'So,' I agree.

Then the memory of what we have done hits us simultaneously and we start to snigger. The girl smooths down the hem of her dress – again I try and fail to avoid gawping – and stares ruefully at the ruined fabric.

'Shall we pretend we didn't decimate this place and we're sitting down now, beginning the conversation?' I ask.

'That sounds good.'

'You first.'

'No, you first.'

'But I insist,' I say. Ever the gentleman. Also, I have no idea what to say. How can I interest her, intrigue her, fascinate her?

'So,' she says, 'what brings you to France?'

'Ah, just hanging around, really,' I tell her, taking a swig of my beer. 'Came over in the spring with a university friend who thought he was *un grande artiste*. Anything to avoid work and real life, I thought. Ended up half starved in a squat with these glumly creative characters. Moody drinking by candlelight, talking about smashing *le system* and starting *le revolution*. Eventually we had … um, a difference of political opinion. They kicked me out. Been knocking about in hostels ever since. My dad showed me how to fix cars and in Paris there are plenty of broken cars. The troubadour mechanic. Where spark plugs fail to spark, he'll be there.'

'You speak French, you fix cars,' she raises an eyebrow and I feel a twinge of pleasure so sharp that it's almost painful. 'A true polymath.'

'Ha, I'm barely a monomath.'

A good line, I tell myself, and one that raises a smile. But she is not drinking. Does that mean she is not staying? The girl gazes over my shoulder. She lifts a forefinger – the nail is short, closely bitten, painted a vivid green – and the waiter appears again, evidently praying these British vandals will pay up and he will be rid of us. But it's too soon, far too soon. The girl must stay, how can I convince her to stay? I can't shake the certainty that her staying is vitally important.

'*Mademoiselle?*' the waiter asks. He is even sketching the figures of the bill on his pad.

The girl fixes me with a stare from over the top of her sunglasses, a speculative glance too brief to translate. 'Brandy,' she says. I don't think I have ever felt such enormous relief.

'*Et un Cognac pour moi aussi,*' I say smoothly.

The waiter winces, his shoulders slumped as he returns once again to his bar. There is silence between us but somehow it is anything but uncomfortable. The waiter returns to my table – our table, now – and sets down two balloons of brandy, generously filled. The girl smiles. There is a tiny triangular chip in one of her front teeth. The sort of minor blemish you would only notice after being very close to somebody, yet haven't we just met? No matter. I pick up my drink and toast her. Despite her coffee-stained dress, she is still radiant, enchanting, mesmerising… and still so far out of reach.

'To new friends,' I propose.

'New friends,' she agrees.

We clink glasses.

'What's your name?' I ask, at the exact moment that she gulps down a huge slug of brandy. The liquor has a powerful kick which catches her unawares. She coughs and splutters for some time before finally choking out, 'I'm sorry, I'm not having much luck with drinks today—'

I laugh. 'It's lucky for me. If you hadn't dropped that coffee cup, we'd never be having this conversation.'

'I'm Hannah,' she says. 'Hannah Allaker.'

She takes a smaller sip of brandy. Her tongue quests over those full red lips, tasting the burnt tang of the spirit. That mouth... that tongue... how long... how long has it been since I... good God, Stornoway, keep a hold of yourself. She removes her sunglasses and stares at me. Her eyes are as green as her nails; bright, piercing.

'I'm Euan,' I tell her shakily. 'So how did you end up here at Café Bellevue, Hannah Allaker?'

'Not too different a story from yours. But my tale started in Venice. After uni I went inter-railing. With my boyfriend.'

I feel a plunge in my stomach. 'Is he—'

She laughs at my stricken expression. 'Oh, don't worry, he's gone now. We argued from Venice to Vienna. Then in Munich I found messages from a girl on his phone.' The girl purses her lips. 'I didn't even have the energy for a row. I waited until he'd gone to the bar and walked out of the *brauhaus*. Made like a banana and scrambled.'

My brow furrows at her mangled metaphor, then I realise it's intentional and match her grin. To look at her is a delight but I love to hear her talk. Those droll twists to her speech, those spiky sea mines of humour bobbing below the surface of her words.

'I'm so sorry,' I tell her with blatantly false compassion. 'What a bastard.'

'From the first day of the trip I knew it was over,' she says. 'And to think we'd been together forever, in university terms at least. We were that couple who everyone hated, the ones sickeningly wrapped up in ourselves and our perfect union.'

Her tone is still bright but her mouth has hardened a fraction. Already I can tell that this is a girl who does not forgive easily, if at all. She is silent for a short while, picking at the skin around her nails. I see the flesh near those sculpted cuticles is bloody, almost raw.

'I bet you even had excruciating pet names for each other,' I say, attempting to jump-start the conversation.

'Quite disgusting,' she agrees, folding her arms to hide the abrasions. '*Complètement dégoûtant*. We learned too much about each other. Nothing was exciting, or dangerous, or alluring about him any more.'

'Isn't that normal, though? For most couples?'

'For most couples maybe. Who'd want to be most couples? And who'd want to be normal?' The girl downs the rest of her brandy with a flourish and slams the glass down on the table. 'Let's get out of here,' she announces, her eyes uncannily luminous as if tiny twin flames are capering in the depths of her pupils. 'If we don't go soon, we'll lose the sunset. There's an amazing roof terrace at my hotel, if you fancy another drink.'

The offer, so casually made, takes me aback. Go? From here? With her? It seems an impossible turnaround in my romantic fortunes.

'Okay ... okay then,' I stutter. At my acquiescence I feel a lightness, a sense of a true path taken. I follow her gaze to the shining silver tram that has slid into existence across the road. Her grin intensifies and for the first time I match her smile. I am utterly confused but carried away by her energy, her life, the sheer overwhelming realness of her. I pull out my wallet and fan a spray of banknotes on the table. It's all the money I have left.

Hannah reaches down and grabs a small milk jug that survived the table apocalypse and the waiter's broom. She slips the jug into her handbag. 'A souvenir,' she says, her lips curling as if at a private joke. 'Look, there's the tram across the street. It stops right outside my hotel.'

She offers me her hand. I take hold of her outstretched fingers. She pulls me forward into the tram and the doors wheeze shut. The vehicle picks up speed, leaving Café Bellevue far behind.

5

252 days since the accident

The lights were low in the bedroom. She sat cross-legged propped up on pillows, swiping through reams of online text on her touchscreen, trying to kill the hours until the dawn light arrived. She heard her husband's snores through the wall that separated their rooms. The wall was only thin but its very presence meant everything.

She could not escape into fiction; books no longer held any interest. Drama and heartbreak were too-familiar bedfellows. Her social media feeds were stuffed with one-time friends proudly displaying successful lives and newly formed progeny. The delighted faces, the gushing messages congratulating themselves on breeding, as if they were the world's first couple to manage such a feat. *So this happened. Our little bundle of joy. No sleep but never felt so happy.* Damn them all.

Craving comfort, she began to click through the old photograph albums stored on the computer. She knew she needed to stop this habit but the pull was so strong; the nostalgia was only sweet because it was rotten. Birthdays, Christmases, Halloweens, Bonfire Nights. Glorious moments captured in a camera lens. So many celebrations, far too many drinks, so much laughter, so many twinned grins beaming back at her. Here they were seeing in the dawn next to the Royal Observatory in Greenwich Park, looking out at the lights of London. Here they were, woozy and red-eyed, clinking plastic glasses filled with whisky at Hogmanay on Princes Street. Here they were, resplendent in colourful cagoules, on top of a hill during that sodden walking holiday in the Lake District. How old had they been, 25 or 26? It seemed like yesterday and it seemed like a distant era.

The walking trip had been his idea. Despite having lived most of his life in Edinburgh suburbia, Euan fancied himself as a rugged backwoodsman capable of lighting fires, building shelters and wrestling bears. *You don't have to pretend you like this sort of thing*, he had told her as she puffed up the hill slope, her face florid, the straps of her backpack gouging tramlines in her shoulders. *The outdoors life ... well, it's not for everybody*. She had stuck out her tongue and told him to keep going – what did he think this was, a macho trial rather than healthy exercise? – but privately his words had troubled her. She wasn't trying to muscle in on his interests; she simply wanted to enjoy what he enjoyed, love what he loved. Later, slumped exhausted next to the fire at the Ambleside B&B – barefooted, her expensive new hiking boots having chafed her toes raw – she told him the truth. She told him why it was so important they enjoyed everything together: her parents had nothing in common and it scared her to think they might turn out the same way. Her parents had no shared interests, no common ground. Even in their home their domains were divided: her mother ruled the parlour and kitchen, forever on patrol for stray specks of dust, while her father would be out in the garden or in his shed, listening to old rock 'n' roll songs on the radio and tending to his witchy-smelling homebrew. It was so very far from her romantic ideal. *It's what you're like, not what you like ... that's what I've always said*, Euan told her. She had smiled at him over the top of her wine glass, trying to feel reassured. But it worried her that any fissures between them might deepen and split into cracks. She wanted them to share everything. She wanted him to think her perfect in every way. She wanted him to have no secrets from her.

But there had been a secret, hadn't there? Maybe one secret, maybe more than one. Something he had hinted at just before their car ended up wedged between the barriers on the railway tracks. Something that haunted her. Something that kept her awake.

Euan had always been a solitary man who kept his innermost thoughts on a tight leash. But in the six months after Jennifer, he had withdrawn from her to such an extent that she didn't know which worried her most – Euan at home, mute and pensive, or Euan off walking or driving, travelling who-knew-where. He had always been a wanderer, but each day he seemed to trek further and further away in both body and mind. However, on the day of the accident, her husband had been less remote and distracted than normal. In fact he seemed to be on edge, his face sickly animated, his eyes flicking around in desperation like a snared rabbit. Less than twenty minutes before the crossing, as they sat opposite one another in the shopping mall coffee bar, he was on the verge of telling her what had gone wrong, what he had done. Innocently, stupidly, she thought it would be better if he told her at home ... but, of course, they never made it home. After the accident it seemed that the secret which had been on the tip of his tongue, nudging at his clenched teeth, had crawled back inside his brain to hibernate forever. Maybe, she reasoned, if she knew what had happened – what had gone so very wrong – she could help bring Euan back to the old version of himself.

In the end, between the hours of four and five o'clock, she was unable to help herself. She was drawn back, over and over again, to the website of the Reel Memory Project. Mellow pastel shades. A soft-focus image of a man and a woman in handsome early middle-age, smiling lovingly at one another, even their crows' feet strangely fetching. The name of the organisation was etched out in a simple black font. One line of text underneath, a slogan of sorts: *We can help*. She managed a wan smile. So many people had tried to help her and Euan. Psychiatrists, counsellors, therapists, even holistic healers. They had declaimed, prescribed, poked and prodded. Every one of them had been found badly wanting.

An icon along the bottom of the screen read: *Learn More About Ree-Mem*. Did she want to learn more? She supposed that she did.

At the Reel Memory Project we have dedicated our lives to reshaping and rebuilding human memory. Phrases which barely made sense flickered before her eyes. *Pioneering research ... astonishing breakthrough ... conjoined hypnosis ... a cure for amnesia ...*

She read on, hardly aware that her heart was starting to boom like a bass drum and a thin layer of sweat had slicked her forehead.

Her fingers danced on the touchscreen, scrolling through the case studies from the Project's patients, the tributes. She fancied she could see digital tears of gratitude collecting around the corners of her screen. The dementia patient who could recall her daughter's wedding day once more. The recovering alcoholic whose lost years had returned to him. The property baron suffering from the later stages of Alzheimer's able to retrieve the location of his will, hidden beneath a floorboard in his childhood home. The sardonic thought popped into her brain that large inheritances often did cause families to take a renewed interest in elderly relatives.

One case study resonated. A couple in Baltimore. The husband suffered a *coup-contrecoup* head injury on his construction site, leading to post-traumatic amnesia. She read the quote from the man's wife over and over again. *We had tried everything and nothing worked ... nothing but Ree-Mem.* The words echoed in her brain. *Nothing worked ... nothing but Ree-Mem.* She was exhausted and confused. Her vision was blurry, fuzzed by fatigue. The thought of strangers poking around in her husband's memories – and the memories they shared and treasured, the memories which made up their marriage – unnerved her. But, as her sister had so bluntly reminded her, they were out of options.

At the bottom of the screen a pill-shaped button glowed. The text below the button read: *Talk to one of our fully-trained medical advisors, 24 hours a day, seven days a week.* She stared at the button, breathing deeply.

She was drawn to Ree-Mem. She was frightened of Ree-Mem. She needed advice, counsel, even a shove in the right direction. She had no one to whom she could turn. Her mother, always conservative, would say *No.* Her sister – eternally impulsive – would urge *Yes.* 1-1, a score draw, no help there. The only person whose advice she craved, the one whose opinion she trusted above all others, was not here to guide her. He was trapped inside the wreckage of his own mind.

What would Euan have done, she wondered, if their positions were reversed?

She thought of the man in the next room; how hard he was trying to be the man she wanted, needed him to be. Maybe this would help. Maybe this would help him.

The button on the screen beckoned to her like a lighthouse beacon to a lost ship. She reached out her forefinger and pressed it.

★

37

The hours that followed dragged heavily. Once upon a Sunday, they might have gone for a walk hand-in-hand or enjoyed a lazy afternoon drink in the garden. Euan could have cooked his infamous Drunken Swine Roast, where he steeped a slab of pork in a bath of cider and left it in the oven until crisped enough to be edible. Instead they glided around the house like ghosts, never touching. At one point Euan turned on the radio, far too loud, and she turned it off immediately. The music reminded her of the days when he was locked inside his coma and she had sat on his hospital bed, his limp hand clasped in hers, playing his old punk rock records – the crashing and howling neutered by the sterile ward – in an attempt to stir brainwave activity. *You call this shock treatment, girl?* Nurse Violet, the one she liked best, had demanded. Back then she had still believed Euan would wake up and want to put on The Damned or The Ramones, maybe ask for a glass of brandy and check how Hearts were doing. Back then she had still believed he would wake up and know her. Back then she had still believed he would wake up as the same man.

The call came when they were sitting watching television in the evening, her on the sofa and him on the easy chair. From upstairs she heard her tablet shrill out a marimba beat.

'Probably my mum,' she told Euan, hurrying out of the room. She couldn't have said why she chose not to tell him the truth.

Scampering up the stairs, she grabbed the tablet from her bedside table and hammered at the green *Answer* icon, fearful that the caller would ring off. The video connection stuttered and fuzzed. Then the screen finally, blessedly, winked into life. She stared into a square-jawed face. The man's skin was the colour of light coffee, his eyes a startling shade of periwinkle blue.

'Is this Hannah whom I have the pleasure of addressing?' the man said, smiling widely and whitely. 'Hannah Stornoway?'

'That's me,' she said with false cheeriness.

The man's smile somehow intensified. 'Hello there, Hannah,' he said. 'I'm from the Reel Memory Project. My name is Dr Scott Calvin. Or Dr Cal, if you'd prefer.'

'Hi,' she said faintly.

The man on the screen seemed to be in early middle-age. Forties, maybe even nearer to fifty. His hair was cropped close to his scalp, speckled with streaks of silver. Suddenly she wished she had bothered to run a comb through her lank hair that day, or at least changed out of her shapeless grey cardigan, which made her feel like a widow in mourning but fit her so well these days.

'My colleague Melissa,' Dr Calvin said, 'has passed on the details of your husband's ... ah ... tragic condition.'

She had spoken to a Ree-Mem advisor during the endless grey of the early hours, giving out sparse personal information, and had been told a Project curator would contact her later. Curator, she thought. Such an archaeological term; as if her husband's memories were exhibits in museum display cases, eternally trapped in still-life.

'Through the magic of telecommunications, I'm reaching out to you in England, is that correct?'

'Y ... yes,' she said. 'That's right.'

'Wonderful, wonderful,' Scott Calvin said, stretching back on his chair. His screen tilted, affording her a view of his office. There were a number of other video screens mounted into the wall behind his head. She saw a grand oak desk and plate glass windows. A large yucca plant stood in the corner of the room, its leaves a shade of chartreuse unknown to nature. 'A charming country,' he continued. 'At the turn of the millennium I had the pleasure of working in a London hospital, although I'm sure the city has changed immeasurably since those bygone days. However, I must confess that I'm yearning for a return visit, and what with the Project's expansion ... but we'll come to all manner of administrative tedium in good time.' He finished with a good-natured chuckle.

'Right,' she said, uncertain whether a response was required.

'Mrs Stornoway,' Dr Calvin said, drumming his fingers on the desk. 'Hannah. I already have a rough drawing of your husband's predicament. But please, so I can fully understand your case, would you shade in between the lines?'

She pushed the bedroom door closed with her big toe.

'He ... he was driving,' she said. Her throat was too dry and she felt her cheeks flush because hadn't she just started with a lie? 'His car was hit by a train,' she rushed on. 'He was in a coma for three months. Physically he recovered. But when he woke up, all his memories were gone. Everything. His life, his childhood. Me. He didn't remember anything.'

She realised she was on the verge of tears and fanned her eyes. She did not want to cry. That would be weak. Whatever faults and flaws Hannah Jane Stornoway possessed, weakness was not one of them.

'Please take your time, Hannah,' Dr Calvin said. 'I'm a neuro-psychologist by trade, but believe me, much of my work here at Ree-Mem is as a counsellor.'

'Euan woke up,' she said, her fingertips working at the lump in her throat. She remembered the explosion of joy she had felt when the phone call came from the hospital; the news that he had opened his eyes and was even attempting to vocalise. Well, that joy had dissipated with shocking speed. He was not Euan. He was a man who had once been Euan. 'One day he just ... he just woke up. It was nothing to do with me and for some reason that hurt. There was no premonition, no psychic link.

I was in the bath when the phone rang and I thought it was my mum ringing with her latest neighbourhood watch update and I nearly didn't bother to answer. It was the hospital. The doctor – he sounded so young – told me Euan was awake, sitting up, confused but otherwise fine. They thought his memory would return, given time, even somewhat impaired, but it never did. Nothing. He remembered nothing. We've been trying to … cope … ever since.'

'Coping must be almost impossible,' Calvin said, 'when your husband looks exactly as he did before his accident, yet internally you are strangers.'

She could only nod. The doctor had summed up her feelings for Euan so succinctly. What was more, he was not judging her for those feelings.

'The first thing we tell the partners of our patients,' Calvin went on, 'is that they should never feel guilty. Our entire personalities reside in our memories, so without our memories what are we as humans? How can we interact with each other without memory? How can we love? How can a relationship endure without our minds delving into our past experiences and informing us that – yes! – this is the person we adore above all others?'

She nodded again, miserably. It had taken a man she had never met before to tell her the truth.

'The treatment we perform here at Ree-Mem,' Dr Calvin said, 'is a procedure we call conjoined hypnosis. Temporal lobe stimulation. Inside the temporal lobe we find the capricious little seahorse we know as the hippocampus. You see, Hannah, the hippocampus is one of the few areas of the brain capable of growing new neurons. In other words, reforming memory. Now, Hannah—'

She leaned forward, biting on her bottom lip, the beating

of her heart so loud she wondered whether Dr Calvin could hear it.

Then one of the monitor screens beeped loudly and the doctor rolled his eyes.

'Forgive me, Hannah,' he said, rubbing at the salt-and-pepper stubble around his jawline. 'Duty calls. One of my assistants will be in touch shortly – if, that is, you wish to learn more about the process. The process and the treatment.'

'Do you … do you really think you can help us?' she asked, almost struck dumb with disbelief.

Dr Scott Calvin nodded, a smile of unshakeable certainty creasing his broad face. 'Ree-Mem can help you, Hannah. We can help you and Euan. I guarantee it. Now, until next time we speak, I wish you and your husband the very best in your lives.'

Then the connection was broken and the screen flicked to grey.

6

Hannah and I: Our first meeting (later)

The Panorama of Montparnasse

The girl with hair like a magnesium flare. I remember her from the café, I remember we caught a tram together, but that was so many brandies ago and now her name dances on the tip of my tongue. Where is she now? The alcohol and the remorseless heat of the afternoon have blurred my mind. I seem to have found myself on an elegant rooftop terrace that looks out over Paris, sitting underneath a stone archway covered with climbing roses. There are at least a dozen tables up here but right now I'm alone.

Then the door to the terrace bangs open and the blonde girl – Hannah! Of course, her name is Hannah! – appears. Triumphantly she brandishes a bottle of red wine.

'Hello, you,' I say.

'Hello, you, too,' she replies. 'Drinks are served.'

I have already fetched a brace of glasses from I know not where. 'We don't have the waiter to help us now,' I tell her as she sploshes in the wine. 'Anything we break we'll have to clear up ourselves.'

'I don't think we'll ever be allowed back to that café,' Hannah says. '*C'est la vie*. Should we toast to something different this time?'

'Ah, why change a winning formula?'

We raise our glasses, say the words – *new friends* – which now seem very familiar, clink and drink. She smiles and I return it, again desperately trying to think of something to say. Humour? Poetry? I stare out over the Parisian cityscape, searching for inspiration. The skyline is an achingly lovely picture postcard – can anything so perfect be real? The panorama looks like a beautiful lie. The first stars are peeking through the orangey smog haze, crystals floating in the ether. With the sight of the stars comes a thought.

'I … I always … always wondered,' I start haltingly, 'that when they sent a dog into space, what would have happened if aliens had spotted it.'

Hannah crinkles her nose. 'Whatever are you talking about?' she asks. In the gloaming it's difficult to read her expression.

I push on. 'They'd have the wrong impression from the initial encounter, right? They'd presume dogs were the ruling species, and this brave soul was the leader, the pioneer. So they come down and observe us … and, get this, their suspicions are confirmed. Dogs really are the ruling life forms. They're the masters and humans are servants. Because we feed them, groom them, clean up their crap. Even when we take them for walks they're one step ahead. So, dogs are Planet Earth's dominant species – right or wrong?'

Hannah stares at me silently. That perfect porcelain face is entirely still, a theatrical Noh mask betraying no emotion. I bury my face in my wine, wondering whether I have made an enormous fool of myself. I'm drunk on beer and wine and brandy and I'm drunker still on her presence; giddy and delirious. But seriously, Stornoway, that's no excuse. Dogs? Aliens? Inwardly I groan. What the hell was I blathering on about?

'Have you mentioned this theory to anybody else?' she asks. Dumbly I shake my head. 'I wouldn't,' she says. 'Ever.'

'Why?'

'Well now,' she whispers, leaning forward in her chair, an eyebrow raising, 'you don't want the dogs to know you've sussed them out.'

Then we are both laughing and I feel as if a gate that was slowly falling shut has magically swung open. I want this evening to last for the rest of my life. I don't want to go back to my grimy hostel with the exposed wiring in the shower block and the greasy pillows and the beds around me creaking from furtive, muffled liaisons. This girl has already led me into a better, brighter world. When we walked through the hotel's marble foyer earlier – swaying a little, almost but not quite hand-in-hand – I could see the bow-tied concierges were itching to throw me out. But while I'm with Hannah, I'm untouchable, I'm golden.

'How the hell can you afford a hotel like this?' I ask. 'I thought inter-railing was all about ten-to-a-bed dorms and wringing out your undercrackers in rivers. This doesn't seem gritty enough.'

Hannah shrugs, replenishing our glasses. 'When my mum heard Danny had left, she wanted me to come home straight away. Terrified about a young girl abroad on her own, heaven forfend. So I promised to stay in decent hotels. No more backpacker doss houses for little Hanny. Borrowed money from my sister. She's got a decent job, she can afford it. I cleaned up a bit and presented my sweet self at the front desk. Been here two days, seeing the sights, walking the streets, failing to hold cups of coffee correctly. But tomorrow's my last day. Next week's chock-full of job interviews in London. I've even started looking at house shares. So very grown up, isn't that awful?'

I don't want to talk about London. I don't want to talk about leaving. I want to talk about Paris; the here, the now, with her. 'Did you see everything you wanted to?' I ask. 'I felt like I should go to the Tuileries, the name's so pretty. I mean, Christ, I come from a city which has areas like Niddrie and Dumbiedykes. Places that sound like infectious diseases.'

She walks her fingers up my arm, setting off tingling explosions in my brain. Her smile arrives slowly, patiently, insuppressibly. 'I don't think I quite managed to see everything,' she says softly. 'But you know what, I found everything I needed.'

Then her lips are on mine and she tastes of wine and wonder and the skyline burns red with unearthly heat and the blood rushes in my ears and when at last we break apart I am gasping for air.

We stare at one another for some time, breathing heavily, almost combative; as if what we have experienced was less an embrace than the first blows of a boxing bout. Emerald eyes, flaxen hair; I was wrong when I thought of her as a typical English rose. Now, silhouetted against the setting sun, she is a Viking goddess.

'As first kisses go,' Hannah says, 'that sets something of a gold standard.'

My poise is so very cocky and suave, my eyebrow raised Bond-like as if this sort of thing happens to me all the time, but my thoughts are whirring frantically. I hope I haven't given her unrealistic expectations. Three brandies, half a bottle of wine and countless beers are not the ideal catalyst for sexual performance.

'It's getting late,' she says, almost casually, 'I'm thinking of heading inside. Were you hoping to follow on behind, perchance?'

'I'd follow you anywhere,' I tell her. 'Absolutely anywhere.'

She tries to smile but it is as if a shadow has passed over us. Her face seems to change. I see her not as the extraordinarily pretty and vivacious girl who entranced me in Café Bellevue, but as the beautiful woman she will undoubtedly become a decade or two in the future. I can fall hopelessly for her as she is now, with her sharp tongue and arch humour and flashing green eyes. But it fills me with such strange joy to know that she will become more, so much more. I feel certain I have been granted a glimpse at her future self; that I have foreseen her in a state of grace.

Rising from my chair, I take Hannah's hand and she leads me from the rooftop terrace towards the dark open maw of the stairwell. I follow the girl wherever she chooses to take me.

7

255 days since the accident

Days later, once the exact details of her conversation with Dr Scott Calvin had receded, the doubts began to creep in. Who were these people at the Reel Memory Project? Why had Dr Calvin offered to help them so readily?

In her darkest moments she told herself it would be foolish to think that the Ree-Mem Project would be different to any of the other treatments, with the added certainty that their methods were at best dubious and at worst immoral. This venture would be a pointless, expensive waste of time. Exactly like all the other pointless, expensive wastes of time.

Then she thought of those glowing tributes on the Project's website, those grateful, tear-stained faces in the documentary. Something somewhere did work, that much was clear.

Nevertheless, the process of memory retrieval still worried her. Dr Calvin had been infuriatingly vague on the mechanics. Only that solitary phrase – conjoined hypnosis – offered any insight. She had pored over every scene of that television documentary but there was little elaboration of their methods. It appeared that the mandate for accepting the treatment was keeping the process confidential. Amid the wild speculation she uncovered online, she harvested scatterings of information that seemed to be rooted in truth. *They strap you together inside this big tank*, one web forum user had posted. *Then they make up this false image – like a movie scene – from fragments of your history. Then they hypnotise you, so you go right back into your past. Pretty crazy, huh?*

Pretty crazy, she agreed. But even if the Reel Memory Project was capable of sending her and her husband into their past, she had no idea how this was supposed to bring back Euan's memory.

It wasn't only the mechanics of the process that concerned her. If the treatment worked, and she found less and less reason to doubt that it did, it was frightening to think of the consequences. Ree-Mem was playing God with the human psyche.

Her phone tinged. It was time for her second transatlantic meeting with Dr Scott Calvin.

'You and your husband first met—' here Dr Calvin consulted his notes '—in Paris not quite a decade ago. You conducted a long-distance … ah, correspondence … for a number of years, then began cohabiting soon before your marriage four years ago. A rather extended courtship. Was the relationship intimate at first, Hannah, or did you begin as friends?'

'Jesus,' she gasped, feeling herself blushing, wondering if the webcam would pick it up. 'What specifics do you want? First kiss, first … whatever?' She thought of the minimal time-lapse between the first kiss and the first *whatever*, wondered what the doctor and his colleagues would think about that, and flushed ever more crimson. 'We'd had a lot to drink, it was a one-night-stand … I mean, I'm not sure I'm comfortable … maybe we could say we kissed and leave it at that?'

Dr Calvin laughed deeply, disarmingly. 'Honesty and trust are the key elements here, Hannah. We need to be totally honest with one another, we must have complete trust. They're your memories, after all. Soon they will be Euan's memories too.'

'It's a bit intrusive.' She bit down on her bottom lip. Now she wasn't thinking of that all-too-hasty race to her hotel bed. She was thinking about the day at the railway tracks.

'The process is intrusive by its nature. You will be sharing intimate and perhaps painful memories with strangers. Highly qualified strangers, of course.' Here Calvin tapped the triangular gold nameplate on his grand oak desk, embossed with a string of letters. 'I assure you my interest is entirely professional, indeed necessary. However, if you find the process distasteful ...'

'No-no-no,' she said quickly. 'We met in Paris,' she went on, 'I found work in London, he was living in Edinburgh. We kept up the long-distance relationship for a long, long while. Lots of train journeys, lots of endless phone conversations. Then finally he came down, because I needed him to. We moved in together. Married, no ... no kids. But everything was fine. Everything was brilliant. Everything ... everything until ...'

She stopped abruptly, suddenly overwhelmed. She thought of the sparks of euphoria that fizzed through their relationship, the silly jokes impenetrable to anyone else. Not his proposal, their wedding day, their times of Great Romance. Just Euan's droll displays of thoughtfulness. The notes he slipped into the pocket of her jacket for her to discover halfway through her working day: *Missing you already* or *I'm jealous of any man who sees you looking as beautiful as you do today* or *I'm watching you – turn around*. His blue marker pen scribbles on the fruit in the bowl on the kitchen table, *Unlike this banana let's never split ... You make a mango wild ... I think we make a lovely pear*. The old photographs of them that he would wedge in the sun visor of her car or tuck into her winter mittens. Not the big things. The little things, the corny things, the foolish things. The gestures that showed he cared so much. The gestures she feared she would never see again.

'Please take your time, Hannah,' Dr Calvin said. 'Tell me, what was your husband like before the accident?'

She let out a feigned laugh, trying to harden her heart. 'Strong. Manly. Irresistible. Or at least he thought so. Verbose when he had nothing to say, clammed up when it came to emotions or big decisions. It took some time to split that shell. Never told me what was wrong. Typical Scotsman, my mum always said. Needy, self-centred, prone to self-pity at the bottom of a glass.'

'You seem,' Calvin said levelly, 'more comfortable with discussing his faults than his finer qualities. His remoteness, you say—'

She nodded and he gestured for her to continue but she found herself unable to tell the doctor what he needed to know; it was too much like a secret. She still treasured the moment she first saw Euan break down and cry because it was also the first time she knew that not only did he love her but he needed her too. He was a proud man and it had taken an enormous leap to surrender himself emotionally. It had happened when she was visiting him in Edinburgh while his mother was in hospital. Euan had moved back into his family home to help out his father – the Stornoway males co-existing in a sham of matey-masculinity, kicking footballs in the garden and watching action movies. When she arrived, the house was a pigsty and the bins were overflowing with crumpled beer cans. Dinner consisted of cheese toasties dipped into scorched mulligatawny soup. *Not exactly haute cuisine*, Euan's father had said as he placed the bowl delicately before her on the table, *Iris is the head chef in this house, I'm afraid*. She watched his hand tremble as he reached for his pint glass, saw his lip quiver, and realised how close this burly, hard-looking man was to falling apart. The three of them ate their dinner almost silently, then watched television and made stilted conversation until Euan made a great show of yawning and saying she must be tired after her long journey from London. Up in his room, hermetically sealed since his teenage years with plastic rugby trophies on the shelves and a *Hearts, Hearts, Glorious Hearts* poster tacked to the wall, he had sat on the single bed, and she held his hand and waited for him to talk. *I'm not sure I'm coping with this*, the man who would become her husband said at last. The words came in an apologetic rush, like a confession, and his candour cracked a fracture in her heart. *I don't know what to say to my dad. It's not like there's a ... there's a fucking car manual for cancer. You can't take a busted part out and put in a new one and everything's fine. He fixes things, he's always fixed everything, and he can't fix this and I can't help him and I don't know what to do*. She had shushed him, stroking his hair, hating to see him suffer but also strangely proud that – finally, finally! – he had opened up to her, his carapace of self-sufficiency cracking. *It's not just that*, Euan went on, a solitary tear trailing down one cheek, *I can't imagine you being the same way. I always thought I'd be fine on my own, but everything's different now you're in my life. I couldn't cope if you went away. I wouldn't be able to go on*. She held him and comforted him and whispered promises that she would never go away, that she would always be there for him, that they could conquer anything together.

The urge to cry was far stronger this time. 'It's ... Jesus ... I don't know,' she stuttered to Dr Calvin, 'it's easier for me to remember the ways he used to drive me mad. It's a way to keep myself sane, if that makes any sense. But even his flaws were somehow adorable. Yes, he was proud and conceited and distant at times. Sometimes he'd go away for a while and I'd have no idea where he was or what he was thinking. But … he always came home to me. He was kind and considerate and loyal and funny. And he loved me very, very much. Or at least I thought he did, before that day on the tracks. I thought he needed me. I thought he would never leave me. I was wrong about that, badly wrong.'

The tears threatened once more and this time she conceded defeat. She cried like a child, uninhibited and soaked with self-pity.

'Let us move on,' Dr Calvin said softly once she had stemmed the tears. 'Would you like to know how the treatment works?'

She sniffed. 'Yes. Absolutely.'

'The medical specifics will be explained if you decide to move forward with us. But I've no doubt you want to know what you – and your husband – must do. I can promise you, Hannah, that in my decades of work with amnesiacs, the memories are always, always there. They are simply sunk too deeply for the conscious mind to dredge up. The memories are spinning around – fragmented, independent of one another – in the depths of your husband's mind.'

'Really?' she said. She felt a rushing sensation, a feeling of being pinned back by a force beyond her control, her body an aeroplane taking leave of the earth. 'You mean … you mean that Euan's memories are still in his head?'

'Oh yes indeed, Hannah,' Dr Calvin said emphatically. He formed twin circles between the thumb and forefinger of each hand. 'These fragmented memories have a repetitive, looping quality, which is why we call them reels. Memory reels. As in reels of cinematic film.' Now the name of the Reel Memory Project made sense – vaguely she had thought *Reel* was a deliberate misspelling of *Real*, stunt-branding like *Krispy Kreme* or *Irn Bru*. The doctor went on, 'These memories still

53

exist but they are not linked together, which is why your husband's conscious mind cannot access them. That's where our little brand of trickery comes in. We manufacture these reel scenes as a catalyst to create true memories. And the neatest thing is, you're in charge.' He chuckled again. 'It's the film of your life, after all. You're the director and you write the script.'

'I write the script?'

Dr Calvin nodded. 'What you, Hannah, must do is link these memory reels inside the hypnotic state. Link the reels together and pull them to the surface. Then, God willing, the Euan you loved will come back to you.'

She held up her hands to stop him. 'Wait, back up there, I'm lost. How do I get into these ... reels, as you call them? How does Euan, when he can't remember a single moment of our time together?'

'We will need certain artefacts – portals, we call them – from your shared history. Keepsakes or mementos, physical objects. One of our great breakthroughs at Ree-Mem was the understanding that touch acts as an electric shock to the memory.' Dr Calvin lolled back in his chair and she had the feeling he was preening a little. 'A breakthrough moment in our early years saw us uncover the location of the last will and testament of a tycoon stricken by dementia. We were at a loss as to how to unlock his memory until one of our researchers mentioned Proust's madeleine – the taste of the cookie resurrecting that great man's childhood. Of course, we experimented with food and drink, but found them insubstantial. The reels slipped away as soon as the food was consumed. We realised we needed a memory marker that was more permanent, more physically substantial. In this pioneering case we used a shard of the stone wall of his home – a humble brick, Hannah! The brick, of course, worked as the portal. We delved into this poor gentleman's subconscious and located his will, hidden beneath a floorboard in the attic. All by using a small physical object as a portal to his mind. The same principles will apply quite as successfully in your husband's case.'

'Does it have to be—'

'Almost anything at all,' the doctor said with an expansive wave of his arm. 'An item of jewellery, a plush toy, a shot glass from Euan's favourite bar. The feeling of these physical objects will spark miniaturised explosions in your husband's subconscious and drag him back to these pivotal points of your life. You will provide our team with a short script of each scene, as much as you can remember.' He wagged his forefinger playfully. 'Exactly what happened, no cheating. Using photographic and olfactory manipulation in a state of medical hypnosis, we will reconstruct these moments from your past.'

'Like a movie scene,' she said, thinking of what she had read online.

'Exactly like a movie scene.' Calvin grinned his wide, gleaming grin. 'These reels will allow you and your husband to interact with one another inside the hypnotic state. It is a fallacy but an incredibly effective fallacy. You will re-live your relationship with Euan, right from the moment you first met.'

She thought of experiencing those moments once more. Basking in snapshots of a relationship that faded her previous lovers into insignificance. To feel again that love which frightened her and bewitched her simultaneously.

There was a darker pull too; she had to admit it to herself. She wanted to bring Euan back, of course. Bring him back and hold him and love him. Then, after she had held and loved him, she would find out exactly what he had done.

'Your job, Hannah,' Dr Calvin went on, 'is to relive your husband's memory of you. Not only do you write the script – in this movie, you're the hero.'

'I'm the hero?' she repeated, a faint smile playing around her lips.

'You're the hero. And the audience – your friends at Ree-Mem – are all rooting for you. You need to pull your husband out of one scene and lead him on to the next. Splice the reels together to create a narrative of your relationship. These will, in turn, stimulate his brain into retrieving yet more memories. Once you have linked those reels, Euan will remember everything. Absolutely everything.'

'And that works?' she asked dubiously.

'In 99 per cent of cases,' Calvin said. 'It works unbelievably successfully.'

'What if we're the one per cent?' she said.

'Then,' the doctor said, 'it means that I have failed. The Ree-Mem Project shall waive your fee. In its entirety.'

She bit down on her bottom lip. 'I wanted to talk to you about this, doctor. I mean, we don't have that much spare cash, and—'

Dr Calvin batted away her worries with a breezy sweep of his hand. 'All wearisome logistics, Mrs Stornoway. Hannah. With this potential case being one of our initial forays into the European market, I'm sure we can come to an arrangement. Providing, that is, you are willing to grant Ree-Mem a little, ah, positive publicity.'

The medic's smile intensified. The grin was so huge that the little computer screen seemed far too small to contain it. She should have felt suspicion or at least cynicism; that familiar grim certainty that Dr Calvin would not be able to help, just like no one else was able to help.

But somehow this time, this treatment, felt different. She felt her resolve stiffen.

'Where do I sign?' she asked.

8

261 days since the accident

Her mobile rang with an unknown number as she stabbed her trowel at the stubborn yellow weeds that sprouted around the corners of their garden. She pulled off her thick gloves and tapped the phone's screen. She could already hear the honeyed flow of Dr Calvin's speech patterns, his cheerful grandiloquence. The way he made her feel as if the sole purpose of his life was to help the Stornoways, time and costs be damned. She knew there had to be a catch somewhere. These were professional people, the very best, and the very best always demanded the most money. How the hell could they afford to pay for the treatment? She wished she was able to pin the doctor down on his administrative tedium and wearisome logistics, but she was always swept away by his confident rush. *Slick patter*, the old Euan would have called it, sucking at his front teeth in the way he always used to when dubious about somebody. *Quite possibly a bullshit merchant.* But that Euan wasn't here any longer. Without the assistance of the bullshit merchant with the slick patter, there was no chance of Euan returning.

'Hello?' she said, her nerve endings tingling.

'Morning, Hannah!' said a female voice. 'It's Carrie here.' For a second her mind was as blank as that of her husband. She had no idea who this person was. 'From work, you know?' the caller added uncertainly.

Then she remembered: Carrie was the office secretary. They had worked together for almost three years before the accident. Carrie had a tumble of strawberry-blonde curls and a toothy smile, but she was struggling to dredge up any further knowledge about her. She seemed to remember a fiancé named Declan, wedding plans, lots of agonising about canapés and the just-right colour of the bridesmaids' dresses. 'Hello ... hello there, Carrie,' she said, relieved to have remembered. 'How's the prep going for the big day?'

There was a slight pause. 'The wedding was two months ago, Hannah. It was great. We'd have loved you to have come.'

'Oh,' she muttered, feeling foolish. Had she even replied to the invitation? 'Sorry.'

'No problem,' the girl said. 'Anyway, Mr Porsing wanted me to call – he's in Beijing at the moment, big deal happening – to say we're not, you know, not expecting you back anytime soon.' The secretary let out a nervous giggle. 'I mean, look, keep this hush-hush of course, but you were a perfect employee and you can take as much time as you need with your ... you know, your ... thing.'

Carrie stopped, lost for words. She thought of her workplace, her manager. Michael Porsing, the CEO, had been extremely supportive in the grim months after Jennifer. He had been even more supportive after Euan's accident, but she knew his patience could not last forever; she was an employee, not a charitable cause. She couldn't say she was desperate to return to work – financial marketing, after all, was not a vocation that set the imagination aflame. Come the apocalypse, no one would be begging branding statistics specialists to save them. But it paid well and she was trusted to lead teams. More importantly, she missed having a role in life that did not revolve around her amnesiac husband.

'Thanks,' she said. 'Tell Michael I appreciate that. And best of luck with the deal.'

'We wish you could come back,' Carrie said. 'We're all thinking of you here.'

'Thanks,' she said again, with feeling this time.

'Bye then, Hannah. Good luck.'

'Goodbye,' she said and clicked off the receiver. Her working life seemed like events that had happened to someone else, perhaps in a dull movie she had once seen. Euan had been supportive of her career, if not enamoured of the London lifestyle it entailed. That, of course, was before Jennifer. After Jennifer, Euan had viewed her job with sullen resentment, as if by leaving each morning to catch the train she was abandoning him. She would have minded less if – once, just once – he had opened up to her, told her how he felt, broken down in tears. Instead he wallowed alone in miserable silence. She was sure he was keeping something to himself but she could never ask him directly. She had been his partner for long enough to know that any secrets would be sealed inside Euan's brain until he alone chose to unlock them.

Later, after the accident, she wondered why she had not noticed the distance between them cracking into a chasm.

Euan had received the news of yet another treatment with his usual calm acceptance. He was used to it by now. The first stage of the Ree-Mem process – the initialisation, as Dr Calvin termed it – was starting the next morning, and she thought they could make that evening something of a celebration. She had painted her face and put on a dress, and insisted Euan wore a smart shirt, and as she took his hand in the taxi, he looked at her with honest surprise.

The restaurant's low orange lamp-lighting smeared their features into soft focus. Chintzy paintings hung on the walls. She was pleased this place was loud; bragging conversations, plinking piano keys, clinking glasses, the scrapings of serrated knives against greasy plates.

The restaurant was recommended by her mother and exactly as aggressively uncool as she had predicted. The steaks looked as thick as a hardback book and she suspected they might be every bit as tasty. The waiter led them towards their small booth and furnished them with oversized menus. She ordered a bottle of the house red.

Euan was quiet, thoughtful, as she set out what she knew about the Ree-Mem Project in between gulps of wine. Eventually he turned his attention to the menu. She reached out a hand, tilting his jaw until their eyes met, until his focus was on her alone.

'How did you like your steaks before?' she said encouragingly. 'What did you always order? Come on, Euan. I bet you can tell me.'

He clenched his teeth, jaw muscles twitching. 'I think … I think … ah, it's not coming.'

'Why not try,' she said quietly, 'for me.'

He scanned the menu for inspiration. 'I'm really not feeling like—'

She stroked the ball of her thumb against the stubby bristles on his cheek. 'I bet you know, really,' she said. 'Come on, Euan. You can win this game.'

To her shock, Euan slammed his hand on the table in frustration. The crockery jingled. A few heads turned in their direction.

'I want to remember,' he said urgently, his fists clenching and unclenching. 'I want to remember, not pretend. It shouldn't be this hard.'

She placed her hand on his. 'Please, darling. This is why we're doing this Ree-Mem thing. They'll help you.'

'They can do it?' he asked. 'Can they do it?'

'I think so. I hope so.'

He offered her a glance she could not quite read. 'Until then, would you tell me,' he said, his tone carefully measured even as she saw a tic twitching his upper lip, 'how I liked my steaks before the accident?'

'Always sirloin, always. Rare sirloin, very rare,' she said with a weak smile. 'French rare. The cow's still breathing.'

The waiter arrived at their table, notepad poised.

'Sirloin steak,' Euan said, staring at the tablecloth. 'Rare. Very.'

She took a huge glug of wine. 'Fillet,' she said. 'Medium-rare.' The waiter nodded politely and glided away. She drank more wine. 'Euan,' she said, 'honestly, you don't have to prove a point.'

'I just want to be him,' he said. 'I want to be the man you loved so much.'

The simplicity of his statement blew apart her defences and she felt naked, exposed; a mass of raw flesh and exposed nerves.

'You will be,' she said, somehow forcing out a halting laugh. She wanted this evening to be special, to be intimate, for him as well as her. 'You will be that Euan again. That's the point of this … this rigmarole.'

'I'd have liked to have met him,' he said. 'Sorry, that sounds a stupid thing to say.'

She shook her head. 'After what I've learned this past week, nothing sounds stupid any more. I can barely believe in reality.'

'I see his pictures all over the house,' he went on. 'It's like … it's like a mirror reflection that distorts in the corner of your eye.'

At last the steaks arrived and her husband dug into his sirloin. She watched him eat, her lips tilting. She felt hope but also a pinch of unease. In the past week Dr Scott Calvin had remained in contact. His emails were always businesslike but there was no mistaking his excitement when he wrote that the Ree-Mem Project had secured a temporary headquarters a short distance outside London. *We shall be freighting over the necessary equipment at the nearest possible juncture.* How could you not be intrigued with a phrase like that? She decided to spark Euan's interest.

'I'm looking forward to seeing what the Ree-Mem machines look like,' she said. 'Do you reckon they'll be all weird and unearthly, like alien machinery in a sci-fi movie?'

'As normal as possible I hope,' he said. 'This is about trying to get back to normality.'

She nodded. 'Normality's the best thing ever. Normality sounds like heaven. Just me and you. Hannah and Euan. Being incredibly boring together, forever.'

'Is that enough?'

She nodded fervently, even though she thought his question slightly odd. 'That's all I want. For you to be you again. We were best friends, not just lovers. We were two halves of the same person. We knew everything about each other.'

That was true, or near enough to the truth that she could have passed a lie-detector test. In all honesty, she recalled, during the early years of their relationship Euan had taken a little while to reveal himself. She had told herself it didn't matter if he rarely spoke about love and commitment; the romance and the intrigue and the sex were terrific. She was sure he would open up eventually. Give himself over to her after enough time had passed. She was proven right. He had been a wonderful husband. Until Jennifer, at least, and what came afterwards. But she couldn't let herself think of those times.

She hoped he hadn't seen the shadow cross her face. Fortunately he was smiling, his placid nature restored. Nowadays Euan never seemed to be angry for too long. 'It's exciting in a way, though, isn't it?' he said. 'Being part of something as big as this. Something which can give you everything you want.'

Her fork paused on its journey to her mouth, her hand quivering. 'You really mean that?'

He stared back at her openly. 'Of course. I want this to work, Hannah. I wake up every day and I know I'm not the person you want me to be. It's as hard for me as it is for you, you realise?'

She felt a lump form in her throat. She reminded herself that she was not going through this treatment alone; the man sitting opposite, the man with the silver wedding ring and the same surname as her, the man who couldn't remember why he was the most important person in the world, would go through it with her.

'So ... this is the way, isn't it?' that man went on. 'This is the way for me to return to how I was, how we were. The best of times. We're going right back to the start, you say.'

'To the very start,' she agreed. 'I've sketched out what happened for the Ree-Mem guys to create their scene. It all came back to me. Perfectly.'

'When we met—'

'In Paris.'

'And you—'

'Dropped a coffee cup and drenched myself. Then you stood up and knocked over your table and your beer went flying. We smashed up the whole café in a matter of seconds. It was such an elegant, graceful way to begin our relationship.'

He laughed but his smile faltered. 'I know this because you've told me,' Euan said. 'It doesn't mean anything because I can't remember it.'

'That's okay,' she reassured him. 'I can remember. I can remember well enough for both of us.'

'Are you sure what you remember will be the same as me?' She blinked as she felt a tingle of static race up her spine, the mellow orange light in the restaurant momentarily blurring to a murky grey. 'I mean, I don't know,' he stuttered, his face flushing, 'maybe you'd want to change things. If you're writing the scenes for both of us, I mean. If there was a part of your life you hated, then you could make it all better. Wouldn't you want to do that? I might, I don't know. Wouldn't you?'

She shook her head firmly. 'I wouldn't want to change anything about our relationship,' she said. 'It was perfect. We were perfect.'

'Perhaps I wasn't a very good person,' he said, staring gloomily into his glass of wine. 'Back before. There must have been a reason. The accident, you know. The crash I caused. There must have been a reason that I did what I did.'

'Euan, please don't,' she said. She reached across the table and he grasped her hands, clinging to her with desperation, and she thought that any other diner in the room would see them as a young couple who were very much in love. 'We're trying... we're having a lovely evening here. Don't worry about the past. I'll take care of it.'

'You'll take care of it?' he repeated.

'Absolutely,' she said. 'I'll make everything perfect again.'

9

Hannah and I: Our first year

The Party at 74a Palmertach Street

So here I am, semi-drunk, trapped in an awful party where the theme of the evening is London Underground station fancy dress. I'm wearing the clothes of a 1970s tennis player: headband, white polo shirt and tight shorts, Green Flash trainers. I have misplaced my wooden racket somewhere.

I'm waiting for a girl I barely know but can't get out of my head. I don't want to be here, but I can't leave because she's the only reason I am here in the first place. I sit, I drink, I watch as silhouette figures gyrate to the endless thump of the music.

The party had seemed a good idea at the time. *I'm heading down to London in a few weeks,* I told Hannah on the phone. *My old uni flatmate lives right by Spitalfields Market. He's having a party – fancy dress, London Underground stations, daft but fun. Proper DJs, plenty of booze, good-looking company. Fancy it, aye?* I have been invited to a party in London. Hannah lives in London. Surely I can invite her to the party without anything being too weird or confusing? It's a perfect point of convergence. If everything goes badly wrong I can dampen my embarrassment with alcohol, insisting that it was only a relaxed meet-up. I almost convince myself I'm not coming down to London for Hannah alone. Most people travel five hours for terrible house parties, don't they? As I reach again for my beer, I sense a presence beside me. I look up with an expectant, hopeful smile.

A girl. But not the one I'm waiting for. She's tall and angular, with a shock-cut fringe of black hair and a large hooked nose that should make her ugly but is oddly fetching. Her jaw is strong, almost masculine. I catch a scent of a perfume like rich, dark honey. She is dressed as a French maid, but a bridal veil hangs over her forehead, masking her dark eyes.

'Nice outfit,' she says. 'What did you come as?'

Self-consciously I smooth the white fabric of my short shorts. The headband prickles against my scalp. 'What do you mean? This is what I wear every day.'

'A joker, right? Should I sit down, Wimbledon?'

'If you like,' I say. My voice is carefully neutral. I don't want Hannah to walk in and see me talking to another girl. But it doesn't look as though Hannah is coming.

'Only if you can guess who I am.' She straightens her petticoat, swishing the veil from her forehead. A thinly sculpted eyebrow raises, the left corner of her mouth tilting in a sly half-smile. I know this gesture. I'm sure I've seen her somewhere else. I've never seen her before in my life.

'You're Maida Vale,' I tell her.

Perching herself neatly, proprietorially, on the arm of my chair, the girl taps the tips of her fingers together in mock applause. The black-painted nails are long and slightly curved. 'Perceptive,' she says. She draws out the word in plosive bursts, her mild accent spiking the syllables. Behind the blur of the veil, her eyes are bottomless pools. 'So what else do you recognise?'

'What do you—'

Then there is a sound of a scuffle and a squeak of outraged vinyl. One of the guests, a fat lad wearing a monk's cowl – Blackfriars, surely – has thrown up over the DJ booth. In the chaos of pushing and shouting, a body tumbles against my chair and it tips and I am toppling backwards – falling, falling, rolling, confused, flailing, falling.

Lying on the dirty carpet I stare up and Hannah is standing over me. Her posture is so elegant, her left foot hooked around her right leg, and my gaze travels up her slender legs to her short simple grey dress. She looks so beautiful and serene and fresh and clean and, oh, the rest of my little world is a fraction less seedy and scruffy by the virtue of her presence.

Hannah is rubbing at something in the corner of her eye as if trying to stem tears. Probably a speck of dust — the flat is very dusty.

'Great party, Euan,' she says. 'Have I arrived a few moments before the police get here?'

At last order has been restored. The sounds of chatter and laughter return. The music is switched on again; softer this time, a classic soul track. I can't see the dark-haired girl in the French maid's outfit anywhere. No – there she is, slipping away through the throng. Her movements are strange. Jerky freeze-framed steps, at odds with her earlier grace. One moment I can see her looking back at me, that secretive smile still on her face, the next she vanishes as if she has slipped through the solid wall.

Shaking my head to remove the dark girl from my mind, I usher Hannah onto the armchair. I locate a fresh bottle of beer on the table and pass it over, kneeling in front of her. 'Hello, you,' I say.

'Hi, Euan.' Her voice is cool. Are we strangers again? 'I see you're as committed as ever to slapstick comedy.'

Wasn't it Hannah who dropped the coffee cup, then knocked over her own table in Paris? I should reply with something funny, a lightly flirtatious jibe, but my mind's a blank. 'It's been a while,' is all I can think of to say.

She picks at the skin around her fingertips. 'Yes, it has. It has been a very long while. You're right about that.'

We sit in silence. I take a restorative swig of my beer but realise in the disarray I have picked up a bottle that has been used as an ashtray. Grimacing, I swallow the mouthful of ash and stale lager. Reacquainting with a beautiful girl never happens like this in the movies.

'You're Wimbledon, right?' Hannah says. She motions to the headband. 'The tube station. The outfit.'

'This is what I wear every day,' I tell her. Again I cast an eye around for Maida Vale but she truly has disappeared.

'I'm not here to judge you. But the guy over there is definitely Barking,' she says, pointing to a man in a dog costume. 'His friend in the clown suit is either Piccadilly Circus or Oxford Circus.'

'Oxford, I think. Look at the mortar board.'

'Good point. I passed Blackfriars on the stairs, he was in a bit of a state. And the guy in the white tuxedo is Bond Street. Then there's the girl with a massive permed wig who I thought at first was High Barnet, but judging by her football shirt I reckon she's Liverpool Street.'

'And you're—'

'Not wearing London Underground fancy dress. Correct. Didn't have time to change after work.'

'I thought you were Angel,' I say. Hannah's eyes narrow. She thinks I'm playing with her — feeding her a terrible chat-up line — and she couldn't be more mistaken. 'I've missed you,' I blurt.

Suddenly it seems the packed, sweaty room is freezing. The dancers are stilted shadow puppets. The only warmth is directly in front of me.

'I've been thinking things over,' I say quickly. 'I wanted to get in touch before now, I really did. I don't know, I just—'

'Just wanted to think things over?'

'Yes, I've been thinking things over,' I say, then reconsider. 'Hang on, haven't I already said that?'

Hannah smirks. 'Keep going, Euan,' she says, 'this time next year we could be laughing together. Or I could just be laughing at you.'

The Hannah Allaker version of a pick-up line. I remember the way she loves to twist words, skew phrases, defy conventional conversation. 'Do you come often here?' I chance.

The smirk splits into a full grin. 'You must have fallen from heaven and hit the earth. It would explain why your face looks that way.'

'Do you believe in love at first sight,' I press on, my heart racing, 'or do I have to lock you in my basement until Stockholm Syndrome takes effect?'

'Rather there than this place,' she says, staring around our shambolic surroundings. 'I'm afraid to touch any of the furniture in case I catch something.'

'It's nothing like Paris,' I say.

'No,' she agrees, 'it's most definitely nothing like Paris.'

Her tone is flat, even downcast, and that worries me. Everything should be like Paris; we should be like we were in Paris. But the fact of the matter is that we're in a dingy east London flat, not sitting outside Café Bellevue in Montparnasse, and I hope – I hope so very much – that this simple accident of geography hasn't ruined everything.

'Does that matter?' I say in a small voice. 'Does that ... does that change things?'

Hannah traces a forefinger around the rim of her beer bottle, seemingly lost in thought. I look at the girl and think of every reason I've remembered her. I know I'm staring but I can't possibly look away, it would be like refusing water to a man dying of thirst. I remember the little details: the spray of freckles on her nose, the minuscule triangular chip in one of her front teeth. Her hair is a little longer now, pulled back in a ponytail. But most of all I've missed her eyes. That incredible shade of green that has danced through my dreams these past months.

'I've been telling myself,' Hannah says, her voice almost inaudible over the party music, 'that I shouldn't get too hung up on one memory. Paris. The city of love, or at least the city of ill-thought-out hook-ups. A day of boozing in burning hot sunshine. Meeting an intriguing stranger. These things have ways of playing tricks with your brain, frazzling your mind. Maybe I thought what the hell, it's only one night, a final frivolity before reality kicks in.' She turns to stare at me and I feel like a spotlight has been shone in my face. 'And who better to share that night with than a mysterious – if slightly inebriated – hunky Scotsman?'

This is a challenge. Whether I leave this party alone or with her depends on how well I rise to this challenge. There is no question about that. So what do I have to offer?

'I travelled five hours to get here,' I tell her humbly. 'Five hours ... just, you know ... just so I'd see you again. Even if it's only for a few minutes.'

She purses her lips. 'You came down just for me?'

'Sort of, aye.'

'Are there no willing ladies north of the border?' she asks archly.

'Scotland has a low population density. They've all heard of me. They know my terrible reputation.'

'Whereas now you've forewarned me of it.' She rolls her eyes. 'Do try to be serious for a moment, Scotsman.'

Maybe I don't have to try. Maybe I should stop messing around before I lose her again. Chastened, I kneel before her and take her hands in mine. She stares at me but does not pull away. 'The longer I went without seeing you,' I say, my voice unsteady, 'the more you seemed like a mirage, a dream I once had. I can't believe you're really here.'

'I'm as real as centaurs or unicorns, don't you worry about that.'

How much does she really care? How important is this second meeting to her? Has she thought of me anything like as much as I've thought of her? In that all-consuming way, where you can't concentrate on anything but the memory of that other person, where the sound and colour have faded from life. I've tried to be cool, I've tried the jokes and banter. So instead I settle for naked honesty. This could be humiliating. This could be incredible. This could be the start of something or the end of everything. This could be … ah, what the hell, here goes.

'You can try to convince me you're not some mythical goddess,' I say with only a half-smile, 'but I'm afraid I'm not going to believe you. You can try to convince me that Paris was a one-night … whatever … but it was something more, I'm sure.'

She laughs a small laugh that sounds oddly like a sob, tracking her fingers up my jawline. Her thumb slips around to my mouth and I kiss it gently. She is here, she is actually here with me. Our lips are barely inches apart and I'm drowning in the sensuousness, the realness, the now-ness of her. I want to kiss her – I need to kiss her – but as I lean towards Hannah there is a cracking sound. For a second the room shakes as if the house has been struck by an earthquake, the solid walls oscillating, the music warping out of any natural beat. We stare downwards and I see my knee has shattered a seven-inch vinyl record that must have fallen to the carpet in the earlier chaos. Hannah bends and picks up the splintered black circle, placing it into my left hand and closing my fingers over the top.

'A gift for you, Euan,' she says.

Holding the broken record, I trace the groove, running a fingertip over the jagged black edge. The tracks feel sensuous, pregnant with meaning. The touch sparks a strange flare of excitement but trepidation deep within me, as if I'm part of a bigger picture I'm too blind to see, but for now I'm happy to live in the moment. 'Will the record still play?' I ask.

The girl smiles a little sadly. 'Oh, it'll still play. You'd be surprised at how well it plays.'

Just what is she talking about?

10

272 days since the accident

She had been unsure what to expect from the Reel Memory
Project's temporary base. Certainly not an unlovely industrial
estate at the furthest reaches of the London Underground lines.
As she stepped towards the entrance to the warehouse, her
shoes crunching on the gravel, it took some resolve not to
flee back to the safe confines of her car. She supposed she had
hoped for a gleaming, newly furnished hospital wing, or perhaps
a miniaturised version of the Project's skyscraper in Seattle.
Instead there was an ugly grey block with a handful of security
guards loitering outside. This did not, she thought, look like a
place where dreams would come true.

Once she was inside the complex, however – after the guards
furnished her with a pass emblazoned with her digital likeness
– her disquiet vanished. The metal beams of the roof pointed
to the heavens like an aircraft hangar, while the decor was a
melange of upmarket hotel lobby and hipster loft apartment. The
vast open space made her feel small and insignificant, yet it was
strangely comforting. Now that she was here, everything would
be taken care of for her. The concrete walls were shaded by blue
light, white leather banquettes and huge yucca plants studded the
bare floor. Video screens hung on chains from the roof, showing former patients gushing compliments about the Project's

life-changing work. Extraordinarily good-looking receptionists in cobalt blue uniforms were perched behind the *Welcome* desk while orderlies in pastel blue scrubs scurried about on errands. There was even a video crew – young, punky-looking men in ripped jeans and short-sleeved black shirts, swooping around the atrium with handheld television cameras. She felt the gaze of a lens fall upon her, only for a moment or two.

In the centre of this industrious chaos stood Dr Scott Calvin, head and shoulders taller than the rest of the Project's workers. He raised out his arms to greet her, enfolding her outstretched hand in both of his huge palms.

'Hannah,' he said expansively, 'thank you for trusting us.'

'Is all this for me and Euan?' she said, staring up at the doctor with a certain awe. She was eye-level with the man's broad chest. His image reduced by the size of her computer screen during their online chats, she had not expected Dr Calvin to be so physically imposing. She felt dwarfed by the man and dwarfed by the occasion. 'I mean, what's with all the cameras?'

'Ree-Mem will see … ah … around two dozen other patients during our time here,' Calvin said with a smirk. 'Our residency in your fair isle needs to turn a profit, after all.'

At once she realised how stupid she had been to think the Project was solely for the benefit of the Stornoways. She and her husband were not special. They were patients, numbers, one case out of many. If their treatment failed, they would only be a statistic.

She looked up into the doctor's face, every fibre of his being radiating tranquil confidence, and some of her worries melted away. He believes, she thought. Even if he's a fantasist, deluding himself, lying that he's found the cure, he genuinely believes.

'Won't you come into my office?' Dr Calvin said. 'We have so much to discuss, Hannah.'

★

'Circular.' Scott Calvin formed an O-shape with his hands as he reclined behind the great desk. She was amused to see the neuropsychologist's Seattle office was recreated with prissy exactitude in this temporary home. 'Memory is circular. A recollective palindrome. This realisation was our greatest breakthrough. It came from a simple question – why do we recall some scenes of our lives so vividly, yet we cannot remember a conversation that took place yesterday?' Calvin drew a symbol on his notepad and held it up. 'What does that shape look like to you, Hannah?'

She stared at the drawing of a figure of eight turned on its side. 'An infinity loop,' she said.

Calvin smiled, bending to his pad again. He held up his drawing. Now the figure of eight had been replicated across the page in interconnected circles.

'Our memory reels,' the doctor said. 'Each loop is a separate memory. For you, myself, the entire non-amnesiac populace, the reels are connected seamlessly. For your husband, each individual memory is a separate loop. For Euan the scenes are disconnected. His brain cannot link these loops together, which results in his amnesiac state. There is a pad and a magic marker on the table, Hannah. Could you please draw a similar shape?'

Baffled, she picked up the felt-tip pen and began to draw. The first infinity loop appeared easily, but when she tried to link it into the doctor's shape of interconnected circles, the lines wavered and her drawing spiralled into a confusion of blue ink.

She threw down the marker pen. 'Messed it up,' she said. 'Sorry, Dr Calvin.'

'Oh, I just go by Dr Cal,' the neuropsychologist beamed. 'But it's harder than it looks, isn't it? The only way to draw a succession of infinity loops is to track around the previous circle before embarking on the next. With your arrival inside your husband's memory loop, Hannah, the scene will begin to spool. It is your job to lead Euan into the next reel before it returns him to the beginning of the loop. Connect the reels before the scene ends. Bring back his memory.'

'And if I can't do that?' she said, thinking of the warnings she had read about the treatment, remembering the documentary footage of protesters outside Ree-Mem's office in Seattle. 'What happens if I get it wrong? What happens if I can't connect the reels?'

Calvin blinked, rubbing at the back of his neck. 'The reel degenerates,' the doctor said. 'I must tell you this before we continue. Once you have started to connect the reels, you cannot go back. You have only one shot at this Hannah, I'm afraid.'

For some reason she thought of her wedding day. She remembered the vicar who married them warning that marriage was full of self-sacrifice and duty, and she had been delighted to disagree. That was before the accident. After the accident the duties never stopped. The duty of the hospital visits when he was in his coma. The duty of staring down at her husband's limp and battered body, shrouded in white blankets, wondering what she could possibly do to bring him back to life. The duty of never voicing the question that chanted mantra-like in her brain throughout the grinding days and endless nights: why had this happened, why?

Then Euan returned, physically at least. There were more duties for the dutiful wife. The duty of living with a man who looked like her husband and moved like her husband and talked like her husband but was not Euan, not Euan in the slightest. The duty of smiling encouragingly as he leafed through their photograph albums of golden years gone by; smiling even though the emptiness in his expression tore her apart inside.

After Euan came out of his coma, he was a stranger. It was almost – almost, almost, almost – as if he had not wanted to remember.

She stared at Dr Calvin, feeling as much a prisoner of her memories as her husband.

'What do I have to lose?' she said.

'Good, good, excellent.' Calvin clapped his hands briskly. 'Now, I would like to offer you a brief introduction to the treatment. A trailer, a sneak preview. You have already emailed the photographs for the first stage of memory reconstruction. And you have the portals, I take it?'

During the past week, on the Ree-Mem Project's instructions, she had ransacked her home and her mother's house searching for objects that reminded her of each stage of their relationship. Dr Calvin had asked for a selection and assured her that many more would be needed. *Assemble a physical scrapbook of your marriage. Little treasures which you can hold in your hand. The shape of the objects bores into your shared memories, which is why we call them portals. They act as catalysts to push Euan, in his hypnotised state, into each reel with you.*

Uncovering the portals had been somewhat morbid, like overturning gravestones. The first, the milk jug from the Montparnasse café, had been easy to find. That was where their shared memories had started, and unfortunately she also knew where those memories would end – at the railway crossing. Dr Cal's boundless confidence had given her strength, so she decided it would be better to dig up the most unpleasant portal next, to get it out of the way as early as possible. Which was why she had spent the previous day scrabbling around the embankment by the railway line, wrapped up against the morning chill. No trains ran on those tracks now; there had been a number of near-misses at the level crossing before the accident. A pale and shivering beachcomber, she had scoured the straggly grass of the embankment with her hands. Eventually she had uncovered her dark treasure: a splintered shard of metal, torn from their car on impact with the train. She slipped it into the back pocket of her jeans and left quickly. Now she had the first and last portals: the Café Bellevue milk jug and the neon green triangle of metal, shorn from the wreck of their car.

'I found the things you asked for,' she said. 'The portals for the first few years of us. Worthless junk, really.'

'Worthless?' Calvin said with an easy laugh, standing up and motioning towards the door. 'I suspect, after what I'm about to show you, you'll understand the portals are anything but worthless. But I've bored you enough with talking. Come, Hannah, now that we are friends, you must meet my children.'

She followed the doctor along a narrow, twisting corridor until they came to a white door. Calvin swiped a passcard, the door swung open and they proceeded into a smaller corridor, the floor marked with blue lights. She was aware of an insistent humming sound. He stopped before two more doors, marked U and D, and swiped his card again, taking the door on the left. The room was as dimly lit as the corridor, with blue floor stones providing the only illumination. The humming sound increased to a heavy mechanical burr. As her eyes adjusted to the gloom, she could make out an enormous smooth oval shape.

'Please meet my first child,' Calvin announced. 'Una.'

'Dr Cal, I can't—'

'You can't see too well. And you have questions. All in good time, Hannah. I prefer patients to experience the process in innocence rather than assumed knowledge. Every question shall be answered in good time.'

The doctor pressed a button on the surface of the egg-like

dome and one of its sloping sides whickered open. The interior of the oval was lit pastel blue, picking out the contours of a sunken leather seat. Electrodes winked on the armrests like the lights of a Christmas tree.

'Hannah, do you have your portal to take into the pod?' Calvin asked. 'The portal for your personal reel?'

She nodded and delved into her handbag. She pulled out her childhood doll, now scuffed and tatty with her wiry blonde hair matted and stained. Amy.

Calvin motioned her inside the pod. 'Please sit down,' he said. 'Make yourself comfortable.'

The air inside the machine smelled unusual but not unpleasant: light and fresh with a faint tang of camphor. The tiny hairs on her arms had pricked up, she tasted adrenaline on her tongue. The fear was now diluted with anticipation.

'See you on the other side,' Dr Calvin said. 'Enjoy your memory, Hannah.'

The side of the pod slid downwards and sealed her inside with a low clunk. She moved her right hand over the glowing crystals that studded the interior of the machine, watching as the lights merged into a miasma of green and blue. Her left hand closed around the doll for comfort.

I I

Hannah, aged six

Saving Amy

The atmosphere inside the pod had changed. Instead of the medicinal aroma there was now freshly mown grass and the sweet scent of honey. The colours of the crystals that studded the machine's walls had intensified into lawn green and clear blue sky. Her eyelids fluttered upwards and she took deep calming breaths of that beautiful air. She felt her heart rate dropping, the hand clutching the doll growing limp as she felt heat prickle her skin. The warming glow of the crystal lights... the warming glow of the lights... the warming glow of the sun on her bare arms.

She had thought she was wearing black jeans and an orange jumper, which had shrunk in the wash and clung a fraction too tightly, but now she was clad in a red and white gingham dress that fell easily on her flat chest.

'What is this place?' she whispered.

The air in the pod... the pod... what was the pod? How silly to think she was indoors. She was in the garden of her childhood home and she was six years old and breathing the clean freshness of a summer's day. There was a pleasant citrus zip on her tongue from an ice lolly. She was sitting by the side of the garden pond, the pond that was so big she told her school friends it was actually a lake, almost an ocean. The pond was very, very big and very, very deep. Her daddy had made her promise – *swear, Hanny, swear it* – never to swim in the pond, never-ever-ever. But she was happy to sit on the grassy bank with her feet trailing in the water. She was trying to read her book but really just basking in the afternoon heat, listening to the birds cheeping, hearing the far-off buzz of a lawnmower, watching dragonflies dance in the hazy air.

It was hot, it was sunny, and that was good because Amy liked it when it was hot. She knew Amy missed the sun. Amy came from Happy Valley, California, a small town on the coast where the sun always shone and each day was full of surfing and roller-skating and drinking soda with ice-cream floaters at the diner that looked out on to Freedom Bay. She had been given Amy when Sassie went away to big school. The doll and the book that came with her, with the words *Hi! My name's Amy Sausalito!* on the cover in bright pink letters. She had asked her daddy how to say Sausalito and he had told her, so now she knew. She spoke to Amy when she woke up every morning and when she went to bed every night. Now Sassie had gone, Amy was her best friend and never too far away.

Speaking of Amy, where was she now?

She stared around the garden and could see no sign of her doll. She had brought Amy with her, she could have sworn it. Amy had been with her at lunchtime; they had shared egg and cress sandwiches. Amy had been with her when they were watching television, before Mummy told her it was far too hot to sit inside all day; she should make the most of the good weather and go and play outside. So she had taken her book and Amy and gone to sit beside the pond. She started daydreaming and the next thing she knew, Amy wasn't there. She was alone beside the pond.

The pond. She gazed into its black depths. It was hot, so hot.

Amy liked to swim. Amy loved the Pacific Ocean. Amy loved the water.

Perhaps Amy had dived in when she wasn't looking?

She poked a fingertip into the murk, peering closer. Maybe Amy was hiding at the bottom. But she had sworn she wouldn't go in the pond – not even to paddle, since Daddy had told her the rocks at the bottom were slippy and she could fall and bang her head. Surely, though, Amy wouldn't let her slip?

She bit down on her bottom lip in an agony of indecision. The pond was very big and very deep. It was filled with long green plants, with flowers like thick brown sausagey fingers that Daddy called bulrushes. She knew she was never supposed to go in the pond. But Amy was swimming in there somewhere. She had to get Amy back – had to, had to, had to. Since Sassie had left, Amy was her only true friend and she told her everything, absolutely everything. She felt tears pricking at her eyes. She wished she knew what to do.

Perhaps if she took a big long jump, she could make it past the rocks and into the deep water? No, better to be careful. She placed one bare foot then the other into the pond. Her feet looked ghostly white underwater. She stepped forward, a pace at a time, calling out Amy's name. The bottom of the pond sloped downwards sharply and soon she was up to her knees. She traced her fingers on the water's surface, pushing past the clumps of bulrushes, desperate for a sight of Amy's bobbing blonde pigtails. She felt the water lapping at her thighs and hoiked the dress up to her waist, knowing Mummy would be cross if she got it all wet. Surely Amy couldn't have swum out so far?

Then she heard a voice yell her name. She looked around and saw a familiar figure racing across the garden, clutching a far smaller figure in his hand. She saw what he was carrying and she felt her heart might burst with love. Daddy – yes! – Daddy had found Amy. She grinned up at the approaching shadow. Daddy really was running fast, his eyes wide, his arms outstretched. Merrily she waved back and turned and took a step towards him. He had found Amy. Everything was all right now, everything was fine.

As she stepped towards her daddy, she felt something slimy and icky shift beneath her feet and her balance betrayed her and she fell backwards, going under the shockingly cold water, kicking and floundering. The bottom of the pond had shelved away and there was nothing to push against, no way to boost herself back to the surface, nothing but emptiness. She couldn't see and she couldn't breathe and she felt the nasty bloated fingers of the bulrushes that had somehow clamped around her legs pulling her down to the very bottom. Her mouth was filled with the dank stink of the pond and her dress had somehow wound around her legs and she knew she needed to kick, kick, kick her way towards the thin shimmer of sunlight breaking through the water, but she couldn't find the strength.

She felt thick arms grasp her and yank her upwards and she was pulled to the surface, the sunlight blinding her streaming eyes, taking huge hacking breaths, staring into the huge sweating face of her father as he held her tightly against his chest and asked why had she gone in the pond, didn't she promise never to ever-ever-ever go swimming there, oh Hanny what were you thinking, please never scare me like that again.

Then the scene fell away entirely and she was floating in non-space.

12

272 days since the accident

Retching, choking, the taste of brackish pond water filling her mouth, she sat up, rubbing at her eyes. Her hands went to her face but came back dry. She blinked and moaned and for a moment she had no idea whether she was in the past or present. She was sitting on a leather seat inside a womb-like capsule adorned with glowing crystals. One of the walls opened and a face, not that of her father but of a stranger, stared down at her. Names that meant almost nothing flew through her mind: Euan. Dr Scott Calvin. The Reel Memory Project.

Reality returned. Her name was Hannah Stornoway. Her husband Euan was an amnesiac. The man staring down at her was Dr Scott Calvin, although he just went by Dr Cal. He was a neuropsychologist from Seattle who would help them.

This same man had transported her back to her childhood.

The doctor supported her as she climbed out of the pod and led her along the darkened corridors. Calvin's white-walled office with the vast desk and the yucca plant seemed absurdly drab after the heightened reality she had experienced inside the pod. He helped her into a chair, fussing around her like a schoolmarm before sitting down next to her. The shadow images of the reel – the garden, the pond, her doll, her father – were still imprinted into her corneas. She shook her head, trying to shake her mind free from the illusions. A cup of orange squash was pressed into her hand. She sipped the syrupy liquid, her breathing slowly coming under control.

'That was a sneak preview?' she said, remembering what he had told her. 'Jesus, talk about an understatement.'

Slightly smugly, Dr Cal raised an eyebrow. 'Did you enjoy your memory, Hannah?'

She nodded, then shook her head and laughed in disbelief. 'My childhood was inside that big white egg,' she said. 'Oh my God. Everything. I saw everything so clearly.'

'Why did you choose that memory?' the doctor asked, making a church's steeple out of his fingers. 'How did it make you feel?'

She thought for a moment. She had found the doll in the attic of her mother's house while hunting for portals and recalled that summer's day and her father, and how much she missed him. Would she have drowned? Probably not. But she remembered her daddy saving her nonetheless. She remembered the love she felt for him, nestling into his shirt as she coughed out the last of the pond water, soaking the blue chambray. At best, she thought, the reel of her falling in the pond would be like a video game or an animated movie. She had been wrong. She had been so very wrong.

'Because I never expected the treatment to work,' she said. 'Or at least I never expected it to work quite the way it does.'

'On this day in your childhood,' the doctor told her, 'we artificially melded the scene of six-year-old Hannah's garden to provide an immersive sensory experience. The smell of mown grass and the sensation of sun rays on your face created a reconstituted moment. Our photographic manipulation team took the image and created a multi-dimensional vision beamed through the crystals, while our olfactory chemists brewed the aromas piped into the pod. The hypnotic state allows your mind to accept the mirage. The portal you are holding in the form of your doll triggers the spooling of the memory. After that... you do the rest.'

'It's not real,' she said disbelievingly, 'but I thought... I thought...'

'The scene is chimeric. Your mind carries out the rest of the illusion. And we will perform the same trick with Euan's memories of you, Hannah. Every one of them. Every key memory of your shared past, right here in this building.'

It was real. It was so real it took her breath away. It was unlikely, it seemed impossible after the year she had endured, but it was real. These people could bring back her husband. That wasted flower of hope in her heart was alive – and blooming.

'In the pod,' Dr Calvin went on, 'you and your husband will be able to interact fully inside your shared memories. Within the reels Euan will believe he is living the experience. There may be confusion, a feeling of a truth dancing away. Before the incident that robbed him of his memory, your husband was an intelligent man so he may feel suspicion. We have only two rules. One is that you must make your reel memories as honest and true-to-life as possible. The second is that you must not, under any circumstances, let Euan know that he is inside a reel. If Euan is made aware of the treatment before you have successfully linked the reels, our process will collapse like a house of cards. Do you understand, Hannah?'

'Understand what?'

'For this treatment to succeed, we must move quickly. The moment we begin to link the reels is the moment we begin to stimulate his brain into memory recovery.'

'Which means—'

'Your first reel will exist in isolation. You can see it as a practice. A safety reel, if you will. But once we have started to link reels, we cannot go back. We cannot stop the treatment. We must move forwards. Always. We can't leave Euan living halfway in the past and halfway in the present, now, can we?' The medic laughed. He refilled her squash and she realised that her hands were trembling. 'That just wouldn't do, would it, Hannah?'

'No,' she agreed, wishing she could feel a fraction of his certainty, 'not at all.'

Once again, she felt as if she had been steamrollered into acquiescence. She had questions, so many questions, but for some reason she found herself unable to voice them in Dr Scott Calvin's presence. She supposed it was the overwhelming confidence of the man, muddled with her own desperation for the treatment to work, which struck her dumb. It was only later, driving home, when she replayed the scene in her mind – creating her own miniature mental reel – that the tiny voice of disquiet spoke out. It spoke and spoke.

Euan cooked for her that night, a steaming bowl of claggy pasta and tomato sauce, and she wondered why the simple food felt like a last supper. There was red wine, rather too much of it, and she felt able to tell her husband how the Ree-Mem Project worked, or at least as much as she knew. The portals, the pods, the conjoined hypnosis. The artificial reality of the past.

Once she had finished he was silent for some time.

'Wow,' Euan said at last, twirling his fork around a stubborn strand of taglierini.

'Wow,' she agreed. 'Definitely wow.'

'This is it. The start.'

'Another start,' she conceded. 'One more fresh start.'

'But you really think it'll work? This time?'

The question was a loaded gun. She traced her thumb around the rim of her wine glass. Dr Calvin had warned against telling him too much, but what had happened earlier – seeing her childhood inside the machine – threatened to scatter caution to the wind. She wanted to tell him it would work. She wanted to let him know everything would finally work out.

'I think so,' she said carefully. 'It's got a better chance than everything else we've tried.'

She saw Euan was unusually alert. His gaze, so frequently muddy and unquestioning after he woke from his coma, was bright. 'What did you see this morning, Hannah?' he asked.

The recollection of that foray into her childhood was still so vivid and she let out a deep breath that was almost a sob. She wondered whether she trusted herself to reply. 'Something that gave me hope,' she said.

'Good,' he said, abruptly putting down his fork, still staring at her with that odd intensity. 'It's a big day tomorrow.'

'Certainly is,' she agreed. She busied herself with the sloppy, tasteless food, silently praying for no further questions, but Euan was animated now, eager for answers. In that moment she wished for Dr Cal's certainties.

'So then,' he said, drumming his fingers rapidly on the table, 'if this ... this conjoined hypnosis treatment works, I won't re-member any of what's happening now?' A tic crossed his face before he continued, 'I won't remember this chat, this meal, the way I can't even cook dried pasta properly?'

She was unable to meet his eyes. She shook her head, trench-ing up a forkful of ragu. 'You know that, Euan,' she said. 'We've been through this, over and over. You'll go back to how you were before your accident.' She felt her throat constricting and took another swallow of wine. 'You'll remember your old life, you'll remember me. But you won't remember this. You won't remember how you were after the accident.'

'Why do you want me back so much?' her husband asked, his

face split with a peculiar semi-smile. 'I mean, I know I want to be me because I know I'm not me. I've been told that enough times. But this isn't just about me. It's me and you, isn't it? I can't have been that wonderful all the time, surely?'

A treacherous part of her mind agreed that Euan George Stornoway was most certainly never wonderful all the time. She loved his words: his knowingly silly jokes, his stories, the way he could cultivate roses in her cheeks with a well-chosen compliment. But at times that silver tongue could sharpen into a blade. During arguments he would choose the one vicious, unforgiving, perfect word that would cut her just right – like a butcher selecting the correct blade – and cleave her into pieces.

She loved his confidence but this easily segued into arrogance. She knew the effect he could have on women. Irritatingly, Euan knew it too. His gaze tended to linger on its subject for a second or two longer than was polite, although she could not deny that many girls found the effect flattering. She remembered introducing Ewan to her work colleagues one Friday night soon after they moved in together in London, and feeling slightly put out at the lingering looks between Ewan and one of the staff interns – a half-Chinese woman named Jasmine with raven hair that fell to the small of her back. Over the course of that evening in the city wine bar, she caught the pair of them gazing at one another at least half a dozen times. Eventually, when Jasmine sashayed off to the ladies' room, offering another smoky glance as she went, she confronted him. *Didn't your mother ever tell you it's rude to stare?* she hissed into his ear. He raised his eyebrows, feigning innocence, and she dug her elbow into his ribcage, pretending to be coolly amused but actually a little hurt. *I was only window shopping, gorgeous*, he had grinned, only slightly abashed. *I'd never actually try anything on for size.* She loved him. She trusted him. But trust didn't extend to naivety.

Then there had been the bleak six months before the day at the railway tracks; the time after Jennifer but before the accident. Where were those great long words of his in those grey months? Suddenly her husband had nothing to say. Did he really think he was protecting her with his silence? She wanted him to speak, needed him to speak. She would have welcomed his frustration, his anger, his regret, his tears. But his silence, his lack of emotion, pushed such a great distance between them. They could be sitting together on the living-room sofa and the few inches that separated their bodies was a bleak void. Irrationally she had wondered whether she could even touch him, as if an invisible yet impermeable sheet of glass had slid between them. *He's gone blank*, she told her mother. At that time, with the accident several months in the future, she had no idea what going blank truly meant.

She was tired and half drunk and heartsick and she knew she would regret the words tomorrow, but she couldn't stop them spilling out.

'You could never bear to be wrong,' she said, tightly gripping the stem of her glass. 'You could be bloody-minded and petty and needed constant reminders of how amazingly brilliant you were. You got into arguments with taxi drivers if they took the long route home. You'd sulk for the whole afternoon when Hearts lost. You took jokes too seriously and serious things as a joke. And when I needed you, really needed you, suddenly you had nothing to say. You went away. So no, if that's what was worrying you … no, you weren't that wonderful all the time.'

She stared at him and suddenly her husband let out a bray of laughter. She stared back at him, her heart thumping. Euan never laughed much any more. Euan's sense of fun had been shorn from him along with his memories. But he was laughing and now so too was she, and their cold house grew a fraction warmer.

'That's good,' he said. 'That's … that's really good. I mean, I was starting to dislike this other guy, the other me, the perfect me. Captain Wonderful. I was starting to resent him a bit, I think.'

'I keep on reminding myself of your stupidities,' she said, 'your mistakes, your annoying habits. Your bad side. Because I loved your bad side every bit as much as your good side.'

Euan reached across the table and took her hand. He said, 'I wish I could remember. I wish I could come back.'

She squeezed back tightly. In that moment she wanted to love this version of her husband – pale, quiet, unable to remember. But he could not remember her and therefore he could not truly understand her, he could not truly know her and he could not truly love her. No matter how hard he tried. Shorn of his memories, he was not the real Euan.

'You will remember,' she said. 'You will come back. I promise.'

13

Hannah and I: Our second year

The Fire Almost Dying, the Ayrshire Coastline

The sound of my bare feet slapping on wet sand rouses Hannah, whose head is bowed as if in reverie, and I run straight towards her, meaning to leap her and our campfire in one mighty bound. But as I prepare to jump, she sees me and squeals and rises up, and collision is inevitable. Well done, Stornoway, the sober part of my brain tells me, you're about to knock this girl unconscious with a flying knee to the forehead. Instead I drag my left foot underneath my right, tripping myself, and I tumble to the ground and pitch up against Hannah in a jumble of salty, sandy confusion.

'Idiot,' she grins, the flames picking out her cheekbones with artistic subtlety. 'Where have you been?'

I indicate the pile of splintery driftwood that I dropped a few paces away. 'It took ages to find more wood for the fire,' I explain. 'That fisherman'll be furious when he finds his boat.'

She kicks a shower of sand into my face, my open mouth. 'What was that for?' I protest, grains gritting against my molars.

'I love sandy-haired men.'

'Oh, very good, how long have you been working on that one?'

'No more than an hour.'

She flicks her hair away from her forehead and stares out

at the Firth of Clyde, a thick streak of searing orange light separating the blackening sky from the sea. The horizon could be the edge of the world. I can see two trawler ships, waiting for the tide, facing one another as if adversaries – or lovers. The coastal air is tinged with the heady scent of charcoal. The low light cracks into shimmering fragments on the ripples of the surf.

Hannah passes over some wooden skewers, expertly smoothed and sharpened to points, and a bag of marshmallows. 'Here. Brave hunter need food.'

'Did you make these yourself?' I ask, holding up a skewer. She waggles a penknife in my direction and nods. 'You're quite the outdoors girl,' I say, impressed.

'Girl Guides, camp craft, first class,' she says, snapping off a military salute. 'Whittled till I could whittle no more.'

I spot the machine stamp on the base of the skewer and pick her up on her lie. 'You bought them somewhere, didn't you?'

'Busted,' she concedes with a laugh. 'Boutique camping store in Kentish Town. Bohemian outdoors merriment is so in this season. Designer wellies, patchwork ponchos. They call it glamping. Glamorous camping, you know?'

'Sometimes,' I say heavily, 'I think I'm not long for this world.'

'Before you expire prematurely, would you toast a lady a marshmallow?'

I thread the rubbery pink and white sweets onto the sticks and balance them over the embers. The marshmallow flesh blossoms blackly and I pass one to Hannah.

'Tough on the outside, gooey inside,' she says, chewing contemplatively. 'Rather like you, I think.'

'You don't understand. I'm pure evil, angel.'

'Should I be worried that I'm in the middle of nowhere with you? Why did you drag me all the way up here anyway?'

What can I tell her? We have been seeing each other for thirteen months now, but each time it has been on her home turf – yet another flit to London, yet another endless train journey hoping that things are the same as they were last time. It seems I know so much yet so little about this girl. I'm playing Blind Man's Bluff with her personality. Warmer, warmer, colder, colder. I feel I've known her forever and I don't understand a single thing about her. But she is here, she is here with me, and in her presence I'm happy to believe in miracles.

So I decided to see how the land lay between us. A few days up at The Lodge. The Lodge – capitalisation apparent when my parents told their friends about the cottage, as if it was a whitewashed duplex on Malibu Beach. My father, a mechanic from a family of nine, thought owning two properties was the apex of personal achievement. Stornoway Lodge is a glorified shack on the wind-blasted Ayrshire coast, with temperamental central heating and a leaky roof. But The Lodge is ours – and more importantly, this weekend it's empty. I had rhapsodised to Hannah about the craggy beauty of the coastline, the serene soundtrack of lapping surf and cawing gulls. She had said *Yes*. My acceptance of her rejection – *It's okay, that's fine, no problem* – very nearly slipped from my lips. *Sure, I'd enjoy a break from London*, I heard her say. Her words were so damned casual, and there was me pacing my living-room floor, gripping the handset so tightly my knuckles had turned white. *Can I catch a train there, or is it horse-and-trap past Kilmarnock?*

I can't help smiling at the memory. Grinning so widely my mouth actually hurts. But I'm unable to stop.

'Hey, laughing boy,' Hannah nudges me, 'the fire's going out.'

'You're the one with the knife,' I say. 'Trim down half-a-dozen strips of wood, build from the bottom, stack any damp ones round the edge so they dry off. Keep the blaze going.'

'You've got an answer for everything. I'm almost fooled.'

'Fooled?'

'About you being the outdoors type. Maybe you're only bullshitting.'

'I do know never to camp out in remote parts without warming sustenance.' I rummage in my bag and bring out the bottle of Calvados.

'No whisky?' Hannah asks. 'I was preparing myself for a lecture on the heady single malts of McLocharlachloch. Dreading it, in fact.'

'Whisky would have been clichéd. And since we're out of earshot of any hairy-arsed Highlanders, I'll admit I prefer brandy. It's our drink, isn't it?'

'Our drink,' she agrees. We clink glasses – clinking as much as a plastic cup can clink – and drink. Hannah isn't finished with me yet though. 'You wanted to avoid clichés, eh?' she says, raising an eyebrow. 'Surely not as clichéd as inviting me up to these fabled remote parts and pretending you're a big macho backwoodsman?'

'It's not that,' I mumble. 'I'm not trying to impress you.'

'Why did you bring me here then?'

'I can … I can talk to you … talk to you properly here,' I say, blushing. I bury my face in the spirit, relishing the burning as it slips down my throat. She waits until I feel able to continue, her chin tilted slightly, the wind playing with the strands of her hair. This is something I forget when I'm not with her: her stillness, her grace. 'The words never come out right when I'm in London. Everything's too fast or slow. I can't keep up with the rhythm.'

The girl blinks, biting down on her lower lip. 'Oh, Euan,' she says, her voice cracking, 'I was only teasing. I love it here, really I do. I love being here together. Just us two.'

I smile back and I am about to tell her how I feel, how I truly feel, but my words falter and die as I stare out at the coastline. There is a mist rolling in off the sea, a slow but methodical onslaught of greyness. Just my luck. We were enjoying a perfect Scottish sunset and now the weather is turning. But there's something oddly unnatural about the fog. Something wrong in the way it moves in a steady, unstoppable creep. There's also something wrong about the way it smells so lifeless, choking away the sweet scents of burned driftwood and toasted sugars and Hannah's floral perfume. It almost snuffs out the glow that her presence has stoked inside me. Wispy tendrils begin to reach out from the mass of fog. For some reason I feel a sneaking pull towards the grasp of those crooked fingers.

Only minutes ago, Hannah's yellow hair was burning as brightly as the campfire. Now it seems the vibrancy of those colours has been swallowed by the shadows. But this is the moment, yes, this is the moment, and her head is on my shoulder and my arm is around her waist. Her hair is impregnated with the charcoal scent of the fire. The sunset is streaked with flaming orange once more. I must have imagined that weird fog. Too much brandy and emotion.

'I keep thinking,' I murmur, 'that I need to say something witty or interesting or shocking. To keep your interest.'

'How about I imagine your amazing words and we can skip to the next step?'

'The next step?'

An eyebrow raises a fraction. 'Where you kiss me, you adorable imbecile.'

'Ah, that next step.'

Our lips come together and for the next few minutes time loses its meaning. The blood roars in my brain like great breakers crashing on jagged rocks and when we finally break apart, her eyes are moist.

'What happens now?' Hannah asks.

'What do you mean?'

She sighs. 'What is this, Euan – what are we? A fling? A holiday romance? An *affaire de coeur*? Christ, you've dragged me up here to the wilderness. Such geographical displacements don't occur just for ... well.'

'Well, what?'

'We always seem to be a little too far apart for comfort,' she says, which seems a strange thing to say when we are wrapped up in one another. 'I don't know what you get up to when I'm gone. Am I some plaything to be picked up or put down as masculine urges require? Am I one of a few, one of many?'

I shake my head emphatically. 'Of course not.'

'Because I do believe in having an open relationship.'

I cough out disbelieving laughter. 'Sorry, what?'

'Yeah, I'm very open about how badly I'll kill you if you ever mess me around.'

I smile but I can tell she's not joking. The emerald gems of her eyes are sparkling but hard, so hard. 'You don't have to worry. There's only you, angel.'

'You would say that, wouldn't you, when you've just kissed me? What about the times when I'm not here with you – can I trust you then?'

'You're always here with me,' I tell her. 'You're with me constantly. I walk down the street and keep thinking I've caught sight of you in a shop window, walking next to me. You're forever in my mind, my thoughts. My memories.'

Turning away from me as if hiding something, Hannah stares out at the shoreline. Does she see what I see? Her body stiffens uncomfortably. That odd fog is back now, definitely. It has reached the edges of the dying campfire. A rope-like wisp curls lazily towards us, floating in a curious arc, its tip curving into the shape of a question mark. There is something chilling about its languorous drift, like a cobra waiting for the precise moment to strike.

'We should go,' she says quickly. 'It's ... too cold. We need to leave. Back to The Lodge.'

'Oh aye? And what happens when we get there?'

Hannah tracks her tongue over her front teeth in a mischievous grin. I must have imagined that strange look of distress on her face, which is now alive, alight with the crackling glow of the fire between us. There's no fog. I'm seeing things. I'm letting my imagination run away with me. I should think only of her.

'Well now,' Hannah says primly, smoothing down the front of her top, 'a good girl like me can't promise too much, can she?'

14

275 days since the accident

The array of objects on the metal tray looked like a bloodless autopsy. The portals. The first months of their relationship had been carefully incised and laid before her by the Reel Memory Project; it seemed cruelly reductive. Her husband sat next to her in Dr Cal's office. She had kept a close eye on him on their way here. During the drive his only responses to her questions were curt grunts. He was pale and at times she saw his lower lip tremble.

But they were here now, at the Project's headquarters. The scene had been set, the cast was waiting in the wings and the curtain was about to be drawn up on the stage. It was too late for doubts.

'Are you sure that you wish to proceed with the treatment, Mr Stornoway?' Dr Calvin asked. She thought, not for the first time, that the neuropsychologist had a tricksy way of second-guessing her thoughts.

'I want what Hannah wants,' Euan said, his gaze at the floor. 'She wants me to be me again.'

Dr Cal glanced at her questioningly. She felt oddly guilty, as if their voyage into her husband's subconscious was a party for Hannah's benefit alone. *I'm not the villain here*, she wanted to tell the doctor and his orderlies in their short-sleeved medical scrubs. *It wasn't me who destroyed two happy lives. That was Euan, remember?*

'What do you really think, Euan?' Dr Calvin probed. 'Are you quite certain you understand the results of this procedure, in bringing back the former version of yourself?'

'I want to do this,' Euan said. He stared over at her, she caught a flash of naked fear in his gaze, and she squeezed his hand in support. 'I want to go back to how I was. I want to be me again. But ... I'm scared too.'

'Apprehension is understandable,' Dr Cal said. 'But you do wish to continue with the process, Mr Stornoway?'

'More than anything.' There was a low urgency in his voice and she felt a gush of relief. Three times he had been asked. Three times he had said yes.

'Excellent, excellent,' the doctor purred. One of the orderlies placed two pens and two sheaves of paper in his hand. 'Now, if you would be so kind, would you both sign these forms? A mere formality.' He chortled at his own joke as he passed over the contract. 'Only to give the three of us peace of mind.'

Her eyebrows rose. She scanned the document. There was a baffling amount of legalese but a few words stood out: *The patient hereby agrees not to reveal information to journalists or any other members of the public about the methods of the Reel Memory Project, as well as any personal/professional details about the curator of their treatment.* They were permitted to speak to no one other than a representative from the Project itself. There was another caveat: *Upon completion of the treatment, Mr Euan George Stornoway and Mrs Hannah Jane Stornoway agree to grant the Reel Memory Project interviews, which shall be recorded for promotional purposes,*

*about their experience, as well as publicity videos and/or photographs
as deemed necessary by their treatment curator.*

'I didn't expect this,' she said, her mouth suddenly dry. 'Should
I at least ask a solicitor to look it over?'

Dr Calvin grinned winningly. 'Of course, Hannah – anything
that makes you happy. It's a standard non-disclosure agreement
with a little dose of *quid pro quo*. I'm sure any lawyer would tell
you the same, but these legal eagles take their own sweet time
about things. I'd say the sooner we start treating your husband,
the sooner he'll come back to you.'

Out of the corner of her eye she saw Euan's fingers were
gouged into the arm of his chair, his nails worrying the leather.
'What's this thing about the interviews?' she said. 'We're not
really—'

'Sadly, our efforts at Ree-Mem are not appreciated by certain elements of society,' Dr Calvin said, tutting like a school
master indulging an errant pupil. 'Doubtless you've seen
the mob with their silly placards outside our Seattle headquarters. The non-believers. In the Dark Ages they would have
brandished pitchforks, I'm sure. They would rather shut us
down and see our patients returned to their amnesiac states.
A wonderfully Luddite mindset, don't you think? So that's
where you and Euan can do us a neat little favour.' He held
his arms out wide as if to embrace the entire world, believers
or not. 'Some positive publicity. After we've successfully treated
your husband of course. The more people who know of the
immense positive benefits of our work, the better. The better
for all of us.'

The pen twitched in her hand as if the doctor had cast a
spell on it. His expression urged acquiescence. The light in his
eyes was disturbingly eager. She felt a sense of control slipping
away from her, just a fraction.

Quickly she inked her name at the bottom of the page, feeling that if she delayed she might lose her nerve. This was real, too real. The contract was signed. Up until now there had only been words and thoughts. The ink on the paper was physical evidence that they had stepped over a boundary, chosen a path. There was no turning back. She stared at her husband, his head bent over his paper in concentration. He was writing his full name, Euan George Stornoway, in small careful letters. The signature could not have been more different from his former flamboyant scrawl. A million tiny cuts, she thought miserably.

Dr Calvin nodded towards the orderlies. One of the men placed a hand on her husband's shoulder and led him away. She was seized by a sudden urge to reach for him, to call him back to her, but the words wouldn't come and her plea atrophied on the tip of her tongue.

Alone with Dr Calvin, the silence grew uncomfortable. Then the medic reached down to take the milk jug that she had stolen from the Parisian café bar named Bellevue. His slender brown fingers wrapped themselves around the porcelain. He lifted the jug like a grail, running a forefinger over its chipped handle. Their first portal.

'It was the best we could find,' she said. 'We nicked it from the café where we first met. As a souvenir. Sorry if it doesn't work.'

'No, a fine choice,' the doctor said. 'The physicality is vital in conjoined hypnosis. Photographs can help take you into the reels, but in physical interaction they are insubstantial. You need this portal to bring up Euan's buried memory and start the scene spooling. You've heard of the phrase, *L'amour, c'est un question de peau?*'

She shrugged. 'My French goes as far as *bière* and *café crème*. You'll see in the reels.'

'Love, the French say, is a question of skin. They mean, I believe, touch. As I told you before, Hannah, touch is an electric shock to the memory. We always remember the texture of the carpet of our childhood home, the way it rubbed against the soles of our bare feet. It is the same for the feel of a long-forgotten toy in our hand, or a paintbrush between our fingers. Or, most presciently, the touch of a lover's hand.'

'Euan and I can touch each other inside the reels?' she asked, then let out an embarrassed giggle. 'Sorry, I mean—'

'You may physically interact with one another exactly as you did when the memory was first formed,' said Dr Calvin, tactfully ignoring the innuendo. 'Now, would you follow me through to the treatment room?'

Again she walked alongside the doctor down that narrow, blue-glowing corridor until they reached the doors marked *U* and *D*. This time Dr Cal swiped his card to open the door on the right. As her eyes adjusted to the neon-pricked gloom, she saw there was another pod in this room, far larger than the one in which she had experienced her childhood a few days ago. A conjoined pod; the egg shapes twinned. The machine hummed quietly. Its smoothly sloping wide walls seemed to vibrate.

'Our most recent and beloved creation,' he announced. 'Duessa.' Now she understood the reason for the *U* and *D* letters above the doors to the treatment rooms. 'Now, if you please—'

Stepping closer, she saw her husband slumped in one of the slanted seats – an unconscious, shallow-breathing form, his cheekbones picked out by the low azure light – and her breath caught in her throat.

'He's under,' the doctor said simply. 'A textbook hypnosis.'

'When he's asleep,' she said, 'when his scar's concealed, he looks identical to the back-before. When he sleeps I can trick myself into believing that when he wakes up everything will be better.'

'We're only at the start of the process, Hannah. We will get there, I promise. Your husband will wake up, one day soon, and everything will be better. But we have many miles ahead of us.'

She bit down on her bottom lip. 'Or many reels?'

He nodded. 'So to business.' He clapped his hands. 'The portal for this reel is the milk jug you, ah, removed from the Parisian café where you met. All that remains is to bind you together to share the physicality of the memory.'

The doctor moved over to the cabinet that hung on one wall. He pressed his thumb into a small crevice that glowed a faint green – a fingerprint scanner, she presumed – and a hatch slid open. He returned holding a thin leather strap in one hand. She noticed the inner loop sparkled with scores of diamond-bright electrodes. Pressure points, Calvin had told her. The electrode belt would heighten the tics and flinches of their muscles, translating them into body motion.

Her eyebrow arched as she assessed the leather strap. She couldn't help herself. 'From your personal collection?' she asked.

The medic's lips narrowed but she could have sworn she caught a glint of amusement in his eyes. 'The electrode yoke is vital for the conjoined treatment, Hannah. The nerve impulses in your muscles will translate into motion in the memory. If you break the seal with your partner—'

'I know, I know, *un question de peau*. Okay, strap me in.'

She eased herself into the pod's reclining chair, trying to

avoid looking at the inert form of her husband. His hypnotised state was too close – far, far too close – to his coma.

Her left arm was crossed at the elbow with Euan's right arm. The band was wound around their limbs from elbow to wrist. The rubber whispered against her skin like the cold, not-quite-dry hide of a reptile. Her husband's flesh seemed to creep against hers. The fingertips of her free hand drummed a staccato rhythm on the armrest of the chair.

'As this is your first time in conjoined hypnosis,' the medic went on, 'we shall take everything very, very slowly. You recall what I told you about this scene being isolated, a practice reel? To overburden your senses would be unwise. When I notice even the slightest resistance, I shall bring you out. But I assure you that you have nothing to fear.'

The medic guided her fingers around the crockery stolen from Café Bellevue so many years ago. Her husband's hand closed over hers and she gasped. The lights in the room dimmed a fraction.

'Watch the crystals,' Calvin said, his voice a trickle of warm syrup. 'Breathe deeply. Breathe deeply.'

The crystals that speckled the pod were blurring and fuzzing into a kaleidoscope of impossible shades. They pulsated with the rhythm of her rising and falling chest, flickering from a sheening silver glare to a reddish-brown glow then to sunlight.

The edges of reality slipped away. The interior of the pod was ablaze with colours. Suddenly she could see a familiar street, a bistro with circular tables and aspidistra framing the cave-like entrance. She knew it was a construct, a recreation by skilled hands, a multi-dimensional photograph. But could photographs really offer moving images, sounds and smells?

The soft voice of Dr Calvin still echoed. *Breathe deeply, breathe deeply, breathe deeply*. But there were more sounds now, which drowned out his words. From somewhere indefinable she heard shouts from a marketplace, the hum of trams whooshing past, the clink of glasses on metal table tops. She smelled tart foreign hops and the unctuous aroma of frying meat. It was all coming back to her now. Sinking down, letting go, she let the rocking wave wash her away to the past.

The sensation that first overwhelmed her was the smell. Griddled steak and tarry *Gauloises* smoke and diesel fumes from taxi cabs. The ripe, pungent melange of odours that seeped through the streets of the 14th arrondissement.

This was Paris. This was really happening. Not a jerky stop-motion film, no theatrical artifice, no smoke or mirrors. This was reality – or whatever passed for it in her husband's shattered mind. She was sitting on a seat outside a Paris bistro that was so wonderfully familiar and yet strangely skewed. The café was not quite as she remembered; she was sure it had changed since she had last sat on the outside terrace. She was positive that she would have recalled the twin aspidistra framing the doorway into the bar's interior. The tables had been wicker, not metal – hadn't they? – and covered with blue-and-white gingham tablecloths. There were roadworks going on a few streets away – how had she forgotten the frantic yammering of the drills? This was the place, it must be the place, yet it was not quite the place she remembered.

It took her a few moments to realise her recollection of the bistro had been corrupted through the passing of years. This was exactly how it had been.

Exactly.

There he was. Sitting alone at the table, a glass of beer in his hand, a plate of steak-frites resting before him. The shirt with a smattering of oil stains, rucked up at the back, at odds with the sleek tuxedo of the waiter. The peeling skin on the tip of his nose, always his most vulnerable point for sunburn. Even his extravagantly relaxed posture, trying so desperately to look as if he belonged, as if this was another day in the louche continental lifestyle of Euan George Stornoway. The young man who was sitting three tables away would one day become her husband. But that morning he had been only another British tourist attempting élan in an unfamiliar district in an unfamiliar city in an unfamiliar country.

This was Euan. This was Euan on the day they first met.

She raised the drink towards her lips. That warm, bitter, smoky aroma of good ground coffee filled her nostrils. Oh God. This was real. This was really real.

She realised, in this recreation of her first sight of Euan, that the tug she felt towards him went far beyond looks and physique. She had never known the meaning of the word *attraction* before; not truly. She remembered being struck by two enormous jolts: twin blows to the head and the heart. Those shocks were coming now, racing towards her as the scene played out, and she was unsure if she could bear the glorious agony.

The first hit, at the raise of his hand in greeting, short-circuited the wires in her brain, dropping her IQ approximately a hundred points. In her confusion she picked up her coffee by the saucer instead of the handle.

The second hit – at the words *Hello, you* framed on that young man's lips – sapped the strength from her muscles and the saucer tumbled from her grasp and the cup fell, exploding against the edge of the table, and porcelain tinkled to the ground. She leapt to her feet, her dress stained and soaked. The young man whose name she knew and didn't know stood up too, in his haste knocking over his own table, his glass going the same way as her mug of *café crème*, and streams of beer and coffee merged on the Parisian cobbles.

She stared at Euan. He stared back.

That was how it started. Again.

15

275 days since the accident

She looked up into the startlingly blue eyes of Dr Calvin. 'That's enough for the moment, Hannah,' the medic said. 'I believe it was plenty of excitement for your first reel.'

She patted her legs, half convinced she was still standing on the cobbles outside Café Bellevue, her dress soaked with coffee. 'I was moving,' she said. 'I was on my feet.'

Dr Cal shook his head. 'Think of it like a dream. You might dream of tumbling from an office block, flailing and kicking. Any observer would see only tiny eye movements and the occasional twitch of your limbs.'

She looked at Euan's unconscious form. 'Did I do okay?' she asked. The doctor nodded and a sunny smile creased his cheeks, which she matched.

'Extraordinarily well for your first experience,' he said. 'But this is only the start. Now you have experienced the first scene, we can move forward through your shared history – taking Euan with you, of course. You need to loop through these reels and link them, dragging Euan from one memory to the next. Remember my drawing of those merged infinity loops, Hannah? Each reel is a separate loop. Your job is to stitch every scene together to provide a memory narrative that plays out flawlessly. Just like a movie.'

'It's not everything, though, is it?' she said. 'We met today, again, but what about before I met Euan? How will he remember the days before Café Bellevue, his parents, his childhood?'

'Do you remember what I told you about the hippocampus, Hannah,' Dr Calvin asked, 'so very early on in proceedings?'

'It's the part of the brain that can ... that can ...'

'The part of the brain that can grow new neurons. Give birth to memories. Each reel sets off eruptions in your husband's medial temporal lobe.' Schoolboy-like in his enthusiasm, the doctor mimed an explosion by clenching his fists, then spreading his palms wide. 'Boom! I'm in Paris, how did I get here? Boom! Where are my family, my friends? Boom! Who is this beautiful lady sitting opposite me? The reels are jump-starts for recreating millions, billions more memories.'

She stared pleadingly at Dr Cal. 'Can we go back again?' she asked. 'Back to Paris, to Café Bellevue?'

'Not today. Tomorrow, after you've rested. It would be dangerous to overburden you. The stresses of meddling with the subconscious are not to be underestimated.'

The electrode yoke that bound her with Euan was disengaged. She pulled her fingers free of her husband's grip and his lack of resistance spoke more than words ever could. She was ushered to the uncomfortable sofa and handed a cup of squash. Two of the Project's orderlies descended upon the limp form of her husband. One was white, one was black, they both stood well above six feet and they hefted Euan's body onto the padded gurney as if he was weightless. They would be taking him through to the recovery room where he would be slowly returned to consciousness. She wondered what passed through his thoughts while he was brought up from the hypnotic state.

Was there a moment, a tiniest fraction in time, in which the imagery of the reels flickered in his mind?

Dr Calvin placed a hand on her shoulder and steered her away from the scene. She was happy to go with him. The sight of Euan on the stretcher – his unresisting form, his shallow breathing – brought back too many memories of the coma.

In his office, which she had already begun to think of as her debriefing room, she sipped at her orange squash, her gaze at the white wall. She almost expected the taste of *café crème*.

'Once you start to connect the reels,' Dr Calvin said, busying himself with the folders and files on his grand desk, not troubling to meet her gaze, 'they will only sustain you for a solitary loop. Two loops are extremely unadvisable. By your very presence in the reel, you are corrupting its internal structure.'

'But these are all things we've lived through. Surely if he's trapped in these individual memories spinning around, he won't notice—'

'His psyche wishes him to remain in this fugue state, that much is evident. You must push through this, Hannah, if you wish your husband to return to you. When you finally begin your journey inside the reels, you will need to proceed most rapidly.'

She stared hard at the doctor. His posture was not as relaxed as normal and she saw a vein pulsing in the centre of his forehead. 'There's an *otherwise* coming, Dr Cal,' she said. 'Isn't there?'

Calvin offered her a slightly uncomfortable smile. 'Otherwise,' he said, glancing away for a moment. He wiped his lips with the back of his hand as if he had a bad taste in his mouth. 'Otherwise we may put the stability of the reels at risk.'

She remembered that first conversation with Saskia about the Ree-Mem Project; it seemed like years ago now. The fears that had been cast out of her mind as excitement took hold. *They wiped a woman's mind ... she went into a trance and never came out.*

'Will Euan be in any danger?' she asked. She tried to keep her tone level, businesslike, but her voice cracked on the final word. Her fingers were clenched into fists, crumpling the brittle polymers of the cup into constituent atoms.

'Oh no, not in the slightest, I assure you,' Dr Calvin said. 'But for this treatment to succeed, speed is absolutely of the essence. From the moment we enter your husband's subconscious, his psyche will recognise there has been an intrusion.'

She bit down on her lower lip, the nails of her right hand digging into the skin of her left palm. Had she expected everything to be so simple? Of course not.

'Once we begin the treatment, we cannot turn back,' the doctor continued, recovering his poise. 'The reason I chose you, Hannah, is you have the mental strength to follow the process through until the endgame. We ascertained this from psychological evaluations since the very moment you first reached out to Ree-Mem.' He brought the tips of his fingers together as if in prayer. 'In addition to my professional judgement, of course.'

Despite her misgivings she felt flattered. 'Thanks. I think. But why wouldn't I go through with it? To the endgame, as you call it. I want my husband back.'

'Oh, if only it was that simple,' Dr Calvin said, lolling back in his chair. 'During this treatment you will revisit the entire history of you and Euan. Some scenes will be magical, others less so. All to provide your husband with a full and frank account of your relationship. There may be painful experiences ahead. You do not need a medical professional to tell you that.'

She remembered the conversation between her and Euan only minutes before the accident; a secret on the tip of his tongue but never voiced. It had been a terrible year for them and he was remote and glum. Some days, in those bleak months after Jennifer, he left her – only to clear his head, he assured her – and each time he left she wondered whether he would return. In response, she tried to be the light to his darkness – cheerful, supportive, even manically happy. She flung herself into the role with as much commitment as any West End star; the supportive wife to the disconsolate husband, in a miserable play performed to an empty auditorium. She was so wrapped up in playing this character that she hadn't realised something had gone wrong, badly wrong, with Euan. If they had driven straight home on that summer's day, he might have revealed everything – and that tortured her. While her husband lay in his coma, she checked his phone history and emails, each time feeling a sticky sense of shame, but there was nothing more sinister than updates from his family and his best friend Barry. In the end she never found the answers. When Euan woke up there was simply too much else to endure. There were far greater issues in their lives.

'So, Hannah,' the doctor went on, 'there may be times when you find the process difficult. You may struggle with your emotions, you may feel pressure. Even think of quitting.'

She shook her head. 'I don't quit anything. Ever.'

'Atta-girl,' he gave her the thumbs-up with both hands. 'However, I must impress on you that once you have started this process you must end it. You must not, must not, quit the treatment. And just as you need to connect every one of the reels, you are also forbidden from altering the past. I realise the temptation may be there—' the doctor winked '—but you must resist it. Otherwise we risk fragments of fabricated memory sparking into Euan's brain. Any deviations from the true memories would confuse him, skew his perspective. Leave him unsure of who he truly is.'

She blinked. 'That doesn't sound … I mean, I don't want to question your methods or anything, but, I mean …'

'The process is entirely safe, of that you have my word.' Dr Calvin favoured her with his familiar booming chuckle. 'So long as you keep to the path that we have mapped out. Just outline the scenes to the best of your memory and we'll do the hard work for you. Then link those damn reels, Hannah. Don't wander off the path.'

She woke the next day flushed with excitement. That feeling she had known as a child on Christmas Eve or the morning of her birthday. Anticipation crackled through her body like a succession of electrical shocks. Sunlight cracked through her curtains and the unremarkable Hertfordshire countryside looked gorgeous that morning.

They had been here before, her and Euan. They had been promised breakthroughs, recoveries, miracles. Cognitive therapists, subcutaneous thiamine implants, static charges. She had agreed to every treatment with good will and tolerance, even if that mask of cheerful resilience had started to slip. Her belief receded in ever-decreasing circles. Then, as all hope seemed lost, the Ree-Mem Project had entered her life. Since that day, everything was progressing with uncanny speed.

Now another treatment. But here was the crucial difference: the process worked. God, did it work. What sort of memory could bring back smell, touch, taste? What sort of memory could bring back the dead?

Because the old Euan was dead. But yesterday afternoon he had been returned to existence inside the Duessa pod. Returned to life, returned to her. If the Ree-Mem Project could raise the dead, surely curing amnesia was not beyond its capabilities.

She was seized with inspiration. They were sitting at the

kitchen table eating breakfast, Euan engrossed in the sports reports on his computer screen. Carefully, to avoid attracting his attention too early, she nudged her empty mug of tea to the edge of the table. The lip of the cup hung over oblivion before the final touch of her fingertip sent it falling. The mug hit the ground with a dull crunch. He glanced up at her, then at the wreckage on the floor.

'Damn,' she said. 'How clumsy.'

She headed quickly towards the store cupboard and removed a broom and dustpan. She poked the brush at the shards of the cup with stagey distaste, as if prodding a dead rat.

'Euan,' she said, feeling a fresh shiver of anticipation. 'Euan … Euan … who's this? Who's this?' She arranged her features into an expression of woe. 'Who's this? Aah, these 'orrible Breeteesh folk … they come to mah loverlee café, they brek mah loverlee crockeree … bah, 'ow I 'ate them.' She grinned at him. 'Who's that, Euan? Who's that?'

'The waiter,' he said. His voice was flat. She realised there was no memory here, only a lesson learned by rote. 'The waiter at the café where we first met.'

Her smile crumpled at the edges. I'm treating him like a dog, she thought miserably. Who's this … what's that … here, boy, roll over, play fetch. What was she hoping to achieve?

'Do you—' she started.

'It's an old joke, isn't it? We used to do impressions of the waiter. We used to mimic him. Laugh at him.'

'Yes,' she said, feeling ashamed. 'You're right, it wasn't funny. Well, it was to us. I mean, if you'd seen his face …'

'I know because you told me. After I woke up. Not because—'

'Not because you remember,' she finished for him. 'Right. Okay. No problem.'

Wordlessly she cleared up the detritus, then went upstairs and lay on her bed. The stresses and the strangeness of the previous day overwhelmed her and she let herself go. She sobbed until she felt she must have cried out all her feelings for her husband, leaving her body a husk. But that wasn't true. No matter how frequently and intensely she mourned Euan as he had once been, there was no closure, no end to the grief.

The next day she answered the doorbell to find a young stranger on her porch. He introduced himself as a reporter from a national tabloid newspaper. The journalist sported a scrubby beard that any mother would have ached to rub off with spit, a shiny silver suit and a hopeful demeanour.

'You're the lady with the fella who's got no memory, ain't you?' he demanded. His voice was a queer mixture of upper-class breeding and affected cockney twang. 'You're the one what's having that sci-fi treatment done, yeah? Mind if I come in for a quick—'

She stuttered an apology and closed the door in the young man's face. Evidently the arrival in Britain of Dr Calvin and the Ree-Mem Project had sparked more interest than she was prepared for. Leaning heavily against the door, the old animated Disney musical *Fantasia* crossed her mind. She had loved that film as a child, particularly the Sorcerer's Apprentice scene. The thought of it frightened her now. She had put the brooms in motion, set them alive and capering, but she had absolutely no idea how to make the dancing stop.

16

281 days since the accident

The camera was on her again. The small video crew was ever-present in the Ree-Mem Project's foyer, whizzing around with their hi-tech kit, conversing in terse jargon. They seemed to focus on her particularly when Dr Cal greeted them at the start of each day of reels. She was sure that one day a lens had even tracked her driving away from the industrial estate. But she could hardly tell Dr Calvin to turn off the cameras, could she? Not with all he was doing for her and Euan.

'Another flaming documentary,' the spiky-haired receptionist informed her wearily. The nametag on his cobalt blue tunic read *Jonas*, he spoke with an Antipodean twang, and since he was the only member of the Ree-Mem desk staff who didn't seem like a perfectly coiffed automaton, Jonas was her favourite. 'Good publicity, the bosses tell us,' Jonas went on, raising a pierced eyebrow. 'The drive towards greater public sympathy, they say. Sympathy for the devil, right? You've seen the rent-a-mob outside. Couldn't miss it, could you?'

There was now a row of tents set up outside the Ree-Mem base, a few feet away from the chain-link fence and the security entrance. A dozen protesters had watched them silently, perhaps judgementally, as she swiped her security pass with the guards and drove into the complex. They had tied blue ribbons to the fence, which fluttered in the breeze. She hadn't felt threatened; they looked more like down-on-their-luck university dons than an angry mob. She supposed Dr Cal would call them the non-believers. Their leader appeared to be a thin, animated woman with straggly grey hair and a scruffy overcoat of indeterminate colour. The woman was brandishing a small hand-lettered sign that she couldn't quite read. The larger placards disturbed her though. The violently scrawled slogans. *Brain butchers*, that was the most common. *Whose mind will they wipe next? No thanks for the memories. God will judge you.*

'What do they want?' she asked.

'To shut us down,' Jonas shrugged. 'Same as always. You sort of get used to it, Mrs Stornoway.'

One of the cameras was now bobbing over her shoulder, demanding attention like a neglected pet dog. She couldn't understand why the film crew were focusing their attentions – and lenses – on her and Euan. They were nobodies; inconsequential and easily disposable. There were no high stakes in their particular game. If Dr Calvin failed to bring back her husband the world would keep turning. The Project would not collapse into dust. They treated the rich and powerful, the famous and fortunate. Whatever became of the little lives of the Stornoways would make no impact whatsoever. However, Dr Cal didn't see it like that, she reminded herself. From his very first words to her, he had acted as if the apex of his career – his life – would be to save Euan George Stornoway.

'What are they doing to me?' her husband asked.

How could she explain? How could she possibly explain? The truth was that they had spent the past week living in their past, or at least the Reel Memory Project's recreation of it. Euan was understandably inquisitive about the treatment and she had no idea how to respond. He always wanted to know what happened in between their arrival at the Ree-Mem headquarters and his surfacing from hypnosis in the recovery room. But she found it difficult to speak to him about the process. The situation was too mundane; a married thirtysomething couple making dinner in their unremarkable commuter-belt house. It was a world away from the science-fiction madness of the last few days. She remembered how handsome Euan had looked in his early twenties. How young, how reckless, how carefree he had been. Her too. They could do absolutely anything together. They could be whatever they wanted to be. She hadn't reckoned on how much revisiting these memories would hurt. It was sweet pain, but it was still pain.

'They're doing what's best for you,' she said lamely.

'They're doing what's best for me?' Euan repeated. His voice quivered and his left eye was blinking and watering. A little disconcerted, she realised that this was a nervous tic the new Euan shared with the pre-accident version of her husband, the 'tell' in his poker-face whenever he was apprehensive.

'They're doing what's best for us,' she tried again. She placed his dinner in front of him and stood back from the table, staring down at the dark curls of his hair, a few flecked with grey, the thick whorls starting to recede very slightly in the centre. She thought of the memories locked away in that head. It was irrational but she could not help thinking that real life was not here but inside the reels. Everything she yearned for was in that Duessa pod, even if Dr Cal called it a fallacy. True emotion, true life, true love lay inside the humming, egg-like machine. There the colours were vibrant, the scents zinged through her brain, her synapses crackled like fireworks with every touch of Euan's hand.

'It's tough not knowing what's going on,' her husband

said, listlessly prodding the potato mash blanket with his fork. 'Anything could be happening to me in there, absolutely anything. I'm a little—'

'It's fine to be scared,' she cut in. Her voice was bright and brittle. She realised that she was using the same artificially comforting tone as the hospital counsellors they had been assigned after Euan surfaced from his coma. 'I'm scared too. It's a scary thing to go through, for both of us. But it'll all work out fine.'

'Are you … are you sure?'

She placed a hand on the nape of his neck, then on a whim placed her lips against the soft skin. 'Quite sure,' she said.

The touch seemed to comfort him. He relaxed and started on his meal. She tried to do the same but her appetite had disappeared. Somehow, everything she tasted and smelled and touched in the reels seemed far more real than real life.

Earlier that week they had come out of the Café Bellevue reel together, holding onto his hand with a crushing grip, making sure he caught that tram with her. Then there had been the rooftop terrace looking out over Montparnasse, where he had come out with that nonsense about dogs and aliens, and she had told him about her new grown-up plans for her new grown-up life, and that was merely a preamble to what had been agreed without words when she invited him back to her hotel. Or had the contract already been signed, she now wondered, when she first sat down at Café Bellevue after they wrecked the place? A one-night-stand with an attractive stranger, the final fling of youth, before embarking on the true adulthood of work and responsibility. Why not? She would never see that attractive stranger again. Almost certainly.

Only it hadn't worked out like that. They had exchanged numbers after the night in her Montparnasse hotel room, and even though she thought of him often during the weeks that followed, she never expected him to call. Only he had called. He had called and the connection – faltering, feared broken – was forged anew.

Each time after a Ree-Mem session she felt split in two. Emerging from her debriefing in Dr Calvin's office, waiting for her husband in the corridor outside the recovery room, she barely knew whether she was the mid-twenties Hannah Allaker or the early-thirties Hannah Stornoway. She felt dazed, almost drugged. She was actually thankful that nowadays her husband didn't ask too many questions because she felt ill-equipped to give answers. They had been leaving the Ree-Mem complex when the camera crew surrounded them on an unknown purpose, the crew barring their passage. Her husband had to duck to avoid a low-swinging boom mic cracking him around the head. He had apologised. The old Euan, she thought, might have made a staunch effort to insert the handle of the microphone in a place where handles were never meant to go. Then, as if on an unspoken order, the film-makers dashed off. Staring across the lobby, she watched them attach themselves to a large entourage clustered outside one of the other treatment rooms. A white-haired man – she was certain she had seen him before, either on television or in a long-ago film – was being wheeled out of the double doors. His hands were clasped tightly to the blanket around his legs and his expression had the same tranquil, maddening blankness she saw on her husband's face every morning.

They had now spent a week inside Euan's fractured memories. Dr Cal assured her constantly that the reels were a mirage, an effective fallacy, but still she wondered whether the doctor was playing down the uncanny power of his own treatment. It felt real, so real. She had been returned to Paris, then the house party in London, then the Ayrshire coastline on her trip up to

Euan's family cottage. There had been an innocence about him back then; an uncertainty that was strangely, deeply affecting. She remembered the way his speech had flitted from glibness to utter sincerity. He had been nervous, she realised now, trying so hard to be cool and casual. There was nothing casual about travelling from one capital city to another on the off-chance he might reacquaint with a girl with whom he had only shared a one-night-stand. Only this time, seeing the memory again, she heard the yearning in his voice, masked with bad jokes and corny chat-up lines. He wanted her, he needed her, but he was unable to tell her directly. Back then she had barely known Euan at all, she had no understanding of his character. It was later that she realised how difficult he found it to open up emotionally. Perhaps it was a fear of rejection, perhaps it was simply immaturity, but maybe it was an essential part of him. She hadn't known the true Euan until later, much later, in their relationship.

Even now she wondered how well she had known him.

Now she watched that man, changed immeasurably from those recently revisited early days, as he sat on the sofa in their living room. He was sipping from a bottle of beer and watching the television, the sound low. The evening news had finished and they were on to the regional updates. She was about to go back to her nightly portal-searching duties when something on the screen made her pause. She recognised that industrial estate, the chain-link fence and the half-concealed block of the Ree-Mem building. The news reporter at the scene was speaking to the bedraggled-looking woman with grey hair who they saw protesting outside the Project every day. She couldn't quite make out the words.

'Let's watch something else,' she suggested.

'No,' said Euan, and she blinked. 'No, I'd quite like to see.' His voice was calm but there was an eager undertone. He thumbed the remote controller and the voices on screen rose. She had become so used to his endless agreement that this minor rebellion troubled her.

'—only wish the government or the police would do something about these so-called scientists,' the grey lady said, pulling at the washed-out lapels of her coat. 'It's the people I feel sorry for, the people who've been tricked into this evil thing, they don't know what they're letting themselves in for, and I just wish—'

She snatched the remote controller and killed the TV with a sharp dig at the power button; Euan looked at her, then back to the screen. She had a sudden but strong urge to hurl her glass of wine at the television, blinding that black eye which stared back pitilessly.

'Maybe put on some music,' she suggested brightly. 'I've got work to do.'

Leaving him staring into dead space, she spent the next half-hour fruitlessly searching for portals for Dr Cal's team, trying to put the news programme out of her mind. At one point she was rummaging in the bedroom wardrobe and found herself looking at Euan's three work suits. The first – a tatty blue serge number known as The Old Suit – had been a mainstay of every formal event for almost a decade, even when the material at the knees was wearing thin and moths had nibbled the cuffs. Then there was The Best Suit: a grey houndstooth-patterned three-piece, bought at foolish expense from Savile Row only a few months before the accident. Behind that rested The New Suit, a department store off-the-peg item in a dull shade of charcoal. The only thing interesting about The New Suit was that one day Euan had gone to work in his houndstooth suit and returned home in the charcoal one. He also had a small but deep cut below his left eye. *Some pisshead in the pub knocked his glass of red wine all over me*, he had told her. *Told him he had to pay for the dry cleaning, turned into a bit of a tear-up.* At the time she had wondered what sort of man spent his lunch hour getting into fights in pubs. She wondered what sort of man went to work in one suit and came home in another. Nevertheless, she had let the matter slide. She was still healing from Jennifer.

It was in The Old Suit that she had loved him best. Feeling slightly foolish but unable to stop herself, she slipped her arms into the jacket and brought the fabric to her face, tears springing to her eyes as she inhaled the corroding remnants of his old scent, the peppery aftershave he used to wear. Then her hand slipped upwards and her fingertips touched the edge of what seemed to be a small box. There was a book of matches in the inner pocket of the jacket. It must have dropped through a tear in the lining and come to rest at the hem. Spiky black lettering stamped on red cardboard boasted: *A day wasted is never a wasted day.* There was a logo reading *Blackout Bar* and a telephone number. She remembered when Euan had last worn that tatty old suit; he had not come home from work that night and his phone was off and she had been frantic. Euan turned up the next morning, stinking of stale booze, mumbling an apology about missing his last train and staying on a colleague's couch. He could not meet her eyes.

Turning over that book of matches between her fingers, she told herself she would not call that number. So why was she already holding her mobile phone?

Because, her waspish mind-voice insisted, her husband had kept secrets from her. Oh yes, he had indeed. All that time he had spent away from her in the early years, helping his family in Edinburgh while she concentrated on her career in London.

What exactly had happened when he was absent from her life? Even when they lived together, Euan was a great one for going off wandering. His usual resolution for any conflict was to go out for a long walk or drive. Heading to places she never knew, because he would never tell her. Sometimes he didn't come back those nights.

She had loved her husband. Trusted him too. But here was a mystery that needed to be solved; only a little puzzle, maybe inconsequential. It would be so simple to ignore but surely, she told herself, that would go against the point of the process. A full and frank account of their relationship – that was what Dr Cal wanted. That was what she had promised him. Perhaps the Ree-Mem treatment could explain everything, in time, but she wanted to know now.

Her husband had stepped into the shower five minutes ago. She guessed she had another two or three at most. She realised she was sweating. Tracing the letters stamped on the book of matches, she held the phone to her ear, listening out for the rush of the shower.

'Blackout Bar,' a voice rapped. 'What you want?'

Thrown by the confrontational tone, it took her a moment to gather her thoughts. 'Um … hi. Hi there. I was wondering … I met … I met a guy in your bar, and now I don't know where he's gone, and I—'

'You was here last night, yeah?'

She felt her cheeks flushing. 'Um, no. Over a year ago, in fact.'

There was a long pause. In the background she could hear clicking pool balls and crunching rock music. 'A year ago. Did I hear that right?'

'Yes.'

'You joking, girl? I'm busy here.'

Desperation took hold. 'Look, I know it sounds mad but it's

important. Really, really important. He's quite a tall man, dark curly hair, Scottish accent. He might have been looking lonely. Or lost.'

'Girl, we have lots of lonely single men in here. It's that sort of place.'

There was a mocking laugh, then the sound of the connection breaking.

She dropped the matches as if the phosphorus tips had burst into flame. She knew that this process was not about judgement or recriminations. *Something's gone wrong*, he had told her, and not twenty minutes later their car was wedged between the barriers of the level crossing. The crash erased the knowledge of whatever had gone wrong and it seemed it would forever remain a mystery. Sternly she told herself to quit playing the detective game. There was nothing to be gained from rummaging in those unlit corners right now. Only suspicion, only torment.

But her urge to know the truth, as ugly as it might prove, still burned. What exactly had her husband hidden from her before the accident? What had she hidden from herself?

17

Hannah and I: Our fourth year

Sisyphean Heights

I slip to the ground and my fingers dig into the wet soil of the mountainside. Microscopic specks of volcanic rock crush into the soft flesh underneath my nails. The smooth soles of my shoes have been skidding on the wet pathway and now they've spilled me. Sneakers. Bloody sneakers, what sort of numpty would wear sneakers to climb a crag? Me, apparently. Sneakers and jeans and a thin suede jacket, now sopping wet and hanging like a rhino's skin on my back. It had been so calm and beautiful when I set out, however many hours or days ago, with only a slight chill in the air, no hint of the turmoil to come. I can imagine the marker on my gravestone, roughly hacked into the marble. Here lies Euan George Stornoway, junior civil servant and failed amateur mountaineer. A fellow of infinite jest and a silly irresponsible prick.

But still I press on up the slope, dipping my head against the push of the wind. I pat the pockets of my jacket and uncover two objects. One – a small black box – I cannot open yet. But the other finding is a minor treasure: I pull out the small bottle of poor-quality brandy procured from I know not where. Perhaps I should save it for a moment of true desperation, but if this isn't an emotional crisis, then what is? What possible reason could I have to yomp up a blasted rock in rapidly declining weather?

When I look up, rain streaming down my face, I see a figure standing on top of a rockfall a dozen yards in front of me. She's dressed even more inappropriately for the weather than I am. No jacket, only a small black T-shirt exposing her flat stomach, her taut olive skin. Her arms are bare despite the viciously cutting wind. Biker boots and purple jeans the colour of a fresh bruise. A razor-slashed black fringe. A wickedly curving mouth, sensuous though a little cruel. It is impossible for her to be dressed in such skimpy clothing in this awful weather and not be shivering, but she seems completely unconcerned about the storm. She raises a hand in greeting.

She knows me. I don't know her, or at least I don't remember her. What does she mean to me? What have I done to her?

Blinking, I wipe my face against my sleeve and when my vision clears the girl has gone, if she was ever there in the first place. Panting heavily, I pick my way over a rockfall and make for the summit. It has stopped raining with incredible suddenness and the sun dries my hair. Reaching the top of the crag at last, I see Hannah leaning casually against a cairn of stacked stones. The relief is almost unbearable. I contemplate throwing myself into her arms but the fact she looks so cool and graceful stops me in my tracks. Barely a strand of hair, spilling from beneath her twee striped bobble hat, is out of place. Her cheeks are not even flushed. Somehow the rain showers seem to have missed her. She looks like a model for an outdoor clothing catalogue. I, meanwhile, must look as if I have challenged the mountain to a square-go and lost badly.

'Remind me why,' Hannah challenges me, 'you decided a restful holiday would involve hiking in the Scottish Highlands?'

'It's not a hike, angel, it's a hillwalk,' I puff, trying to ignore the tearing pain in my left side. 'Tranquil amble. Healthy exercise.'

'Which is why you're three steps from a heart attack?'

'Shouldn't have got so drunk last night,' I admit, sitting down heavily on the rocks next to her.

Yesterday Hannah took the train to Edinburgh. I met her at Waverley Station in a flash car borrowed from my dad's chop-shop and we drove for hours to the grandly shabby hotel overlooking the great loch. The suite, booked for three nights, cost half my monthly income. Sadly, Stornoway Lodge is currently occupied by my eldest sister Edith and the two miniature replicas of her errant husband. No Lodge for us. But I hope this place will remind her enough of our wonderful weekend on the Ayrshire coast two years ago. I feel certain the success of my plan relies on those happy memories.

Except last night I lost my nerve and tried to restore my confidence with far, far too much booze. Eventually Hannah, worn out by the two long journeys, went next door to bed and I stayed up, knocking back drink after drink, peering at the fuzzy picture on the television screen until my brain was equally fuzzy. Eventually I fell asleep in the chair, waking with a cricked neck and breath like a chemical toilet. My girlfriend made no mention of my foolishness this morning, but did I detect a certain coolness in her attitude? A slight lessening of affection? Maybe the time will never be right. Maybe I have blown it already.

What can I offer her? Are we playing out endless holiday romances? Can any relationship survive such a distance? The thought of her living alone in London – meeting new people, exciting people, people who want to take her from me – tortures me. Which is why I have to ask her. Simply to know. To forge a sense of permanency, or else the uncertainty will drive me insane.

Hannah, meanwhile, seems lost in a daydream, unaware of my mental turmoil.

'Look at this place,' she says, casting an arm over the scene. I'd admit it is a pretty impressive sight; a picture postcard of the Caledonian pastoral idyll. Even the rain has ceased for a few minutes. On a normal day the verdant swoop of the valley, the calm ripples on the loch and the snow-tipped peaks in the distance would have sent my soul soaring. But not today. For the first time in my life these majestic sights are flat and washed out because the unfathomable beauty stands directly before me.

'What a sight,' I agree. 'You sure you don't want to move here?'

She sighs and pinches the bridge of her nose. 'Euan, please—'

'I was only joking,' I protest. My previous attempts to convince her to move to Scotland inevitably end in arguments.

'I wish I could believe that. When you're joking you make the remark and smirk slightly and lean back for approval. But when you're trying out an idea, testing for my reaction, you lean in and squint slightly.' She raises an eyebrow wryly. 'I'm afraid I know you too well.'

My hand is clasped on the box in my inner coat pocket, resting over my heart. 'Do you really, angel?' I mutter.

'What was that, Scotsman?'

'Nothing.'

That eyebrow arches again. 'I really hope it's nothing. We can't change this scenario, darling. Your life is in Edinburgh, mine's in London. I wish we could spend more time together, I really do, and you should know I'm totally committed to us and making this relationship work, however hard it may seem at times. But I'm … I'm in a good place at the moment. The boss likes me so there's lots of opportunities. And these opportunities will keep me down south for the foreseeable future. I wish I got the same salary for teaching loveable urchins or adopting kittens but, Jesus, there isn't any money in that sort of thing.'

Rubbing at her eyes, she stands up from the rock and walks to the sheer edge of the path, staring out over the void. Unable to contain myself any longer, terrified of losing my nerve again, I take this opportunity to bend down on one knee. Eventually Hannah turns back to me. She takes in the sight and freezes as if caught in an endless moment by the shutter-click of a camera.

Then she blinks rapidly and manages to say, her voice cracking, 'Good grief, Euan, what are you doing?'

Staring up at the girl, her grace threatens to steal away my words. I take a deep breath and begin, 'Nothing... nothing in my life was ever as good as I hoped it would be. I hated school, then I was bored by university and I've been even more bored by work. Everything has been mediocre, everything has been disappointing. Apart from you. Apart from being with you. Being with you has been so far beyond any of my hopes or expectations that I'm struggling to cope with the idea that this is reality.'

She moves very close to me. 'Euan... what are you saying?'

I pull the little black box from the inner pocket of my jacket and fumble it open. I pinch the ring tightly between thumb and forefinger. I tell her simply, 'I can't not be with you.'

Hannah's eyes are so very wide. She says weakly, 'Please tell me you haven't proposed with a double negative.'

Reaching out I take her left hand. 'If this ends right now, and we go off and live separate lives and try to be happy, I won't be able to forget you. Every time I do something that reminds me of you, the memories of our past will obliterate any enjoyment of the present. You've ruined me for everyone else. I can't live without you. So ... I thought, you know ... will you marry me?'

A single tear tracks down Hannah's cheek. 'I want you to promise me one thing,' she says, her voice not quite steady. 'Promise that at our wedding we won't have that awful poem read out, the one about how we're hilariously mismatched and get on each other's nerves, but despite all these flaws we still love each other. Because I can believe in a flawless love. I really can. Everything else in our lives can be a disappointment, I'm fine with that. But I ... I want us to be perfect.'

'So that's a Yes?' I ask.

Her hands go first to her mouth, then to her leaking eyes. She laughs in disbelief. 'Oh, fucking hell, I forgot. Yes, of course it's a fucking Yes.'

There is a sensation in my stomach like the moment an aeroplane leaves the ground, either to take flight or crash and burn. It is at once exhilarating and terrifying.

'Such special eloquence,' I laugh with relief. 'But thank you, anyway.'

Holding the ring tightly – a vivid picture pops into my brain of it falling from my grip and bouncing over the edge of the mountain – I remove the woollen glove on her hand and slide it onto her finger. The ring fits so well. It fits like it should have been there long ago, as if it should have been there always.

Still clasping Hannah's bare hand, I push myself to my feet and we embrace for so long that seconds and minutes and hours lose all meaning.

'I love you,' she says when we finally disengage, 'so very, very much.'

'I love you too,' I say. 'Look, I realise I've, well, sprung this on you a bit. I needed to know you felt the same way as me before I made any other decisions. I'm aware there's a lot of things we need to sort out, but I honestly promise you that—'

She shushes me. 'Not now, Euan. Later. There's more than enough time for the details later. Let's enjoy the now.'

Pulling me close once more, she places a tender kiss on my cheek. It is impossible but her hair smells slightly smoky, as if still impregnated from the fire at the beach so long ago.

Eventually Hannah breaks the embrace. She reaches down, digs into the earth and picks a small shining stone from the ground. I realise she is taking a souvenir of the occasion – the girl has always been a magpie, an incorrigible thief – and I smile knowingly. But as she pockets the volcanic rock, there is an expression of unutterable sadness on her face.

'I don't want to go,' she says. 'I don't want to see what happens next. I want it to be like this forever. I want to stay here with you forever.'

She breaks down crying and I drape a clumsy arm around her. I can't understand why my girlfriend – no, my fiancée, good God, I have a fiancée – has dropped from elation to despair in a moment. All I can do is hold her and wait for her personal storm cloud to pass on by.

'I wish I could at least go back to the start,' Hannah says, her voice choked. 'I really want to see this one more time. I think I could live out the rest of my days playing this scene over and over again.'

I blink, truly confused. 'I don't understand. I don't follow you.'

She is fanning her fingers underneath her eyes, as if the imperceptible backdraft will stave off further tears, and the gemstone on the third-left finger twinkles in the sunlight. Then the light fades as if a switch has been flicked and the diamond is dull and listless. Its shine is covered in shadows. Both of us have picked up on a shift in the atmosphere and I sense a storm coming. As if on cue there is a warning chuckle of thunder. On the horizon a dark cloud – wraith-like, almost formless – edges slowly towards us. The ground beneath it darkens. I've seen mist before, I'm Scottish after all, but never mist that moves like this. It creeps.

'What on earth is that?' Hannah says, pointing.

'That, my future bride,' I say, striving for humour in spite of my unease, 'is classic Caledonian springtime weather.'

We watch the fog as it lazily eats up the landscape. I can even smell it. The clean natural scents of the Highlands which I love are being swamped in an airless haze and I'm finding it hard to breathe.

'That's weird,' Hannah says. 'It didn't … we didn't … this seems wrong.'

'How do you mean wrong?' I feel a little hurt. I've just proposed. She said Yes. Everything is perfect. Nothing can be wrong, surely. Except this stupid fog.

'I think we need to leave,' she says. We look around and see our path down the mountain is blocked by a colourless wall. The mist has crept up right to the edges of the rockpile we're standing on. I don't have any desire to hike down in this weather. Hannah reaches for my hand. 'How would you feel,' she says urgently, 'if I asked you to step off the edge of this cliff with me?'

I should tell her that she sounds insane. But love is insane and I can tell this is a test.

'Walk off the top of the mountain?' I grin. 'That sounds terrific.'

We shuffle forward until the tips of our shoes are hanging over the edge of the cliff. I can't see the bottom of the valley for the mist. Then the greyness parts, only for a moment, and instead of the rocks and bracken and heather far below us, I see a room. A familiar room. Fairy lights and tinsel and a Christmas tree that has had its top branches sheared off, giving the green spines a weird flat-top haircut. Unable to believe what I'm seeing, I peer closer, laughing in the face of gravity. Then the mist closes upon the impossible sight.

'Hannah,' I say slowly, 'what is this place?'

'The best place,' she says, holding me close, trying to kiss away my worries. 'The very best place in the world.'

Wherever we are, it's both real and unreal, and I feel certain that if I don't go with this girl, I will be stuck here forever.

Clutching one another so very tightly, we step off into the void and take flight.

18

Hannah and I: Our fifth year

How Lovely Are Your Branches

'Oh, you have got to be kidding me.'

I hate this tree. At this point in my life I have never hated anything more than I hate this tree. I have carried this nine-foot monstrosity up four flights of stairs; straining, swearing, sweating, grunting, swearing, more swearing. My chapped hands are reamed from holding onto the rough bark of the branch, there is sap running down my nose, a hundred prickles indent my face. My right eye is reddened from when a branch, caught against the frame of the front door of our flat, swung back and rudely poked its long finger halfway into the socket.

Now the tree is finally in our flat. The only problem is that it is at least a foot higher than our living-room ceiling, bent over like an osteoporosis-stricken old man. That won't impress Hannah at all; she wants a gorgeous tree for our first Christmas as a proper, engaged, rings-on-finger-and-wedding-plans cohabiting couple. Hitting on a solution, I pad into our little kitchen alcove, rummage in the top drawer and pull out the huge scissors that look more like garden shears. Humming to myself, hearing an orchestra horn section toot triumphantly in my brain, I snip and hack at the branches until the tree is small enough to fit under the ceiling. Dragging it across the living room, barely caring about the freely shedding pine needles, I lever the tree upwards and wedge it in place, then collapse back on my haunches, panting but proud.

I realise Hannah is standing in the opposite corner of our living room. I'm not sure how she is here already. I could have sworn she had been out posting Christmas cards – but no, she is definitely here, resplendent in a tartan skirt and furry white jumper with strands of red tinselly wool across the front. She is rubbing at her mouth, the way she always does when she's trying not to laugh.

'It's not funny,' I tell her in a warning tone. 'That tree was really heavy.'

Her eyes are too wide, too innocent. 'I never said anything was funny.'

'Just the look on your face.'

She pouts innocently. 'What look on my face?'

'Hannah said she wanted a massive Christmas tree. That's what she said.'

'Hannah said she wanted a lovely Christmas tree. Euan translated this, somehow, as Hannah wanting the biggest Christmas tree ever found in northern Europe.' She straightens out the branches and I try to avoid noticing the amount of foliage that falls to the floor and embeds itself in our carpet. Her brow furrows as she assesses the damage. 'Wait … what have you been doing to this poor innocent tree?'

'I think the needles are starting to drop already,' I say lamely. 'I had to snap a couple of branches to get it inside. Then gave it a wee tidy. Spruced up the spruce, you know?'

'Euan—' she starts.

'What?' I say. Her eyes tick-tock from me to the tree and back again, gauging my reaction. She is rubbing at her lips again. 'What?'

'Darling, I don't know how to tell you this—' She points at the top of the tree, at the exact spot where the angel is supposed to sit.

'Oh, you have got to be kidding me.'

There is no tip to the tree. Only a flat-topped wedge. In my desperation to get the tree inside our flat, I have hacked off the highest branches.

'It's not the traditional Christmas tree shape,' Hannah says, kneeling beside me. 'It's more of a—' She sketches out the flat lines with her hands.

'A Christmas quadrilateral. It's the new trend.'

'You've got an answer for everything, haven't you?'

We collapse against one another in laughter. The tree stands in the corner like a mute, pensive party guest. As our laughter tapers off, we take another look at the mauled branches and start to laugh again.

'I think you need a drink,' says Hannah at last. 'Then at least when our guests are here you can blame that regrettable attempt at horticulture on the booze.'

'That sounds like a grand plan.'

She leaves me with a kiss on my reddened forehead and I hear ice clinking into glasses. Nothing like Christmas spirits to get you into the Christmas spirit. Plus wearing stupid festive jumpers, wandering around garden centres in search of trees, being driven slowly mad by the same jingly-bell songs on an eternal loop. Plus checking out the range of terrible gifts on offer. I wonder at what point garden centres became the one-stop-shop for festive tat. Neon-glowing snowmen, Santas that dance and play techno versions of carols, elf and reindeer costumes for the kids. I pat my jacket pocket to reassure myself. My gift is still there.

'Do you think we're getting old?' Hannah calls through the hatch that divides the kitchen and living room.

'How do you mean?' I ask, knowing already.

'Going to garden centres on a Saturday afternoon. Hosting dinner parties.'

'As opposed to what, exactly? Going to raves in cold muddy fields? Listening to music so edgy it's unlistenable? Taking drugs we can't even pronounce? I'm happy to be past it.'

'That doesn't sound much fun,' she agrees, returning with glasses in hand. 'Here, Rudolph. Carrot for nice reindeer.'

I stare at the yellow gloop in the glass she has passed me. 'What on earth … are we out of brandy?'

'It's a Snowball cocktail. Alcohol and custard.'

'Two of my favourite things.' My fiancée snuggles up beside me. I drape an arm over her shoulder. Her hair smells of cinnamon. There is a pinprick glow of heat in her pale cheeks. She'll never know how lovely she looks right now; I can't tell her, can't even begin to tell her, the words won't ever come out right. 'Now three of my favourite things,' I add.

We clink glasses, staring at the tree. The room already smells of pine sap. I think back to the childhood Christmases with my family, my parents, sisters, grandparents, the rarely-seen aunts and uncles and cousins who turned up en masse and apparently uninvited; the house rocking with beautiful chaos. This year, however, we have decided it will only be the two of us, in our apartment, together. The two of us and our massive flat-topped tree.

'It won't look so bad with a few bits of tinsel over the top,' Hannah says reassuringly. 'Those fairy lights will make all the difference.'

Stagily I slap my hand against my forehead. 'Damn, I knew I'd forgotten something.'

She stares at me. 'You mean you didn't buy the fairy lights? That was the plan, wasn't it? I thought that's why you headed back to the gift shop while I was queueing in the café.'

'I got distracted,' I admit.

'Oh Christ, you didn't go to visit Santa, did you? You can't go round sitting on strange men's knees, Euan. Behind the beards and the jolly ho-ho-hos, some of them are quite danger-ous. Disreputable itinerants, drifting from grotto to grotto, hell-bent on finding out whether you've been naughty or nice ...'

I pull out the small plastic bag in my pocket. 'I bought this instead.'

Hannah blinks. 'An early Christmas present?' she asks.

'Something like that.'

'Shouldn't I wait until the big day?' She shakes the packaging. 'Hmm, nothing rattling – interesting. You could wrap it up and put it under the quadrangle ... the tree, I mean.'

I place my hand on hers. 'I think you should open it now.'

She says nothing. She opens the bag and pulls out what I have bought her. She holds up a tiny pair of red elf boots with green trim and gold felt buckles. The sizing tag reads zero-to-six months. Her lips part as if she wants to say something, many things, but no sound comes out.

'We've got a lot going on at the moment,' I say, my heart thumping. 'What with the wedding and moving out and every-thing. But I know you like to plan ahead. So ... you know ... just so you know, it's like a promise.'

'A promise?'

I nod. 'Just so you know. I'm ... I'm ready for this sort of thing, whenever you say the word. I know I'm not very good at telling you what's on my mind, what I want from life, and I know that's hard for you. But I know exactly what I want

– love and marriage and everything that comes with it. We've had a lot of adventures in our time, but … but I really feel I'm ready for a different sort of adventure. I realise I'm not going to change the world but that's fine because we have our own world together. I'd only care that I was growing old if I was growing old without you. There's nothing more that I want from life. Only you. You and whoever else comes along.'

Hannah turns over the child's boots in her hands. 'You pick your moments, Scotsman,' she says finally. 'You certainly do. As if I haven't got enough on my mind right now, eh?'

'You can put it to the back of your mind now,' I say. 'Forget about it.'

She stares at me again, then laughs and I feel enormous relief. Another bridge crossed, or at least stumbled over. Why do I make such heavy weather of these things? Why do I find it so difficult to open up to the person closest to me?

'Oh, forget about it,' Hannah says, digging me in the ribs. 'Forget about it, great advice. In my mind I've bought the cot and converted the spare room into a nursery. In my mind I've finalised the list of baby names. You know what us females are like.'

Placing a kiss on her forehead, I happen to glance out of the window. It looks as if winter has bit hard into south London. The crisp blue December sky has taken on a sickly pallor. The fog is so thick it even seems to have crept through the gaps between the windowpanes and into our apartment. I can barely see the far end of the room. I think of mentioning the strange mist to Hannah but everything is perfect between us and I refuse to let the slightest shadow spoil our day.

'If it's a boy he'll be called Euan,' I tell her. 'Like me, like my dad. All my dad's brothers were called Euan too.'

'Sorry, what—'

'Makes things simple for Mum – you and you and you and you, come get some scran.'

'Ah, another shit joke. A lifetime of shit jokes. Is this really what I've signed up for?'

'That and more. So much more.' She kisses me on the lips. I return her kiss with interest. 'Do you like your Christmas present?' I ask.

'I do,' she says, taking my hand. Her eyes are red and her lower lip is trembling. 'I really do. I love it, in fact.'

'Good,' I reply. 'I hoped you would.'

'I'm going to pop these boots up on a shelf, out of sight of anyone except us,' Hannah says. Her tone is matter-of-fact but there is a slight hitch in her voice. 'Then, when the time's right for us, we can take them down and put them on our very own Christmas elf. How does that sound?'

'Better than anything,' I say, my voice barely a whisper.

She kisses me again. There is heat in our embrace but the room is now freezing. Above my head the ceiling lights pop and fizz, the filaments flaming out simultaneously. The sky outside has turned from daytime to dusk in an instant. Hannah doesn't seem to notice.

'There's no way I'm waddling down the aisle looking like I've swallowed a beachball,' she continues. 'So until then, I think it's best we stick with practising.'

'Have we got time to practise before Barry and Shona arrive?'

Her hand slips onto my thigh. 'We'll make time.'

'Splendid.'

My fiancée takes me by the hand and leads me towards the bedroom. We are so wrapped up in one another that I can almost ignore the darkness descending around me in a localised eclipse. Surely it's just an odd refraction of the sunlight, my mind playing tricks on me. Everything is golden, everything is perfect, I tell myself. Even though the air smells so strange, so lifeless, as if the oxygen has been sucked out of the room and I'm choking in a vacuum. Then I feel a sudden savage lurch, like an invisible blade twisting inside my stomach, and I stop in my tracks, almost going to my knees. One moment I'm walking behind Hannah and the next her grip has slipped and she is a great distance away, nearly out of sight. Just seconds earlier I was intoxicated by her vivacity, her life, the glow we make together, and now she's a shadow figure, a silhouette. That damned fog is everywhere around me now. I wonder if this is a waking dream or hallucination because I'm alone in this blackened room and Christ, it's cold, and instead of my fiancée's warmth I feel another presence behind me, not a friendly one.

'Hannah?' I call, trying not to let the fear show in my voice. I can't see her anywhere. 'Angel, what's going on?'

'She won't be here for you,' a voice swims out of the mist. Female but definitely not Hannah, the tone arch and slightly accented. 'Not much longer anyway, the way you're going.'

'Who are you?'

There is a low chuckle, somewhere to the side of me now. The aroma of honey fills my nostrils and clogs my brain with its sweetly rotten musk. 'As if you don't know, Euan.'

'Well, you know my name and I don't know yours, so you must be a voice in my head.'

Another sly giggle. 'That's true enough. Doesn't mean I'm not real.'

'Euan?' Hannah shouts. 'Euan? Are you there?'

At the sound of her voice the greyness evaporates. It seeps

from the scene and Hannah and I are standing opposite one another in the blessed normality of our living room. We are only a couple of yards apart. No one else. I realise my left eye has begun to water.

'What the hell happened?' I demand, masking my fears with anger, as if Hannah is somehow to blame. 'What's going on?'

'I don't know,' Hannah says. 'Please ... please, you need to come with me right now.'

I stare at her outstretched hand. 'The room just disappeared. You were gone or at least far away. Something weird happened.'

'Uh-uh,' she says. She shakes her head violently, her blonde hair flying. Her eyes are wide and too bright. 'I've been here all along, you adorable imbecile. Maybe that cocktail was a bit too strong for you.'

'But you just said—'

'I said we're going to bed. Any problems with that, Scotsman?'

She silences any further protests with a deep kiss. There is a desperation in her embrace. At last I take her hand and she grips my fingers so tightly that I wince. She leads me out of the room and the stuffy warmth of the flat is blown away by a draught of balmy springtime air that no central-heating system has ever managed to replicate. The soles of my black formal shoes are clacking on the stone floor ... wait, stone? Formal shoes? I'm certain I was wearing battered trainers. Battered trainers and faded blue jeans, but now my legs are clad in smart suit trousers. The scuffed wooden doorframe of our apartment bedroom has formed into a sandstone archway. I can smell flowers, I see a flash of whiteness; a sweeping gown of incredible purity. I need to ask Hannah what the hell's going on but she's setting a fair old pace to the bedroom and I don't want to lose my grip on her fingers, scurrying to keep up.

As we leave I cast another wary glance behind me. The other presence – the unknown woman with that insidiously mocking tone – has vanished.

But that doesn't mean she was never there.

19

286 days since the accident

Shifting uneasily on the slippery white sofa, she placed the baby booties in her bag, not wanting to look at them ever again. In an unknown room inside the complex, Dr Cal's colleagues were bringing Euan back to the present day. Reaching for the cup of orange squash as if its sickly contents were lifeblood, she tried to stop herself shaking. Whenever she thought she was reclaiming control there was another lightning strike from a disinterred memory. But now there was something else. Dr Calvin picked up on her concern.

'What is it, Hannah?' he said. 'You can trust me with anything.'

'I think there's something in the reels,' she said unwillingly.

'Something in the reels?' Dr Cal repeated. His tone was relaxed, even teasing. 'Other than the entire romantic history of you and your husband, you say?'

'There's this... this fog,' she said, attempting to mimic the doctor's relaxed air. 'It's probably nothing. But I saw it. Definitely. This grey fog.'

He was still smiling but his eyes had narrowed. 'Hmm, how very peculiar.' He drummed his long fingers on his thighs. 'I suspect it may be a mild corruption of the photographic manipulation, a visual flaw. I shall raise it with the imaging team.'

'It was creeping in on us,' she said. 'The fog. It was creeping. Once it had rolled over the scene, I couldn't see anything left. Like it was trying to swallow the whole reel.'

Dr Calvin pursed his lips as if carefully chewing over a mouthful of an unknown foreign food that might turn out to taste ferociously bitter. 'That is somewhat ... ah ... interesting. At what point does this fog start to encroach on the memory reel, Hannah?'

She swallowed. 'At first it came out of nowhere,' she said, 'sneaking in at the end of the loop. In the most recent reels I can see it right from the start, the very second I enter.'

'It covers—'

'It eats up everything around us. The imagery of the reel vanishes into the grey.'

'The script for the scene that you gave our imaging team ...' Dr Calvin cleared his throat. 'It was accurate, was it not?' She stared back at him, genuinely perplexed, and he held up his palms in contrition. 'I apologise for any rudeness; only past patients have been known to attempt to rewrite history.' He laughed dryly. 'Say, if a proposal was not as heartstoppingly romantic as one partner might wish. A damp squib, as I believe you British call it. You would be forgiven for wanting to make it better. But even a tiny – and well-intentioned – alteration in the reel can lead to vast corruptions in the reconstituted memory.'

She shook her head. 'Everything has happened exactly as I remembered. The proposal on the mountaintop, the day close to Christmas when he finally told me he wanted kids. They were two of the most important moments of our relationship, doctor. I wouldn't change them for anything.'

Calvin grimaced, rubbing at his mouth. Abruptly he stood

up and took refuge behind his vast desk. 'Hannah, would you please tell me something?' he said, doodling on a jotter. The good humour had dropped from his voice completely. 'Your husband wasn't hiding anything from you, was he?'

Her skin prickled. She felt a lurch of nausea. She didn't want to answer Dr Cal's question. 'I felt like I'd nearly lost him in that last reel,' she said. 'He seemed so far away. I was scared. What's going on?'

'You realise, Hannah, that our presence in your husband's mind is invasive?' Calvin said. 'In a similar defence mechanism to the way our white blood cells detect and destroy germs, Euan's mind may be attempting to cast us out. We can decipher the fog as his mental immune system fighting against the process. Nothing more.'

'So we're the infection,' she said. 'That doesn't sound like nothing more, doctor. That sounds like something we should be worried about.'

'We are not the infection,' Dr Calvin wagged a finger. 'We are the cure.'

'The cure for what?'

'The cure for his condition!' he announced, his cheeriness restored. 'And we shall cure it, make no mistake. Euan Stornoway was … is an intelligent man. By this point in the treatment, his subconscious will have recognised that something is amiss. These creeping greys are his psyche rebelling against our intrusion, I'm certain of it. It should not present a problem, Hannah – there is nothing to fear. But do keep your husband away from that fog.'

'Why?' she demanded. 'What's in the fog? What is the fog? You're not telling me something, I know it.'

The doctor now seemed unnaturally engrossed with some paperwork on his desk. 'If you'll excuse me, Hannah, I'm an extraordinarily busy man and sadly our time together today has drawn to a close.'

'What happens if I lose him in that fog?' she pressed again. 'I thought I was looping through my husband's memories, making him better, and suddenly he's fighting us with his own mind. What sort of mad treatment is this? What are the consequences if something goes wrong?'

The doctor scribbled a few notes on a pad and she was sure the words were meaningless.

'Please, Dr Cal, you have to tell me.' She sprang up from the sofa. His eyes flickered with momentary alarm. She bent over his desk, trying to snatch his pen and paper, and Calvin pulled away from her. 'For God's sake, you've got to tell me what I'm dealing with here.'

'I could press this button beneath my desk and have four orderlies here quite rapidly.' He smiled but the coldness in his voice drew up a barricade between them. 'In a jiffy, as I believe your quaint British expression has it. I do hope it won't come to that.'

She held up her hands in apology. 'Please,' she said. 'I didn't mean … I don't want you to think …'

'I would prefer it if all future conversations between us took place on a professional basis.' He steepled his fingers. 'I would also prefer it if the methods of the Reel Memory Project were not questioned by its patients.'

'Thanks for your help,' she said sourly. 'I suppose I'll have to do this on my own.'

'Hannah,' he said. 'You can't.'

The lack of emotion in his words was worse than anger. Up until that moment she had always thought that Dr Cal was on her side. The neuropsychologist's smile was still plastered to his face but now it resembled the rictus grin of a corpse.

Her heart pounding, her legs wobbling, she escaped the office. The documentary crew was buzzing around the foyer again and she shunted her way past them.

'Mrs Stornoway! Hannah!' a voice trilled. 'Mrs … Hannah! Please!' She turned to see a tall, eager-looking young woman in a bright blue trouser suit trotting towards her. She wore horn-rimmed spectacles, carried a clipboard and a gold pen was stuck in her stacked mess of blonde hair. Two smartly-dressed middle-aged men trailed in her wake. 'I'm so glad I've caught you here. Treatment going well? Dr Cal taking good care of you?'

'What … what?' she stuttered. 'Who … Dr Cal …'

'He's great, isn't he?' The woman half turned to beam at the two men. They stared back impassively.

'He's quite something,' she muttered. She thought of the chilly way in which Scott Calvin had shut her out once she threatened his ordered existence. That empty smile.

'Great. Great-great-great. Now I know you're picking up your husband in a tick, but these two lovely gentlemen are from the medical regulatory board, and I thought as you've been such great sports so far, you could maybe fill them in on your experience with us guys at Ree-Mem.' The girl tittered for no reason she could comprehend. 'Give them a rundown on how well you're doing. How safe the process really is.'

There was a lurch deep in her guts as if the gravity in the room had been displaced. The aircraft hangar roof dipped and flipped, closing in on her. 'You've got to be kidding me,' she said, aghast. 'Here? Now?'

'Leave it, Letitia.' The dry drawl of Jonas carried across the vast room. 'Try to pick your moments better, love.'

The two men in suits seemed nonplussed as she stumbled away from them. Keeping her head down and her shoulders hunched as if to ward off any further intrusions, she made it across the foyer to the recovery room. Euan was sitting on a row of chairs with an orderly either side of him, looking pensive. Did he realise his subconscious was attempting to sabotage the treatment, she wondered. Did he know he was trying to stop himself from returning to his real self?

She didn't talk either as she signed them out at the reception desk. Fortunately Letitia had vanished but the film crew remained. It was probably her imagination – the stresses of meddling with the subconscious, she recalled, were not to be underestimated – but it seemed as if the camera was following her. She sensed its flat black glare on her back as she led her husband away from the Reel Memory Project.

The doorbell rang and she saw a familiar figure behind the frosted glass. She sighed inwardly as she recognised her mother's tight mesh of ash-blonde curls. She was having enough trouble adjusting to the time-jump charades of the treatment; the psychic residue meant most of her mind was in the past and the present was the façade. She barely knew who she was any more. The woman known as Hannah Stornoway – who had a good job and a nice house and a loving husband, the woman who was slowly but surely healing from a traumatic experience – was on the verge of vanishing. Now here was her mother to make her feel like the wilful little child she had once been, the way she always did.

Summoning up her reserves of patience, she opened the door. 'Hi, Mum,' she said, as cheerily as she could manage.

Elaine Allaker stepped over the threshold with stateswoman-like grace, handing her daughter her imitation fur coat. 'Good afternoon, cherub,' she said, standing on tip-toes to place a tickling kiss on the side of her face. Her nostrils quivered. 'Hanny, there's an awful pong in here.'

'Haven't had much time to clean up,' she said, feeling those familiar shameful flowers bloom in her cheeks, the reaction only her mother could provoke. Their home had begun to smell peculiar to her too. She kept picking up the damp, marshy scent of a house that had been shut up for years.

She wanted to tell her mother, *Been digging up my husband's memory all week, Mum. Tiring work, you know? Sorry that the mantelpiece isn't dusted and there are a few stains on the carpet and fragrant petals aren't scattered in your wake.* Instead she said nothing.

'How is—' her mother made a small charade with her hands that seemed to indicate her husband, The Patient.

'Euan's fine, Mum. He's out for a walk. Christ, it's not like he's had a bloody leg lopped off or anything.'

'Language, dear,' her mother said mildly, following her into the kitchen.

'Tea, coffee, something to eat?'

She could see her mother's practised eye taking in the mass of crockery in the sink, the mouldy cafetiere, the smeared tinfoil takeaway cartons that had made it almost to the bin.

'No, thank you,' she said hurriedly. 'A glass of water if you please. I'm only here for a short spell. Your sister is moving out, so I thought I'd remove myself from under her feet.'

She felt a twinge of melancholy as she ran a dusty glass under the tap. Sas was a friend and an ally, one of the few she still had left. Most of their old gang had dropped off the radar once the Uterus Express chuffed into town. She supposed the same should have happened to her and Euan, with the move out to the commuter town and the plans for the spare room with the pastel-shaded wallpaper and the tiny bed that would soon be occupied by a tiny form … and why exactly was she thinking about Jennifer again?

'Saskia's going back to San Francisco?' she asked.

'Oh no, she's moving into some rented flat in town. She says she's staying in the country a while. To – and I quote her here – get her head straight.' Her mother's voice dropped low and complicit, as if her elder daughter might have followed her to the house and even now could be eavesdropping outside the door. 'I think she's even been meeting up with that horrible biker chap she was so keen on at school. Silly girl.'

She tried to conceal the smile playing around her lips. She had always rather liked her sister's old boyfriend Robbo, with his crooked grin and the tattoos creeping out from under the sleeves of his leather jacket. He seemed far more genuine than the flash-suited City boys and dreadlocked trust-fund hippies who preyed on Saskia's impulsive nature.

'Anyway,' her mother said, with a what-can-you-do roll of the eyes, 'are these American doctors looking after Euan then? I read a piece about them in the newspaper the other day. They didn't mention you two.'

She shrugged. 'I'd hardly expect them to. We're not exactly the most important patients on their list.'

'The reporter,' Elaine said, staring forbiddingly at her over the top of her glass, 'implied that this organisation called Ree-Mem was in fact a group of charlatans promising everything and delivering precisely nothing. There was also some mention of the dangers of the treatment, so they call it. A young lady in Portland, Oregon, they suggested, had extremely adverse effects when they—'

She waved her hands to cut off her mother's words. 'That's bullshit, Mum. Typical tabloid stuff. How can the procedure be a total sham, a massive con-job, but still powerful enough to wipe somebody's mind?'

Her mother's eyebrows rose. 'So it does work then, this hypnosis mumbo-jumbo?'

Scott Calvin's words from earlier rang in her ears: *His mental immune system fighting against the process.* She shivered.

'It works,' she told her mother, trying to keep her voice steady. 'I can't tell you exactly why I know it works. But believe me, it works.'

Elaine Allaker dabbed at her lips with her handkerchief. 'Well, you know best, Hanny. The one thing your father used to say was that he could never pull the wool over your eyes. But how much does Euan know? Are his memories coming back?'

She shook her head. 'We won't know until the end of the treatment, Mum. It's all or nothing. Dr Cal explains it as the old Euan and the new Euan. The Euan of the back-before and the Euan we have now. The old Euan's personality is floating underneath his conscious mind. Once I've linked the reels together, he'll swim to the surface. Meanwhile, the new Euan—' strangely she felt a lump in her throat '—will vanish completely.'

'And everything will be fine.'

She felt a sensation like a trickle of icy water. Again she recalled Calvin's diagnosis: *These creeping greys are his psyche rebelling against the intrusion.* Why was her husband trying to shut her out? What exactly was he hiding from her?

'Y … yes,' she said, 'I suppose it will be.'

A line of concern formed between her mother's brows. 'How do you mean, dear?'

She dug her fingernails into the palms of her hands. 'Sometimes I can't help but wonder,' she said, 'whether he wants me in his head at all. I know a little but I don't know the full truth.'

Her mother plucked at the corners of her handkerchief, shifting in her chair. 'Are you quite sure you want to know all these things about Euan? I'd venture that some of what you find out may be rather upsetting.'

'Yes!' she burst out. 'Yes, I want to know. I really want to bloody know. Doesn't a wife deserve to know? No one ever mentioned it at the hospital; they only focused on making him better. No one asked why he did this to me. So, yes, I do want to know. More than anything.'

A wrinkle of worry appeared between her mother's brows. 'More than getting Euan back?'

'Of… of course not,' she checked herself. 'It's just, I don't know, it tortures me. Only knowing half the story. Like a book with a block of pages torn out.'

'And this treatment will tell you everything you need to know?'

She hung her head. The small mauve crescents in her palms grinned knowingly up at her. 'I hope so,' she said. 'The whole truth.'

20

Hannah and I: Our sixth year

Do Us Part

My footsteps echo on the stone floor of the empty church. Restlessly I pace from altar to arch, past the rows of empty pews, breathing in the cool musty air. There is an uncomfortable stillness in the atmosphere, not the state of grace promised by the bridal magazines that Hannah has taken to hoarding beneath her bedside table. There is nothing transcendent, nothing wondrous, nothing that stops the heart and fills the soul with joy. There is only loneliness here.

My shoes pinch at my feet, the collar of my white dress shirt chafes at my stubble rash. I have followed my father's advice and checked for any pricing labels that may be hanging on stubbornly. I am dressed for the occasion, but the occasion seems to have forgotten to dress up for me.

If this is a wedding, why are there no guests?

I reach for one of the bouquets tied to the ends of the wooden benches with twine: white roses and heather. But the petals are crisp and brittle and the fragrant purple shrubs smell not of the moors of my homeland but of decay. I clench my fingers and the flowers crumble to dust.

Stepping quickly to the grand sandstone arch at the entrance, I stare out at the churchyard. A thick sweep of fog is edging across the gravel path, snake-like feelers entwining around the crumbling old gravestones. Hannah had hoped for a wedding reception soaked in balmy sunshine, she's been checking the forecast for days with ever-increasing glee, but now we seem doomed to share our first glass of champagne as a married couple in a dingy haze. I could even use it as an opening joke in my groom's speech – Highland mist specially imported for the occasion – but the sight of the spreading grey blanket saps the humour from my thoughts. It smells wrong, it moves wrong. It just is wrong. The whole scene is all so very wrong.

Then I hear a faint stab of organ music. The solitary chord pummels at my brain before disappearing with unsettling suddenness.

There is a blur of motion to my left, a snatch of brittle conversation. A whiff of cloying old-lady perfume and a shout of laughter. There is motion in every corner of my vision; the church is empty yet not empty. I stare at the white roses that I am still clutching and the once-dead petals are malleable, fragrant and alive. The organ pulses once more, the music insistent this time. I race back to my place at the altar.

At once I realise the church is full, packed to the cobwebby rafters. The rows are stuffed with guests; a sea of enormous hats and ill-fitting suits. I catch the eye of my mother – she appears to have stolen her hat from a Spanish conquistador – and drop her a wink. She blows me a kiss and surreptitiously wipes away a tear. My father seems distracted by the long bare legs of a trio of Hannah's university friends on the other side of the church, where my fiancée's family sit in a polite and demure row, their hands clasped on their laps.

There's only one face that I don't recognise. Sitting alone in a pew right at the back of the church is a girl with ink-dark hair cut raggedly across her forehead. She is wearing a leather biker jacket that seems pretty incongruous in this formally dressed congregation. She looks up at me. She beckons me to her. Her fingernails are long and black. Shaken for reasons I can't understand, sweat springing out on my brow, a sickly taste on my tongue, I stand still at the altar. I'll stay here until Hannah comes. I look down at the stone floor. I don't want to see this uninvited guest.

'Ready for this, big man?' Barry asks.

Turning, I blink, staring into the square-jawed face of my best man. He grins at me, exposing the missing front tooth – knocked clear from his head in a rugby scrum – that he promised to have fixed for the wedding. I must have zoned out for a short while there; the emotion of the day coupled with a few nips at Barry's hip flask for strength and sustenance.

Happily I pull my oldest friend into a bear hug. Paul McGuigan – re-christened Barry decades ago by our boxing fanatic headmaster – is dressed in an identical morning suit. The waistcoat strains at his barrel chest and he has done the best he can with what remains of his gingery hair. I think of how Barry recently separated from his long-term girlfriend Shona, the mother of his two children, and that I haven't been there for him as much as I should have. But he's always been there for me. In fact, everyone is here for me, here for us; for Euan Stornoway and Hannah Allaker, soon to be Hannah Stornoway. Can this be real?

'You feeling okay?' Barry asks, and – yes – this must be real because I can smell on his breath the whiskies we drank in the vestibule earlier, the alcohol not quite masked by diligent application of toothpaste. 'Look a little spaced out.'

'Sure,' I nod, dropping into our familiar shadow-boxing routine and aiming a jab at his torso. 'The Colinton Cannonball, on his way to the ring. Proudly undefeated.'

He counters my punch and pretends to uppercut me. 'Last-minute nerves, Storny?'

'More nervous about your speech. I really think I should take a look at it before you get going.'

'Ach, you'll be fine. If you've never done anything at all wrong your whole life, you've nothing to fear.'

'Is it too late to change my best man?'

'Well,' my friend shrugs, 'it's too bloody late to back out now, that's for sure.'

The music swells enormously in volume – the organist is really testing the church's old pipes – then cuts out, leaving the final note hanging in a delicate cadence. The vicar steps forward. He silences the crowd with a raised finger like a skilled orchestra conductor and nods genially at me. His lips are moving, he is declaiming to the congregation, but I cannot hear a single word.

The crowd rise to their feet as one. The organ strikes up once more. Not the triumphant tooting of the Wedding March, which Hannah hates, but a tranquil descending arpeggio like the trickling of water down a mountain stream. The music is so utterly, completely Hannah that I have to bite down on the inside of my cheeks to stop myself bursting into tears.

Unable to resist, I crane my head over my shoulder towards the doorway. Hannah is framed underneath the stone arch, her uncle Tony clasping her arm. She is wearing only the lightest touch of make-up and her white-blonde hair hangs simply to her shoulders. Her dress is not the meringue monstrosity we had mocked at friends' nuptials, but a simple silvery-cream gown that shimmers in the late summer light shining through the church windows. The sun has fallen on her bare shoulders, blasting away that weird mist from earlier. She is so beautiful that she is almost not of this earth. My emotions are snared in some romantic purgatory between fear and lust and hope and love.

Halfway down the aisle, Hannah stops, staring at me as if truly seeing me for the first time. Her eyes are moist, her lower lip quivers. I have the strangest feeling that we are the only two real people in the entire world.

She mouths four words that I am unable to make out. Or maybe I don't want to, because it seemed as if her lips are forming the words, *I can't, not yet.*

Then she vanishes.

My bride-to-be vanishes. She disappears from the scene. The guests – Barry, my parents, her mother and sister, our friends, the aged aunties in the preposterous hats – vanish with her.

I call out to Hannah but my voice echoes in the emptiness.

Heartsick, headsick, my stomach moiling, my vision flickering, I reach for the pew to steady myself and grasp a handful of crumbling rose petals. Once more the flowers are dead.

What has happened is impossible, unbelievable. Surely this is no dream, no hallucination. Hannah was here, inside the church with me, then she was not here. This feels real and yet suddenly the inconsistencies are far too glaring. How can a church be full one moment, then empty the next?

Is everything I see an illusion? I feel like a marionette, dancing a stilted jig at another's bidding.

A beacon of understanding glows in the darkest corners of my mind. The truth, I am certain, is known only by the girl with hair like a magnesium flare. Clapping my hands to my head, I let out a low moan. Around the pews, beneath the wreaths, coils of fog push hungrily towards the altar.

21

290 days since the accident

'Hannah!' There was no mistaking the panic in Scott Calvin's voice. 'What the hell are you doing?' She was halfway out of the pod, disengaging the electrode yoke that bound her to Euan, rubbing at the sticky smear of lubrication on her arm. 'Hannah, why in God's name did you leave the reel—' The doctor's eyes were almost bulging out of his skull.

'No,' she said, holding up a warning hand, leaning against the smooth white wall of the Duessa pod for support. 'Not now. Later you can scream and shout, tell me off all you want. But now I need some time alone.'

Then she was gone, stumbling from the treatment room, away from her comatose husband. Her eyes burned as the harsh light of the complex dazzled her, her guts cramping as if an acid-footed spider was dancing inside her. She thought of Dr Calvin's words from her first day at the Project. *You must not, under any circumstances, let Euan know that he is inside a reel.* But she knew he had seen her; his head turning to drink in the sight of his fiancée in her bridal gown as he stood at the altar, and then she had ripped herself from the scene. Had she blown it? Had she ruined everything? She wouldn't know until she went back inside the pod to see if she had damaged – or even broken – the reel. Could she relive her marriage yet again, knowing how it had ended? Right now she didn't know if she had the strength.

There was a commotion in the Ree-Mem lobby. A gaggle of reporters was clustered around a makeshift stage with a video screen backdrop. She had to step back sharply to avoid being trampled by two cameramen. Then she saw a familiar face in the crowd – it was the reporter in the shiny silver suit, the one who had turned up on her doorstep that morning right at the very start – and the young man's eyes widened with recognition and he began to push his way through the throng towards her. She felt as if she might be sick; she needed peace, solitude, fresh air. There seemed to be no air in this vast cacophonous space. She had to get out, right now. Close to panic, she slipped in between two workmen shunting pallets, spotted a double door marked No Exit and tumbled through, slamming it shut behind her.

She leant with her back against the door, the breeze cooling her reddened cheeks. There was an impulse – a dangerously strong compulsion – to walk to her car and simply drive away. Drive to a far-off place where they had never heard of conjoined hypnosis or portals or linking reels.

'Awful, isn't it?'

It took a second to locate the source of the voice. She was not alone in the alley at the back of the Ree-Mem building. A tall lady with close-cropped hair, perhaps in her early seventies, was staring at her imperiously, a cigarette dangling between her forefingers. She was wearing a navy-blue trouser suit and her scrawny frame appeared to be composed entirely of angles. Her expression was that of a scientist who has uncovered a new species of tropical bug: intrigue mixed with mild concern and a hint of disgust.

'Cigarette?' the woman asked.

She hadn't smoked in years, had given up entirely before

they started trying for a baby. But she reached for the proffered packet anyway and the elderly lady helped her light the cigarette, chasing her trembling hand with an ornate platinum lighter. She sucked at the white tube, taking the nicotine hit, craving any form of comfort – she supposed if someone had passed her a crack pipe, she would have taken it gladly.

Acrid smoke plumed between her lips and she spluttered. The tobacco tasted like the tarry *Gauloises* she and Euan had smoked in Paris. But that was only an illusion, just like every one of the illusions of the Reel Memory Project.

'Awful,' the woman repeated. 'Such a circus. Once you let the Press poke their grubby noses into anything, they turn it into a circus.' The woman's thin rouged lips curled into a sneer. She could make out a trace of a clipped European accent, perhaps German or Scandinavian. 'They are the clowns but they think they are the ringmasters, am I not correct?'

'Are you a patient?' she asked, barely aware of what she was saying.

'Young lady,' the woman huffed, 'do I look like a brain-dead zombie?'

'No. Sorry.'

Her new acquaintance pinched the tip of her half-smoked cigarette between thumb and forefinger, removed a small silver case from the breast pocket of her jacket and placed the stub inside.

'My sister,' she said, 'with unfortunate timing suffered a stroke midway through the revision of her will, the silly fool. Her ingrate daughter is contesting it. Therefore we have submitted ourselves to this dire charade to ascertain the correct testament and the proper attribution of funds and property upon her passing. Doubtless you are suffering similar family travails.'

She could not bring herself to share any more intimacies

today, especially not with this forbidding lady. 'Something like that,' she said.

Staring intently at her, the woman tilted her head to one side until her hooped earring was brushing her left shoulder blade, her lips pursing. Then her mouth crooked into a small, vicious smile. 'You're not *that* couple, are you?' she said.

She blinked. 'That couple?'

'The camera crews. The documentary. Such a dreadful PR stunt, but even an *ingénue* such as myself can ascertain that this … this company, if you can call them such … is desperate for the positive publicity.'

She shook her head, feeling a nauseous churn in her stomach. 'I think you must have confused us with some other couple.'

'Then I wish you the very best of fortune with your pursuit,' the woman said, a finality in her words. With a stern nod she straightened the lapels of her blue jacket and stalked away.

Later, when she had her emotions under control – or at least locked in a box where they buzzed and pulsed like a stirring wasp nest – she found her way back inside the complex. Dr Calvin was waiting in his office, leaning against his desk, his posture unsettlingly still. The look on his face frightened her. She had become accustomed to his confident, slightly patronising manner. She had never seen anger in him before.

'I just … I don't … I just couldn't,' she started. 'I'm really sorry. I felt, I don't know, emotionally blitzed. I couldn't take seeing my wedding day again. It was too much.'

'What did I tell you?' Dr Calvin said, his lips pulling back from his teeth in a snarl, every word punctuated by the slam of his hand on the desk. 'You stupid girl. After everything we've done for you. We give you a few simple goddamn rules to follow. This is how you repay us?'

'I couldn't,' she gasped. 'I didn't know—'

'Hannah,' the doctor said, stepping towards her with menacing deliberation, 'you do remember what I told you before you started to link the reels? You never, never, never alert the patient to the artifice of this project? You never, never, never let the patient know that they are in a reel. You do remember, don't you?' His huge fists clenched and unclenched. 'How difficult is that, Hannah?' he demanded, his voice rising to a shout. He was kissing distance from her now. 'How fucking difficult?'

She shrank away from him, her back against the wall, her fingers scrabbling for the door handle that had somehow slipped far out of reach. She had never heard the doctor swear before. She had never seen him lose his temper. She had never thought those twinkling blue eyes could look like jagged shards of ice. He loomed over her, hulking and furious, his shoulders heaving. Then abruptly he turned on his heel and stalked back to the desk, slamming his large body into the chair. He picked up his pen and pad and began to draw concentric circles on the paper, holding the magic marker like a baton, bearing down as if he hoped to drive the nub of the pen through the paper, even through the wooden desk.

'You deviated from the path clearly laid out for you by highly experienced medical professionals. You ignored my advice and your vanishing from the scene will have alerted and alarmed your husband.' His words came in a rapid-fire babble. 'Your husband's mental immune system will be concentrating all its efforts on eliminating the alien presence. That is how things are and they will only get worse. I tell you these facts for the betterment of your treatment and because I have staked my considerable reputation on the case of you and your husband. Time is going to be running very short for you now.'

Shaking, on the verge of tears, she hung her head, holding

her hands to her temples. 'I promise I won't do it again. I'll follow your instructions, I'll stay on the path, I swear.'

'I think we should leave this for today,' Dr Calvin said. His voice was brusque but he was calmer now. The furious circling of his hand had slowed, as if the drawing was his method of self-hypnosis. 'I'm afraid that you are not yourself today. When you next go into the reel of your marriage, it is vitally important that you keep clear of anything unusual in the scene. Inconsistencies, faults, something alien to your memories. Something that worries you. Perhaps that grey mist you mentioned. Perhaps something else.'

'Something else?' she almost wailed. 'You mean this isn't enough? This isn't a happy stroll down memory lane, doctor. It's a ghost train.'

'Indeed.' He drummed his fingers on the oak desk. 'At the onset of any treatment we carry out a thorough psychological analysis to ensure the non-fugue patient has the mental strength to carry the process through to its conclusion.' He scrunched his drawing into a tight ball and dropped it into his waste paper basket. 'I blame myself that you have fallen short of my expectations, Hannah. My hopes for you.'

With a flick of his forefinger he sent the pen rolling off the edge of his desk. It hit the carpet with a dull thud that sounded so very loud in a room that still reverberated with his rage. He let out a long sigh that ended in a groan of frustration, slumping backward in his chair. At least he was calmer now.

'I need this, Dr Cal,' she said urgently. 'Euan needs it too. And we need you. We can't do this without your help.' Swallowing down her fear, she stepped towards him. The large man in the room with her seemed like a stranger. She saw a coldness in those periwinkle blue eyes. Something between her and the doctor had fractured. It was possible that it could never be mended.

'When you go back inside the reels,' Dr Calvin said, his tone soft but pitiless, 'keep your guard up, Hannah.'

Keep your guard up, her brain repeated as she steered the car into the driveway of their home. Keep your guard up against something indefinable, something unknowable, something you can't possibly fight against. Great advice, Dr Cal, she thought bitterly. She had wanted to say more to him back there in his office but instead she had bitten back her words, choking down the bile. Now she really owed the doctor; she had made a mistake and was in his debt.

'Can I ask what happened in there?' Euan said. She looked over at him and saw his brow was sweaty, his hands fidgeting nervously. He knew something was wrong.

She shook her head. 'You know I'm not allowed to tell you about what goes on inside the reels, Euan.'

'Still, though,' he said, affecting nonchalance, 'it's ... well ... it's my mind you're messing around with here. It's my fault I'm an amnesiac, so any problems in making me better are my fault too, aren't they? So maybe I can help.'

She stared at him closely. Throughout the treatment she never let herself wonder too deeply where Euan went after their time in the reels was over. She knew that the Project's orderlies wheeled him away and brought him up from his hypnotic coma, but she had no idea where his mind wandered to during those times. Did images of the reels ever reverberate in his brain, like a dream half caught in those sludgy moments between sleeping and waking?

'It's tough,' she admitted. 'It's tough emotionally, I mean, not physically. I'm seeing the entire history of our relationship for the second time and sometimes it's too much to bear. Right now I'm struggling.'

With a sudden violent movement her husband slammed his fists against the dashboard, letting out a bark of frustration.

'Euan!' she snapped. She couldn't take any more anger today. 'Euan, stop that right now.'

At her command he placed his hands flat on his thighs, his shoulders heaving. 'What's it worth?' he sobbed. 'How terrible must I be to live with, if this is the alternative?'

'I'm doing this for you, Euan,' she said. 'Everything is for you.'

'Is this so bad?' he asked, squeezing his eyes tightly shut. That worried her too, because that was what he had been doing before that day on the railway crossing, closing his eyes to shut her out. 'Am I so bad?'

Sighing, she leant across the divide between them and wrapped her arms around his neck. He submitted to her embrace. Every time she felt she had given all the emotion and support she could possibly give, there was still another tiny chunk left to be torn out of her soul. *Who guards the guards, Hanny?* a voice whispered in her brain. *Who looks after you while you're looking after everyone else?*

'You're fine, Euan,' she said. 'You're fine. But you're not entirely yourself.'

He broke away and stared at her. 'But I ... I quite ... I quite like being me,' he said. 'I like being this me, not the other version of me. Because I know what that other version of me did. I know exactly what he did.'

'Do you?' she whispered. She wanted to tell him everything. She knew she had to tell him almost nothing. 'What do you know?'

'You've told me,' he said, near tears again, his breath hitching. 'You've told me everything. I hate knowing, I hate myself. I parked my car on a railway track and waited for the train to take me away. I nearly killed myself and I risked your life too. What sort of man would do something like that? You know, I quite like not remembering why I did it. I love it, in fact.'

'This is for you, Euan,' she said again. That was the truth, she told herself. Of course it was all for him, how could it not be for him? Her entire life was dedicated to restoring her husband to his former self. There was nothing selfish in her actions, nothing selfish in the slightest. 'It's for you. You know that, don't you?'

'It's for you, Hannah,' he replied, and the certainty in his voice was strangely chilling. 'It's for you as well.'

22

Hannah and I: Our sixth year

Do Us Part

The organ music swells from a low hum into a bone-shaking crescendo and I chance a look over my shoulder. I see a figure framed by the sunlight beneath the stone arch of the church and feel a strange mixture of love and fear. The girl proceeding towards me, holding onto the arm of her uncle Tony, is evidently not of this earth. The occasion has granted her an eerie grace; she does not walk towards me, she glides like a spectre.

Hannah reaches me as the last pounding organ note hangs in the atmosphere. Her pale skin is daubed with only the lightest touch of make-up and her hair hangs simply to her shoulders. I remember the conversation in which she laughed off the idea of the veil. *A veil? Really? You know what I look like, Scotsman. You've seen my face enough times so why should I hide it?* She had been lying naked on the bed, her hair fanned out on the pillow, my fingers tracing the concave swoop of her stomach. *Using that logic,* I had replied, *why even bother spending all that money on a dress?*

Her beauty has stolen the breath from my lungs and I am drowning in air. At once I understand the source of the fear – somehow this does not seem real. I fear my beautiful bride may be a beautiful illusion and this marriage is a mirage.

As if understanding, Hannah stretches out her hand and I

cling to it desperately, reassured by her warm touch. I cannot speak but my lips frame a silent, heartfelt request to please, please, please take me away from this place.

But first we must be married.

The vicar's lips move but I can hear no words. We have rehearsed these moments and I mouth along too; there is no sound in the church but a ringing in my ears, as if I have been partially deafened by a chaotic punk rock gig. Loving and honouring. No obeying, though; Hannah had insisted on the removal of that line, and I had smirked at the idea of an outdated religious edict ever causing her to reconsider her independence. Richer, poorer, better, worse. God, who wrote these platitudes? What relationship ever failed in the good times? Why the hell are we agreeing to this anyway? These words bear no relevance to our relationship, to Hannah and I, to the world we have made together. A one-size-fits-all promise, now swap rings before the best man loses them – hoorah, you're spliced forever, now let's get drunk and dance badly and wake up tomorrow wondering how to get red wine stains out of those nice clothes.

I remember something Hannah told me years ago. I think she was trying to be hopeful about our budding relationship – her natural idealism shining through, even as circumstances pulled us in opposite directions – but instead it worried me. *I know we both have our individual flaws*, she had said earnestly. *But together we can be perfect ... can't we? Can't we, Euan?*

Perfection. Such a strangely insidious word. I can only promise to try.

But how about something more realistic. Can you love your partner when they seem entirely unlovable? Can you bear them when they're hungover, grouchy, irrational? Can you give comfort to them when you don't understand their problems, can you stop yourself screaming at them when they're picking away at your insecurities like a scab? Can you laugh at their bad jokes when no one else is even smiling? Can you look forward to a time years from now when their beauty will be faded and crumpled and worn like an old photograph? Can you tell yourself how lucky you are to have met them when they tell you they wish they'd never met you? Above all, does the thought of being with this person until the day you die – this one single person on a planet of however many billion alternatives – leave you feeling nervous, confused, scared… and still you can't wipe that enormous smile from your face?

Is that perfection? Is that enough for her? Is that enough for us?

My hands trembling, I stare into Hannah's eyes as I slide the ring onto her finger and I realise that I have been voicing my thoughts out loud. The whole church has been privy to my rambling internal monologue, but the girl who stands before me at the altar seems to be the only one who has heard.

She bows her head in a slight nod – a queer mixture of amusement and pity, joy and sadness – and that gesture is enough. The acceptance of me and all my faults and fractures is so much more than enough.

'Hello, you,' I say weakly.

'Euan,' Hannah says, 'we have to go.'

The vicar is pronouncing something to the assembled throng – probably something quite important – and this entire momentous day feels like a charade.

'What's wrong?' I ask. 'Can I at least kiss the bride?'

The girl, who I suppose is now called Hannah Jane Stornoway rather than Hannah Jane Allaker, smiles even though her eyes are shining far too brightly. 'Of course,' she says, 'but quickly.'

She leans forward and places a kiss on my lips. It is unutterably tender. But it is not enough, nowhere near enough. Too brief, too functional. This is our wedding day, this is our first kiss as husband and wife. Why is she in such a hurry?

'Are you going to tell me what this is about?' I ask.

'Euan, please,' Hannah says, her voice wavering, 'look around you.'

My attention has been so focused on my bride that I have taken in nothing of the scene. A thick fog has entered the church. It is so dense that it seems to swallow everything it covers. Slender strands reach out like a plant's feelers, slipping stealthily through the rows of wedding guests. The mist reaches my family, a cirrus of smoke coiling around my mother's chest – the colours of her bright red dress fade immediately to a dull haze but she sits statue-still even as she dissolves – and I lunge forward, meaning to pull her free, but Hannah holds me back, gripping my arm with surprising strength.

'What's going on?' I ask frantically. 'Please tell me. There's something wrong with what's happening, isn't there? There's something wrong with us.'

'Don't think about it,' she says. 'Concentrate on me, Euan. Think only of me.'

But I can't stop myself staring with shock and dawning horror. The mist is devouring the church. It swallows every one of the guests and no one does a thing to stop it, their faces ghoulishly blank even as they are consumed. Our families have disappeared entirely. By my side Barry is standing statue-still, his strawberry-blond hair and ruddy cheeks colourless, his beaming features erased into nothingness. I try to shout a warning to my best friend, grab him out of the colourless void, but my voice cracks in the lifeless air and he fades from sight. Now the fog descends upon the altar, reaching towards us. I feel a strange but unshakeable certainty that this is my fault; an awful, deeply buried knowledge threatening to burst from my subconscious.

'There's something wrong with me – isn't there, Hannah?'

The girl refuses to meet my gaze. 'We have to go,' she says once more, but I am paralysed, as if my shoes are welded to the stone floor.

'I'm not going,' I say. 'Not until you tell me what this is all about.'

She reaches for my hand again but I pull away. This is wrong. This is all so wrong. The creeping greys are nearly upon us now. The only features of the church that I can still fully make out are the stained-glass windows and the stone arch of the door. As I stare up at the ancient daubed glass it bends into a warped rainbow of sickly whirring colours. There is a crumbling sound of tortured slate as the roof flexes in on itself, inverting its steeple into a sharp point that is pointing directly down at the altar. The church is crunching in on us, the descending steeple aiming towards Hannah and I like a dagger. I can't move. Still I can't move.

With a gasp of fright, my new wife grabs me and kisses me deeply, an embrace with the true passion of a wedding day kiss. The intensity of her kiss jolts me back to my senses and the paralysis breaks.

'We can leave now, I think,' she says.

'I think so too.'

We turn to face the exit. The sandstone arch glows faintly as we take stumbling steps towards it, trying not to think of the slate-shaded, cold-reeking mass that constricts around us until the church nave is barely the size of a small tunnel. If we don't get out soon, we'll be crawling. Then wriggling on our stomachs. Then I don't know what. The organ music strikes up again, but the notes are now flayed and mangled chords that defy rationality.

'Keep going,' Hannah says. 'Keep hold of my hand, Euan. Don't look back.'

We move swiftly towards the open doorway, which now holds the only light of the scene – an impossible light, a horizon of burning orange – and by the time we burst through the archway we are running.

23

Hannah and I: Our sixth year

Retsina Sunset

The sun sinks into the ocean, the glowing orange ball splintering into a thousand shards on the waves. The taste of resiny wine is in my mouth, my skin is salt-scurfed by our dip in the sea that afternoon. Fishing boats, moored either side of the jetty, bob on the tide swells. At times an unbearably sweet scent washes over me, an aroma both freshly floral and slyly exotic, perhaps jasmine. I have to hand it to my wife – Christ, it still feels odd saying that word, rather than girlfriend, partner or fiancée – she knows how to pick a honeymoon destination. It was worth her endless online research, which I had largely ignored. Scrolling through screen after screen of mysteriously similar photographs of pale sands and crystal-clear waters and whitewashed hotels, all the locations seemed identical, until Hannah had spotted the picture of the jetty. This was where we would go. It was perfect.

The hotel staff have dragged a table onto the wooden boards so we can spend our first evening in Zakynthos watching the sun go down over the Ionian Sea. Relaxing back in my chair, I stretch my bare toes out towards the water. Yes, this is a place of utter contentment.

The only thing missing is my wife. Has she been gone long? It is so difficult to say in a place like this, where time seems to lose its meaning.

Hannah will be here soon. Surely. I think of her in that simple but evocative white dress, the flimsy fabric floating bewitchingly away from her thighs. I bury my nose in my glass of retsina, letting the wine wash sensuously around my tongue. The first couple of sips had been like knocking back paint stripper. Curiously, now that the second bottle has been demolished, I have rarely tasted anything more delicious.

I see Hannah pacing towards me down the jetty, holding what looks like a miniature amphora. Her shoulders are slumped. Her head is bowed.

'Hello, you,' I say as she nears the table, 'what on earth's the matter?'

She perches on her chair and sets the small ceramic jug down between us. She folds a sheaf of her hair back over her right ear, the way she always does when she is hiding something. 'Sorry, what?'

'What's wrong, angel?' I press her. 'You're worried, I can tell. What is it?'

My wife shakes her head. 'Nothing at all, dear husband. All is good. In fact, the barman at the hotel, the nice young one with the moustache, gave me this.' She taps a forefinger on each of the amphora's handles. 'Says it's the really good stuff that the locals drink around here. Either that or they're playing a joke on the idiot British tourists and it's some horrific gut rot that melts through metal.'

Evidently she has decided to keep whatever troubles her a secret. Instead I reach for the amphora, getting a whiff of what smells like raw ethanol, and stare at the lurid cartoon painted on the pottery.

'This long-lost masterpiece,' I say, aiming for the nasal, snooty tones of an art critic, 'depicts a man with the head of a cow engaging in sexual congress with a buxom young lady. Actually, she seems quite happy with this turn of events.'

'Don't you remember the ancient mythos about the virgin princess and the horny minotaur?'

'You tell me, you're the intellectual one. The classical scholar.'

She scoffs. 'I had three years at private school before my dad's first business went belly-up. It's not like I spent my teens nose-deep in Euripides.'

'You know, that's my one and only classical joke,' I say. 'Euripides trousers? Eumenides trousers!'

My wife sighs theatrically. 'Oh dear. Is it too late to change my mind about this marriage?'

'Sorry, you're stuck with me now. No big thing, aye? Just forever.'

Hannah stares directly at me, then casts a concerned glance around us. 'We can't stay here forever though,' she says. 'Don't try to lull me, Scotsman.'

I shake my head, confused. 'This is our honeymoon. We have all the time in the world.'

Even as I say those words a chill breeze begins to wrap around me. While I have been distracted by my new wife, the scene seems to have changed. The sun is not setting, it is dying; its amber glow now a dusty, dirty open wound. The water that laps against the wooden struts of the jetty appears to be as sludgy as an oil slick. But what captures my attention is a strange fog that sweeps in a low arc from across the bay. It has already covered the sloping nubs of the mountains across the water. What truly unnerves me is that this mist does not roll as mist should; it creeps stealthily, as if trying to catch us unawares and fall upon us.

Hannah half rises from her chair, tipping the contents of the amphora into my empty wine glass and slipping the jug into her handbag. 'I'm getting really cold,' she says, 'can we go inside? Please?'

'You said you wanted to stay here to watch the sunset,' I protest. 'What happened back at the hotel?' A strange thought strikes me. 'Were you even at the hotel anyway? Where exactly have you come from, Hannah?'

'Euan,' she says, taking my hands in hers, 'I really wish I could tell you. But … Jesus, how can I put this … figuratively and literally I'm in two places at once and I'm so confused and scared right now, and you need to trust me here. Do you trust me?'

In mute acceptance, I nod. I don't understand … or perhaps in some way I do and I'm hiding the truth from myself. The greys are now completely covering the waves either side of us, edging over the boards of the jetty. The air, once so warm and fragrant, is cold and dead-smelling. I feel the presence of the fog tugging at me like turbulence trying to pull down an aircraft. The happiness of the evening is lost. Instead I feel a numb hopelessness flood through me, chilling my bones, freezing each joyful thought.

'Do you trust me?' Hannah demands again. Her eyes are blazing, her posture imperious; a classical goddess herself, beautiful and pitiless. It could be my imagination but I think that the ugly creeping mist has receded a fraction, frightened away by the full-beam radiance of her beauty.

'Of course,' I manage to choke out.

'Then finish your drink and let's go.'

I down the contents of the little amphora and the taste is as appallingly potent as I'd feared. My eyes start to stream, my throat feels as if I've swallowed a lump of white-hot coal. Coughing and spluttering, half blind, I hold onto Hannah's hand as she leads me … where?

Our footsteps echo flatly on the wooden slats of the jetty.

I hear my wife's breath come in rasps. She is afraid, she is upset, and hadn't I promised myself that I would protect her from harm, to comfort her in the dark times, to be the dutiful husband who would make her world such a better place? Yet here she is protecting me, comforting me, leading me to what I can only assume is safety. There is confusion and there is fear but there is guilt too; I feel as if I have failed Hannah. How can I be the man I want to be for her when faced by these joy-sucking greys?

Encouraged by my bleak thoughts, a coil of the mist reaches around my ankle, twisting and pulling. This is no illusion. I feel the fog tug at me, first tentatively, then with more ferocity. There is a compulsion to let it take me – to submit to the mist and have it drag me to whatever fate I would face alone. Somehow these creeping, grasping greys seem real and my wife is the mirage. Is she even here at all? I can't for the life of me remember why I'm here on this jetty facing the bleakest of sunsets, and the woman with white-blonde hair standing in front of me is almost a stranger.

Hannah sees the look on my face and her lower lip quivers. Something in my expression has spooked her. 'Stay with me, Scotsman,' she says. 'Tell me where we are, Euan. Tell me why we're here.'

'We're … we're on our honeymoon,' I say. The coil of greyness has wound around my leg; the sensation is like being tickled by the fingers of a corpse. I don't need to tell Hannah that for a moment I couldn't remember why we were in this terrible place. I couldn't even recall if we were married.

'One hundred per cent correct. And what do people do on their honeymoon?'

'They … they …'

'They love each other,' she says. 'They remember all the reasons why they love each other. Don't they?'

Yes, I can think of all those reasons. Can't I? Surely? Even that fleeting contact from the greys has blitzed them from my mind. I know that I love my wife but right now I don't know why.

Then Hannah gives my arm a mighty pull – almost wrenching it from its socket – and the thread around my ankle is broken and so too is the unpleasant spell it cast. We race down the jetty towards the sandy path that leads to our hotel. We are so close to the safety of the lobby with its palm trees and marble floors and smiling waiters, and then this madness will be behind us. But only moments before our feet hit the sand there is a cracking noise underfoot and we have to leap backwards as the boards start to disintegrate in front of us. The wood warps and snaps, splinters flying off into the fog, and our safe path has become a splintered mess. The hotel in the mid-distance melts into a misshapen lump, as if the whitewashed walls are made of wax, then the ooze collapses into a puddle on the ground. A forgotten chamber of my brain tells me that the hotel was never there in the first place; it was only a representation of something indefinable in this collapsing world of sand and fog. There is no way out and nowhere to go. Hannah stares at me, her eyes wild, and clutches at me with desperate fervour. Slowly we pace backwards away from the debris, hand-in-hand. My wife's jaw is working as if she is whispering a mantra under her breath, or possibly a prayer.

'What is this?' I breathe. 'This is impossible. This can't be real. Is this a dream, Hannah? Where are we?'

She says nothing. She knows. She knows more than me at least. If we had more time maybe she'd tell me, but now more boards of the jetty are splintering as if from blows by a huge unseen hammer, and with each horrendous cracking sound our safe space grows smaller.

We turn and there is only a grey mass.

'Back,' Hannah wheezes. 'Can't … can't go that way.'

But where else can we go? We turn again and the mist is coming in from all sides, flanking us. Hannah gnaws on her bottom lip, blinking rapidly.

Then, as if seized by a burst of inspiration, she grabs hold of me and kisses me deeply, overbalancing us. I stumble backwards – or has she pushed me? – and we topple together into the lapping waves of the Mediterranean. But as we hit the water there is no splash, no sensation of being drenched by the surf, only an empty dryness. We hold onto each other as we fall through a gloomy vacuum that has neither warmth nor colour, and I hear a wispy echo of a finger-plucked guitar, a flamenco tune that stutters and veers out of key. It seems as if we might fall forever and I cling to Hannah, terrified of what will happen if I let go.

24

294 days since the accident

'What the hell is it?' she asked. She was still clutching the portal from the last reel – the small amphora, taken from a Greek island hotel on a honeymoon that now seemed indistinguishable as dream or reality. 'It's like the grey's killing the scenes. They start to fracture then disappear. I'm trying to do what you told me, link the reels as quickly as I can, but how can I link Euan's memories when they're corrupting all around us?'

'But you still completed the reel. Didn't you?' A nervous tic was pulsing in Dr Calvin's jawline. 'Please tell me that you linked the reel successfully, Hannah. You ... we cannot afford any more mistakes.'

'I got out,' she said. 'But barely. The exit was covered by the fog, so I found another. Improvised. I don't even know if I messed up or not, I had to think quickly. What's going on, Dr Cal? What's happening to us?'

He shook his head. 'Another time, Hannah. You do your job and I'll do mine.'

The doctor was halfway out the door when she spoke again. 'I won't play your game,' she said loudly, hoping her voice would carry into the corridor, even into the lobby area. 'Not until you come clean with me.'

Dr Calvin turned and stared at her. She saw cold dislike

on his face. It hung there just for a moment before his calm professional demeanour returned. It was impressive, she thought, the way he had made that scowl disappear so quickly. *In a jiffy*. He stepped back into the office, dragging his feet. 'I do beg your pardon?' he said.

'Very nice turn of phrase,' she said. 'You're really brushing up on your English gentleman speak. By the time the documentary comes out you'll hardly sound American at all.'

'Hannah, this is absurd, I don't—'

'I figured it out,' she went on. She was surprised at how quickly the answers had come to her. 'With all the other puzzles I'm trying to solve, this one was easy. The cameras. The fact you didn't ask for money. The contract we signed agreeing we wouldn't talk to any journalists, but we had to agree to all those interviews with you.' She laughed humourlessly. 'I suppose I should be flattered. We're younger and better-looking than the Alzheimer's patients you usually treat. We'll look good on the documentary, and in the adverts, and on your website. We can help you in your war against the non-believers. Only problem is, we didn't realise we'd enlisted.'

Dr Cal's face was fighting a battle between anger and resignation. 'I never lied to you,' he said finally, slipping behind his desk and reaching for his jotter pad. 'I was quite open about our request. For you to grant Ree-Mem some positive publicity.'

'If the treatment works,' she replied. 'Right now I don't know what's going on, only that everything is going badly wrong. I wish I didn't have to trust you, but I'm so scared right now and you're the only hope I have left.'

He shook his head. 'We have found it is rarely in patients' best interests to know too much about any … inconsistencies … in the treatment. Far better to keep their mind on the task in hand. Do you really want to know, Hannah?'

'Yes,' she said simply. 'Yes. You owe us that much. Tell me everything I need to know about the greys. What they are. How to fight them. And what they'll do to Euan if they catch up with him.'

Dr Calvin drummed his fingers on the desk. His gaze was at the far wall, his expression blank. The silence stretched out. 'I have seen this phenomenon occur only once before,' he said at last.

She remembered that first conversation with Saskia about the Reel Memory Project. It seemed like years ago now. She remembered the fears that she had cast away carelessly, as excitement about the treatment took hold. *They wiped a woman's mind*, she had told her sister. *She went into a trance and never came out. I want my husband back. Not a vegetable.* Suddenly it seemed there was too little oxygen in the room. She fought for breath, cold sweat on her brow.

'The woman in Oregon?' she asked. She knew already.

'Indeed,' Calvin replied. 'I should not tell you this, Hannah – it is highly unprofessional and breaks almost every regulation we have – but there are similarities in the cases. This lady from Portland had attempted self-deliverance in the bathtub with pills and a plastic bag. Like your husband, she woke up shorn of all memories after her attempted suicide.'

'My husband's crash was not a suicide attempt,' she said. 'It was an accident.' Clenching her jaw, she managed to choke out, 'An accident that he caused.'

Calvin held up his hands. 'No matter. Regardless, like you and your husband, the Project reached out to this poor couple. Her partner went into conjoined hypnosis with her. Midway through the process of connecting the reels, he began to describe rolling waves that would wash away the scene entirely. The black waters, he called them. We pressed on with the treatment, going back over the same reels in an attempt to smooth out the memories. Foolishly, as it turned out. After the lady emerged from the final reel, she had no memory of anything before her suicide attempt. No memory of anything afterwards, either. Her mind ... her mind was nothingness. No past memories – and no future ones either. We judged that her brain had performed a ... a reset.'

The flatness of his final word sent a spidery tickling sensation down her spine. She took a deep breath, her hands clamped on the amphora like a drowning sailor to a lifebuoy. 'A reset?' she repeated.

Reluctantly Dr Calvin nodded. 'Her mind returned to the post-coma state, the amnesiac state. She lost the memories she had formed since waking up from her ... her accident. A failure, Hannah. Some years ago, when the procedure was still in its infancy, but admittedly a failure. Our failure.'

'So where is she now?' she asked. There was a taste of rancid adrenaline on her tongue. 'That woman from Portland? I see you've kept her out of your flashy promotional videos.'

'She is rebuilding her life,' the doctor said. 'It is not easy. We have given them every, every support.'

'They signed up to get their old lives back,' she said. 'You made things worse. So much worse. Because you thought you knew what you were doing.'

Dr Calvin started to speak and she felt as if she had left her body and was floating somewhere in the ether between reality and reels. For once there was none of the neuropsychologist's usual eloquence. The complications were set out in short, terse words: Euan saw her entering his mind as an attack; if she did not link the reels quickly and successfully, his brain would erase everything. Not simply his memory. His motor functions too, his conscious mind. His brain would hit the reset button. She would be left with a husband who might never emerge from his hypnotic coma.

'This would only occur if the treatment was to … fail,' Dr Calvin finished, 'and I assure you there is only an infinitesimal possibility of this occurring. But if the reset does occur, Euan will enter what we call a non-transient global fugue state.'

'In other words, he'll become a vegetable,' she said. 'Mental oblivion. Is that what you're telling me?'

'Hannah, I'm not sure you understand—'

'No, *you* don't understand!' Leaping to her feet, she slammed her hand on the armrest of the white sofa so hard that the embossed nameplate on Calvin's desk toppled over. 'You don't understand anything. Six months I've spent with him, six months of trying to make him realise who I am, who he is, who we are. And now we could lose all that? He's different now but I've already lost him once. I can't lose him again. Don't you see?'

The doctor steepled his fingers, his tongue flickering over his lips. 'Therefore you must press on, Hannah, and quickly. Move through the reels as rapidly as you can.'

'Oh, more reels!' she cried. 'Brilliant, that's your answer for everything. The only answer to any problem is more reels, more Ree-Mem, more blundering around trying to find a way out while my husband's memories are collapsing around us. Well, fuck you. Fuck your Project.'

With a desperate sob she hurled the Greek amphora at Scott Calvin. It missed by some distance and shattered on the wall, leaving a reddish stain on the white paint. Their portal, the last remaining physical evidence of their honeymoon, was now lying in a dozen pieces on the floor of the doctor's office. The cheap little jug she treasured had been broken and the memory itself had been broken by her husband's mind. She felt broken herself. She knew she would never think of her honeymoon again without seeing the scene viciously warped inside the reel. The anger running out of her like water down a drain, she collapsed back on the sofa and began to cry. She had known there would be risks in this treatment. But the knowledge that her husband's subconscious was trying to wipe her from his brain – as if she was a virus, an infection, a blood-borne parasite – was almost too much to bear. She wondered how much more of this treatment she could stand. How long before the overwhelming pressure sent her screaming and gibbering into a padded cell.

She realised Calvin was kneeling in front of her. She saw a vein pulsing in the centre of his forehead. 'Ree-Mem shall not let the same thing happen to your husband, Hannah,' he said. 'I give you my word.'

'How can you?' she said. 'How can you give me your word when I can't believe anything you say?'

'The moment you entered your husband's subconscious was the moment he began to fight against the intruder, as you were informed with due diligence early on in the process.' His words arrived in a rapid bluster. She could make out a blush on his dark skin. 'The only way to beat these attacks by Euan's mind is to stay one step ahead of them.'

'We can't stop—'

'We cannot stop the treatment, no. If we stopped now, with your husband's memories brought only halfway to the surface, there would be a risk of random fragments of the pre-accident Euan's memories appearing in the post-accident Euan's mind. Like performing an operation without stitching up the patient. We must continue, Hannah.'

She breathed out heavily. She felt anger flash through her again and held onto that burning, frazzled emotion; it was better to feel rage than despair. Her fingers were clenched into fists, the nails digging cruelly into her palms. 'That's your great medical advice?' she snapped. 'Just carry on regardless? Cross my fingers and knock on wood and hope I don't accidentally turn my husband into a zombie? This is his mind we're talking about. This is our life, don't you see? Jesus! Jesus Christ.'

'Just think of the reward, Hannah,' Dr Calvin urged. 'Think of how you'll feel when Euan comes back to you. I want you to hold onto that thought, Hannah. I need you to hold onto that hope.'

'I never should have done this,' she said miserably. 'I never would have started this if I'd known the risks. Why didn't you tell me? Just why didn't you tell me, Dr Cal?'

He tried to take her hands in his and she pulled away from his touch. 'The risk is an inherent element of the cure,' he said. There was a ragged wheeze of desperation in his voice. 'As with any surgical procedure there may be ... complications.'

'Complications,' she repeated, her hair hanging lankly over her face like a shroud. 'Do you know the dictionary definition of *complications*? Making a complete mess of something that you made sound very simple. Isn't that the truth, Dr Calvin?'

The doctor bit his lip and looked away. It seemed, for the first time in the process, that Dr Cal had no answers.

There were always complications. Complications had brought them to this point, after all. What complications would spring up next, she wondered. Well, it was obvious. Dr Calvin had told her that they could not halt the treatment now, and as much as she didn't truly trust him any longer, there was no mistaking his sincerity when he said they must press on. *Like performing an operation without stitching up the patient.* They couldn't stop the process or it might do even more damage to Euan. Now they were about to enter the worst memories of their lives together and her mental defences were at an all-time low. How stupid she must have been, at the start of the process, not to recognise the direction in which they were heading. Then she realised she had not been stupid but rather blind. She had been so consumed with wanting to bring back the original Euan, so swept up in those incredible memories of their early years together, that she had forgotten how bad their lives had become ahead of the apocalypse on the train tracks. Circumstances had exploded beneath her like a rocket fired into the stratosphere and it took most of her strength simply to cling on.

She sighed, shaking her head, and bent back down to the plastic crate filled with domestic detritus that she had never got around to throwing away. She couldn't think of the time shortly before the accident, she couldn't think of the reset. She still had work to do. Unfortunately, Dr Cal was right. They had to continue.

The garage was cool and pleasantly oily-smelling. Since the accident she had used it as storage space for everything they would never use again. Cocktail shakers, curling tongs, squash rackets, an encyclopaedia of instruction manuals for kitchen gadgets, Christmas tinsel, old batteries, a string of electrical cables that looked worryingly nibbled. She knew what she was looking for. No other portal would suffice. She knew it would be here somewhere: the cardboard carton containing a slim white plastic strip with a digital readout. She knew she had kept it as a strange souvenir, but amid the tumult of the move, the kit must have become separated from the other bathroom supplies.

She delved deeper into the box. Both her and Euan had been terrible with clutter, and there had not been time before the accident to sort their possessions into neat, compact piles. Her hand closed around a small solid slab.

Her brow furrowing, she pulled out the unknown object and stared at it. Euan's mobile phone from his old workplace.

She suspected he was meant to have given it back after he was sacked a few months before the accident. There was no possible reason for him to have kept the handset.

Holding her breath, her forefinger caressed the power button.

A train horn hooted in the distance and she jumped – the conversation with Dr Calvin about the reset had shredded her nerves – and her hand closed involuntarily around the phone. The screen lit up. She stared at the device and felt fear shudder through her, as if she had trodden on a fault line and the earth's crust was shifting beneath her feet. She wanted to switch off the phone. Switch it off and stash it away and never think of it again. Then three melodic chimes beeped up at her. Instinct forced her to stare. There were three new messages on the phone's home screen.

'You can't hide from this'

'The situation is the same I made up my mind'

'If you want no part that is fine but you will regret'

She read them again and again. She wondered how long those three short messages had been floating in the ether, never answered.

The phone's battery expired and she was left holding a blank, dead screen.

'Are you okay, Hannah?'

She spun around with a small shriek, her hands flying to her face. The phone skittered away beneath Euan's dusty old workbench.

'What the—'

'I came to see if you wanted anything,' her husband said. He was standing in the open doorway of the garage, holding a tall glass of lemonade. Ice cubes jingled merrily against the glass. 'Maybe a cool drink?'

'No!' she gasped. 'Get out, Euan.'

The expression of hurt on his face broke her apart a little. Her mind whirring, she was forced to remind herself that he was innocent of any of her old husband's past sins. Gritting her teeth, she prayed for calm. Surreptitiously she dabbed at her eyes with her sleeve. She didn't want Euan to see her like this, to think that her pain was because of him. Anything she had seen was the fault of the old Euan.

'I'm sorry, that was uncalled for,' she said, pushing herself to her feet and going to him. She held out her arms. After a moment's thought he returned her embrace and she squeezed him tightly, guiltily. 'I'm pretty on edge right now,' she went on, 'it's not your fault. It's … it's …'

'Tough to pick through those old memories?'

'It's junk. Old junk. Nothing more.'

'Maybe you should throw out all that old junk,' he said neutrally. 'Maybe that would be best for everyone.'

She took a pace backward and stared at Euan for some time. His left eye began to water but he did not drop his gaze. Then abruptly he turned on his heel and left her standing there alone.

25

Hannah and I: Our seventh year

The Test

There has been a change, such a seismic shift, yet all we can do is laugh about it. I am lying on the bed in our flat in the Victorian mansion block, listening to our upstairs neighbour fail to master finger-picking on his acoustic guitar. I suppose the guitar is better than the techno music he plays late at night, but it seems as if he has been playing the same tune for hours, perhaps days. No matter; our offer has been accepted on the new house in the little hamlet outside the commuter town. We have already started to divide our possessions into cardboard boxes. London will soon be part of our past. Home Counties suburbia here we come.

It is not only the music upstairs that seems to have been going on forever. It also appears that my wife has spent an inordinately long time in the bathroom.

Eventually Hannah emerges, naked, holding a white plastic strip. She is staring at its small digital screen with a queer pout on her face, in the midst of a smile and a frown. Her left foot hooks around her right leg. It's her regular stance when she is caught between nervousness and excitement. The exact same posture as when we saw each other for the first time after Paris, at the party in Palmertach Street. I wait for her to speak but she is silent and eventually I can bear the tension no longer.

'Is it a thing?' I ask.

'It's a thing,' she says. 'One day it may have a name. A name, wants and desires, hopes and dreams. But for the time being it's a thing. It's a girl, by the way. Don't ask me how I know. But believe me, I know.'

I feel a giddy looping that travels from my brain to my stomach and back. This is a physical confirmation. But mentally, somehow, she had known right from the very night. I fight a losing battle with an enormous cheek-splitting grin.

'Are you proud, then?' she says, dropping face-first onto the bed. I start up in alarm, already nervous for our unborn child. Surely a pregnant woman should be more careful with her body? Christ, I wish I understood more about these mysteries. 'Feeling like the number one stud in the stallion farm?' she continues. 'Praising your little wrigglies on such a dangerous mission, nobly accomplished?'

'You know, I think I read somewhere that the gent's sperm hunting down the lady's egg isn't quite true. It's actually the egg that reaches out and traps the sperm. This is your fault, conceptually speaking.'

'Gosh, sorry. This is definitely my problem. Along with look-ing like the side of a house for months, childbirth, breastfeeding, screaming-based insomnia. My problems. But hey, you put the bins out twice a week so we can call it evens.'

'Ach, it'll be brilliant. You'll be filled so full of love for the little sod that you'll have three times the energy. Probably.'

My wife sniffs dubiously. 'That's not the half of it. I'll be worn out, knackered, dowdy, covered in baby fluids. And you'll feel jealous that I can't treat you in the princely way you've become accustomed to. Honour you with my body and soul, that sort of thing. You'll be with your friends in the pub, whinging that your wife doesn't understand you. How you used to have such great fun and now she doesn't pay you any attention because she's distracted by a piffling little thing like child-rearing. Then you'll turn into a total walking cliché and start screwing your secretary. Oh, the evil that men do.'

Finishing her tirade, Hannah pouts with mock sullenness, then sticks out her tongue.

'I'm not evil, angel,' I grin, 'I'm so much worse than that.'

Knowing exactly what's coming, she holds up a warning finger. 'Don't you dare. A lady in my condition—'

'You need to be punished for saying those terrible things about me.'

She shrieks as I pounce. Rolling on top of her, I plant a knee on each shoulder, pinning her down to the mattress with gentle pressure. With careful precision I begin to tickle her under the chin, always her weak spot, until she dissolves into giggles, shunting me off her. We lie together, hand in hand, staring at the ceiling. Thankfully the acoustic assassin upstairs has put away his weapon.

'Are you sure we're emotionally mature enough to be parents?' I ask.

'Probably not,' says Hannah. 'Maybe it'll come to us in a flash.'

'I think most mums and dads are winging it,' I tell her, tracing my fingers over her flat white belly, wondering what it will look like plumped and swollen. Swollen with my child. Jesus Christ on a rusty chariot, my child. 'I remember when I first realised my parents were fallible,' I hurry on before emotion overwhelms me. 'It was a summer's day – I can't have been more than seven or eight. I was kicking my football up against the garage door and managed to hoof it onto the roof. Couldn't get up there on my own. So I went round to the side of the garage and got my dad's ladder. I didn't know how to put it up and I put it round the wrong way. I was halfway up the ladder when it collapsed in on me. There was this moment – this absolutely perfect moment – where I was staring at the sky, thinking how it was so incredibly blue and amazingly huge. Time seemed to stop. I wasn't falling but floating.'

'Can I predict,' Hannah says, 'that the youthful Euan Stornoway was, in fact, not floating but falling.'

'Quite right,' I tell her. 'Anyway, I was going backwards, set to crack my silly little head on the concrete of the driveway. Death, brain damage or a nasty bump, who's to say? But that moment stretched out, and I was falling, falling, falling from what seemed like skyscraper height, and then suddenly someone caught me. Mrs McInnes from next door had vaulted the garden fence like an Olympic athlete – despite her gammy knee – and caught me. And then, missing their cues by a minute, my parents came out of the house and ran to me. There was this strange look of betrayal on my mum's face because someone else was the saviour. I've always wondered what would have happened if Mrs McInnes hadn't been watering her begonias that morning and had a clear sight of me about to fall. Funny, I never looked at people the same way after I fell from the ladder. I knew I couldn't rely on anybody to help me in life. When I fell, no one would catch me.'

'Apart from Mrs McInnes?'

'Even the redoubtable Mrs McInnes. Her being there was dumb luck.'

'I'd have saved you,' Hannah says, 'or at least died trying.'

'I bet you would,' I tell her, squeezing her tight.

Her bottom lip begins to droop. 'You have to let people help you, Euan,' she says. 'You've got to let people in. Otherwise you'll find yourself… you'll find yourself pretty lost.'

'Yeah, sure,' I say, now feeling somewhat troubled. 'I know that, angel.'

'Do you really, Euan?' she asks. 'I'm not sure you do.'

My childhood tale was a joke – I think – but my wife has taken it strangely seriously. The smile has dropped from her face completely. Somehow Hannah looks different: older, sadder, more drawn and weary. Noticing me noticing, she hides her face in the pillow.

'I wish we could stay here,' she says, her voice so muffled her words are almost inaudible. 'Back when I still had hope. Back before... before...'

'Hannah, I don't understand—'

'It's nothing,' she insists. 'Leave it, Euan, okay?'

I blink. 'Okay,' I say, not understanding.

Then I notice that the edges of the room seem to be fuzzed and colourless. The painting hanging on the wall, a print of Monet's *Water Lilies*, is now opaque, its shading indefinable, hidden by an ashen fog. I blink, rubbing at my eyes, wondering what's going on, but the mist encroaches still further. The room is starting to fade into nothingness, the wooden floor disappearing from view, the greyness creeping towards our bed.

Hannah notices this too. She sits bolt upright, her eyes wide with panic.

'We need to leave here,' my wife says, lines of concern furrowing between her eyebrows. 'We need to get out of this scene right now.'

'Sorry... scene, what... what are you saying?'

'Euan, we'll never get anywhere if you keep questioning me.'

The room is starting to shake, trembling as if struck by a localised earthquake. The window distorts inward, the glass bending impossibly, convex then concave like a billowing ship's sail. Outside should be a scruffy south London street, terraced houses and shops and a distant sight of the greenery of Clapham

Common, but I can see nothing through the endlessly warping glass.

A thin strand shoots out of the miasma and coils around my wrist like a bracelet. Its pull is weak but insistent. As the rope of fog tugs at me I feel a strange swamping sensation, as if it's constricting the flow of blood to my brain. My mind feels fuzzy. What are we doing here? Hannah has told me some news. Good news, I'm sure, but what? Something... something... something to do with ... her, and us, and our future? Then I spot the white plastic strip on the bedside table, the pregnancy, and I remember. But I don't remember quite enough.

'What's her name?' I say shakily. 'If you're so sure it's a girl, what are we going to call her?'

'Jennifer,' Hannah says, her voice scratched and strained. 'We're going to call our little girl Jennifer. You know this, Euan. Don't you?'

Jennifer, of course. Jennifer.

The strand breaks off and disappears into the haze. I stare at my wife in mute fright. Our first child, if we do indeed have a daughter, is going to be called Jennifer. It's Jennifer for a girl and Jamie for a boy. Hannah and I agreed those names years ago. But in those few seconds, as the rope of fog bound to my wrist, I couldn't remember. I couldn't remember the three sweet syllables of the name of my unborn child.

'Jennifer,' I gasp out. 'Of course. Jennifer. I'm ... I'm sorry.'

Hannah's green eyes are wide and wild. She takes my hand, pulling me up. The greyness is all around us now; we are trapped in an ever-decreasing circle. Our bed is an island in the fog. The rest of the room has vanished.

'Where do we go?' she demands in panic. 'How do we get out?'

More coils of mist are nudging over the corners of the mattress. Reaching. Probing. Hoping to grab.

'What's happening, Hannah?' I cough out. 'Is this real? It can't be real, surely?'

'Hush now, Scotsman,' she says. An ache of a smile crosses her face. The smile is so sad – so pregnant with loss and hopelessness – that I would do anything, absolutely anything, to make her never smile like that again. 'I've got an idea. Do you remember why I was trying out that pregnancy test in the first place? What brought us to this point?'

'Yeah, I mean, yes, obviously, but what—'

'Let's do that again.'

'Here? With all this going on? What the fuck?'

'Something like that. Trust me here, Euan.'

I give up trying to understand and take her in my arms. As we sink among the sheets and she sighs beneath me, I feel a plunging sensation as if we are falling through the bed itself. The periwinkle blue blankets fold around us, cocooning us in a gentle embrace, and as we fade through the room, wrapped up in each other, I see an impossible scene. The tatty wallpaper of our bedroom is blurring away. It morphs into the blank whitewashed walls of a hospital. I see uncomfortable-looking plastic chairs and linoleum flooring. I can smell the cleaning chemicals, hear the beeping of heart-rate monitors and the low comforting murmurs of medics. For reasons I can't comprehend, the sight of that hospital ward sends a horrible chill through my body.

26

Hannah and I: Our eighth year

Jennifer

This is not a place where good things happen. The reek of antiseptic, the whisper of rubber soles on plasticky tiles. There are people around, people in blue uniforms, and none of them speak to me but I know they are watching. What are their feelings? Pity, regret or blank disinterest? How desensitised do you become when you work in one of these theatres of human suffering? When sickness and misery are vital components of your trade, surely you have to block out the horrors around you, or go insane yourself?

I sit on the hard chair staring at the posters on the hospital wall, reading the signs but not taking in a single word. What is a man supposed to think at a moment like this? I have been in this place for some time, yet I cannot recall the specifics of my journey here or how long I have been waiting. I suppose this is for the best. The one thing I remember is that I knew from my first step into our house that something was wrong; life had gone badly awry, fate had pulled the rug from underneath us with a callous hand. It was in the atmosphere, thick and oppressive. I recall calling out to my wife and hearing nothing.

I had padded through into the living room of our new country home. No Hannah. The television had been left on a channel showing a classic comedy series and the laugh track burbled and chuckled mindlessly. I tapped the button on the remote control and the laughter died. The sudden silence seemed to deafen me. In that moment I became truly scared.

'Hannah?' I called. I thought that I heard a noise, a low whimper, from upstairs – or is that my memory tricking me?

Close to panic – for no good reason, I tell myself now, only that instinctive dread – I had walked up the staircase and paced towards our bedroom. Quickly, not running, there was no reason to be alarmed, obviously; my seven months' pregnant wife had simply driven down to the shops or taken a late-afternoon nap ... she had forgotten to turn off the television ... there was a simple explanation and we would laugh about it later, my idiotic paranoia ... my mistake ... dear God, let this all be a silly mistake ...

There was no Hannah in our bedroom. But the door to the bathroom was open and inside I saw ... I saw ...

No. I can't allow myself to remember that scene.

Instead I sit and wait on the chair outside the hospital ward, a prisoner of my memories, willing my mind to become a blank.

Eventually the door opens and I am allowed inside the room to see Hannah.

My first thought, unforgiveable in its casual cruelty, is how old she looks, how drawn and haggard. There are huge purple half-moons gouged underneath her eyes, her lank hair is the colour of rotten straw, and her posture as she sits on the bed is slumped and defeated.

'You can see your wife for only a few minutes,' a doctor says quietly to me as she steps away from the vast construction of metal and fabric that calls itself a bed. 'Remember she's tired and in pain.'

It is such a long, long walk from the doorway to where Hannah is sitting. My feet keep sticking to the floor. I have to fight a low instinct to turn and run, flee from the awful scene. But where else is there but here, and who else is there but her? There seems to be nothing real in the world but Hannah. Just as the good times had filled my life with joy and laughter, the bad times – and there are no worse times than this, how can there possibly be worse times? – swamp every aspect of existence with pain and heartache.

Eventually I reach the bed and sit down next to her. I take her hand and her fingers hang limply in my own.

'I'm sorry,' I say. I have no idea what I'm apologising for, only that some form of condolence is required and I have completely run out of words for the occasion. What words would fit? What words will ever fit again?

'I'm sorry too,' she says.

'How are you feeling?'

'It doesn't hurt as much as I thought it would,' my wife says. Her voice is so empty, so lifeless. 'I think they gave me something for the pain.'

'Good,' I say, nodding with idiot fervour. 'That's good.'

'The doctors said the same thing was likely to happen if we tried again,' Hannah says, her gaze at the blank white expanse of the wall. A nervous tic is pulling one side of her mouth up into an awful humourless smile. She swallows twice, deeply, then continues, 'It's something ... something wrong with me, with my body. It's my fault.'

She starts to cry – not a crashing tidal wave of grief but slowly leaking tears that seem as if they will never stop – and I shush her, trying to calm her as best I can. I realise that I'm not strong enough to give her the support she needs. Hannah has often accused me of having an answer for everything and now I have no answers, not a single one. I had always flattered myself by thinking I was a good husband: the romantic gestures, the jokes, the laughter. Now I realise that my self-congratulation was worthless. The good husband is not the man who can admire his wife's beauty and rip her out of her dress. The good husband is the man who can sit beside the pale, frightened woman who has lost her baby and speak the words that will comfort her.

But those words won't come. The words won't come and the tears won't come either. My father – a good man, but a pitiless man – always used to tell me never to go crying about anything that I couldn't fix. But how can I fix this?

'Please don't cry,' I tell her lamely. 'You're … you're still here. That's all that matters.'

'We'll be fine, you and me,' she says. I realise – a moment too late – that this is a question, not a statement. 'Won't we?' Hannah asks, her tired eyes enormous, pleading.

'Of course,' I agree. I would say anything to make her stop looking at me in that way, begging for the solace I cannot give.

My wife nods tiredly. She catches sight of something over my shoulder and flinches as if slapped.

'What is it?' I ask, following her gaze. The edges of the room have fuzzed into grey. At first I think it might be smoke, that there is a fire in the hospital, but there is no burning odour. The mist smells flat and dead, like the air in an abandoned warehouse or the brackish scent of a lake that can sustain no life.

'I want to go,' Hannah says. That drifting tone is gone from her voice as if the sight of the greys has shocked her back to life. 'We need to leave here.'

'Hannah, we can't … you need to rest, get better …'

'Euan, if you love me you'll get me away from this place,' she says. 'We can't be here any longer.'

I nod. What else can I do?

There is a small onyx-shaded vase filled with a sprig of fake flowers on the bedside table. Hannah picks it up, unceremoniously throws the plastic daisies on the floor and conceals the vase in her lap.

'They took away Jennifer in this place,' she says quietly. 'I'm going to take something from them, something we can remember her by.'

The mist has now reached the end of the bed. Quickly, but as gently as I can, I help Hannah into the wheelchair left by the hospital orderlies at the side of the bed. She lets out a single gasp of pain that rakes at my conscience like nails against flesh.

'Things will get better,' I say, placing a kiss on her forehead. Her skin is moist yet cold to the pressure of my lips. 'I promise.'

'Oh, Euan,' she smiles sadly, 'if only that was the truth.'

My wife is about to say more, but a probing tendril shoots out of the mist and latches onto a spoke of the wheelchair and she lets out a harrowed moan. The window in the far wall shakes as if walloped by an unseen breeze. With rotten ripping noises, the linoleum panels pull themselves out of the floor and begin to form blockades around Hannah's bed. The walls lose their comforting solidity and bend inwards, cocooning us in an ever-tightening ball. Grief-sick, my mind hazy from confusion and lack of sleep, I accept the impossibility of what is happening. We are being wrapped up so very tightly in this hospital room and I'm certain that once there is no possibility of escape, the greys will fall upon us. I barely care. Life as it is seems meaningless. There is little point in us leaving without Jennifer. How can we carry on without her?

'No,' says Hannah. Her voice is barely a whisper but firm. 'No, stop. I'm not letting you have this one. I won't let you ruin this.'

I don't fully understand what she means but at the sound of her voice – as frail and cracked as it is – the fog recedes.

The twisted chaos of the room unravels, springing back to an unremarkable hospital ward. The room is still murky but now I can see the green glow of the exit sign and the doorway beneath it. For a moment there I was almost ready to let myself go, submit to whatever was happening, but then I heard the resolve in my wife's voice. Despite everything, everything she has endured, she isn't ready to give up. My heart fills with wonder at her phenomenal strength. Suddenly, at this shaft of light in my bleak thoughts, we have been granted an escape route.

But is this all my fault in the first place? Is it me doing this? Have I caused the greys to come?

'We need to go!' Hannah shouts, snapping me back to reality. 'Euan, we need to go right now.'

Gripping the wheelchair's handles, I push her forward but the fog swoops down in a sheet, closing off my path. Spinning her round, the rubber tyres shrieking on the plastic floor, I can't see the exit sign anywhere. I can't see anything but grey.

'Please, Euan—' my wife gasps.

Knuckling the sweat from my eyes, I catch sight of the doorway and see there is a room beyond this room. Not a hospital corridor. A kitchen with low candlelight to distract from the scabby decor. A house that should have been a beautiful family home but is already falling into disrepair. It is a cold house. No one will ever laugh there again. But there is nowhere else to go. So I take hold of the handles of Hannah's wheelchair once more, grit my teeth and push her rapidly towards the green exit sign, already knowing there is no exit from whatever hell we are in right now.

27

300 days since the accident

'Are you okay?' he asked. She turned her head towards him, barely seeing him through tear-blurred eyes. Most of her mind was still lost in the past trauma of yesterday's reel, aching for what had been taken from her. 'You look so sad,' he went on. 'Can I help?'

She shook her head. She knew it was her imagination, a vicious trick of the mind, but the lower half of her body hurt exactly as it had done after the doctors took what remained of Jennifer out of her. That scraped-out sensation. A three-syllable name sang endlessly in her head like a mantra; she wished she could turn down the volume. She wished for blackness, blankness. She wished she had never started this crazy, awful process. She wished she could go right back to the start. On that morning, still reeling from the recollection of her lost child – a grief so violent it stabbed like horror movie strings, piercing her over and over again – she even wished she had never met Euan.

'Should we ... should we go out for the day?' her husband asked. 'We've got the day off from the Project, haven't we? Only, you know, if you want to, I mean.'

His gaze met hers for barely a second, then flicked away. He had no idea, absolutely no idea, what the pair of them had been through. But now she wondered whether that was such a bad thing. The sheer innocence of his offer, the way his cheeks were flushed and his breath was coming fast, dragged her mind away from Jennifer. She was grateful for the distraction, grateful to him.

The train wheezed to a halt and they disembarked. She could not say exactly why she had chosen this place; there were pleasant country walks closer to home. But there was something oddly fetching about the man-made reservoir where they were heading. The way the sun seemed to trap itself in the bowl-shaped lake, painting the scene in mellow gold. The way the trees bowed over the water, their leaves reflecting off the surface in a mirror image.

She bought a cheap bottle of rosé at the high street grocery store before they came to the lake. Fizzy, sugary stuff that she was sure would never feature on any Michelin-starred restaurant's wine list. They found a seat beneath the branches of one of the sycamore trees studding the bank and Euan dug the base of the bottle into the mud of the shallows to let the water chill it. They sat in silence for some time until she could bear no more and pulled the wine free of its makeshift cooler – a spray of silty muck spattering on her floral dress – popped the cork and splashed generous measures into their plastic glasses.

They drank and looked out across the water. On the other bank a young family – mother, father, baby and toddler – were packing away the remains of their picnic into a haversack. The elder child tottered around on her stumpy legs, picking up then dropping paper plates and cutlery, hindering more than helping. Jennifer would have been about that age now, she thought.

'Did we ever want kids?' Euan asked. Shocked, she stared at him and he gazed back innocently. He really didn't know, she realised. He had simply picked up on her emotions, like an animal scenting another's sickness. The accident had robbed him of his memory but it could not take his natural empathy. 'Before, I mean,' he added.

'We did,' she said carefully, 'but, well, it never happened for us.'

He offered her a shy smile. 'Not for want of trying, I'd imagine.'

A deep mechanism inside her, so long dormant, began to creak slowly into operation, the cogs – rusted by disuse – slowly starting to turn. 'How do you mean?' she asked.

He coughed nervously. 'Well ... Jesus, I mean, you're a beautiful woman. A man would be mad not to find you attractive.'

'We were together for almost a decade before ... before what happened,' she said, laughing with a lightness she did not truly feel. 'I'm sure you solved all the mysteries of female anatomy quite some time ago. You see each other at your absolute worst. Hungover ... sweaty and irritable after the gym ... runny-nosed with the flu. There isn't much romantic intrigue left when you've spent a third of your lives together.'

'I'm not sure about that,' he said.

She stared down at her lap, realising that her palms were damp and her heart was ticking a beat or two faster than normal. She looked up at the man who she knew and yet did not know. He was staring at her, his lower lip trembling slightly. Her vision suddenly heightened, intensified by a jolt of adrenaline pouring into her veins, she drank in his image. The dark tousles of his hair, his eyes crinkling at the corners, the stubble on his jawline. The feeling she had experienced the first moment she saw him at the Café Bellevue in the 14th arrondissement juddered through her body like a surge of electricity. That feeling was dangerous, she knew – perhaps even fatal – but the sensations were delicious.

'I think—' Euan started, blushing ever more crimson, and

she had no idea what he was about to say – what he might propose – because at that moment a violin chord pierced the silence around the lake.

The musician – sitting across the water, close to the picnic spot the young family had vacated – was a young man with a scrawny frame and an oversized nose. His posture was awkward but his head rested upon his instrument as if surrendering himself to a capricious yet irresistible mistress. He was not busking, she realised. He hadn't spotted the pair of them, concealed beneath the bending branches of the sycamore tree, and he thought he was alone. The violinist had simply come to a quiet place to play the music he loved.

She recognised the tune: wry, sly and evocative. Her sister, who preferred the guitar but had an irritating ability to pick up any instrument almost instantly, could fiddle a passable version of that sinuous tango. *Por Una Cabeza* – known to Saskia as *Pour me one more glass of Cabeza*. It was a tune that spoke of lingering glances, red wine that soaked the tongue, intimacies embarked upon that seemed so perfect in candlelight. Their fallacies would perhaps be displayed mercilessly in the morning's harsh glare, but in that moment, their transgressions were so very right.

'Do you want to dance?' Euan asked suddenly.

She sputtered out a confused laugh, then realised he was serious. 'What? Here? Now? With you?'

'Nobody's watching,' he said, his voice quiet but implacable. 'Why not?'

The cheap sparkling wine had raced to her head, the bubbles fizzing and popping in her brain. The old Euan hated to dance. She even had to cajole him into a first dance at their wedding, and felt a twinge of annoyance as he made a great show of trudging her around the floor to the Fifties doo-wop song they had chosen, before body-popping during the chorus – the guests had loved his clowning, she had not. But the very same man – or rather, the same man who had changed beyond measure – was holding out his hand to her, a simple yearning in his gaze.

'Screw it,' she said finally. 'You're right. Why not?'

He helped her to her feet, clumsily knocking over the empty bottle as he did so, and she giggled and hiccupped. Matching her smile, he held her in the time-honoured ballroom pose and began to turn her slowly around the copse, and the inch or so between their bodies felt like miles. The music melded into a slower waltz, mellow yet mournful, and Euan pulled her closer, nestling his head into her shoulder. He placed a tiny, hopeful kiss on her neck and she did not pull away. A thousand thoughts raced in her brain and she decided to rescind them all, only for this moment, and surrender to the blissful blankness.

After some time she realised the violinist had packed up and moved on, yet Euan still clung to her, his heartbeat thumping against her chest. There was wetness on her neck and she knew he was weeping. A chill breeze bristled through the browning leaves clinging desperately to the trees. Over his heaving shoulders she could see the sun fading fast. The darkness descended rapidly, the dying light painting them as featureless silhouettes against the mild ripples of the water.

28

Hannah and I: Our eighth year

Michelin Stars

The atmosphere is shaded sullen. I am in the kitchen of our house stirring a casserole on the stove. Hannah is out drinking with her work colleagues. This has been a regular Friday night occurrence over the past two months. She barely touched a drop of alcohol when she was carrying our baby, but now there is no baby – now there will never be a baby – she can do as she pleases.

There my thoughts go again; I was thinking about nothing much in particular and suddenly we come back to Jennifer. What happened to Jennifer and what I did afterwards, when I was weak and drunk and falling apart.

There is a knock at the door. Not the front door of our house, signalling Hannah's return home. The knocking is coming from inside the pantry. Knowing, dreading, moving as if in a dream, I move towards the door. I pull it open and see her there. The dark girl.

'Hello, you,' she says.

She is wearing the summer dress she wore the last time I saw her. When she needed to tell me something but I wasn't brave enough to allow her to speak. I'm not brave enough now either.

'Get out of my fucking head,' I hiss.

'*Git ootah mah fookin' heid*,' she mimics. She pushes her thick black fringe away from her eyes; that gesture I always found so oddly fetching. The last time I saw those dark eyes they were clouded by tears aching to spill. Her trying to talk and me finding every reason not to listen. 'Oh, Euan. Your accent sounds so macho when you're angry.'

I press my palms to my aching temples. 'This isn't you. This is my home. You were never here.'

'Well, this isn't you either, Euan, is it? And you're not really here either. So doesn't that make us a fine couple?'

'Shut up.'

'You wouldn't listen to me before. Now maybe you'll listen. Maybe you'll listen to yourself—'

The dark girl's words are cut off as I slam the pantry door shut. She was never there at all, obviously. A walking talking daydream. There's enough going wrong in reality without being tormented by my own imagination. I wish there was a way to stop my brain. I wish there was a way to blow my thoughts to shards of dust.

I can't live with what I've done and I can't bring myself to tell my wife and shatter her faith in me. What possible way out is there from this personal hell I've created?

I've blown my career. Too many days turning up hungover or not at all, so there went the job. Invited to seek alternative employment elsewhere ... or, as my dad would call it, the sack. On reflection I deserved it.

I've blown things with my family. An innocuous query from my mother about arrangements for Audra's son's christening turned into a telephone screaming match because the thought of childhood celebrations seemed incomprehensible at a time like this. I said unforgiveable things that I did not mean. My mother was in tears. My father and my sisters have united against me and I have to admit that I deserve it.

Now we come to my wife. I've done something that, if the truth ever emerges, will blow apart my relationship. And I shall most certainly deserve it.

I am swirling down a vortex that swallows anything good in life. A vortex that I think I might name Jennifer.

My wife has moved on from Jennifer and I have not. She still hurts, she still aches, but she believes that the worst is over. I fear, I fear so very deeply, that the worst is yet to come. My fault, my mistake. She does not know yet, but surely it is only a matter of time. What will happen when she does know? All I am certain of is that the grey won't fade. Guilt, depression, fury at my own weakness. What a potent mixture that is, what a killer cocktail. Black clouds and red mists converging into an insidious grey that creeps and crawls over everything in my life. A grey that drowns joy and suffocates love.

But now I hear a key turning in a lock. Hannah is coming through the front door and I must keep my thoughts to myself.

She takes a couple of attempts to hang her coat on the peg in the hallway. She totters through to the kitchen. I have made the most of the space we call our own, there is low light and soft music. I was hoping the glamours would distract her from the dirty windows and the peeling paint on the walls, my best efforts at creating the illusion of an enchanting French bistro inside our kitchen. There are even candles on the table, although they have now burned down to flickering nubs. She fails to notice any of my efforts at keeping our romance alive.

'Hi there,' she says. Her cheeks are pink and her eyes are too bright and the febrile scent of alcohol hangs about her in an invisible mist.

Pointedly I stare at my watch. The time has just passed eleven o'clock. She promised me that she would be home for eight, or nine at the latest. 'Hello,' I say. My tone is level. My voice is calm. 'I tried to call. A number of times, in fact.'

'Oh, right,' she says. 'Went for a few drinks after work. Phone was in my bag. Can't have heard it. What are you cooking?'

'The same thing as I was cooking three hours ago. When you were supposed to be home.'

I dole out the beef stew onto a plate. The dining set of Scandinavian ceramic stoneware was purchased by one of Hannah's elderly aunts as a wedding present. The expensive, fashionable crockery looks incongruous in the tatty kitchen. We did mean to decorate the house when we moved in, we had grand plans for doing up the place beautifully, but then... well, then Jennifer happened.

'It's only a bloody casserole,' my wife says mulishly, taking a seat at the table and digging into the bowl. 'We're not talking Michelin stars here.'

I pause, tightly gripping the handle of the serving spoon. 'Thank you for your appreciation of my hard work, Hannah. Spending my day making something nice for you while you were out boozing.'

She snorts. 'Climb down off your cross, Stornoway. You could have come out with us, had some fun for once.'

'With those Bullingdon bellends you call colleagues? I'm hardly their sort of person. Urgh, nasty lower-class Pict – quick, flee back to our ivory towers.'

My voice wavers on the last syllable. I have heard – has Hannah heard too? – the sound of the pantry door unlatching. A low, sneaky sound. The light in the room flickers and fades and an icy breath tickles the back of my neck. She can't be here, she can't possibly be here. I struggle to keep my gaze on my wife.

Hannah sighs. 'It's not their fault they were born into money.'

'The right school, the right friends, the right contacts. Life's just so easy.'

She takes a great gulp of her wine. 'I know how you've been feeling but you really shouldn't blame others for your problems, Euan. You're in quite a negative headspace.'

'Oh, good grief, here comes the psychobabble.'

I'm feigning anger. I feel only fright. I hear boot heels click-clacking on the stone flagging of the kitchen floor. The candlelight has taken on a sinister hue and the background music is flitting discordantly, jumping out of time. A shadow falls over my wife, blotting out the white-blonde halo of her hair. The dark girl is behind Hannah now. She stretches out an arm, raising a curved black nail as if to tap my wife on the shoulder. Reveal herself, reveal everything. Then she steps back into the gloom.

'Listen to yourself, darling,' Hannah scoffs. She hasn't noticed the stranger, the intruder; not yet. Feeling my left eye begin to water, I glare back at her, desperate to keep her attention on me. She can't see. I won't let her see. 'You're upset when I don't take an interest and you're upset when I do.' The fire in her eyes dims and she places a placatory hand on my arm. 'Euan … please … I'm really trying here. I'm trying to support you because I know you're finding things tough right now. It's been a horrible year for us both. But I'm moving on and I need you to move on too.'

I feel the greys begin to shroud my vision. The colour is starting to fade from the scene. It is as if my own rotten thoughts are projecting waves of toxins, poisoning everything good.

'I don't know how to move on,' I say, and I am close – so, so close – to telling her the truth. No, not now, not tonight. But the confrontation is on its way, like a train hurtling down the tracks, and I pray for just one more night, one more week, one more month before the collision comes. 'I don't think it'll get better.'

Hannah stares at me for a long time and her expression begs for reconciliation. 'You need a break from all this,' she says, topping up her wine. 'When I get that next promotion we can have a massive, awesome holiday. Maybe Japan like we used to talk about, or go out to see my sister in San Francisco. Maybe both places. First class all the way, my treat.'

'Am I supposed to be impressed?' I sneer. The greys have reached us, they are nearly at the table now. There are greys in our house and greys in my brain and, oh God, what I would give for an end to this. 'Well done for rubbing it in that I'm skint and unemployable. Is that the most you want from life? Making money? Being the big jet-setter?'

The dark girl, now perched neatly on the kitchen counter, blows me a kiss. She's pleased with me. I feel nauseous, my saliva tasting acidic.

'I know we can't have kids, Euan,' Hannah says fiercely, 'but that doesn't change our marriage, does it? My priorities ... well, they're different now. I'm never going to be the good little wifey sitting in the corner with my knitting, gazing up at you adoringly. That's not what you signed up for.'

'So why go on with this then?' I ask, barely aware of what I'm saying. I feel a chill and see thin strings of fog curling inquisitively around my ankles. The way I'm feeling right now, I can't even be bothered to fight it. 'We can't have a family. You don't seem interested in being a wife. You don't even seem too interested in me.'

'Maybe you should try to be a little more interesting then,' she replies. 'Actually bloody do something rather than moping about the house. It's not easy for me to come home to a husband like a caged animal.'

I feel my self-loathing turn in on itself; making a blade of the sharp edges of my guilt and twisting it back at my wife. 'I made the compromises for you,' I tell her. 'I'm living the life you want to live. So can you at least try to give the impression, even if it's a lie, that you don't regret saying Yes to me?'

'I wish I could say that I've never regretted marrying you,' Hannah whispers, her body trembling, 'and I'll do almost anything for you, Euan, but I won't ever lie to you.'

The room rings with a stranger's laughter. A switch flicks inside me. I grab Hannah's bowl of stew and hurl it at the kitchen counter, towards the dark girl. The crockery clatters musically as it shatters against the wall. She isn't there any longer. She has vanished again. But I can still hear her mocking laugh echoing in my mind.

Hannah leaps to her feet, backing away from me. We stare at the wreckage I have made. The threads of fog have entwined into a thick rope that snakes around my lower legs, binding to me like a second skin. In that moment, embraced by the grey, I cannot remember a single good thing about my wife.

'Sometimes you can be an impossible person to live with,' she says, her lower lip quivering.

I tell her, 'Sometimes you can be an impossible person to love.'

Hannah stares at me, her mouth a wide-open O of shock and betrayal. Then she turns, overbalancing on her stupidly high stilettos. I reach for her and catch her before she falls; a painful parody of a classic romance. I have held her this way so many times but now it feels as if I am holding a mannequin. I am holding Hannah and the greys are holding me and somehow she seems colourless, as if the life has been drained out of her. I try to think of the times I loved her beyond measure, the times she made me laugh, the times when I felt that to know her made me the luckiest man alive. But there's nothing, absolutely nothing. She feels like a stranger to me. How can I tell her that I love her when I can't even remember why I love her?

'Please, Euan,' she says. 'You don't need to be this way. This isn't you. This isn't the man I married. Why are you doing this to yourself?'

Staring down with fuzzed vision, I see her tears have stained the front of my sweater. The sight of that little damp patch, her emotion made physical, jolts me back to some sort of sanity and that rope of fog that was holding me snaps immediately.

'I'm so sorry,' I tell her. 'For a moment there—' I can't finish. For a moment there I couldn't even remember my wife's name, let alone what she means to me.

'We need to get out,' Hannah says urgently. 'We need to leave right now. This house ... this place, it's sucking the life from us.'

But the scene all around us is shrouded. The kitchen and the table have almost vanished. The candles are vague misty pinpricks of light. We are standing on a patch of carpet the size of a vinyl record.

'There's nowhere to go,' I say. 'We're trapped.'

She shakes her head. Her mouth is set in a stubborn pout: my wife's don't-mess-with-me face, which I've seen often enough in our relationship. 'Don't say that. I'll never give up on you, Scotsman. So don't you dare give up on me.'

I take her gently by the shoulders. 'But, Hannah ... where can we go?'

She stares at me for several moments, then breaks into a shockingly unexpected peal of laughter, and at the melody of the sound the fog rears back like a frightened animal. 'Why, we can go anywhere we want, Euan. We can go absolutely anywhere we want.'

Hannah drops to her knees and plunges her fingers into the

carpet. Her hands sink into the material as if it was mud. She arrows her fingers, then splays them wide and a hole emerges in the centre of our living room. The carpet and floor have taken on the consistency of treacle. Almost forgetting the mist, I watch in fascination as she pulls out gloopy strands that shine with iridescent, impossible colours. My wife's hands are dripping with thick liquid that used to be solid wood and tough fabric. She digs some more and the hole grows wider and wider and this can't be real but as long as I'm with Hannah I'm willing to accept the impossible as my new reality. The hole is now a tunnel and at the end of it I can see a prismatic light shining faintly, like the reflection from a shattered mirror.

'Dig with me, Euan,' Hannah urges. 'If we can't go out, then we'll go down.'

So I drop to my knees with her and as she takes my hands in hers we plunge together through the hole in our floor. As we tumble towards the splintered light of that tiny yet somehow vast mirror, I cast one final glance over my shoulder. Our home – our once happy home – has been consumed entirely by the greys.

29

Hannah and I: Our eighth year

Broken Reflections

There's a pact that I've struck with my conscience. Privately I'll repent, I'll beat myself up every single minute of every single day, I'll submit to every torture my mind can devise, so long as Hannah never finds out. If she finds out it would destroy her and that would destroy me. So I mouth this meaningless pact, this worthless charm, my mantra to keep the horrors of guilt at bay. Please let her never find out. Please let her never find out. Surely that isn't too much to ask for? Surely, surely, surely some mistakes can pass unpunished?

The broken pocket mirror dangles between my limp fingers. I have been away, that much I know – far away from my wife. Where did I find this worthless keepsake, why do I still have it with me? As a homecoming present it leaves something to be desired. The jagged pieces of glass splinter my reflection into a face that is almost unrecognisable. Then I hear the door open and I slip the mirror into the back pocket of my jeans like a magician's cheap trick. Hannah need never know.

'So you came back,' she says.

She is framed in the doorway, her face flushed, a few strands of hair plastered to her forehead. I can't read her. I can't read her expression, her voice; I'm sure I used to understand her. Is she happy, relieved – or furious? I can't feel any warmth. Did she even want me to come back? We are husband and wife, yet an onlooker would mistake us for strangers. At this stage in our relationship I wonder whether we really know each other at all.

'I needed some time alone,' I tell her.

'Did you get it?'

A difficult question to answer. I have been gone for, I think, a week. Maybe ten days. Somehow the time slipped away from me. A few days with my parents, a few days crashing on Barry's couch. A night at a budget chain hotel next to a motorway intersection when the hangover mists were making me a danger to other road users. I left because I couldn't stand to be with Hannah and I came back because I can't stand to be without her. I know that I can't live without her. Yet this life we now live together is consuming the good things we used to feel about one another; slowly, inexorably eating up our happy memories. My fault, inevitably.

'I've missed you,' I blurt out.

Her eyes narrow. 'Then why leave?'

'I don't know.' This, at least, is honesty. 'I thought … I just thought we needed space from each other. We were killing each other. Making our lives a misery.'

'And you thought,' she says, perching down on the armchair, 'that bailing out on me for an indefinite period of time would be a successful way to achieve marital bliss?'

She is definitely furious. One facet of Hannah's personality is that the more emotional she is, the more she tries to cover up her feelings with elaborate speech. It's knowing little quirks like this that remind me how much history we share – and how few secrets we hide from each other.

But there are enough.

'It was a shit idea,' I say.

'Yes. Yes, it was.'

'I should have told you where I was going.'

Her fingers are bunching into fists with each breath. 'You can't just leave and expect me to be waiting here for you.' Her voice is cold but her lower lip is trembling. 'You can't do that again, Euan. Ever. That's not how relationships work.'

'No. I realise that now.'

'You acted like a child, a spoilt child. You're over thirty. You need to be a man. A man who faces up to life and the bad things that happen. You need to open up to me, not shut me off. You need to be a man who actually talks to his wife, rather than clamming up and running away.'

I bow my head. 'I know. I know.'

Unbelievably she is trying to smile. *Han always makes the best of things*, I remember her sister telling me years ago. That will to make the very best of the very worst; what I would give for some of that hope, that wild optimism which soaks through her nature. 'They're our problems, Euan,' she goes on. 'We can make it through this together. But you have to – you must – tell me what you're thinking, what you're feeling. I'm your wife, remember? You can tell me everything.'

She's wrong, so very wrong. I can't tell her. I can't tell her anything that matters. I can't tell her anything. She doesn't know the first thing about me. She doesn't know what I'm capable of, she doesn't know how much I can hurt her. She doesn't know that this is more than the carousel of domestic discord that every couple rides at times in a relationship. It feels like something has snapped, something is irreparably broken.

I'm so close to telling her. I can't ever tell her. Guilt is so hellishly fertile. Every little twinge of regret gives birth to more and more shameful recollections until the combined effect leaves me breathless, gasping for air. If only I could be rid of these tumours growing fat inside me. If only I could start again.

'Do you still love me?' I ask. I need to hear her say these words even though I don't deserve them. Even though, if she knew everything about me, what I've done, she wouldn't say it. She would never say those words again – ever. But I need to hear her say these three simple words or else I'll fall apart entirely.

'I love you,' she says. 'Of course I still love you, Euan. I love you more than anything. You're the most amazing husband and the most wonderful person I've ever met, but ... but ... you can also be an irresponsible prick.'

Sighing, she beckons me over and I go gratefully, nearly crawling across the living-room floor in deference to her. The house keys in the pocket of my jeans dig into my thigh; I can't tell her how close I came to flinging these keys into the Water of Leith one drunken night staggering through Dean Gardens, to make our mental divide physically permanent. I can't tell her that I came so close to never coming home again.

Hannah draws me to her and I'm so glad my face is still crushed against her chest so she can't see the expression on my face; if she had seen it, only for a second, she would have known everything. She is so close to the truth, yet she will never guess because she trusts me. If I was a better man I wouldn't have put myself in this impossible situation. If I was a worse man I'd be able to fabricate my way out of it. In essence I'm horribly mediocre. There's no good or evil, right or wrong. It's not black and white. It's just grey, everything's fucking grey.

'I think about her every day,' I tell her.

'So do I, Euan,' Hannah says. 'She was part of me for seven months.'

'No one should ever have to talk about their kid in the past tense. It isn't right. It just ... just shouldn't happen.'

'I know, darling,' says my wife.

'I don't know how to make things better.'

She pulls me close again, gripping me tightly as if she could squeeze all the unhappiness out of me, and the broken mirror that I have concealed poorly – where did it come from? Why is it even there at all? – falls out of my pocket and hits the carpet with a dull thump.

Hannah stares bemused at the shattered glass on the floor. Has she seen what I just saw – dark eyes, dark hair, a sly smile – reflected in a warped kaleidoscopic image?

'What the hell is that?' she says. 'Where did you get that mirror?'

I wish I could tell her that I don't know, but somehow I do. I wish I could tell Hannah the truth. Everything is broken. My father's words from decades ago echo in my brain, *Don't bother crying to anyone about what they can't fix*. My dad was right. No one can fix this; not Hannah, not anybody.

'A present,' I say desperately. 'It's stupid, I know. It … it doesn't mean anything.'

'Everything means something in this place, Euan. Don't lie to me.'

I know she's right. Because a second ago I was retching in the lifeless air and now there is febrile warmth breaking through the dead haze. There is a scent of a spicily exotic perfume, a scent of fresh human heat. My clothes feel soaked with soapy water even though I am completely dry. I know if Hannah looks at the broken mirror again she'll see the reflection of that face. A person who is a stranger to only one of us. Smears of kohl etched around eyes so dark there is no shading between the pupils and iris. The dark girl.

'I'm coming, Euan,' she whispers. 'I'll soon be there. Then you'll have to tell her. You won't be able to lie and bluster out of this one. Not even you.'

I fling the mirror away and it is swallowed in the fog. Hannah is too distracted looking for a way out of the swamped room to notice. Small mercies. Surely, though, she saw the flash of that reflection? No ... no ... no, I'll never let her know, never let her see. But the room is changing around me and surely she must notice this? The walls have changed. Instead of the dull yellow living-room wallpaper, a hangover from the previous owner, inked patterns are swirling into definable shapes. Now boxes of presents are etched on the walls, their bows wrapped around one another in a sideways figure-of-eight, an infinity loop, because someone here just likes presents. Not Hannah, no, someone else. Someone else I thought I'd got rid of a long time ago. Someone who's demanding to be seen, to be known. No. No. No, I can't let my wife know, I can't let her see ... rather the greys than this ... rather oblivion than this ...

Now the fog is my friend. Now the fog is my salvation. There is no chance of Hannah seeing anything else in the pocket mirror now; the mists have deadened the reflection. The dull air has swamped and choked that evocatively spiced perfume. No darkly flashing eyes, no seductive smile, no black-painted fingernails and purple jeans. Hannah won't see, Hannah can't see, because there is no colour in our world any longer. The room has disappeared around us. My wife clings to me and it is her, not the fog, that should be my salvation. But I fear – I fear so very deeply – that I am well past saving.

'What's wrong, Euan?' she demands. 'What the fuck is wrong with you?'

'I'll tell you,' I say, not knowing whether this is an empty promise, only wanting to be away from this place. 'Get me out of here and I'll tell you everything.'

A weak golden glow pierces the haze and a small passageway appears, a tunnel barely large enough for us to crawl through.

There are sounds coming from the end of the tunnel: muted clatterings of crockery, innocuous jazz music, a hiss of escaping steam. Hannah is pulling me away with her, pulling me from the greys, but I feel an equally deep pull towards them. Rather the cold embrace of whatever is inside that fog than face the truth.

30

Hannah and I: Our ninth year

Malvue

This seems like a shoddy, sad imitation of our first meeting. A man, a woman, a coffee bar. Except this is not the 14th arrondissement of Paris, it is a franchise outlet in a commuter town's dingy shopping centre. Our backing soundtrack is saccharine light jazz instead of the shouts of market traders and the whoosh of trams. There will be no brandy for us today, no weaving walk in the moonlight along the cobbled street to her hotel. No Montparnasse rooftop nightcap, no laughter, no kiss with the twinkling Paris skyline as our backdrop.

We are so very far from where we started out. I fear we are at the end of our journey. I wish I could go back to the beginning. I wish that with all my heart, with every fibre of my being. But we cannot retrace our steps. It's our own fault if we wander off the path.

What would the 23-year-old Euan George Stornoway make of the man sitting here today, stirring his coffee while a soundtrack of self-justification whines away in his head, waiting for the girl he first met at Café Bellevue to arrive so he can tell her the news that will destroy her world? Would he be angry, bitterly disappointed? Or would he simply be confused? It was a mistake that got out of hand and the consequences are simply phenomenal.

That same woman is nearly a decade older now but still so beautiful she turns the head of every man she passes as she picks her way carefully through the café's maze of chairs and tables. The surface of our table is clean but rubbish is piled up beneath the furniture, almost out of sight.

I reach for my drink to avoid catching her eye – suddenly certain that if our gazes meet right now my wife will see through to the filthy core of me – and I realise that next to my coffee mug is a new arrival. A small box. It is gift-wrapped with twin bows encircling one another. A present. Someone here likes presents. I don't. Because I know that whatever is in the box is not a gift, it's a nasty surprise.

The box begins to rock gently. My heart hammering, I peer closer. The sides of the present are oscillating as if from blows by tiny fists and feet. There's something inside. Something almost but not quite alive.

'Why don't you take a look inside?' the voice of a not-quite-stranger calls from the coffee shop's serving counter. 'See what you ignored before.'

No, I won't look up. I won't see. More importantly, I won't let Hannah see.

'Hello there, handsome Scotsman,' my wife says, arriving at the table and dumping her bags on the floor. As she shrugs her coat onto the back of a chair, I take the opportunity to sweep the gift box off our table. It tumbles away from view with all the other detritus. 'Jesus wept, you should have seen the queues. Ooh, chocolate sprinkles, decadent.' Her nose wrinkles. 'Are you okay? You've not touched your coffee.'

Greasy sweat slicking my forehead, I chance a glance upwards. The girl at the counter – wearing a purple smock with the words *Trainee Barista* stamped on the midriff – is awfully familiar. I can see her smiling over at me with a lemon-biting grin. She raises her right hand in a mocking greeting while the left cradles the slight swell of her stomach. Black fingernails. Of course.

'Almost ready to plunge back into department store hell?' Hannah asks brightly. 'We still need to pick up some new blankets, a travel kettle and some toiletries for the holiday. Then, because you'll be on the verge of suicide, we can go to the wine section of that posh supermarket, you can pretend to know which bottle of red goes best with our steak and I'll pretend to be impressed.'

I hold onto the sides of the table to steady myself. My vision starts to fuzz. Either that, or there truly is a thick fog slipping around the tables of this coffee bar. 'Hannah, can we talk for a second?' I say.

She blinks. 'Why?'

'Please.'

She perches forwards on her chair, smiling at me. Filling the silence between us, the too-loud jazz soundtrack segues seamlessly from bland to bland. Hannah raises her mug to her mouth and smacks her lips; this is the best cappuccino anybody has tasted, ever. I realise, perhaps for the first time, how exaggerated her movements are, how her happiness comes across as an affectation. My wife is mining every ounce of joy from existence to convince me that life's worth living. This has been happening for months. She's been trying to shake me from my malaise; I am dim and lustreless, therefore she must shine brighter. She is acting for an unappreciative audience of one. And how exactly have I repaid her? It would be so easy not to tell her the truth. Try to forget the knowledge the morning has brought me. Keep our lives as they are, let her live in blissful ignorance for another few months. But then what? Pretend what is about to happen will never happen? She needs to know. I owe her that much.

The strange fog has covered the walls of the café, coating the interior in a deathly haze. The sun beaming weakly through the glass door out to the car park is the only light in the room. It is the height of summer but the air temperature has dropped at least ten degrees as if a storm is coming.

Stop looking for excuses, Stornoway. The only storm is the one you've created through your own stupidity. A whirlwind of vicious grey, closing in on me from every side, and right now I'm trapped in the unsettling calm of the storm's eye, but I can't stay here forever.

'There's something I need to tell you,' I tell Hannah. Then I can't think of a word to say. Instead I concentrate on the delicate coating of chocolate on her lips. Lips that I've kissed a million, billion times; lips I fear I'll never kiss again. The ooze of the music from the speakers above us becomes a shriek, littered with bum notes, but I realise this is a trick of my mind; Hannah's not noticed anything, in fact she's tapping along to the soulless cover of a song we once used to dance to on drunken nights out. She is waiting for me to speak. Eventually she grows tired of waiting.

'It's the music, isn't it?' she says. 'You're past thirty and you've decided to give up on punk and buy one of these light jazz albums they always play in franchise coffee bars. The ones they sell at the counter, with an out-of-focus saxophone on the cover.'

'Angel, please, I—'

'It's okay, I understand,' she says, patting my hand as if consoling me. Oh Christ, she still doesn't understand, she's so obsessed with trying to be cheerful that she's failed to recognise the hell all around us. 'You've decided what's missing in your life – the only thing that'll make you content – is a Marks and Spencer sweater. A nice thick chunky one. You know this is an important step, maybe a tipping point in our relationship. You're not sure how your wife will react to this abrupt slide into middle age. But it's okay, we'll get through it together.'

Steeling myself, I spit out the words, 'Something… something's gone wrong.'

'What, worse than the time you—'

'Hannah,' I cut in, unable to bear this faux merriness, her desperate desire for a happy ending, 'I need you to listen. I really, really need you to listen.'

Hannah's smile begins to slip from her face, her expression crumbling into confusion. Disquiet steals the shine from her eyes. This is so much worse than I thought it would be, worse than I could ever have imagined. Because she is holding onto hope – ever since Jennifer, she has been clinging doggedly to the belief that life might get better – and soon, so soon, she'll be forced to let go.

'I've had some news,' I tell her. 'This morning, while you were in the shower. It… it wasn't good news.'

She winces. 'Your mum? The cancer again? Jesus, Euan, I'm so sorry, I was only messing—'

I shake my head. 'It's not to do with anyone else. Well, obviously it is. No one you know, I mean, but at the end of the day it's all down to me.'

'Darling, you're making very little sense.'

I open my mouth to speak but no sound emerges. I stare at my wife, voicelessly pleading. She is silent too. Time stretches out mercilessly. There will only be one chance to say what needs to be said. I wish I could leap fifteen minutes into the future and discover how this plays out, rewind and start again. I wish

I could see where we go from here. But there is no exit, no way of escaping; the mist has blanketed everything.

'Those times you went away,' she says at last, her voice drifting, 'I never … never thought …'

'It's not like that,' I insist.

'So what was it like?'

'It's difficult to explain.'

If only she could know without me having to tell her. But some part of her – survival instinct, I suppose – won't let herself understand. Whatever she thinks may have gone wrong, she's so far from the truth. She can't imagine, maybe she's refusing to let herself imagine. 'Here's what I propose,' my wife says. Her tone is mellow, supportive. 'We'll drive home and talk properly there. Not in a bloody coffee bar with crap jazz playing over us. You can tell me exactly what's gone wrong. I'll let you speak and I promise I won't interrupt.' She tries to take my hand again and I wish for a better life, that I could have been a better person for her, because I don't deserve her and she doesn't deserve the pain I'm about to inflict on her. 'There's honestly nothing we can't conquer together. Whatever you're going through, I'll be here for you. I promise—'

Her words are cut off by a crash. A small red apple has fallen from – where? The ceiling? Thrown by a customer? The dark girl at the counter? – and landed in the centre of our table. Then another falls, then another, then another. They hit and boom like giant hailstones. We stare upwards but all we see are the tumbling apples, falling through the greys that have shrouded the ceiling. One clips my right ear, which reddens instantly. Hannah raises her arms to protect herself from the rain of fruit but somehow none of the deluge hits her; they are all aimed at me.

'What is this?' she groans. 'What now, Euan? Just what are you doing to us now?'

I don't know. Or maybe I do know and I can't tell her. I feel dampness on my legs. The knees of my jeans are wet and stained as if I've been kneeling in mud. This is a memory... this isn't the right memory... Jesus, where is my mind going? I wish I knew what was really real here.

'What's that in your hair?' Hannah asks. My hands go to my head and come back covered in sweet-smelling purple mush.

'I don't know,' I say, 'I don't understand.' The latter words are true. The first words are lies.

Hannah shakes her head, frustrated. 'We need to go,' she says, 'we need to—'

She stops and her hand goes to her mouth. I look down and see what she has seen. Distracted by the rain of apples, I have ignored the mist. It rises above our table like a cobra set to strike, then forms itself into the shape of a hand with crooked fingers. That impossible fog hand flexes, then clamps down on my wrist. There is no pain, only an immense pressure; a sucking, draining sensation. My wife reaches out but the fog pulls me backwards and she is fading, fading, fading away in the greys.

'Stop this, Euan,' she urges, her voice echoing as if there is a vast distance between us. 'Please make it stop. What in Christ's name are you doing?'

I shut my eyes and breathe deeply and concentrate hard. Because in the moment that the fog took hold of me, I didn't even know the name of the woman sitting opposite me. I didn't know who my wife was any longer.

'Ha – Han – Hannah,' I cough out. I can't see her. I can't see her through the mist. I can only hope that she's still with me. 'Where did we first meet?'

There is nothing in my vision but greys. My wife is some-where here but I don't know where. 'Don't mess around, Euan,' her voice comes faintly. 'What are you—'

'Please, Hannah,' I say faintly, feeling the fog grasp me and flex again, my brain cramping as if everything I know and love is being squeezed into nothingness. 'I need to know.'

'Paris.' The word floats out of nowhere, battering an opening of golden light into the bleakness.

'Where did I propose?' I ask, my voice stronger now.

'On top of a mountain in the Highlands.' That golden glow has become a bright dawn.

'What tube station did I come dressed as at the party all those years ago?'

'Wimbledon,' her voice is almost a sob. 'You were Wimbledon with your stupid bloody headband and tennis racket. Why are you asking me this?'

'Because I'm finding it harder to remember,' I tell her. 'But I know you're Angel. I know that now.'

Hannah's arms reach through the golden gap in the greys and embrace me, and at her touch the clamping hand on my arm releases its grip, and that frighteningly huge pressure – that feeling of having the contents of my mind siphoned away into nothingness – dies away. We are sitting opposite one another in a franchise coffee bar. No falling apples. No greys. No strangely familiar people behind the counter. Nothing out of the ordinary whatsoever. In my relief, I've almost forgotten that I came so close to telling her. I still haven't told her. Maybe I never will.

Then I hear a sound behind me and I turn my head. A low, mechanical, unpleasant sound. It rises inexorably; whooshing and chuntering, almost chuckling. The sound has one purpose and that purpose is destruction. The sound grows louder and louder and the coffee mugs should be juddering and the walls should be shaking and everybody should be diving for cover. But no one else – not my wife nor the faceless customers – seems to hear it but me. That sound, that horrible sound. The sound of a train coming down the tracks.

31

303 days since the accident

'Why are we doing this?' he asked. 'Why are we doing this when it hurts you so much?'

She gripped the steering wheel tightly. Her guts churned and the veins in her temple seemed on the verge of exploding, festooning the windscreen with their precious contents. At that moment she almost wished for her own set of rail tracks, her own hurtling train.

'We're doing this because we can't not do this,' she said. 'There's no other choice.'

'Are you sure?' Euan asked.

She thought of what the neuropsychologist had told her early on in the treatment. Warnings which, like so many warnings, she had ignored because she so desperately wished for her husband's return. The warning that leaving the process before completion would result in random fragments of Euan's memory reels sparking into his brain, skewing his perspective, leaving him bewildered, unsure of who he truly was. She could not take responsibility for cleaving her husband's psyche in two.

'Dr Cal says we have to keep going to the end,' she said flatly. 'We have to.'

'Is Dr Cal always right?'

It was a sincere question. There was no meaning, no subtext.

This version of her husband seemed incapable of hiding his feelings from her. Euan simply wanted to know the truth. Yes, she wanted to say. Yes, Dr Cal is always right. But he hadn't been right about the woman in Portland. He hadn't been right about the creeping greys. He had hidden the truth from her: the documentary, the risks of the treatment, his knowledge of the severity of Euan's condition. That was wrong too. She wondered what else Dr Cal had got wrong. Any little mistakes, any unforeseen bugs in the program. It seemed to her that the past two years had been ruled by a succession of tiny errors. Tiny errors and appalling consequences.

'He's got us this far,' she said. It was a limp response.

'And this is the end.'

'It's not the end. It's the start.'

'So you say. So I've been told.'

Sighing, he stared out of the passenger window as the countryside blurred past them. She could not see the scar tracking down his left cheek. Irrationally she wished she could see that slender pink blemish, the crooked borderline that divided his personalities; physical proof that he was not the real Euan, not the man she had met at Café Bellevue almost a decade ago, not the man with whom she had fallen in love. He was not Euan. She wanted the old Euan back. She needed him back.

Didn't she?

They drove in silence until she reached the turning to the industrial estate. The Reel Memory Project's headquarters reared up against the skyline. It was a bright and clear day but the dull slab threatened to block out the sun. She wanted to press the brakes, kill the engine, rest for a while. But they had an appointment to keep with Dr Scott Calvin, their final session. The endgame. The time for conversation – for contemplating who they were and what they had been and what had been lost and found – had long passed. They could not stop now.

The small camp of protesters outside the chain-link fence had disappeared like dirt washed away by a downpour. Only the stubborn remnants remained. Some of the tents were evidently abandoned, the zips jingling as the canvas flaps waved in the wind. The one person she could see was the middle-aged woman with the knotted grey hair. She was sitting cross-legged, her gaze vacant as she stirred a pot bubbling on her camping stove. Her sign was propped up against her tent. For the first time she read the words inked neatly on the placard: *This is not the answer.* But if this wasn't the answer, she thought, then what was? She offered the grey lady a listless wave and was surprised when it was returned, and with a smile too. She drove on towards the gates which parted to let her through, past the familiar stern nods of the guards.

The car pulled into their regular parking spot. After today it would be given over to a new patient, a new case for Scott Calvin and his team. Perhaps a couple a little like themselves: desperate, clean out of options, but clinging onto that final shred of hope.

They slammed the doors shut and walked together towards the Ree-Mem headquarters. There was barely a sound but for the tweeting of birds. The gritting of their footsteps on the gravel was very loud.

Then Euan paused.

'I've enjoyed getting to know you,' he said.

She didn't want this conversation. Not here, not right now, not with everything else she had to endure. She wanted it to be over. She wanted to finish off this awful treatment and go home with her husband. Sit down, pour a very stiff drink and let him tell her what he was supposed to have told her before the accident. Then sleep for at least a year, probably two. That was all she wanted. She didn't have the strength to deal with these fresh – oh, why not use Dr Cal's words? – complications.

'You've always known me,' she replied. 'You'll know me a lot better when we come out of this building again.'

'That's true enough,' Euan said. He managed a twisted smile that plucked out a melancholy tune on her conscience. 'But I have always known you. Like this, I mean. I woke up and you were there. You said you were my wife. You said we had been together for years. I had to trust you right from the very start. You could have been anyone. You were telling me things I couldn't remember, and I was trying to be someone I didn't recognise at all. We didn't make sense to each other. Maybe that was why it was so hard at first.'

'Euan, I don't know—'

'I mean, I could have fallen in love with you all over again.'

The simplicity of his statement stole the breath from her lungs and her vision swum to grey. She thought of the day by the lake when they had danced to the violin player. She thought of his tentative half-smile. The way he asked for nothing but her continued presence in his life. She thought of the way he had agreed to the Ree-Mem process so readily, how he so rarely questioned her motivations, her obstinate insistence in pressing onwards with this lunatic treatment. How he was willing to sacrifice his own existence to bring back the previous version of himself.

She loved him. No, she loved him as he had once been. But that Euan had become so confused and corrupted in her brain that she had no idea who her husband had been before the accident.

The Euan standing before her now, well … she knew everything about him. He had arrived in her life as a fully grown, fully functioning man who could walk and talk but had no knowledge of what he had once been. She had been there for almost every moment of his short existence. For love and for duty, she had tended him. Comforted and consoled him, tried to spark his memories with stories and photographs and silly games. Eventually, her sanity almost at snapping point, she had guided him into the path of the Reel Memory Project. She had been a good wife, a dutiful wife; all with the intention of casting this Euan away as soon as the old Euan returned. If she and Dr Cal succeeded, her husband would return to her as he had been before that summer's day ten months ago and this man would disappear uncomplainingly into the ether. Understanding exploded in her brain and it was the sickest joke she had ever heard. Today was a day she would commit murder. Today she would kill this Euan. She would kill him out of love.

Sensing her distress, he shook his head. 'Sorry. I don't know what I'm talking about. It's stupid but—'

'Euan, please stop talking,' she broke in. Her heart was larruping in her chest, her breath hitching. 'I can't take it. I really, really can't.'

Reaching out, he pulled her towards him and she could not help sinking into his embrace.

'I only wanted you to know,' he whispered quietly into her hair, 'that whatever I did ... did before ... well, I want to tell you that I'm sorry. I don't know why I would have done anything to cause you pain, to ruin our lives. I can't ever know that. I wish ... I wish I could go back and find myself and stop him before ... before he did whatever he did.'

'Euan, please—'

He broke their embrace, holding her gently away from him. She saw that her tears were on his cheeks. She could feel his tears on her cheeks too. Hesitantly he reached out to smooth away the worry lines on her forehead with his fingertips and it was the most tender touch she could ever remember.

'I don't know why anyone would want to hurt you,' he said. 'You're the best person I've ever known.'

She managed a shaky laugh. 'I'm the only person you've ever known.'

He laughed too. 'I think the point still stands.'

At that moment, seeing the depth of trust in his eyes, her resolve wavered. She knew what she needed to do. She had to go into the Ree-Mem building and into her husband's memories for the final time and bring back the original version of Euan. Was that what she wanted, though? Did she really want the old Euan back? The man whose mind, the further she delved into it, seemed viciously fractured – warped by grief and unhappiness and whatever memories still remained unknown to her. Could she ever put that man's mind back together again? Was he the man she truly, honestly wanted?

Dr Cal's voice spoke for her. The time for questions, he told her sternly, was over. Now it was time for action, not thoughts. The endgame.

'Come on,' she said at last. 'We need to do this.'

Euan nodded. He looked resigned but resolute. He ran his hands through his hair, smoothed down the lapels of his jacket, staring straight ahead at the yawning open doors of the Ree-Mem building. She saw his jaw was clenched with the determination of a soldier marching onto the killing fields. He wasn't so innocent; he knew what this day would cost him and he was prepared to confront it, accept it, for her. She felt an urge – sudden but powerfully strong – to grab Euan, pull him back, get into their car and drive away. But Dr Cal had warned her that she had to follow this process through to the very end; in a way, this was all his fault. She couldn't stop what she was about to do. Her heart hardened as her fingertips lightly caressed the book of matches in the pocket of her coat.

The process had become messy, tangled, broken – but she could fix it, she told herself. Once she knew everything, she could fix it. She was quite sure, almost sure, that she could fix it.

So she followed her husband as he made his way towards the doorway. Jonas met them at the foyer, the light from the arched roof of the hangar glinting off the piercing in his brow. The young Australian said nothing but nodded at them both, unable to meet her eyes.

Euan paused before they entered the Reel Memory Project for the final time. He told her, 'After today everything will be better.'

She wondered why the words sounded like a eulogy.

32

The day of the accident

Hannah is crying so hard that I doubt she can even see the road. I shouldn't have let her get behind the wheel. She had seemed fine when we left the coffee shop but at some point on the drive home, understanding had arrowed into her brain. As the first splodges of rain dotted our windscreen, she let out a short sob and stared across at me with an expression of utter betrayal and in that moment I knew all hope was lost. She couldn't lie to herself any longer. Every worry, every suspicion, every dark thought she has ever had about me is chiselling away at her sanity and the anger-anguish is crackling off her. She needs to pull over, compose herself. Instead she keeps driving. Too fast.

A thunderous summer downpour is ringing off our car's chassis like bullets. The sky is a queasy shade of slate. The hottest summer in years and this savagely dreich day is mirroring my thoughts. Visibility is barely a few feet despite the madly flapping wipers. I'm scared that Hannah might veer off the road but a sick cowardly part of me prays for an accident. Anything to avoid the conversation we're about to endure. I have to tell her now; we've gone far too far. I have to tell her. I've promised to tell her. I can't ever tell her.

Up ahead I can see the level crossing. The stop lights and the barrier. We have sat and grumbled amiably here many a time on our drive home, waiting for the fast train to London or one of the clunky old goods trains to rush past. We're coming up to the crossing. *STOP when lights show*, the familiar sign reads, although the fog around us is too thick to see that warning now. She keeps driving. The lights have flicked to red. A train is on its way. My wife maintains a steady pressure on the accelerator, then – with a harrowed gasp like an animal caught in a trap – she pushes her foot down. The car bursts forward. We won't make the crossing. We can't make the crossing.

'Hannah, the fucking tracks!'

We are speeding but time seems to be running in slow motion. Despite my panic – or maybe because of it – I experience everything in minute detail. The grille behind us swoops down. My head snaps over my shoulder and I see the falling metal just missing the tail end of our car. The front wheel judders over the first track. The gate in front of us descends and I see it smashing into the windscreen, slicing us in half. My wife slams on the brakes and we skid to a halt inches from the barrier, my skull thumping back into the headrest, the seatbelt wrapping around my neck as if trying to strangle me. The grille grins chummily back at me with a shark's smile. There are tracks either side of us and a barrier in front and behind. There is nowhere to go. We're trapped.

'Jesus Christ!' I snap. 'What the hell was that? What stupid point are you trying to prove?'

'Tell me, Euan,' Hannah demands, weeping, her forehead resting on the steering wheel. 'What have you done? Just what have you done?'

Caught between fear and anger, I take a deep breath, trying to compose myself. My wife is being completely irrational so I must be totally rational.

'We have to get out,' I say gently. 'A train is going to come. So we have to get out. Now.'

A plastic strap from one of the windscreen wipers has come loose. It is dragging across the window with a scree-scree sound that might drive me insane if I hear it for too long. The muscles in my forearms are humming with adrenaline. I fight the urge to jam my fingers into Hannah's seatbelt lock and drag her out of the passenger door, kicking and screaming.

Instead I mime turning the key in the ignition. Faintly I can hear the tooting of horns on the safe side of the barrier, the onlookers alerting us to a danger that we've somehow missed. 'The car,' I say mindlessly. 'We'll need to buy a new car.'

'Oh, fuck the car, Euan,' she cries, her head snapping up. 'You're worried about wrecking a car? What about us? Did you ever think about us?'

'I'm sorry.'

'No, you're not. Not really.'

She still has the steering wheel clenched in a tight grip. Her bare forearms are shaking, the tendons standing out starkly on her fishbelly-white wrists. In fact her whole body is shaking. With mounting horror, I realise that the railway lines are transmitting their vibrations through our vehicle. I can't see the train, the surroundings are too fogged up. But I can sense it coming. Fast.

'I am sorry. Truly.' I extend my hand to her. The silver band on my third-left finger is the only brightness in the scene. 'If you come out the car with me, I'll explain everything.'

Hannah shakes her head. 'You won't. You'll lie again. You're good at it, you've been doing it for ages. And it was my fault too. I was blinding myself, chanting *yadayadayada* like a kid so I wouldn't understand what you were trying to say. See no evil, hear no evil, right?'

My tongue flickers over my lips. 'No lies. I promise. I'm done. It's just … it's complicated.'

She turns to me. Her eyes are reddened, her face has a corpse's pallor. There is no love left in her gaze; we could be strangers.

'Ah, so the clichés begin.' She manages a tight, sour smile. 'Real life is so very complicated. Isn't it, Euan? I'm not falling for that bullshit. We're not going home. Right now I've got your full, undivided attention. At least right now you'll tell me the truth.'

'Hannah, this is crazy.'

'I'm not leaving this car until you tell me what you've done. Exactly what you've done.'

Slapping my forehead in frustration, I bark at her, 'For Christ's sake, you'll kill us both.'

She starts to weep again. 'And living is better?'

'Yes. Obviously.'

'Are you so sure, Euan?'

'Of course, I mean, I—'

My words collapse and atrophy on my tongue as a dull roaring fills my senses. I think of what happened to Jennifer, I think of how we fell apart afterwards, I think of what I did in my pathetic attempt to feel something other than grief and misery. I try to remember the happiest years of our marriage, those golden times, but the memories seem to have been swallowed by the lifeless mist that's all around us now.

I reach for her hand and she tugs it away. 'Don't do this to me,' I beg her. 'For God's sake, Hannah, don't do this to us.'

She leans in close, kissing distance away from me. She speaks slowly and firmly but I can barely hear her above the chuntering bellow of the train. 'I want. To know. Everything.'

And I'm about to tell her. I need to tell her – if only to get her out, get her to safety. The car is rocking like a boat tossed on stormy seas. We have barely seconds left.

The train's air horn booms and the sound seems to shock Hannah back to her senses. Her green eyes widen and her mouth falls open and she stares at me with an odd innocence; her expression heartbreaking in its simple confusion. In that moment she is not a stranger any longer, sick with malice. She is my wife, and she loves me, and I love her, and we can conquer anything together, but have we left it too late?

Hannah gasps, 'Euan, I'm—'

The driver's door is yanked open. A man with rain-sodden hair reaches in and grabs hold of her. In that moment I see he has a perfectly bland appearance; a faceless hero. Clawing at her seatbelt, the man's arms encircle Hannah's waist and she flies backwards with a startled yelp. Her final words are left hanging in the empty air. A fragile apology, soon to be shattered by the shriek of mutilated metal. The unknown rescuer drags her into the culvert and they slide together down the slippery wet grass, rolling towards safety. The man's body is pinning her to the sodden earth but she is struggling and she stares up and our gazes meet. Hannah reaches out to me but she is so far away. Far enough away that I can breathe a huge, long-pent-up sigh of relief. She never has to know the whole truth. Despite the chaos all around me, I feel a great calmness descend.

Seeing my wife for the final time, I mouth three simple words to her. Then I turn and stare into the blank grey face of my onrushing fate.

The sound explodes and there is nothingness.

33

Betrayal Reels (Volume 1)

The Crossing – Blackout Bar – The Dark Girl

The car rests on the tracks at the level crossing. I feel a strange calm, lethargy easing out the tension in my muscles. My hands are on the wheel, the car is trapped between the metal grilles on the train tracks and I am trapped inside the car, trapped with nothing for company but my own guilt. It would be easy to stay sitting here, letting whatever is about to happen simply happen.

What has brought me to this place? I don't remember driving here. My mind is so damned fuzzy.

'Help,' I say quietly, to nobody in particular. 'Please help me.'

Then I feel a presence beside me in the car. I turn. A woman with green eyes and white-blonde hair is sitting next to me. My wife. I had thought I was alone. Somehow I've dragged her into my disaster. Then again, I suppose it changes very little. Nothing can alter what will happen. So I let my head rest on the steering wheel, feeling its cool leather against my sweaty skin. Car horns hoot around us. Either side of the barrier there must be onlookers, rubberneckers, gawpers. Let them watch, I genuinely don't care any longer. Let them watch the guilty man receive his sentence of execution.

'Reverse,' Hannah says. 'Now.'

'Can't,' I reply. 'Trapped.' In every sense of the word.

'We have to get out,' she says. Her voice is gentle but firm. 'A train is coming. We have to get out. Now.'

She slides the seatbelt from around her neck and lays the palm of her hand on my shaking shoulders. Is she trying to comfort me? Is this the way out? Can I leave the car here – leave all these rotten old memories here – and look forward to a better future?

'The car—' I say.

'Forget the car, Euan. We have to get out. Now. Please.'

'Then what?' I ask.

'We find our way home. We sit down, pour a very stiff drink, and talk about … whatever. And I strongly suspect we'll need to buy a new car.'

'Then what?'

Worrying at the skin around her fingers, Hannah breathes out deeply. 'Well, I suppose we pick up where we left off.'

Feeling a plunging sensation in my stomach, I roll my eyes towards her. 'Great. Wonderful. Such a tempting offer.'

'What do you want?' she asks. She is fighting for control, tenderness tinged with panic. 'What's wrong, Euan? Tell me, please. What the hell's the matter with you?'

I let my head fall onto the wheel again. She reaches out for my hand and I pull it away. 'Don't do this to me,' she says, her voice thick and choked. 'For God's sake, Euan, don't do this to us.'

'I think I've done enough,' I reply. These are my words, surely, so why do I feel like I'm reading out lines in someone else's play?

She speaks to me, screams at me, begs and implores me, but my treacherous brain mutes every word. Finally she pushes herself out of the car and I feel such blessed relief. Hannah has gone and I am alone to face my fate. Surely she will not come back.

But here she is again, rapping on my window. 'Please,' she urges. 'Come on, please.'

In less than a minute Hannah will be rid of me forever. I can only hope she is sensible enough not to look at the final moment. I can only hope that she will move on; that she finds someone to love her, that she finds happiness in life. She deserves better from this world. She certainly deserves better than me.

'Now!' her voice rises to a shriek. 'Get out, Euan, please! Look at me. Please.'

My eyes squeeze slowly shut.

Surely it will end now. Surely. Hannah will run from the car – run to safety, run far away from me – and the train will come and take me with it and my problems are solved. I will depart this life in solitude and my wife will be left with a better memory of me.

But then the car door swings open and time seems to stop.

Hannah is back in the car. She has come back to me. The train is eating up the last few-score yards to the conclusion of its fateful journey. So close now, the car is rocking and I can hear the air horn bellowing, yet she has decided to step back inside the car with me. Why?

'Can't you at least tell me the truth, Euan?'

My shoulders slumped, I shake my head, then nod. I don't know any longer. I barely know what's real.

'What did you do, Euan?' Hannah asks again. Her voice is almost inaudible, yet it echoes in my brain like thunder. 'Tell me, now that we're close to the end. What did you do that was so very wrong?'

I stare at my wife. Her face is so pale it is almost ghostly, her hair is like a burning halo, her eyes are shining emeralds. She is an angel; but this is an angel of vengeance, hard and pitiless. I know that after I have finished my short, unpleasant story she will cast me from her life forever. The train is coming. But somehow I know it won't arrive until I have finished telling my wife what I must tell her. It doesn't matter any longer. I'm done.

Defeated, I take Hannah's hands in mine.

'Let me tell you a story,' I say. 'Let me tell you what went wrong.'

The boy was drunk, falling. There was a can of cider in his left hand and a small squat bottle of brandy tucked neatly into the inside pocket of his jacket. The knuckles of his right hand were swollen and purpled from a confrontation he could scarcely remember. One or two drinks with a work colleague had turned into five or six, then the colleague had fled back to his Surrey commuter belt nest. But the boy had the taste of alcohol on his tongue and such a horrible howling emptiness deep inside. That vacuum needed to be filled, if only temporarily.

So he continued his lonely stumble around the backstreets of the East End of London, squinting against the ugly glow of the streetlights, kicking through the rubble of discarded takeaway cartons and beer cans. He was almost praying for the smash of a bottle over his head or the press of a blade into the small of his back. A young man with a sway in his swagger, wearing a slightly tatty old suit with a smear of blood on his white shirt. He might as well carry a sign reading *Please Mug Me*. He would welcome the boots in the ribs, the cracking of his skull, thank his attackers for bringing down the shutters on reality. Anything to fill the hole which had ripped open in his soul after that day at the hospital, after Jennifer.

He stopped to urinate against a graffiti-daubed railway bridge, resting his forehead against the low wall. The rough bricks felt wonderfully cool. He heard the screech and whine of a train passing underneath the bridge, craning his neck to see the blurred lights of the carriages carrying weary workers back to their homes. But there was no home for him any longer, only a house that seemed so dreadfully empty in the absence of its expected arrival.

He thought of the cards on the mantelpiece. Those carefully worded condolences – *Sorry for your loss* seemed to be the most popular, as if their friends and relatives somehow felt the need to apologise. Hand-drawings and watercolour paintings of flowers and trees, images of newly blooming life. They were mocking him. One day, when Hannah was out, he had snapped and stuffed the cards into a black plastic sack and thrown them away. When his wife returned, she had stared at the empty mantelpiece and he ignored the hurt on her face. It was better that the cards were out of sight. It was better that they did not talk about it. No one could help them. No one.

Hannah tried to talk about Jennifer and he met her words with chilly indifference. It seemed no words would fit right, no words would ever work again, so he said nothing. Instead Hannah talked constantly to fill in the gaps. She spoke of wanting to go back to work, of painting a seaside mural in the spare room that was to have been Jennifer's room, of visiting her sister on the West Coast of America. Yes, she spoke of everything and nothing and each one of her words sounded like an accusation. Because it was his fault, all of this. His faulty sperm, his inadequacies as a man, his failure as a husband. For better, for worse, for richer, for poorer, in sickness and in health. They had pledged these vows to one another but what had they really known of the bad times? Up until Jennifer they had experienced only light. They were hopelessly unprepared to make it through the darkness.

Shambling on autopilot, he realised he had followed the path of the railway tracks to the vastly yawning metal structure of a train station. He could catch the last service in fifteen minutes. Within an hour he could be in bed, nestling into Hannah's warmth, inhaling the fresh hay scent of her hair. They could wake up together and plan their future. They had so much to do, so much to see together. Life had bent and bowed them yet they would not be defeated. They were stronger than that. Together they were unbeatable, unbreakable.

But while these pleasant fantasies drifted through the boy's mind, his feet took a path of their own – stumbling across the street towards a place with thumping music and dingy lights and a wide-open door, welcoming him inside.

The bar reeked of stale beer and sweat. It was packed and humid, every shuffling step bringing a jostle or a sharp elbow in the ribs. At the bar he ordered a continental beer that his drink-slushed tongue could barely pronounce and a double whisky. Hoisting himself onto a stool, he knocked back the harsh spirit, then buried his face in the lager. A quiet voice questioned whether Hannah might wake in the night and wonder why he hadn't returned. But at this point that worry seemed like a very small worry indeed.

The people in the bar were a strange mixture of the capital's after-dark fauna. City workers in smart suits rubbed elbows with green-haired punks, market porters standing stoically alongside hardened alcoholics with red-raw faces. No other circumstance but a need to keep drinking could have brought them together. There was no better place to be because there was nowhere else to go.

So where did he fit into this scene? Where was the faction for heartsick, grieving young men for whom the night out – for whom life itself – had taken a depressing turn? There were no friends for him here. Only people who had no one.

He had someone. That was what he should have remembered when the waves of melancholy threatened to drown him. He was not like these people. He had someone special waiting for him.

Suddenly the boy felt lonelier than he could ever recall. This was not where he needed to be. He belonged at home, with his wife. He drained his beer in a huge gulp. If he ran fast he could get to the station in time, make the last train. Home within the hour. Home to Hannah. The next day – he had waited so long but, please God, not too long – they would talk about Jennifer. He would open up to her, tell her exactly how he felt. He would listen to her too, finally; hold her close as she screamed out everything she ached to say. He would make it all right again. He would talk, he would listen, he would be there for her. Tomorrow was the start of the rest of their lives together.

Then a hand fell on his shoulder.

He turned and stared into huge, wide-spaced dark eyes; the shading between pupil and iris indefinable. The girl was tall and slender with a shock of black hair hanging over her forehead in a ragged fringe. She tilted her head, showing off a slightly hooked nose that should have made her ugly but was oddly fetching. Her jaw was strong, almost masculine. She wore a leather jacket and purple jeans that clung to her thighs like a second skin. He caught a scent of rich, dark honey.

'Will you protect me?' she said.

He blinked.

'Those guys have been hassling me,' the girl went on, hooking a thumb over her shoulder at a group of City boys playing pool. He noticed two of them – a short weasel-faced man and a chubbier friend with buttery curls – were eyeing up her denim-clad rear. He saw the twin leers on their faces and felt a twist of anger in his gut. 'Not that you don't expect it in a place like this, but I really don't want to walk out of here alone in case they follow me.'

'I'm really not sure—'

'I saw you come in,' she said. Her voice was clipped, full of staccato notes. 'You could be looking for someone. You could be meeting me here.'

'So if I pretend—'

'So if you pretend to be my boyfriend, they might piss off.'

He saw a white track of scar tissue running through the hairs of her eyebrow, perhaps a piercing from years ago that had healed over. Her features seemed slightly too big for her face – her eyes, her lips, her nose – but somehow this made her even more attractive. The girl was electric; as if he could touch her skin and the explosive charge would fling him right across the room.

The boy laughed, the hit of double whisky now throbbing through his skull. Suddenly that resolve to leave was very shaky indeed. 'I'm sure I can try,' he said easily. 'What's the worst that could happen?'

'What's that accent?' the girl asked, casually placing a hand on his wrist, sending a tremor shivering through the muscles of his arm.

'Scottish,' he said, finishing his pint, 'and since we're already fully embroiled in this charade, would you care for a drink?'

'Is this the Celtic charm I have been warned against?' she asked, a suggestive smile crossing her face. Her mispronunciation of Celtic – *cell* instead of *kell* – somehow charmed him even more.

'That's really more of an Irish thing,' he replied, his tongue feeling thick and sludgy, his words threatening to tie themselves up in knots. 'It's the lilting accent. We Caledonians sound drunk or aggressive, generally both.'

He could tell the besuited pool players were looking at him now, sizing him up. Invincible with drink, he fixed them with an icy stare until they dropped their gazes and returned to the game.

'It's a beautiful country, Scotland,' the dark girl said. Her own accent filtered in and out of her words like radio static; a transatlantic drawl with occasional spiked consonants. Maybe Eastern European by way of American films? It was impossible to tell.

'Scotland's the most beautiful country in the world,' he agreed with woozy nostalgia, signalling to the barmaid and ordering more drinks. This was not really happening, he thought – perhaps he had fallen asleep watching a movie that had imprinted itself on his mind, or maybe he was dreaming and sleepwalking. 'So long as you avoid north-west Edinburgh, south-west Glasgow and the whole of Dundee. Up where I'm from, the chances of getting your head kicked in outside a pub like this are quite high.'

'The place I come from originally, it only has one bar. Very rough bar. Outside there, last summer, a man had his head cut off.'

His eyebrows shot up involuntarily. 'Good grief.'

'Yes.'

'I take it you try not to spill anyone's pint there?'

'No. Especially not the pint of the local bobby. He's a really violent guy. You say this word, right – bobby?'

'You can say it, but you'll sound like you're from the Thirties.'

'A joker, right?' She blew out her cheeks in mock exasperation.

'English confuses me. The language, I mean. I've lived here five months and nothing makes sense. Why so much slang, why do London people have so many different words to people from elsewhere?'

'I don't know. It's how we bond with people from our hometown, I suppose. And shut out strangers. Wouldn't want to accidentally make friends with somebody, would we?'

The dark girl laughed. 'So we're both foreigners here.'

He paid for the drinks, then with a complicit wink she ordered a brace of tequila shots. Surreptitiously – without allowing himself to think about what he was doing – he slipped off his wedding ring. His little finger pressing the ring against the flesh of his palm, he made a show of taking a book of matches – emblazoned with the motif *A day wasted is never a wasted day*, below the name *Blackout Bar* – from the bowl on the bar top. Then with one fluid movement he dropped both his wedding ring and the matchbox into the inside pocket of his suit jacket, where the silver band clinked against the near-empty brandy bottle.

'I've been thinking I might save up a little,' the girl said quietly, and he leaned closer to hear her over the background bar hubbub. 'Get a cheap flight back. Get my old job again. No one would have replaced me anyway, I'm sure. No one new ever arrives in my hometown. People only ever leave.'

'Ah, come on, London's not that bad,' he said, feeling himself reeled into intimacies like a marlin accepting the certain fate of the bait and tackle. 'Admittedly there's high taxes, pollution and overcrowding. But on the bright side there's bad nightclubs and binge drinking and the temptation of casual ... eh ... violence.'

She picked up on his stutter before the last word and raised an eyebrow, the gesture so archly seductive, and in that movement the contract was sealed. He felt nauseous and weak and sordid, but also – for the first time in so long – strangely good. This was an emotion almost forgotten; a low emotion certainly, but an emotion other than grief and pain and loss. He remembered his father's words all those years ago: No one would help him through life but himself. So would this help him – help him heal, help him move on, help him forget about Jennifer for one solitary blissful second – or was he simply unable to help himself?

'I'm sick of these people,' the girl said, hooking a disparaging thumb at the pool players. 'Do you want to find another bar? Somewhere with fewer men in expensive suits boasting about the gargantuan size of their ... wallets?'

The way she said the word *gargantuan* – chewing the word over like a delicious morsel – set off miniaturised explosions in his brain. Gooseflesh pocked his arms. He felt suddenly cold then warm all over. Her small pink tongue tracked over her lower lip and the dark girl was plucking the sweetest spots of his emotions like a virtuoso musician and – oh God – how she knew it.

'That sounds great to me,' he told her, wondering why he felt a chill wind blowing through the stuffy stinking air of the bar. He said again, 'What's the worst that could happen?'

Later, much later, he wondered who exactly he was trying to convince. All he knew was that he was trying to fill that gaping hole in the centre of his chest. Casting his gaze upwards he offered a silent curdled prayer. Just for that night let him be a man without responsibilities, troubles, burdens. Just for that night let him be a man stripped of the awful knowledge of Jennifer and the hospital ward. Just for that night let him be a man without memory.

The pair of them scraped back their chairs and made for the

exit. The dark girl – her name, he still didn't even know her damn name – pulled open the door of the bar and gestured for him to follow, steering the boy into whatever future lay ahead.

34

Betrayal Reels (Volume 2)

Marta – Bath Time – Breaking Things

He remembered the cracks in the walls of her flat, covered with multi-coloured fragments of carpet fabric in a failed attempt at bohemian chic. The smell of cigarette smoke and exotically spiced perfume. He remembered the clink of their glasses as they finished off the last of the brandy. Her question – so innocently spoken and yet so loaded. *Are we going to bed now?* His lips were too numb to form a coherent reply and so he had simply nodded.

After it was done, he and the dark girl had lain together, breathing heavily, their bodies coated with a light film of sweat. Her hand stroked the rough sprouting of stubble on his cheek, his fingers traced along the nubs of her spine. He stared at the imprint of tattoo ink on the small of her back. Two gift boxes, their colourful bows wound up in one another, forming the shape of a sideways figure-of-eight. *Why did you get that tattoo?* he had asked her, finally finding his voice. *I like presents*, the girl told him, unfazed by the oddness of his question. *That's understandable*, he replied, *but it's hardly a coherent reason to brand yourself for life.* She had only shrugged and said, *I just like presents.*

He remembered the taste of her. He remembered the contours of her body as she threw back her head and cried out. He couldn't remember the last time he had made Hannah feel that way. He couldn't remember the last time he had felt so wanted, if only for a night.

But it hadn't been just a night.

Impossible colours swirled in the whiteness, then formed into definable shapes. The boy found himself in a bathroom clouded with steam. As the fug cleared he realised who was in here with him. He stared down at the naked girl reclining in the bath. Suds did a poor job of concealing her breasts; the flesh flushed pinkish with the heat of the water. She fixed him with a challenging stare.

The girl's name was Marta. The boy did not know how he knew this.

'I believe there's room in here for one more,' she said, stretching out languorously in the tub as if to disprove the point.

Uncomfortably he smoothed the front of his houndstooth suit jacket. The fabric was fine and pleasing to the touch – a pointless expenditure on Savile Row to prove that he was a success, a mighty man, a fellow of consequence in the world. He had bought the suit soon after he met Marta. The soft material was like armour. When he was wearing that suit he wasn't himself. He could be another person, a totally different Euan George Stornoway. A man his wife would never know.

'Thanks for the offer,' he said, 'but I'm already dressed.'

She dug her fingers into the bubbles and blew him a kiss. The bird's nest of foam came to rest on the front of his suit trousers.

'Hey,' he protested faintly, wiping away the suds. The bubbles had left a small island of moisture on the fabric of the crotch. The significance of the stain was not lost on the boy.

The girl rolled onto her front with the grace of a seal. She knew, he thought. Christ, she knew exactly what she was doing to him – had he ever met someone whose every physical act was loaded with such sensuality? Through the light spattering of bath suds he could see that now-familiar tattoo on the small of her back, the gift box bows wound together in the dual circles of infinity.

'I have to get back now,' he said. But his voice trembled, so weak and acquiescent.

'Oh, do you now?' she asked. The heat of the bathroom, the heat of her, made him dizzy. He wasn't in his right mind when he was with her. He wondered if he could plead temporary insanity. A madness that had lasted almost two months.

Kneeling beside the tub, he ran his index finger along the nubs of her spine, tracing over the inked flesh of her back, then – hating himself but unable to stop – he allowed his hand to slip further down into the warm embrace of the water. The girl giggled, kicking her heels, churning the bathwater. A soapy wave sopped over the rim of the tub and splashed the cuff of his jacket.

'Now look what you've done,' he snapped.

'I can do a lot more.'

'I'm sure you can,' he said. 'But I really have to go.'

Instead she scooped a measure of water in her hands and poured it over his head. He didn't even see it coming. Choking on the sick soapy taste, he pushed back from her, his vision shrouded. His eyesight returned to see Marta send another cascade at his shirt with a kick of her foot.

'Now you try and go,' she said with a smug smile.

'Bitch,' he gasped, blinking away the stinging liquid. His clothes were soaked and clammy, the floor of the hotel bathroom a tiled lake. A man could drown in an inch of water, he remembered somebody telling him once.

There was no going back to the office now. Hooking his arms around her, he pulled her over the side of the tub, relishing the glimmer of shock that crossed her face in the momentary shifting of control. The girl landed on top of him; a soft, slippery form. As he raked his nails down her back she let out a sharply drawn breath, cursing him in her own language. His lips mashed down on hers, their teeth connecting. She straddled him, pushing him down, the back of his head colliding painfully with the unyielding porcelain of the bathtub, the pain bringing him back to some sort of sense. He held out his palms in wordless appeal. His gaze tracked over the gentle curve of her stomach, the deep rise and fall of her chest, then finally to her face. An almost childlike pout played around her lips. The kohl had run from her eyelids, streaming down her cheeks in dark tears. He could not tell whether she was excited or furious.

'You have to go?' she said.

'I only wanted—'

'You get what you wanted and then you have to go, right?' she demanded.

'Marta, please, I—'

Her lips twisted and her hands went to her cheeks, pulling down the skin, turning her face into a fright-mask. 'Please shut up.'

'I don't understand, I thought we were only—'

'Just fucking shut up,' she snapped, taking a swipe at him. Her black-painted nails dug into the skin below his cheekbones, abrading a few layers of flesh. With a heave he shunted her body off him. Her bare back hit the bathroom door, slamming it shut; the sound as loud as a bomb. The make-up bag perched precariously on the rim of the sink toppled over. Her pocket mirror spilled out and broke on the tiles. He caught sight of his face and the glass shards reflected a splintered mask of guilt. He tried to go to her but slipped back down on the sodden floor, hitting his head again on the side of the tub, and everything was chaos in the steam and sweat.

They stared at one another like boxers who had landed knockout punches simultaneously and were only just coming back to consciousness.

He wiped the back of his hand against his cheek. It came back bloody. 'That really hurt,' he said. She stared back, sullen and defiant. Despite everything he still wanted her. He wondered what they could be without complications. Then he realised he was thinking of Hannah – his wife, his love, his life – as a complication in this affair, and the certainty hit him that he must be one of the worst men alive. He should have ended it after the first night. Or the second, or the third. Now their affair had become routine – skulking around behind his wife's back, meeting for afternoon sessions in the sort of hotels where rooms could be hired by the hour – and the reasons for starting it were unclear to him. He had only wanted an escape from the grey routine that had entrapped their lives after Jennifer died. An escape from the unspoken accusations – Hannah didn't even realise she was making them – as she repainted the baby room and made plans for a future that would never be brightened by a child's laughter. Her miscarriage had all been his fault; the doctors told him differently, but he was certain of it. He could never give Hannah what she needed to feel complete. Then Marta had stumbled into his life at the exact point at which he was most vulnerable. He had only wanted to feel like a man again – a strong man, a potent man, an attractive man – rather than a miserable failure. But there were no excuses. The dark girl was collateral damage in the internal war of his life and now he had hurt her. He didn't even want to think of the suffering he would cause his wife if she ever found out.

Shuffling over to Marta on his knees, he pulled off his soaking suit jacket and laid it around her bare shoulders in a meaningless gesture of gallantry. He gathered up the splinters of the pocket mirror and tried to piece them back together.

'I'm sorry,' he said.

She shook her head. 'I'm more sorry. I break things. I always have done. I can't help myself.'

'What do you mean?'

'Do you want to hear an old story?' she asked, resting her head on his shoulder. He could not push her away. Not when she was looking at him in that way.

'If you like,' he said.

'When I was six years old, my big sister had a toy. One of those … those great big balloons that children bounce about on. What are they called?'

'Space hoppers?'

'Space hoppers,' she nodded, tenderly wiping the blood off his cheek. 'Always jealous of it. Not allowed one myself – too young. But one day when Lili was out with her friends, and my parents were in the garden, I went into the shed where the space hopper was. I only wanted to play with it, but I broke it instead. Took a hammer from my father's toolbox, twisted the claw into the balloon until it popped. Bang. No more space hopper.'

'Did your sister know it was you?'

She laughed. 'You're supposed to be the smart guy, Euan. Who else was it going to be? I had to pay her back out of my pocket money for nearly a year. All for what? I couldn't have the toy, so I broke it. Funny, right?'

He shrugged again, placing a kiss on her forehead. 'Kids can be nasty like that. They don't realise how cruel they can be.'

'Grown-ups too,' said Marta. She pushed him away, holding him at arm's length, the sombre blackness in her eyes threatening to swallow him whole. 'Why are you doing this to your wife? What have I helped break?'

He was about to answer – the words were right there on the tip of his tongue – but suddenly the bathroom dissolved, and they were somewhere else entirely.

35

Betrayal Reels (Volume 3)

A Picnic – Messy Endings – The Phone Call

The air smelled of freshly mown grass but there was an electric tang in the atmosphere promising a storm. The first drops of rain had already started to land on the girl's shoulders, seeping down in small rivulets to the hem of her summer dress. She was holding a basket in her hand, swinging it back and forth.

'Marta—' he called.

There was a low growl of thunder and the clouds exploded. The rain plastered his white shirt to his chest within seconds. The dark girl's dress was clinging to her body like a second skin. He felt no yearning, only a tired revulsion – not at her, but at himself. He wondered at what point their affair had become routine; a parallel marriage, with a little more intrigue and a great deal less love. But still they had pushed on, blindly driving towards something impossible to catch, destroying everything pure in their wake. She broke things, and so did he, and they couldn't stop themselves. Just a cruel trick from whichever celestial engineer designed them – an in-built fault in the system, a malicious bug in the program.

'We should go back,' he told her.

The girl's hair was hanging over her face in a shining black cowl. 'Go back where?' she said.

'I don't know why we came here,' he said, sinking down into

the long grass, feeling the moisture seep through the tough fabric of his jeans. 'I don't understand any of this.'

'We came for a picnic,' she said, lifting the basket like a prosecutor displaying the first item of evidence. 'A fun day out in the sun, right?'

Then he remembered why he had brought her here, to the pleasant copse by the man-made reservoir in an isolated suburb at the end of the train line. This place had no memories for either of them. This was a place where they would not be disturbed. This was a place where he could leave her.

The dark girl knew it. Before it had even happened, she knew it.

'This place is quiet,' she said. 'Is that so nobody can hear me scream?'

'Is that what you're planning to do?'

She shrugged. The casualness of the gesture couldn't mask the pain on her face; twisting her lips, dampening her eyes. 'Perhaps.'

Instead she pulled a roll of bread from the basket and hurled it at him, missing by some distance. He stayed sitting down, his hands clasped as if in prayer, mouthing the speech that he had been rehearsing for days. *We aren't right for each other ... I won't ever make you happy ... this is my fault ... this is all my fault ... I'm sorry.* The contents of their picnic basket thumped around him. A carton of potato salad. A wedge of camembert. Then Marta found a packet of apples, ripped it open and began to throw. She threw hard and her aim was good. There seemed to be far more apples than could conceivably fit into one punnet; the rain had been replaced by a torrent of hard fruit. One apple clipped his right ear, which reddened and stung.

'Bastard,' she spat.

'Marta, please,' he said, shaking his head, suddenly very tired. 'This doesn't solve anything.'

'Fucking selfish fucking—'

He bowed his head, feeling the fruit slam against his chest, his shoulders, his arms. 'This is just childish,' he muttered.

Standing over him now, the girl grabbed a packet of blueberries and mashed the fruit into his hair. Sticky dark sugars mixed with the rain and ran down his face. Wiping the purple mush away from his eyes, he stared upward to see her swinging a glass bottle of ketchup down towards his forehead.

'Jesus!' He rolled quickly to the side, sweeping his right leg under hers and bringing her to the ground with a wet thump. 'What are you, some kind of psychopath?'

He pinned her to the soft earth with a knee on each shoulder. 'Drop the bottle,' he told her calmly. She snapped at him in her own language. 'Drop the bottle, Marta,' he repeated, applying a little extra pressure to her arm. With a curse, she let go of the bottle and he tossed it away into the bushes.

'Are you going to be calm?' he asked.

She breathed out heavily. 'Okay.'

'Promise?'

'Whatever.'

They disengaged and she pulled her knees up to her chest, rocking back and forth.

'I'm sorry,' he said. 'I don't even have to tell you why we're here. Maybe because I knew you'd scream and shout, so I took you to this place so no one would hear you. Because I'm a coward. This … everything … was so, so wrong. You don't deserve this. You deserve to be rid of me.'

'I can't get rid of you,' she said. 'What you put in me.'

'We have to end somewhere,' he went on, barely hearing her. 'I never had any good reasons for starting it. Maybe I just wanted to feel something that wasn't grief or sadness. Only for a short time. I never thought anyone else would get hurt. I have to live with that. It's time for me to grow up.'

He stood, unable to meet her eyes. For a second it seemed she was about to tell him something, then her mouth snapped shut like a trap. It was better that way, he told himself. The only words they could say now would wound each other, badly.

'I'm sorry,' he mumbled again. 'This is all my fault.'

He turned to go, but Marta wasn't finished with him yet.

'Hasn't everything worked out nicely for you, Euan?' the girl called after him. 'It's your wife, your Hannah, who I feel sorry for. Look to her, if you can turn away from your own reflection for a few moments. You won't tell her because you're not that sort of guy. Instead she'll see it in your face. Maybe she won't ever ask. But she'll know.'

Walking quickly, his head down, he knew he couldn't go back to his wife that day. The dark girl was right. Hannah would know. Perhaps she had always known.

Now, through everything, as they traversed the reels of his betrayal, Hannah was a mute and watchful presence – a ghost at this festering feast. There was only one place to take her now.

There had been three phone calls before. The boy had ignored each one. He was constantly on edge; every time that hateful gadget buzzed or bleeped he felt his muscles stiffening, his cheeks tinting crimson as if his body's impulses were conspiring to betray him.

That emptily aching hole in his chest had been replaced by a crushing band of pressure. An unyielding loop that constricted around his lungs whenever he recalled what he had done.

Every night – lying in bed beside his wife, wishing and praying for sleep – he thought of how he had strayed from the path. Where he had gone wrong, what he should have done instead. His mind endlessly replayed the time between the girl approaching him in the Blackout Bar and leaving her bereft at the copse in the thunderstorm. His memories of her sheened so very clear and bright; such a contrast to the greys that swamped his life.

Those memories tormented him. The guilt and shame and regret and heartache had become a cloak that hung around his shoulders; a cloak of deepest grey that he could never shed. The greys coated everything he said, everything he did, everything he thought. The old Euan George Stornoway had died the night he met Marta. Sitting on the train back home the next morning, carefully composing his excuse for Hannah – his head pounding with a sickly hangover, the taste of decay in his spit – he felt he had become another person entirely. Maybe if he had stopped then, seen his betrayal as a solitary idiotic drunken mistake, he could have forgiven himself.

Instead he had continued. They had continued.

After he ended their affair, his guilt and shame remained. Had he really expected any different? His old, happy life had slipped from his grasp like grains of sands whispering through his fingers. Only the greys remained.

But he had to keep on living. He had to maintain the illusion that he was a good husband. He ignored Marta's telephone calls.

On that muggy summer morning his wife was in the shower. He judged that she would not have heard the bray of the mobile phone above the hissing hot water. Holding on to his resolve, he tapped the green *Answer* icon on the touchscreen.

'I told you never to call me again,' he muttered.

The lightly accented voice whispered a few words. His first thought was to switch off the phone – or throw the damned handset out of the bedroom window – but the fear in the girl's voice was so great that he could not bring himself to hang up on her.

'You didn't listen,' she said.

'What was there to listen to?' he said harshly. 'It's over. It's the end. I'm sorry but you're just going to have to deal with it.'

'It's not over. It's just started.'

'What does that mean? You're going to start stalking me? Turn up outside my home and weep and wail until someone notices you?'

'Please,' Marta said, 'it's not about you. It's not about me. It's about someone else now.'

He squeezed his eyes shut, his brain starting to throb. 'What, Hannah? If you say anything—'

'Euan, must I spell it out?' she asked, her voice cracking with fatigue. 'There's someone else now. We made a mistake. I don't know how. You're going to … you're going to be a …' She broke off and he heard her sobbing quietly.

Realisation nudged him in the ribcage, dropped him a sly wink. 'Oh Christ, no,' he breathed.

Marta choked out a disbelieving laugh. 'That's your reply, Euan? Oh Christ, no? Oh Christ, yes. Yes, fucking yes. I'm pregnant. You're the father. How else can I make you understand? If you only—'

Her words were lost as the room pitched and yawed like a madly spinning gyroscope. 'What can you do?' he said faintly.

'There's nothing to do. There's nothing can be done. I don't know whether I waited too long but it's so goddamn big now and I can't make myself… I didn't think it would happen. I pretended I was getting fat. I was scared. I am still scared.'

'This will ruin my life,' he said. He didn't even realise he was speaking out loud.

'Poor you,' she replied. He could tell she was striving for

mockery, for bitter sarcasm, but falling far short. 'You had almost nothing to do with it.'

'I didn't know it would end in this ... this mess.'

He heard a quavering breath on the other end of the line. 'Is that what you call it? A mess?'

'Yes,' he said. There was a coldness to his voice that he didn't recognise, as if he had become another person entirely. 'It's a total fucking mess. So you deal with your mess. I'll deal with mine.'

He clicked off the phone. He stood there shaking, his face shock-pallid. First there was panic, then a stabbing sensation in his chest. His fingers clenched into fists. His eyes bulged, he felt an enormous skull-splitting pressure in his brain. He paced the room like a caged beast, spitting a single obscenity over and over and over again.

He heard his wife's footsteps on the landing and he shoved the phone into his back pocket. Hannah appeared in the door-way draped in a dressing gown, her hair swaddled in a towel. They were going shopping later. How ridiculously mundane. He tried to compose himself as best he could even as his left eye gently began to weep. Hannah padded past him as she retrieved her make-up bag from beside the bed; if she had so much as glanced at him in that moment, she would have seen the truth painted in discoloured shades on his face, surely. But his luck had held. Now he had to get rid of the phone. Maybe, when he was taking out the car, he could hide it in the boxes in the garage – Hannah wouldn't look there – then later on that afternoon, make a pretence of popping out on an errand and throw the fucking phone into a river.

Marta's words echoed in his mind, *I just like presents*.

So what was his present? The gift he had bought with his

stupidity. What would Hannah say when he gave her that present? What would Hannah do?

The answer came to him far too quickly. She would leave him. God knew he had been intolerable enough, even before she found out the whole rotten truth. His wife would leave him and she would never look back. The bonds between them would snap with the frailty of cobwebs. It would be over. No, no, it couldn't be over. He had to tell her. He couldn't ever tell her.

He wished he could go right back to the start. Never do those things. Be perfect for her. Make it all better.

36

Hannah and I: The last year

The Crossing

The train looms over us. The vast shadow is moving yet not moving. We are back in the car, trapped on the railway tracks. Where did we go just then? I've never told my wife anything about Marta. But she saw everything. Everything. Oh God. There's nowhere to go.

'You stupid man,' Hannah says, fanning her fingers underneath her reddened eyes, composing herself in the way she always does, the way I remember she always used to. I can remember so much now, almost everything. 'You fool,' she finishes. Her voice is so quiet, so calm, scarily drained and lifeless. 'You complete fucking fool.'

I can only nod in agreement.

'Why didn't you tell me about this before?' my wife asks. Her tone is almost conversational, as if we have been nattering about the weather rather than exposing my unforgivable betrayal, and that frightens me. 'Why couldn't you tell me about what you did? Why couldn't you tell me about her?'

'I don't know,' I say. 'I knew I had to tell you and I knew I couldn't tell you and so I did nothing. I sunk into this grey horror where I could barely move. Everything ... everything got worse and worse. I felt like my life was a movie, or some tragic play, and I was watching the main character going further and further down until there was nowhere else to go. Nowhere to go but here. To the tracks.'

Breathing heavily, my wife bites down on her lower lip. I think she is going to start talking again in that awful half-dead voice. But instead the explosion comes.

Hannah lets out a raw-throated howl and socks her fists against my chest, my head, my face. She hits me. She hits me again. She hits me so many times that I lose count. She hits me over and over and all I wish is that she could hit me harder.

'You selfish ... fucking ... idiot,' she spits, each word punctu-ated with a strike. 'You fucking ... fucking bastard ... fuck you, just fuck you.' I can barely feel her punches, let alone resist them. I know I deserve a hundred, a million more blows than she is able to give.

Eventually, after I lose track of time, she stops hitting me. She is panting with exertion, her nails digging cruelly into her hands.

'I hurt too, you know,' Hannah moans, her voice breaking on the last syllable and that flayed sound is more painful than any physical violence. 'I hurt more than you could imagine. Did you think you were the only one grieving over Jennifer? Did you think you had to face everything alone?'

Miserably I shake my head.

'I needed you,' she says. 'You weren't there. You went away. I needed you to talk and all I got from you was silence. Long before this accident you're trying to cause, you went away.'

'This isn't an accident,' I tell her. Her eyes flash with either fury or fear. 'I don't ... I don't know how I got here, but I'm sure I didn't want to live with that cloud of guilt hanging over me, poisoning everything. I felt there was nothing good left in this world.'

Hannah is silent for some time. Tentatively I reach out my

hand for her. She stares at me for a moment so long it could be infinity. I think she is going to step out of the car and leave me here alone, forever, and it would be the least I deserve. But at last she takes my hand.

'There was me,' she says quietly. There is a desolation in her voice that is so much worse than her anger. 'There was always me. Your wife, Euan. I could have helped you through. We could have led each other into a better place. Wasn't that enough? Wasn't I enough for you, Euan?'

I can't answer.

As one we look up at the train. It fills my brain entirely, that wide expanse of purest, murkiest grey. My fate is racing towards me at a million miles an hour yet that snub-nosed leviathan is hardly moving at all.

'Now you know what I did,' I say, disengaging from her, 'now you know how I betrayed you, you'll want to leave now. Please, Hannah, get out the car. It has to end like this. Me, alone. This is my accident. This is what I deserve. This is all my fault.'

Hannah traces her forefinger down the left side of my face as if following a track mark that isn't there, and I wonder exactly what she knows and what she is not telling me. What's happening is not real, or maybe it's halfway real, but only my wife knows the truth. She knows everything and unless I follow her, I'll be lost forever in this strange purgatory.

'It was certainly a perfect storm of ruining your life, Euan,' she says slowly, seeming to pick each word with the utmost care. 'Ruining both our lives. Part of me wants to leave you here, to let you get hit by that train again. In many ways you deserve it. But I've seen the alternative. It wouldn't be punishing you. It would be punishing me.' Almost unbelievably, she lets out a brusque laugh. 'You need to come back and face up to what you've done. I'm not letting you get off that easily.'

I sense a shaft of light in the darkness. 'You … you mean …'

'I'm not forgiving you,' she says, staring at her clenched fists. 'Don't think that for a second. There'll be time enough to sort out your personal disasters after this is all over. But I've put my heart, body and soul into this process and I'm not giving up now. Dr Cal was right. I've gone too far. We've gone far too far.'

I stare up at the train. I stare across at my wife. I can barely fathom what I'm hearing. There is understanding, a great comprehension, but it is an uncatchable shadow figure, a silhouette dancing out of reach.

'We can get out of this car,' Hannah says quietly but urgently. 'We can go back. Wouldn't you like to go back, Euan? Wouldn't you like to go home?'

I am crying now. I nod, reaching blindly for Hannah. She takes my hands and squeezes them hard, pressing them to her chest. 'I want things to go back to how they were before,' I manage to choke out, 'I want to be a good person for you, a good husband. I want everything to be better.'

Her lips are very close to mine. 'We can make it better,' she whispers. 'There's no need for this. It never has to happen.'

'It never has to happen?' I repeat dumbly.

'No. We can change this. We can make it better.'

'How?'

'We both get out,' Hannah says. Now she is smiling and she looks so beautiful whenever she smiles but there is an unnerving vacancy in her expression, a sense of sanity glissading away. 'Isn't that great? We both get out, that's what happens. We both get out just in time.'

'We can do that?'

'Yes, we can. I'll fix it.'

'Promise?' I ask, surrendering myself to her. 'Together?'

'I promise,' my wife replies.

Then there is a crescendo of splintering glass and my face is peppered with savagely spiked shards. The interior of the vehicle bulges hugely before the metal splits in two, as if the train is somehow being born through the side of the car. There is a horrendous screeching of tortured machinery and grey clouds bloom behind my eyes, swamping my vision. I try to scream but my lungs are full of the fetid diesel breath of the train, and I know that I have waited one second too long, and I am trapped and there is a phenomenal pressure tightening around my body, squeezing the life from me, and I have no idea where Hannah has gone and my last breaths are the two short syllables of her name before the train consumes me whole ...

But two blood-stained hands reach through the car's shattered windscreen and yank me roughly out into the sunlight, my stomach scraping on the clear jagged triangles of glass still embedded in the rubber frame.

There is an enormous force pushing me back into the car. The pressure seems as if it might bulge my eyeballs right out of my skull. But Hannah has a hold of me – grasping on with preternatural strength, her fingers sinking into my biceps so deeply that I fancy her fingernails might pop straight through the flesh. With a huge heave my wife pulls me from the prison of the car and I am out, free, into the white. She loses her balance and we topple together away from the car in which I experienced my deliverance, my retribution, my ending, hundreds upon thousands upon millions of times over. Still clasped together in a mad embrace we roll away from the accident, slipping off the side of the tracks into the grassy culvert as the sound explodes, shielding her with my body in a parody of a lover's ecstasy.

My vision is shrouded by blinding light and before the scene fades, I catch a glimpse of the dull grey nose of the train mashing against the passenger door of our car with a shriek of twisting metal and the whiff of spent ozone, bunting the vehicle down the hot tracks and out of my line of sight with shocking velocity.

We lie in a tangle of limbs on the grass verge staring at the smoking wreckage of crumpled metal on the train tracks. Every day for as long as I can remember I have been trapped inside that car, strapped into the driver's seat, before the train hurtles into the passenger door with a wheezing crunch. The impact lifts me and hurls me with astonishing strength, like a stone tossed from a giant's hand, and my vision cuts to black. The narrative of this little movie is simple: I am trapped in the car, the train hits the car, the impact of the crash wipes my memory. Until the next day – I say day, it could be the next hour, month or year in this unfathomable place where time moves in circles – when I am reborn and experience the accident over and over again.

But now it is different. I am out. The train hurtled past barely inches from our tumbling bodies but it never touched us. Hannah has saved me. She has saved both of us.

Today is the first day of the rest of our lives.

Breathing deeply, unable to believe I have survived the accident unharmed, I stare down at my wife. Hannah is lying on my chest. She is conscious but barely so. I stroke her white-blonde hair, trace my fingers across her face. It is impossible to believe I tested her love so sorely. But that man, that weak man who did those terrible things, doesn't feel like me any more. Come to think of it, I have absolutely no idea who I am any longer. The past we have lived through seems like it happened to another person.

'Hello, you,' I say.

Her eyelids flutter. Her gaze tracks me slowly, lazily. Then the realisation of where we are slams into her brain and she sits upright, panting. Her hands go to my face, tracing an outline of smooth flesh from the left side of my temple to my jawbone, as if feeling for a seam or indentation that isn't there.

Tears spilling from her eyes, Hannah lets out a yell of triumph – an Amazonian war cry – and lunges forward and presses her lips against mine. I taste salt, I taste her. Her breathing is ragged, almost whimpering, and she is hugging me with such fervour that I feel my ribs might crack.

'You know, I think we can leave now,' she says, her words coming in a gabbling adrenalised rush. 'The train didn't hit us, thank Christ. We can go home and fix ourselves that strong drink I was talking about. Then tomorrow morning I strongly suspect we'll need to buy ourselves a new car. Some atrociously macho monstrosity with massive spoilers or a Batmobile or anything, whatever you'd like. Then we can drive out to the coast – I haven't seen the sea for years, isn't that sad? – and we can have a pint of local ale looking out across the shoreline, maybe some fish and chips, then the day after ... Jesus, there's so much I want to do ... maybe head to Heathrow and see if there's any no-shows and fly, oh God, anywhere in the world. What do you say, Euan? Let's get out of this place. Let's make like a banana and scramble. Let's go home.'

Her face is lit with a wild light. My throat is closed pin-prick tight as if my own body is trying to stop me telling her what needs to be told. She is so dazzling in her excitement. So dazzling, so horribly deluded. Something's not right here. Something's not right at all.

'Hannah,' I say slowly. 'What do you remember?'

She blinks, the intense smile slaloming off her face. 'We were ... we were in a coffee shop. Then we talked about something, I've no idea what, some nonsense. We left. One of us was driving, I don't remember who. Then our car got stuck at the level crossing and we heard the train coming. It was scary. But we got out just in time. Wow, just in time.' Her voice is heartbreakingly childlike. 'Isn't that what happened, Euan?'

My wife genuinely doesn't remember. Our roles have been reversed, if only for a few seconds. She is caught on that muddy stile between waking and dreaming, a halfway-house bridging the conscious and subconscious mind. So much love, so much trust. I wish I could capture this moment forever in a still-life portrait. Because when she does remember, she'll never look at me this way again.

'This scene,' I say, 'what just happened, you do know this isn't real, right?'

She stares at the ground. 'Don't mess about, Stornoway. My nerves are shattered enough from a near-death experience without you getting existential on me.'

'I did get hit by the train,' I tell her. 'I was in a coma for months. Those are the facts and nothing can change them. Look at my face, I don't have a scar – do I?'

'I ... I can't see. The light's bad, I've got smoke in my eyes. What does it matter if you have a stupid scar anyway?'

Harsh halogen beams of comprehension are pinpricking through the fog in my brain; a sunrise of understanding. I don't want to witness what's revealed when the light gets in. I don't want to see this bleak dawn. But it doesn't seem as if I have a choice.

'I'm not the real Euan,' I tell her. I know that much at least. 'I'm not really me and I'm not really here.'

She shakes her head, her hair whipping back and forth. She is stubborn, my wife. We wouldn't have made it to this point if she hadn't been stubborn, and I love her for her sheer bloody-minded will, her refusal to give up. But she needs to understand.

Because thanks to Hannah, I am beginning to understand everything. I know everything. I remember meeting Hannah in Café Bellevue in the 14th arrondissement, I remember proposing to her on the Highland crags, I remember our wedding day. But not just these wonderful cataclysms – suddenly my head is full of the most wonderful ephemera. Times I haven't thought of in years. Rock pooling on the coastline, her barefoot and laughing, the hem of her gingham dress soaked and clinging to her thighs as she kneels to uncover a shore crab from beneath a stone. Me making a great show of skewering the wizened black crustacean for our evening barbecue on the beach, her splashing me in protest and returning Old Mr Crab to his dank, craggy apartment. How old are we here? Where are we, even – Scotland, the south coast, abroad? Then the scene changes and we are on a ghost train ride at a funfair – I think this could be in Leeds or York but I'm not entirely certain – and as the siren sounds and we are plunged into darkness, the sound of crazed discordant Wurlitzer music cranking up, I pull her close to kiss her and taste a trace of candyfloss sugar on her lips. I blink and I am lying on the sagging bed of my parents' cottage in Ayrshire, listening to the hiss of water from the shower – she still can't get the campfire smoke out of her hair. We are embroiled in the benevolent chaos of a Stornoway family Christmas, wearing matching festive sweaters, playing hide-and-seek with my nephews and nieces. We are in the hospital ward for the ultrasound scan, holding hands as the medic smears the goo over her protruding belly and the plastic stick picks out the blurry motion of the small life moiling gently inside her. We are together, we will be together forever. I haven't thought of these good times in far too long because there haven't been any good times in far too long, and maybe the memories are too painful to remember. I need to hold these memories close, to remind myself of who we are and what we are together.

But how much has been lost already?

Because I remember everything and I wish so much of it had been erased. I remember Marta and how I left her, too weak to face up to my mistakes. I remember that I saw no way out and I remember the blessed relief in the second before the train hit my car.

Waking up in a hospital bed with a crippled mind; I remember that now. I remember the Reel Memory Project even though the man I am now should have no knowledge of any of the process. Dr Scott Calvin, the pods, the portals, the treatment, the reels. My new knowledge all comes back to those reels. They have been connected too well. I feel as if I am floating, transcendent, staring down at my pre-accident and post-accident self. The treatment has been an absolute success.

I wish it hadn't been.

Because in this moment – with a knowledge that thuds into my brain with the heaviest of blows – I remember that it was Hannah who parked our car on the level crossing that miserable summer's day. Not me. She's been lying to everyone. She's been lying to our friends and family, the Ree-Mem doctors, my amnesiac self. But she can't lie to me as I am now. I've fucked up so much in my life, but not this. Never this.

The accident was Hannah's fault.

37

Hannah and I: the last year

Fade to Grey

My wife and I lie together on the grass verge, the fields stretching endlessly into the distance either side of us, a safe distance from the site of the accident. I can barely bring myself to look at the twisted and torn hunks of metal a hundred yards down the tracks. If this was reality, there would be an unconscious man hanging upside down in the passenger seat, a man with an ugly gaping tear down the left side of his face. A man who won't wake up for months, a man who'll return to life changed beyond measure. He's still out there and I'm here, although I've no idea where here actually is right now. Are we inside my fractured memories, her manufactured memories, an impossible shared headspace? All I know is that we are both so very far from home.

Shaking my head at the madness of it all, I turn my gaze to my wife. She is rocking back and forth, her head in her hands, her jaw working soundlessly. She turns to me. We stare at one another as if we've never seen each other before. She never knew what I was capable of. I never knew what she was capable of. I don't want to say these words, not when she's been through so much already. But what's the alternative?

'We can't rewind time,' I tell her. There's anger – plenty of it – but strangely it feels distant and almost inconsequential, like a limb amputated through a thick haze of morphine. What wipes out the anger I feel at my wife is a suffocating sadness. We've both done things that are unforgivable, irreparable. 'We can't undo what we did,' I go on. 'We can't change what happened.'

Having lived through our relationship twice, Hannah knows my memories better than I do. She's even added a few of her own. Maybe I can't blame her – if I could live it all again I'd put things right, I'd make amends. But this is memory recovery, not time travel. There is no magic here. No otherworldly presence will float down and smooth out the fractures with a touch of a divine hand. There is only me and my wife, my betrayal and her lies. I wonder how long she spent conjuring up the false reel of me at the wheel of the car. How many scenes she wrote and rewrote until she found the right one to make me confess everything and turn herself into the hero.

The perfect ending for a new beginning: we emerge into the sunshine, all my memories restored – with an added fake memory to keep the jackals of guilt from snapping at Hannah's heels. My wife is absolved of blame. She is clean but I'm still filthy and tainted. She insists on me facing up to my weakness and infidelity – even though she cannot accept she caused the accident that almost killed me. So where does that leave us?

It seems the greys are as much a part of Hannah as they are a part of me. The sunshine of my wife's fabrication has been snuffed out. The vibrant greenery of the Home Counties landscape is fading to a dull mulch, exactly like it was on the day the accident really happened. I feel the darkness begin to creep through our shared minds.

'We need to get out,' says my wife. 'Whatever happens outside the reels, we can't stay here.'

'Right then,' I say, 'so where do we go now?'

'I'll lead you out of this reel. Then it'll be over. The treatment will be complete. The Ree-Mem Project will bring you back to reality. You'll wake up with all your memories restored.'

'They're not my memories though, are they?'

'Euan, what do you mean?'

'You know exactly what I mean.' I gesture towards the mangled metal that used to be our car. 'This, right here. In your reel it was me who caused the accident. I can't live knowing that I'll come out and everything will be my fault. Not just Jennifer and what happened afterwards, but the crash too. After the reels, after what you've done, that'll be my fault.' A sickening thought strikes me, icy disquiet riddling up my spine. 'What the hell else did you change?'

'Nothing!' she cries. 'Nothing, nothing, I swear.'

'Maybe it would have been better if you had rewritten our whole history,' I tell her with a desperate laugh. 'When I come out, I'll still have Jennifer. I'll still know I betrayed your trust. But soon I'll have a wonderful brand-new knowledge – that I tried to kill myself and nearly killed you. Thanks for the fucking memories, Hannah.'

My wife stares at the ground, guilty red smears staining her cheeks. 'I can't take this any more. Whatever happens between us has to happen outside the reels. I just want out.'

She wants out. I want out too. But is there anywhere better to go? We've both caused too much damage to one another. Hannah's rebuilt our shared past but the only future I see is ruptured beyond repair. 'I don't think we can fix this,' I tell her finally.

'Euan, we need—'

'We can't fix this. It's broken, we're broken. You'll always wake up and see the man who betrayed you. And I'll always wake up and see the woman who nearly killed me.'

The thick fog has crept up insidiously, surrounding us. I

know what it is now: a construct of guilt, a miasma of betrayal, a hungry drifting mass of regret. I knew all along that Hannah was involved in some trickery and my mind invented the greys to sabotage her mission. Her manipulations, really, have changed nothing. I created this fog to destroy myself.

'I want this guilt to go away,' I tell her. 'My subconscious knew you were trying to bring back the old me. That's why the greys came. That's why the reels began to fall apart. That's why I tried to sabotage this whole process. Maybe I don't want to be the old Euan again. I broke our marriage, I broke your trust. You could have left me then. You could have started a new life, you could have been happy. I forgot you. Why didn't you forget me?'

'I needed to know,' she cries out. 'You don't understand. You left me with too many questions, they were bursting my brain. I knew just enough to torment me every single moment of every single day. So I had to find out. To know if I was right. And I was right. You never faced up to what you did. I couldn't let you ... couldn't let you ...'

'You couldn't let me get away with it.'

'I didn't mean it like that.'

Calmly I hold up my hands. 'No, it's fine. I understand.' Again there's no real anger, only a joyless throbbing sensation, and that's the truth. 'I'm sorry. I'm still not great at facing up to what I've done. But really, Hannah ... what do I have to come back to? In the end we've changed nothing. It won't get better. We won't get better.'

While I've been talking, I have allowed the greys to surround us. The car, the train, the tracks, the whole of the grass verge apart from a small green patch in which we sit together; every aspect of the scene has disappeared into the ether.

My wife's eyes widen with panic. She springs to her feet,

trembling madly, every muscle thrumming as if a high-voltage electric current is being passed through her body. She stares at me. She understands but she understands too late. The look of betrayal on her face tears at my conscience, but I know what has to happen.

My wife knows too. 'Euan,' she says, her voice almost inaudible, 'you don't have to do this.'

'Look to the man you wake up with,' I say. 'You may find there's more to him than you're willing to admit to yourself.'

Her eyes are wet. 'He's a stranger to me,' she says. 'He doesn't remember our past. He has no recollection of our lives together. He wasn't shaped by the experiences we shared. He can't be you, can he? He can't be Euan, surely?'

'Maybe he's the good Euan. The right Euan.'

Hannah has no answer to that. Instead she stares around us, her expression a confluence of panic and awe. We are the only two people left in existence. The glamours of the reels have collapsed entirely and we are floating in nothingness, the greys lapping hungrily at our feet.

'Can you ever forgive me?' I ask, searching for one last chance in spite of myself. That insane flickering hope that still refuses to flame out. 'Not right now. Maybe not for months, years. Even if it's twenty years from now, even if I'm old and demented and it's ten seconds before I die. I need to know that you might forgive me one day. Otherwise I don't know what I'm coming back for.'

Hannah's head is bowed. 'I can't promise that,' she says, each word forcing its way out through gritted teeth. 'Don't make me say it, Euan. I'm happy to lead you out of here and we can try to start again. But I can't promise I'll forgive you.'

'I can forgive you for the accident,' I tell her. 'I can do that. I'll live knowing the crash was my fault, if that's what you want.

I was selfish before. Stupid and arrogant. I only thought about what I'd lost, not what I already had. Now I understand much better. If I can have you, that's everything. If I have you, I can beat the greys, I'm sure I can. But only … only if you can give me another chance. I think we both need to forgive and forget. What do you say?'

She doesn't answer. It's as if I haven't spoken. Instead she says, 'Get out, please, Euan. This is how it has to end. Get out, if you ever loved me.'

There is no emotion in her voice. My wife has given up on me. She is only carrying the plan to its conclusion. This is simply a nasty chore that must be completed. Just like in that awful hospital ward, when she had to give birth to the little that was left of Jennifer. She's got what she really wanted all along, the entire way through the process; she knows the whole truth.

With hopeless resignation, I reach out to my wife. She takes my hand. Her touch is cold. The greys are all around. Three words, three simple words, are framed on my lips. Somehow Hannah knows where we are going. But as she leads me towards the exit, the greys converge hungrily upon us.

So I let go.

38

303 days since the accident

She came back to the real world with pitiless speed. She struggled up from the chair, clawing at the slippery coil of electrodes wrapped around her forearm. Warm firm hands tugged the electrode yoke free from her arm. She barely registered whoever had helped her. Her attention was on her husband.

Euan lay in the pod, alive yet not alive.

The recollection of what he had told her inside those final reels, what he had showed her, slammed into her chest like a sledgehammer. She had been there every step of the way. Somehow her mind had melded into Euan's as he led her through the scenes that she could never have seen, because she was never there; it was only her husband and the other woman. But she had been watching. Watching as he betrayed her, watching as he lied and cheated, watching as he had chosen oblivion on the railway tracks rather than face up to his mistakes. She raked at her cheeks. Why had she wanted this man back in her life? Why had she wanted to know the truth behind his accident? She should have chosen ignorance; better to live with the false ideal.

Now he had left her again, betrayed her again. She had given him the opportunity to come back, to be himself again. Instead he had chosen to forget her.

Suddenly she wanted to be as far away from this man as possible. Shunting herself backward, tears spilling onto her cheeks, she would have fallen out of the pod had Dr Calvin not rushed forward and caught her.

'Hannah,' the doctor said softly. 'Hannah, please. We must bring Euan up from his hypnotic state.'

Only now did she realise the room was filled with people: the white-coated Ree-Mem curators and the orderlies in pastel scrubs. The atmosphere was that of a freshly opened mausoleum.

'Let him lie there,' she spat. In that moment she could have fallen upon that comatose figure and choked him. 'Keep him trapped in his mind. Thinking about what he did for the rest of his life. Facing up to his actions at last. It'd be punishment enough. Keep him in there.'

'Hannah,' Dr Calvin said again, staring at her curiously. 'Do you really want that?'

She shook her head. 'No. No, I don't. I want him back. But not like he was. I hate him. I still love him. I just … I just don't know any more.'

She sank back with a low moan and let her head fall into her hands, wishing the unknown saviour had never rescued her from the car. The hurtling freight train would have carried them both away. Then she would have forgotten her husband's betrayal. She would have forgotten that she caused the accident. Instead she was left with – well, why not use Euan's own words, the words from the hidden memory he had shown her? – a total fucking mess.

Eventually, when she felt her legs could bear her weight, Dr Calvin helped her out of the pod. She was unable to watch as the Project orderlies took Euan away. Instead of following the neuropsychologist through into the recovery room, they slumped down onto the floor, their backs against the wall, and watched the Duessa pod as its doors hissed slowly shut. Calvin removed a bottle of brandy from the inside pocket of his white coat and passed it over. The taste yanked her back to Café Bellevue in the 14th arrondissement and tears pricked at her eyelids. She let out a low gasp.

'I was hoping this drink might befit a celebratory toast,' Calvin said. His voice was pregnant with emotion. 'I blame myself that it isn't so.'

She supposed she felt some anger towards him, even a dull hatred. Dr Calvin had tried to help them. But he had lied too. He had been using them all along.

'Your husband, Hannah,' he went on, 'an extraordinary case, quite beyond anything... it was my fault for not recognising the uniqueness of his situation. I watched enough of your story to guess the ending. I should have known he was hiding secrets from you, I should have known he would show you something dreadful inside that final reel. But I didn't know enough until we had gone too far. I underestimated the cataclysmic potential of his guilt.'

'Guilt,' she said slowly, passing the bottle back. 'Interesting word, doctor. Don't you feel that yourself? I certainly do. If there's anything that links the three of us, it's guilt.'

'So you feel guilt,' Calvin said, staring at her with the same analytical expression. 'Survivor's guilt, I'm sure. Although I am afraid your feelings are not mirrored on this face of the triangle. Here at Ree-Mem, we did our best.'

'Uh huh, you certainly did,' she agreed bitterly, 'but you didn't do it for me and Euan, did you? You did it for yourselves. We were supposed to be the smiling couple on the documentary telling the world that Ree-Mem had saved us. Rather than the people protesting outside. Waving placards reading Brain butchers.'

A vein pulsed in the doctor's forehead. He drummed his nails on the hard glass of the brandy bottle. 'The hypnotic process, Hannah, as I fully informed you with due diligence at the beginning of our professional relationship, is merely an effective fallacy that—'

She raised a hand to cut him off. 'It's not just hypnosis,' she said. 'Don't fool yourself, Dr Cal. What you people at Ree-Mem do ... it's far beyond a magician's illusion. It's something more, something dangerous. I was inside Euan's memory. I was part of my husband's mind. And he ... he was part of my mind too.'

'Hannah, here at the Reel Memory Project, we can only offer a process that—'

'Your process works, Dr Cal,' she went on. 'Congratulations. Maybe it works too well. I saw things in that pod that I've never seen. Things I should never have seen. I don't think you understand what you're messing with here.'

Staring at the floor, Dr Calvin was silent. There was a grisly similarity between the doctor and her husband, she realised. They loved to talk and talk when there was nothing much to talk about. Then, when the words really mattered, suddenly they had nothing to say.

'What sort of man will I be left with?' she asked tersely. 'A full reset? Will there be anything of Euan left whatsoever?'

'We will know the extent of the ... the damage ... once we have brought him out of hypnosis. But you will have all the support you need from Ree-Mem, Hannah. I give you my word. Whatever trials you face in the future, we will be there for you.'

The doctor did feel some guilt, she decided. Certainly regret. But not for them. For himself – his project, his baby, the child he had birthed and tended. The child that had grown far too big for him to handle or even understand. The child that had grown uncontrollable and destructive.

'I won't speak to anyone about you, if that's what you're worried about,' she said, taking the brandy bottle back. The drink had already numbed that ripe sharp grief, as freshly agonising as lemon squeezed on an open wound, into a listless throb. 'You can tell the TV people, the Press, whatever you want, but I'm not going to say a word. Even if the worst has happened.'

Relief crossed his face, smoothing out the wrinkles on his forehead, and she let herself hate the doctor just that little bit more. She thought how stupid she had been to think he cared about her and Euan. Dr Cal only truly cared about the Reel Memory Project; his fortune, his empire. Now she had the power to cause serious harm to both, perhaps even destroy Ree-Mem entirely. That knowledge only made her feel unutterably weary. She was so very tired. She had gone into this process hoping for answers but now there were only more questions. What damage had Euan done to himself? What damage had she done?

'Come with me, please,' the doctor said, reaching out a hand to her, groping almost blindly. 'We must find out how much of your husband's memory remains.'

Dr Scott Calvin led her out of the Ree-Mem treatment room for the final time. For a second she let the fingers of her free hand trail over the smooth endless curve of the Duessa pod. Then the door swept shut behind them.

Instead of heading back to the doctor's office, she followed him through a set of doors into a low-lit bunker. Euan lay in the centre of the room on a sloping metal chair, staring blankly up at the ceiling. His arms and legs were bound to the frame of the chair with rubber cables. A quartet of medics scurried around him industriously.

'His hands—' she started.

'Merely a precaution,' Calvin said. 'Some of our patients experience quite a ... ah ... physical reaction upon being brought back to reality.'

She wondered what reality was anyway. Was it here, with Dr Calvin and the shell of a man who might be her husband? Or was it inside the reels with their memories? She wondered how many partners of Ree-Mem's patients had begged to stay inside those treasured memory loops. Safer and happier in the perfect past, surely, than a future filled with uncertainty and loss.

But what did the present hold for her? Another rank gift from fate? A basket filled with spoiled fruit? Would she be left with a husband whose mind had been wiped clean once more, to care for as best she could?

Euan opened his eyes. He stared at her. There was everything and nothing in his gaze. In that moment he was the Euan of the back-before, the Euan of after the accident, the Euan of the reset. His eyes were laughing and his eyes were screaming and his eyes were blank as if he hadn't seen her before in his life. There was love and fear and hope and loss in his expression, but also an endless emptiness that frightened her more than she could say. She later told herself that it must have been her imagination – it had only been for a second, after all, that she saw a triptych of personalities vie for possession of her husband.

Then one of the Ree-Mem doctors placed a small metallic mask over the top half of his head. Light flashed beneath the contours of the visor. She watched Euan's face contort, his Adam's apple bobbing in his throat.

'What's underneath the mask?' she asked Calvin, an edge of panic in her voice. 'What are you showing him?'

'You,' he said simply. 'You, him and your shared history. The completed reel of your relationship. We shall know soon enough what we need to know.'

Her pulse quickened. She thought of what she had done to the final reel and whether the fallacy might stir something dormant in Euan's psyche. Fighting for breath, her vision greyed and she tottered slightly. Calvin placed a hand on the small of her back to steady her.

The visor was removed from her husband's face. The doctor holding it – a slim, dark-haired girl with elfin features – whispered into his ear. At times he nodded or shook his head and she realised he was being asked a series of questions. At last Euan craned his head up and looked across the room at her. There was certainly recognition in that gaze now. But not the recognition she had once hoped for: it was the look he had given her every day since he woke up after the accident.

It was not the return but neither was it the reset.

Weakly she raised her hand in greeting. Euan smiled, the look on his face one of total trust. She was waiting for that old familiar greeting to form on his lips – *Hello, you* – but she realised he might leave her waiting forever.

'I need some fresh air,' she told Calvin.

She turned to go and the doctor followed her down the blank white-walled corridor towards the glowing exit sign. Before she reached the door, he called after her, 'Hannah!'

With trepidation she turned. 'You dropped this, I believe,' said Dr Cal. He was holding out the book of matches from the Blackout Bar. She pocketed them without comment, yearning for the safety of the doorway. Instead he laid a hand on her arm. 'Hannah, stay with me a moment.'

'Please, I can't take—'

'I read the news reports about your husband's accident while initially assessing your case,' Dr Calvin said quietly. 'In none of them did I see it stated that he was driving the car. Only that you were rescued by an onlooker and he was not. The only quote, in fact, that I recall was that Euan Stornoway had escaped death by a matter of inches. Had he been in the driver's seat that day on the tracks, he would have been killed. Is that correct, Hannah?' She felt a lurch in her stomach and there was a high tinnitus buzzing in her ears. Calvin's tongue flicked briefly over his lips. 'Or have I ... misremembered?'

'It's difficult to trust our own memories,' she replied. 'Sometimes they're not quite how we wanted them to be. Isn't that right, Dr Cal?'

Beads of sweat were clustered upon the doctor's temples. The pressure of his grip on her arm increased incrementally. 'I asked you for a full and frank account, Hannah. I stressed the importance of honesty in the process. This treatment was about bringing back your husband. Not to satisfy your curiosity ... not to absolve yourself of guilt. This is a phenomenal breach of professional trust that may have far-reaching—'

'I couldn't trust you though,' she cut in coldly, disengaging herself from his grasp. 'I think that makes us about even.'

'You lied—'

'And so did you, and so did Euan, so who's keeping score?' she snapped, furious tears spilling down her cheeks. 'I needed to know, don't you understand? Can't you understand? Yeah, I faked part of the reel, big deal. If he'd realised that I caused the accident, he'd never have told me the whole truth. He'd have kept it shut up inside just like ... just like he did when it really happened. I needed to know. Now I know.'

Calvin held up his hands and sighed. Deep wrinkles were etched in his forehead; the doctor looked to have aged about twenty years since morning. 'Fine, Hannah. It is done, you got what you wanted. So was it worth it? To discover the whole truth about your husband?'

She wiped away the tears and stared defiantly back at him.

'I'm still working that out. I think I'm in shock right now. You know how you feel when a parent dies and at first it's so unreal you feel like laughing? I never expected it to be so bad. I never expected him to be so bad.'

'And what about you, Hannah – how do you feel?'

'Doctor, I'm really not in the mood for psychoanalysis.'

'Answer me, Hannah,' Calvin said. In an instant the weariness fell away from his face and there was an unsettling eagerness in his clear blue eyes, almost a sense of wonder. 'After today we'll never see each other again. You keep your lips sealed tight and I'll do the same, a little more *quid pro quo*. But please, humour me, answer my question. It's a simple question. How do you feel?'

She knew that she didn't need to answer. But somehow this felt like every bit as much a contract as the one she had signed at the beginning of the Ree-Mem process. She and Dr Calvin were in each other's debt now.

'Every day, seeing Euan after he woke up from the accident,' she said, 'I felt guilt. The sort of guilt that makes your teeth feel like they're dissolving in acid. I didn't want to feel that way any more. I couldn't bear the thought that he'd wake up, back to the old Euan, and remember what I'd done. It would have killed us all over again.' One hand was on the exit door. A strong push and she would be free. 'I thought I could make it better, Dr Cal,' she said with a painful smile. 'I tried.'

On the way home, unable to drive any further with a monstrous tension headache pulsing against her skull, she stopped the car on the swell of the hill that overlooked the chaotic sprawl of the capital. As if on an unspoken command they stepped out of the vehicle and sat together on the bonnet, staring out at the vista of sheening skyscrapers and green sweeps of parkland and stubby red-brown houses, as a light breeze played with their hair.

'It didn't work out, did it?' Euan said at last.

'How do you mean?' she asked, dabbing a tissue at her reddened eyes. She was surprised at how calm her voice sounded. Maybe it was because this place was neutral. It held no memories for Euan either before or after the treatment. She could leave him here and he would be safe.

'I'm still here,' he said. 'I remember everything back to waking up in the hospital bed months and months ago, but nothing before that. And if the treatment had worked, it would be the opposite way round, wouldn't it? I'd remember being him. I wouldn't remember being me.'

She reached into her handbag for the brandy bottle. Her hands shook as she fumbled off the screw top. It was impossible to look at him. The experience was still too raw. There had been a moment – slumped against the metal wall of the Ree-Mem building, her thoughts flitting from grief to blankness to black rage – in which she had seriously contemplated never going back in to fetch him from Dr Calvin's orderlies. Only a moment, but a moment nonetheless.

She knew that if she saw his face right now, she would paint over this man's innocence with the expressions of her husband's faithlessness. Euan in the Blackout Bar slyly sliding his wedding ring off his finger. Euan's hands hooked into the dark girl's hair. Euan grey with fright as that same girl told him the consequences of what he had done. Finally, Euan's face as he allowed himself to be shrouded in the creeping greys, choosing oblivion rather than face up to his mistakes. The betrayal reels had been captured in the shutter-clicks of her mind's camera. Mental photographs that she wished she could set aflame; she hated him in every one of them.

As the alcohol began to quell the jagged pulses of hurt, she allowed herself to look ever-so-slowly at the man sitting beside her. She decided she couldn't allow herself to see him that way. This man, she reminded herself as she took three more hearty glugs from the bottle, was different. So very different. He stared back, pulling a hand through his tousled curls. In the mellow early evening light his scar was barely noticeable.

'Talking of memories,' she said carefully, 'what do you remember about me, exactly?'

'I remember what you've tried to do for me,' Euan said. She passed over the brandy and he drank deeply. 'I remember what you tried to do for us.'

Relief exploded inside her like a dam bursting. He didn't know. He never had to know.

'I can try,' Euan went on, his voice hitching. 'You tell me what to do, Hannah. Any time I'm doing something wrong, you tell me. I'll say the lines, I'll be the old version of me. I can't... I can't lose you again.'

'I don't want you to act,' she said, then somehow managed to choke out a laugh. 'You know, I've seen enough charades these past few weeks to last a lifetime.'

'Then I won't be anything like him,' he said. 'I'd never do whatever he did. What he did to hurt you.'

She almost dropped the brandy bottle in shock. She could barely breathe. Time ran in slow motion, then sped up sickeningly. Apprehension shivered through her. She wondered whether he knew something, whether he remembered the whole truth. No, he was staring back at her guilelessly. The same expression she had seen every day since he woke from the coma. He knew nothing about what he had done. He remembered nothing about what she had done either. He was innocent. She supposed she had to thank fate – or maybe dumb luck – for granting her a renewed, pure version of her husband.

'I don't want you to be him either,' she said. Her voice was almost steady. 'I want you to be you.'

'So where does that leave us?'

'That's a little more tricky,' she admitted.

'Please don't leave me,' he whispered. 'Please don't.'

It took most of what little reserves of mental strength she had left, but she reached across and squeezed his arm. 'I won't,' she said. She knew she was telling him the truth. There was love and there was duty. One followed the other. She had no idea whether the love would ever return. But the duty remained. 'I'll stay. I'll be there for you.'

'Where do we go now?' Euan asked. 'Where do we go from here?'

Wordlessly she took his hand and led him back inside the car. She turned the key in the ignition and the engine rumbled into life. The low evening sun – a ball of opalescent orange light – shone directly into her eyes, blinding her to the road that lay ahead.

39

The Aftermath

She had woken from that dream again. The reoccurring dream that seemed far too vivid in its imagery, too eloquent in its telling, to be anything other than a memory.

But it was only a dream, or so she would tell herself upon waking. The dream in which she was holding hands with Euan as he was swamped by the greys. She felt such a great tug and suddenly what was left of the scene at the railway tracks had vanished and the pair of them were floating in non-space, their bodies incorporeal strands entwining endlessly in the ether.

Then they were in the hospital where it had all started to go wrong, on the jetty watching the sun go down over the Mediterranean, inside the church on their wedding day. They were on the mountaintop as Euan crouched down on one knee and brought out the ring from his inside coat pocket, the expression on his face so heartrending in its simple hope. They were not reversing history, she thought with something close to wonder, they were spooling back through their shared past. The campfire on the Ayrshire coastline, the party in the dingy flat at 74a Palmertach Street.

Finally, inevitably, they came to rest at a familiar place. Just like they always did. The pleasant café bar with the aspidistra framing the entrance. She heard the hum of passing trams in the background. The heat of the Parisian day had turned the small circular tables into a chef's hotplate that sizzled to the touch. This was where Euan lived now. Café Bellevue, either in her dreams or subconscious, had become her husband's prison.

She stared at the cobbled street, the intertwined streams of spilled coffee and beer. Shards of glass and porcelain winked in the sunlight.

'Jesus,' a voice said, 'I'm really sorry.'

'You're going to have to do better than that,' she replied. 'Sometimes sorry is nowhere near good enough.'

He sighed. She took a quick glance over. There he was. Just like always. The dark curly hair, still thick without a hint of grey. The peeling sunburn on his nose, the stubble on his cheeks and chin. The plaid shirt smeared black at the waist from oily hands, because Euan could fix cars. The old Euan, the Euan she had known from that searing hot afternoon in Montparnasse until the morning nine years later at the train tracks, could do that. The man who looked like him, the man she lived with now, could not fix cars. A tiny difference. One of about a million, a billion, tiny differences.

Yes, the old Euan had a gift for fixing things, she reminded herself. But the old Euan could break an awful lot of other things as well.

She listened as he played out the charade of ordering brandy. The bad French. The hangdog expression on the waiter's face. His face distorting in the Cognac glass as he raised it to his lips.

'To new friends,' said the man who would one day become her husband.

She shook her head, grinding her nails into the palms of her hands. 'We're not friends. I wish we'd never been lovers. The idea that I was married to someone like you—' She lit a cigarette, reasoning that in this dream or fantasy world, she could smoke as much as she wanted, health risks be damned '—makes me realise what a terrible judge of character I am.'

Her glass of Cognac remained on the table in front of her. Perhaps if she never picked it up, if she never clinked glasses with this man, she could stop everything happening. She could go back to being the 21-year-old girl who fancied that her sunglasses and cigarettes made her look like a starlet from Hollywood's golden age. That girl who could – and would – do anything she wanted.

'Wouldn't it have been great,' she went on, 'if I'd simply left you here? Just finished my drink and said goodbye. Taken that tram alone. Packed my case and got the hell out of Paris. It'd have been a lot neater and simpler. *Au revoir*, you faithless fucker.'

'Hannah,' Euan said, leaning closer. His hand reached across the table to comfort her, caress her. She thought of what he had done. She thought that if he touched her, she might scream. At the last second, sensing trouble, his hand fell back onto the arm of his wicker chair. He let out a groan that seemed to last forever. 'Hannah, you have no idea how much that hurts.'

'You have no idea how much you hurt me,' she said. 'Every day's a struggle, do you realise that? Living with a man who looks identical to you. Every day I wake up and see your face. Your lips coming down on her lips. That tongue of yours, which lied and lied and lied. Oh Christ, I see you. Your face and his face, I can't tell them apart some days. You murdered your own memories and – how fucking funny – now I'm trying to stop myself remembering. Bringing you back to life in him. Every day I see you and I want to kill you. Or leave you. One of the two.'

Smirking, he lolled back in his chair. Even in her mind-voice, her fantasy, Euan still couldn't face up to what he had done. 'Don't you remember the good times?' he asked in that teasing tone she always used to find irresistible. 'The great times? The best times?'

She glared back at him. 'I won't let myself remember any more,' she said. 'It's tainted forever. Roses wrapped up in razor wire. That's all you left me.'

'But it's all worked out so well for you, hasn't it?' Euan said, downing his brandy, his lips curling into a sneer. 'I'm the villain and you're perfect. And now you have a husband who doesn't know any better.'

She thought of the new Euan; his earnest voice and gentle ways. That day at the lake with the violin player, where they had danced to the softly stinging strings, danced in a way she had never danced with the old Euan. When the grief and hate threatened to consume her, she could hold onto that day at the lake.

Suddenly his brandy glass was full again. The cobbles, having dried in the heat, were wet. She could smell the potent reek of spilled coffee and beer, see the shards of glass and porcelain reflecting the sunbeams. In a matter of moments they would be going back to the start of the reel. She rubbed at her eyes to shatter the illusions.

'You can make me whatever you want to make me,' Euan said. He watched as a silver tram slid into existence across the street. She knew that tram stopped right outside her hotel. She felt something in her hand, opened her clenched fist and saw a miniaturised milk jug lying on her palm like a grail. 'So ... we can start again. Can't we, Hannah Allaker?' He raised his glass of brandy in a mocking toast. 'To new friends? New friends?'

Then she woke up.

Her husband knew something was wrong that morning. She could tell by the way his concerned gaze kept alighting on her as she sat morose and still on the living-room sofa, an unread property magazine on her lap, trying to shake the images of their past life out of her mind. He was concerned but said nothing. He was quiet these days, somehow even quieter than he had been in those endlessly dragging months after he emerged from his coma.

Crawling into the spare room bed a few hours before dawn, she had used the excuse of a bad dream for the third time that week. He had accepted it, just like always, and held her close until blessed unconsciousness claimed her. They slept in the same bed but there was no heat between them, simply the unity of capsized souls bobbing in a blackened sea with no shoreline in sight. At times she wanted his touch – anything to feel an emotion other than the deep trauma of betrayal – but didn't feel strong enough to ask. Even shorn of his brashness and verve he was an attractive man, and she thought back to the final weeks of the Ree-Mem Project when he seemed to come alive again. The afternoon dancing at the lake, his choked tribute to her before the final reels. He was so different but somehow the same, reborn a better person, and she wondered why she had been intent on shutting the new Euan out of her life. The visceral, unknowable bond between them could never snap entirely. Perhaps it was merely human nature; part of her still wanted him, and she knew without doubt that he wanted her. She suspected sex might happen again, maybe sooner than either of them expected. A few glasses of wine, a cheesily romantic movie on the television, and instincts would prevail. Not yet though. There was always the chance that her mind might trick her and she would look up and see the old Euan's expression painted onto the face of the innocent, tender man she lived with now. She would think of what he had done, who he had done it with, the product of that union. She couldn't cope with that, she was still too raw. Hadn't she done enough already? Hadn't she made yet more sacrifices? Despite every-thing she had learned about Euan in the reels, she had stayed with him – because this man was nothing like the old Euan. She was doing her duty. This was her penance, her punishment. Surely that was enough?

'Maybe we should go out?' he suggested at last. 'This ... you ... it's killing us in here.'

She tossed down the magazine. The phone call she had made earlier that day was preying on her mind and she was glad of the excuse. Some murky discoveries, long entombed, needed to be brought out into the sunlight. 'That's a good idea. We need to talk, you and I.'

They had come to the lake again, where she felt closest to this new version of Euan. The place had a calmness, almost as if time stopped around that flat expanse of water and they could stay for as many hours or days as they needed. She thought that she needed all the natural serenity possible if she was going to get through this horrible business. They found the copse again easily. There was no fiddle player today nor picnicking family. They were alone but for a small knot of starlings freewheeling above the lake, their bodies creating abstract art in the overcast sky; an endlessly twisting black spray upon the grey.

Easing themselves down on to the soft grass, they sat opposite one another. It was well before midday but she wished she had picked up a bottle from the shop. For courage.

Euan stared at her expectantly. He was cross-legged in front of her like a pupil hoping to learn an interesting lesson from a favourite teacher. He looked hopeful, even eager. For him this was simply a pleasant trip out. Maybe he even thought they might dance later on. The knowledge of what she had to say left a rank taste in her mouth; there was a strong compulsion not to tell him, to let him be innocent. She rushed on before she lost her nerve.

'There are some things you need to know,' she said.

He blinked. 'Things?'

'Some things,' she agreed. 'About how you were. What you did. Back before the crash.'

His tongue twitched over his lips. He looked away. 'I'm not sure I want to know,' he said.

She sighed. 'I'll be as brief as I can. You … we … we had a child. Jennifer. We lost her. You went out of your mind. You made some very stupid decisions. You left me. You came back. But I think in that time away you met someone else. Someone. Another girl.'

She looked over at him and was a little frightened by what she saw. His jaw was trembling, the tendons popping out on his neck like metal cords. 'I'd never do that,' he said, his hands clenched into fists. 'How … how can I … I mean, look at you. You're everything. Absolutely everything.'

The solid earth felt unsteady beneath her. She pressed her fingernails into her palms. 'You obviously didn't think so,' she whispered.

'Well, that man was a fool,' Euan said, his voice almost a growl. 'And I'm pleased he's gone. Fucking pleased.'

His words were like an adrenaline jolt to the heart. She couldn't remember this version of Euan swearing before. There was a viciousness in his tone that she'd never heard her husband use, not since the crash at least. The blood pounded in her veins. 'You really mean that?'

'I don't lie,' he said. 'I don't know how.'

'He did,' she replied. 'He was good at it.'

'I would kill him,' Euan said. 'If he wasn't dead already.'

'There's more. More I need to tell you.'

The anger ran out of him and his shoulders sagged. 'Please, no. I don't want to hear. Please no more. I can't bear—'

She raised her hands to cut him off. 'Don't make this harder for me. I can only tell you this once. I'm not strong enough.'

He squeezed his eyes shut. 'Okay.'

Taking a deep breath, she continued. 'You ended it with this other person. You thought you could come back to me and we'd be fine. Only nothing was fine. You'd made a mistake. She'd made a mistake. You ... she ... oh, fuck it, I'm crying now ... she was pregnant, Euan. She had the baby, alone. You have a son.'

He reeled backwards and almost lost his balance, his face pallid, almost grey. 'What the—'

'They're over in Hungary now with her family. She was going to confront you, show you face-to-face what you'd done, but then the accident happened. She saw the crash on the TV news. Saw your face. She was four months' pregnant and watched the father of her child being pulled from the wreckage of our car. God knows how she felt. I don't even want to imagine.'

'How do you know all this?'

'Because I've spoken to her. This morning, in fact. You covered your tracks badly. You knew you couldn't tie up the loose ends, lie your way out of this mess. That's why—' she felt a choking lump in her throat and swallowed hard, the shameful red flowers blossoming in her cheeks '—you parked your car in the path of a train.'

'Jesus Christ, Hannah.'

'The boy's six months old now. He's fine. They're living with her parents about twenty miles outside Budapest. You know, I didn't even ask his name. Not out of spite. There was just too much for me to take in.'

'Oh God.' His hands were in his hair, squeezing at his temples as if trying to hold in his aching brain. 'Oh no.'

'Yeah,' she said, 'that's what I thought. But here we are.'

'How do you deal with all this on your own? First the reels and now this.'

'I don't know,' she said flatly. 'One day at a time. That's the trick.'

He stared at her with reddened eyes. 'Why haven't you left me?' he asked. 'After what I've done?'

She laughed and the sound echoed across the water, too shrill and jagged to avoid questioning her own sanity. 'Because you didn't do it. That's the tragedy, the sick joke. How can I blame you? How can I punish you? The other Euan did it. And he's drowned in the greys. He's gone.'

'I think I like that,' he said.

'I like that too,' she agreed. 'Also, I'm all talked out. Shall we go home?'

'Together?' her husband asked.

'Together.'

40

The Start

Two months, it seemed to her, passed in the blink of an eye. Life continued. Dr Calvin kept in touch, even though – as promised – he had waived the Reel Memory Project's fee. His emails were professional and polite, yet she could tell he still believed she would go to the Press at some point and reveal everything about the secrets of the Ree-Mem Project; how its founder and public face had tried to manipulate them. Eventually she stopped replying to Dr Cal's messages. There was nothing left to say. Euan, to use the Project's euphemism, had never responded to treatment. He was still the post-accident Euan, the new Euan.

He could communicate with her, live with her, provide the warmth and companionship vital to any relationship. He even made her laugh sometimes. He loved her with a tenderness and loyalty that unobtrusively wound itself around her conscience.

Eventually she went back to work. He made some money doing gardening and odd-jobs for their neighbours, relishing the outdoor labour and the sun on his back. Sometimes she would pass him as she drove to the train station in the morning, digging a rose bed or mowing a lawn; his shirt off, his brow sweaty, the scar on the side of his head faded to a dull streak. He would raise a hand and she would raise hers in return, and she knew that when she returned home that evening, she would find a meal on the table and a bottle of wine in the refrigerator and Euan sitting in his easy chair, turning to drink her in. She would stare at him and for a moment she was returned to the final reels, the betrayal reels, and anger flared inside her. She reminded herself to breathe deeply, breathe deeply, breathe deeply. In the end, that was all the Ree-Mem Project had been good for: how to hypnotise herself. How to forget.

It wasn't this version of Euan who had betrayed her, she kept telling herself. It was a man who looked a lot like Euan, but still another person entirely.

When she watched the television documentary on the Project's time in Britain, she felt almost nothing. No anger at Dr Scott Calvin, only some regret. Whatever the doctor's motives, he had no way of knowing the rancid secrets his treatment would uncover. Most of the hour-long show focused on three high-profile cases: an industrial tycoon, a former politician and a faded celebrity. She knew that if the Stornoways' treatment had been a success, they would have been expected – no, legally obligated – to add their voices to the tearful tributes to Ree-Mem; pawns in Dr Cal's war on the non-believers. Instead they were nowhere to be seen, or at least she thought so on her first viewing. When she watched the documentary again she saw a glimpse of her husband's tousled hair during crowd footage, while one tracking shot captured her standing in the foyer of the building, mostly concealed by the bulk of Dr Cal. They were background actors, little more than scene setting. She was glad of it. Life was easier that way.

Letting go of their past lives was simpler than she had dared to hope for. The photographs, the letters, the portals, the documentation of their old lives, had been shut away forever. It was better that she did not think of the past. It only tainted the present.

In the early hours, in that muddy purgatory between sleeping and waking, she felt the memories slip from her mind, washed away like detritus on the shoreline. Self-hypnosis, that was the key. She repeated the words under her breath like a catechism: she would not hate, she would forgive. Because Euan, as he was now – well, what was there to hate and what was there to forgive?

That morning she was staring critically at her reflection in the bathroom mirror. A woman in her early thirties with blonde hair that a man so very long ago compared to a flare of lit magnesium. The girl named Hannah Allaker – the girl with the whole world in the palm of her hand, the girl who truly believed she would never be bound or beholden to anyone – was gone. Now she was Hannah Stornoway, a woman who had responsibilities, a woman who had lived and loved and lost.

Her eyes had shed that haunted look and that was something. Small victories. Better than no victories at all. She had gone into the Ree-Mem Project hoping for the return of her husband. Instead she was left with a man who looked like Euan and sounded like Euan and yet was not Euan at all. She could live with what he was, she had decided, but she was happier still to accept what he was not. Her memories of that man were too complex, too painful. This new Euan was different.

Flushed with an intangible sense of joy, her feet feeling ballerina-light, she marched into the musty-smelling spare room and flung open the curtains. The day was bright and clear and the sunlight streamed in.

'Morning,' she announced cheerily.

Her husband struggled up from sleep. 'Hi there,' he mumbled.

'We should have a party,' she said. 'A week on Saturday.'

He rubbed at his eyes. 'Any particular reason?' He blinked. 'God, it's not your birthday is it? I'm so sorry, I—'

'No, no. Not a birthday party. An extra-special party. For you.'

A bemused grin spread across his face like that of a child who fears he's being tricked. 'What? For me?'

'That was the day you woke up. Exactly one year ago.' Then, somewhat too late, she reconsidered. 'Shit, unless you think it's a bit morbid?'

Euan shook his head and beamed. 'I suppose it would be like a birthday, you know?'

Then they were both laughing.

Which was why, a week on Saturday later, their little home was crammed with friends and relatives, many of whom she had not seen for years. She was caught in conversation with one of Euan's elderly aunts about the phenomenal quality of life in New Zealand – *honestly Hannah, I don't know why you stay in this country, what with all the overcrowding and the immigrants and the horrible weather even though it's quite nice today I have to say* – when she saw her sister gesturing to her over by the kitchen door. With relief she extricated herself from the aunt, muttering an excuse about checking on the canapés in the oven. Saskia ushered her through the kitchen out into the garden and shut the back door behind them. They leant against the warm brick wall, the party sounds of laughter and music pleasantly muffled.

'I thought you deserved a break from Enochette Powell in there,' Saskia said, lighting up a cigarette.

'Appreciated,' she said, before nodding towards the packet. 'Not got anything stronger than cigs?'

'Afraid not,' her sibling said, placing an arm around her shoulder. 'You doing okay, sis?'

'Sure,' she said. 'I'm fine.'

'Swear?'

'Swear,' she agreed. 'I swear I'm fine.'

'Hannah's always fine,' Saskia said, holding her close. 'That's what Dad told me. Hannah makes the best of everything. Hannah's always fine.'

'Except when she's not.'

'Except when she's not,' her sister repeated. Her voice was a little choked.

She smiled wryly and broke the embrace. 'Any other suggestions for amnesia treatments for us to try? Any more completely mad adventures in medical science-fiction?'

'Nothing,' said Saskia, staring at the ground. 'I'm all out of options.'

'Me too,' she said quietly. 'It's for the best.'

The back door bashed open and her sister's boyfriend stood before them, tottering slightly.

'Where's my sexy lady?' woozed Robbo. He had removed his leather jacket in the heat of the day and there was a splodge of ketchup on his grey Motorhead T-shirt. 'Ah, here she is. Excellent.'

'Sisters are having a private conversation, Roberto Pellicci,' Saskia said. 'It's polite to wait until they've finished that conversation before interrupting. Or don't you understand the meaning of politeness?'

'Nah, I'm a caveman, ain't I?' Robbo said, offering her a gap-toothed grin. He leapt off the porch and flung a shrieking Saskia over his shoulder. 'Gonna club you over the head and drag you back to my lair.'

Smirking, she watched Robbo carry her sister on a lap of the garden as she wriggled and laughed and beat her fists against his back. As they toppled over into the flowerbeds and began to kiss deeply, she felt a hand on her shoulder, a familiar touch.

'I wondered where you'd gone,' she said.

'I thought I might have to throw a blanket over the lovebirds,'

Euan said, hooking a thumb at her sister and Robbo. 'There's children present, you know.'

She giggled. He smiled back, pleased to have made her laugh, the way he knew his old self always used to do, but his grin was soon replaced by a nervous, hunted expression. There was a slight sway in his posture – alcoholic courage, she realised – and it was obvious that one of his questions was coming. Only now she didn't dread the questions. In fact, she welcomed them; they showed he was learning, growing, becoming the man that Euan always should have been. Recently something had changed between them. Something small and indefinable, but most definitely something. A key that had jammed in the rusty lock of her soul was suddenly turning with ease.

'Do you ever miss it?' he said, his words barely a croak. 'The reels, I mean. The Project.'

She knew he was really talking about his old self. But she had forgotten that man, hadn't she? Instead she thought about the visits to that aircraft hangar building in the industrial estate, her troubling relationship with Dr Cal, the mechanisms of conjoined hypnosis. No, she did not miss any of that. As for the contents of the reels, the greys, she would not allow herself to remember them. They had happened to someone else an awfully long time ago.

'No, I don't miss it, why?' she said. 'Hospital stuff, medical stuff's always horrible. How about you?'

'I don't remember too much about the treatment,' he admitted. 'Big building. Lots of lights, smells I couldn't place. Then it was like going to sleep without dreaming.'

'Funny,' she said. 'They were only ever dreams. This is what's happening. This is real life. Right here, right now.'

'I feel like this is a better time than I've ever known,' Euan said, his voice cracking slightly. 'I feel like I'm in the perfect place.'

She did not know how to respond. So instead, on impulse, she kissed him. Just a small, almost-chaste kiss. He was so taken aback that he took a step away from her, nearly tumbling over the rockery, and she laughed again.

'Brandy?' she said, licking her lips, relishing the caramelised taste of the spirit. 'It's barely teatime.'

'Just a little.'

Emboldened, he pulled her towards him and placed a fierce kiss on her lips. She was surprised – not a little stunned – and did not resist. The kiss grew longer and more lingering and the blood rushed to her brain and her poor abused mind was in turmoil, full of uncertain hope.

Finally, they broke away. Simple devotion was painted on his face. There were deep dark pouches underneath his eyes, stress lines carved into his forehead, and a hint of grey creeping into the dark whorls of his hair. But she thought he had never looked more handsome since the day they had met in a little café in Montparnasse half a lifetime ago. They had learned so quickly about each other back then. Their hopes and fears, needs and wants, faults and fractures. She needed to learn Euan again, but that was fine. There was all the time in the world for new memories.

They walked back to the house, their fingers entwined. Euan located the brandy bottle in the kitchen and poured them both a healthy measure.

'I was thinking,' she said slowly, 'that I'd like to go somewhere new. Somewhere different.'

'Like a holiday?'

She shrugged. 'Maybe a couple of weeks. Or even longer, there's nothing much keeping us here. Perhaps a place with blue skies and sandy beaches, fishing boats coming into shore with the day's catch, where people speak a language we can't understand but it doesn't matter. Or perhaps somewhere remote and beautiful, where we feel like we're the only two people in the whole wide world. Somewhere with no memory of us. Simply somewhere we can start again.'

His eyebrows raised hopefully. 'Together … I mean, no separate rooms or … or …?'

'Absolutely not.'

'Are you sure this is what you want?' he asked, the yearning on his face almost too much to bear. 'Is this what you wanted from life?'

She buried her face in her drink. She did not want him to see the traitor teardrop that had slid down her cheek. She felt as if the last of her love for the old Euan had been crystallised inside that tiny drop of salty water. 'This is exactly what I want,' she said at last, surreptitiously wiping her eyes. Placing down her glass, she slipped her arms around her husband and kissed him again for some time longer. The sweetness of his passion stole her breath away. 'This is who I want. You, Euan. You.'

Epilogue

I thought she knew. I swear I thought she knew. When I woke up on the reclining chair in that weird building with all the doctors around me, my wife stared at me and I thought she knew. A second more and she would have seen it in my eyes, who I really was. They saved me by putting the visor over my face. Because inside I was screaming.

Somehow I came back. I thought I had let the greys carry me away. That would have been better, cleaner. I wanted to die, I wanted to let the greys wipe my memory. It didn't happen that way. Something went wrong in the treatment; not only did I remember my life up to the crash, I also remembered my life after the coma and my life in the reels.

I knew everything, absolutely everything. Most importantly, I knew what Hannah had done.

Lying there, my wife's gaze upon me, I had a fraction of a second to make my choice. I could have been my old self, who she hated – or I could be reborn, guiltless and free. In the end, Hannah's actions made the decision for me. Her lies let me live again.

When that pretty dark-haired doctor took off my visor and whispered questions into my ear, I played dumb. No, I didn't remember meeting Hannah at Café Bellevue in the 14th arrondissement. No, I didn't remember proposing to her on Highland crags four years later. No, I didn't remember that we had a daughter, who we lost, called Jennifer. No, I didn't remember how I nearly died on the railway tracks. The lies streamed out like a row of paper dolls joined hand-in-hand.

Maybe I couldn't face up to what I'd done. But neither could my wife. In every way we deserve one another. Now she has got exactly what she wanted: to be blameless, perfect, with a blameless and perfect husband. Hannah won't ever know it but she's given me exactly what I wanted too – a second chance. I can be the man I always should have been. A new, better Euan Stornoway.

Sitting on the bonnet of our car looking out over London, drinking brandy, I thought she was going to leave me. The hurt thrummed off her like radiation sickness. So again I played dumb. I've been playing dumb ever since. How can you blame a man for a crime he doesn't know he committed? That was another person. Another lifetime.

The days pass by slowly. I do my boring gardening jobs and wait for Hannah to come home from work. There will be a meal ready for her, we will drink a little wine, we will go to bed together. I'm glad of her comfort because I don't sleep too well. I wake with a jolt in the early hours, terrified of what I've seen in my dreams – the only place my memories are allowed to live these days – but even more scared that I've been talking in my sleep. Then, seeing Hannah is at peace, I calm myself and nestle back into her warmth. The greys only come at night.

Some days it seems as if my new, happy life is a magnificent castle built from the flimsiest materials. I am the best husband for her. I am loyal and loving and sometimes – when I'm sure it won't arouse any suspicion – even a little bit funny. The castle still stands after more than six months. However, today brings another potential fracture in the framework. The year has just edged breezily into November. The month of my son's first birthday.

Hannah is pacing down the stairs of our house, her hair spilling out from under a comical woollen bobble hat. She always did feel the cold and after Jennifer I wasn't able to keep us both warm. She steps towards me and smiles. Her cheeks are still slightly pink from the heat of the shower. Even in her unflattering duffle coat she'll never know how beautiful she looks right now. I can't tell her because the other man, the man I play now, wouldn't think to tell her.

My gloved fingers fumble with my scarf. She undoes and reties it for me. Briefly she lays her palms upon my chest. Surely she must feel the mad thumping of my heart.

'I didn't do it,' I tell her, an edge of desperation in my voice. 'God, I know that sounds stupid. Because I did do it. When I wasn't me. I know what I'm supposed to have done, what I did do when I was different, because you told me. But I don't know why or how or … oh, I'm sorry, I just don't know how to say this, but I think I mean—'

Stammering, stumbling, I allow my tongue to tie itself in knots and I see only pity on her face. Pity, sympathy and love. Because this is the Euan of the lake, not the Euan of the train tracks, and those two men are strangers to one another.

She places a mild kiss on my lips to hush me. 'I do know what you mean,' my wife agrees, even though she doesn't know a single thing, 'and I know it's scary. But it's still something you need to face up to.'

Glumly I nod. 'I'm sorry for what I did,' I tell her. 'Even though I don't remember doing it.'

'I'll be here for you,' she says. 'Whatever happens.'

I smile in simple gratitude. 'I'm not quite sure what to say,' I tell her. 'I don't know what to expect.'

'Everything will be fine,' Hannah says. 'I promise.'

She takes my hand as we walk across the grass. Regent's Park, a neutral space, should be beautiful but the harsh autumn has turned it desolate. The branches of the trees are craggy, denuded of leaves, and a recent rainfall has left a mulch beneath our feet.

Up ahead I can see a woman sitting on a bench looking out at the swings and slides of the park's playground. She turns and tentatively raises a hand. I remember the olive-shaded skin, the ink-black hair, the slightly hooked nose. I try to calm my breathing, arrange my features into an expression of confused apology. I don't know what I did, what we did together. She's a stranger to me now. A normal person who my mind made into a monster. The Marta of the reels, the dark girl, is nothing like this thin, nervous-looking woman. The two loves of my life are meeting for the first time and there's no animosity between them, only a strange union – while the man who caused them both so much pain is standing here blameless.

A small stocky figure peers out from the folds of Marta's overcoat, clinging to his mother's legs. Here he is. Nothing could have prepared me for this moment. Nothing. I want to run, I want to cry, I want to howl with fright and whoop with joy. His eyes are as dark as those of his mother, but I know the tousled curls have been inherited from his father.

Crouching down on my haunches, I gaze at my son for what seems like days. Marta is refusing to look at me but still she urges him in my direction, holding tightly to his mittened hands so he doesn't fall. He takes a couple of faltering paces forward on his chubby little legs, his red Wellington boots gleaming with dewdrops. The boy's cheeks split into a slight smile, the grin arriving with the aching slowness of a step on the moon. I reach out a hand to touch his face, marvelling at the softness of his skin, the unbearable purity. Then, feeling no resistance, I gather him up in my arms. Such a weight, such a great living weight. A cavity in my heart that I thought would remain torn open forever, an ugly tattered wound caused by Jennifer's death, heals over. I've never felt so happy and what does it matter if I'm acting when the charade is so beautiful? I can keep one step ahead of the greys, I can live this lie, I can live this life.

Hannah slips a hand into mine. She is crying, so bitterly, and I can't imagine what it is costing her to keep the three of us joined in this way.

The words are out of my mouth before I can stop them.

I say to my son, 'Hello, you.'

And Hannah's eyes open wide.

Acknowledgements

If you're planning to write a high-concept thriller / broken love story / speculative sci-fi, you really need an agent who believes in you. Literary giant Harry Illingworth was that man. Eternal gratitude to Harry for hauling the chassis of *Forget Me* out of the junkyard, then showing me how it could look with a turbo booster and go-faster stripes. Thanks to Caz Tudor for her agent recommendation. Sam Morgan in New York came up with a stunning idea to knot the ending together. My editor Ben Willis at Orion provided invaluable vision, direction and encouragement; every editorial meeting should take place over several beers in the dingy alleyway behind The Harp in Trafalgar Square. The team at Orion have also been nothing but fantastic towards a debut novelist with a weird little idea.

As a child, my parents filled our home with books and encouraged me to read them all. Many were not entirely age appropriate. Pulpy airport thrillers and imposing hardbacks; an ancient set of Dickens that smelled of mildew; Sixties counter-culture literature; Matheson and Asimov and (for inexplicable reasons) the complete works of Jeffrey Archer. There was no filter. It was a great time of exploration.

I'd have quit this some time ago had it not been for the endless support of my brilliant, beautiful wife Laura. Over the

five years it took to turn *Forget Me* from concept to book, she
provided me with love, advice, encouragement... and the most
amazing little girl in the world. On that note – hello, Arianne.
Maybe read this when you're a little bit older.

Thanks for the memories...

AJE